COLD TO THE TOUCH

What Reviewers Say About Cari Hunter's Work

"[*Snowbound*] grabbed me from the first page and kept me on the edge of my seat until nearly the end. I love the British feel of it and enjoyed the writer's style tremendously. So if you're looking for a very well written, fast paced, lesbian romance—heavy on the action and blood and light on the romance—this is one for your ereader or bookshelf."—*C-Spot Reviews*

"[*Desolation Point*] is the second of Cari Hunter's novels and is another great example of a romance action adventure. The story is fast paced and thrilling. A real page turner from beginning to end. Ms. Hunter is a master at an adventure plot and comes up with more twists and turns than the mountain trails they are hiking. Well written, edited and crafted this is an excellent book and I can't wait to read the sequel."—*Lesbian Reading Room*

"Cari Hunter provides thrills galore in her adventure/romance *Desolation Point*. In the hands of a lesser writer and scenarist, this could be pretty rote and by-the-book, but Cari Hunter breathes a great deal of life into the characters and the situation. Her descriptions of the scenery are sumptuous, and she has a keen sense of pacing. The action sequences never drag, and she takes full advantage of the valleys between the peaks by deepening her characters, working their relationship, and setting up the next hurdle."—*Out In Print*

"Once again Ms. Hunter outdoes herself in the tension and pace of the plot. We literally know from the first 2 pages that the evil is hunting them, but we are held on the edge of our seats for the whole book to see what will unfold, how they will cope, whether they will survive—and at what cost this time. I literally couldn't put it down. *Tumbledown* is a wonderful read."—*Lesbian Reading Room*

"Even though this is a continuation of the *Desolation Point* plot, [*Tumbledown*] is an entirely different sort of thriller with elements of a police procedural. Other thriller authors (yes, I'm looking at you Patterson and Grisham) could take lessons from Hunter when it comes to writing these babies. Twists and turns and forgotten or unconventional weaponry along with pluck and spirit keep me breathless and reading way past my bedtime."—*Out In Print*

"Truly terrible things, as well as truly lovely things, abound in the mystery-thriller *No Good Reason*. The plot takes off immediately as a captive woman makes her bloody escape and the—Well, this is not a romance, dear reader, so brace yourself. …After visiting America for her last two books, Desolation Point and Tumbledown, Hunter returns to the land of hot tea and the bacon butty in her latest novel. Our heroines are Detective Sanne Jensen and Dr. Meg Fielding, best mates forever and sometimes something more. Their relationship is indefinable and complicated, but not in a hot mess of drama way. Rather, they share unspoken depths, comfortably silly moments, rock-solid friendship, and an intimacy that will make your heart ache just a wee bit."—*C-Spot Reviews*

"Cari Hunter is a master of crime suspense stories. *No Good Reason* brings tension and drama to strong medical and police procedural knowledge. The plot keeps us on the edge of our metaphorical seat, turning the pages long into the night. The setting of the English Peak District adds ambiance and a drama of its own without excluding anybody. And through it all a glimmer of humour and a large dose of humanity keep us engaged and enthralled."—*Curve Magazine*

By the Author

Snowbound

Desolation Point

Tumbledown

No Good Reason

Cold to the Touch

Cold to the Touch

by

Cari Hunter

2015

COLD TO THE TOUCH

ISBN 13: 978-1-62639-526-8

This Trade Paperback Original Is Published By
Bold Strokes Books, Inc.
P.O. Box 249
Valley Falls, NY 12185

First Edition: December 2015

Credits
Editor: Cindy Cresap
Production Design: Susan Ramundo
Cover Design By Sheri (graphicartist2020@hotmail.com)

Acknowledgments

Thanks and a bag of pork scratchings to the good folks at BSB, particularly Sandy, who always gets the sticky end of my e-mails. To Cindy, for being a fab editor, for her sage advice, and for letting me keep the pork scratchings. To Sheri, for the lovely cover. To Kelly, for sweets, laughs, cheesy ball challenges, and making me do "the lift" while driving on blues. I miss you! To her husband, Col, who fielded a few of my more obscure research questions. To Kirsty, for Meg's "we can't fix stupid" line. To everyone who's read my books, sent feedback, written reviews, and become friends. And to Cat—last but never least—who betas tirelessly and loves me to the bottom of my knackered work boots.

Dedication

For Cat

Always

CHAPTER ONE

The water was tepid and straight from the tap, its overriding taste one of chlorine. Trying to ignore the avid gaze of the twelve people seated to her right, Sanne Jensen drank it regardless, wishing she had painkillers to chase down.

"Detective Jensen?"

The curt prompt from the prosecution barrister sent a spasm through Sanne's fingers, and water spilled over the edge of her glass to form a small puddle on the wooden shelf. Unseen behind the lip of the witness stand, she pulled her jacket sleeve down over her hand and used it to clean up the mess.

"No," she said, and the twelve faces shifted back in her direction like a crowd at a slow motion tennis match. "There is no possibility that the chain of evidence was disrupted or that the evidence was contaminated. My partner Detective Nelson Turay and I personally supervised the collection of Mr. Mulligan's clothing, and proper procedures were adhered to at all times."

The prosecutor nodded, an unmistakeable glint of relief in her eyes. "So in your opinion there is no likelihood that Miss Gordon's blood could have been accidentally transferred onto the shirt of the defendant?"

"No. None at all."

"Thank you, Detective. No further questions."

Sanne waited for the judge to grant her permission to step down and then walked across the courtroom. She kept her head high, maintaining an air of professional confidence, although her body felt as if it had been pummelled and her legs threatened to give everything away by simply folding beneath her. Sitting in the gallery, Nelson smiled as she caught his eye, but his expression still bore the strain of the last two and a half hours.

The passageway to the exit was dimly lit and empty. Once certain she was out of sight, she leaned against the wall and wiped her face on her damp sleeve. Her head was throbbing, a dull, insistent beat that had become a constant companion.

"Fucking hellfire." She thumped the wall hard, sending an echo reverberating through the corridor, but the gesture didn't clear her head or work a miracle on her mood; it just made her knuckles sting. Too tired to care, she straightened her jacket and went out to face the music.

❖

"Did I balls it up?"

Sanne's quiet question broke the silence in the car. After meeting her outside the court, Nelson had said nothing, only snarling at a diversion forcing them into Sheffield's city centre, which hardly counted as conversation.

He hit the brakes, avoiding the bumper of the van in front by inches. Red light blazed across his face as he turned to look at her.

"Almost." He raised his hand, his thumb and index finger nearly touching. "You were this close, Sanne. This close to sending four months of work down the drain. She deserved better."

"I know," Sanne said. Sleet battered the windscreen, and wind gusted between the high buildings that lined Church Street. She clenched her teeth to stop them from chattering.

Trevor Mulligan had murdered his girlfriend after an argument about dishwashing had ended with him smashing her face to pieces with a beer bottle. Although he had concocted a story about a random intruder and done a competent job of removing trace evidence, he hadn't fooled Sanne or Nelson for a second. On the first day of his trial, a friend had provided an alibi and the defence successfully fought to suppress Mulligan's previous conviction for domestic assault. Now, on day four, Sanne's faltering performance on the witness stand had threatened to derail the entire case.

She peered out at the shops closing for the day and commuters rushing to catch trams, their collars and hoods drawn tight against the bitter weather, their umbrellas rendered useless by the strengthening wind. Defunct Christmas lights swayed between lampposts, waiting for the council to strip them down. Until then, they lingered unlit, underscoring that miserable period straight after New Year when everyone commuted in the dark, when the weather was at its shittiest and there was nothing to look forward to. With moods at a low ebb and tempers short, it was no wonder that crime rates shot through the roof. The nine detectives in EDSOP—the East Derbyshire Special Ops department—were struggling to keep their heads above the seasonal onslaught of rapes, beatings, and murders that traditionally occurred once the presents and tinsel were stashed away and the credit card bills began to drop onto the doormat. Every member of the team was exhausted, nobody was seeing much of their families, and the seemingly endless brutality was wearing on the most hardened nerves.

Still, Sanne knew, she had no excuses. Sensing Nelson reach over, she turned away from the window. His focus was already back on the traffic, but she noticed a ripple of warm air begin to thaw her fingertips and realised he had switched the heater to its highest setting.

"Do you want to get something to eat?" he asked. "Talk things through?"

The thought of food made her queasy. She shook her head. "I really am sorry about today," she said. "I'll be better, I promise."

He stopped at a junction, knocked the gear into neutral, and pulled on the handbrake, his movements methodical and unhurried. In front of the car, pedestrians jockeyed for position as they began to cross the road. He watched them for a moment before leaning back in his seat.

"Everyone has a wobble now and again, San." His voice had lost its edge, and his gentle tone made her want to hold on to him and bawl. She couldn't bear the thought of losing him as well.

"I've been wobbling for a while now." She drew in a deep breath that smelt of car exhaust and takeaway pizza. "Time to get on with things, I think."

"Yeah, it probably is." Pink and green neon swirled over the dash as he drove past a line of kebab shops. "Easier said than done sometimes, though."

"Aye." Misery crept in over her again. When she finally spoke, she could only manage a whisper. "Ain't that the truth."

❖

The sleet turned to snow as Nelson broke free of the snarled-up city streets, the sat nav muted in favour of Sanne's less convoluted directions.

"It's not supposed to stick," she said, watching wet flakes obliterate themselves on the windscreen. "Not tonight, anyway."

Nelson scoffed, waggling a finger toward the lights flashing on an approaching sign. "Famous last words, San."

The sign indicated the closure of the Snake Pass, the high, tortuous cross-Pennine road linking the cities of Manchester and Sheffield, a link connecting directly to Sanne's cottage.

"It's not sticking here, though," Nelson said, almost to himself. Then, louder, "Let's give it a go, eh? See how far we get." Accelerating past the sign, he began to whistle an off-key rendition of the *Mission Impossible* theme, drumming along with his fingers on the steering wheel. His enthusiasm proved contagious, snapping Sanne out of her glum mood and prompting her to provide backing vocals. He was one of only two people she ever dared to sing in front of.

"Bet you're glad you swapped your last piece of junk for your current piece of junk," he shouted over her finale. "You might even make it into work tomorrow." The streetlamps ended without warning, plunging the road into darkness, and he squeaked in a way that could only be described as unmanly. They didn't have the best track record on this route.

"I'll have you know I'm rather fond of my current piece of junk, and there was nothing wrong with my bloody Corsa either."

She folded her arms, sticking out her tongue in a deliberate attempt to distract him.

He gave a bark of laughter. "Oh no, it was absolutely fine until it attempted to murder us on this very road. You know there's a plaque on that wall we hit, commemorating the fact that we barely escaped with our lives." He spoke lightly but then sobered as he recognised the underlying truth of his words. Although the collision had been minor, its consequences later that night had almost killed them both.

"I say a little prayer every morning to give thanks for the unbreakability of your head," Sanne said.

To her relief, he grinned. "Thank you. Coming from an atheist, that means a lot."

"Yeah, I nick your god for a minute or two. Do you think she'll mind?"

"I think she'll be fine with that."

"How very benevolent of her."

Sanne propped her feet on the dashboard and let Nelson concentrate on the road, the only noise the grinding of his teeth as he negotiated a succession of sharp bends. The snow reverted to sleet before stopping altogether, but the dearth of vehicles travelling in the opposite direction told them that the summit was impassable.

"Drop me off at the top of the track, and I'll walk the rest of it," she said, spotting the approach to her cottage, though the landmarks were softened by snow. The unadopted access lane was steep and treacherous in the best of weather, and the pool car issued to Nelson for their court appearances hadn't come with four-wheel drive. In past winters, she had often abandoned her Corsa in the closest lay-by and hiked home.

"Are you sure?" he asked.

"Positive. Even if you got down there, you wouldn't be getting back up. You're welcome to kip in my spare room, but I reckon Abeni would like to clap eyes on you for once."

He pulled the car to a careful stop at the verge. "I did tell her I'd try to make it home for tea. At this rate I'll be lucky if she's not fed it to the cat."

"So kick me out here and head back to your lovely wife."

"I don't know, San. You're not dressed for a trek."

"Pop the boot for me. I put a pair of wellies in there this morning when I saw the forecast." She was already halfway out the door, the cold air stinging her lungs and pricking her ears. When the boot sprang open, she gripped the cold metal for balance as she replaced her smart shoes with battered wellies. Her feet instantly went numb. She had remembered the boots but forgotten to pack thicker socks.

"Text me when you get in," Nelson said, his brow knitted.

"Yes, Mum." She waved him off, yelling, "You text me too!" as he made a U-turn.

He stuck his thumb up through the open window but yanked it back when the car skidded. Sanne waited until the brake lights disappeared round a bend and then gave him a count of fifty just to be certain that he hadn't slipped into the first ditch. From forty onward, all she could hear was the sharp breeze rustling through the frozen ferns, and her own heartbeat.

"Okay then," she said.

White mist puffed out in front of her, and snow crackled beneath her boots. She pulled on her hat and gloves, looking up to see countless pinpricks in the clearing sky. The clouds released an almost full moon, and she let it guide her path, picking her way around puddles and favouring patches of snow over the icy stones. After a day sequestered in court, she relished the opportunity to stretch her legs. She broke into a clumsy trot, with the wellies slapping against her shins and threatening to upend her into the hedgerows. The first glimpse of lamplight in the window of her cottage made her shoulders sag, though. She slowed to a walk, scuffing her toes against loose pebbles like a reluctant child. She was tempted to keep jogging, to see how far she could get before exhaustion set in and she had no choice but to come home.

Not being prone to dramatic gestures, however, she merely took out her key and unlocked her door.

The kitchen was as frigid as the outside, the logs in the wood burner long since reduced to ash. She didn't have the energy to fetch new fuel and relight the burner, so she settled for the easy option, filling the kettle for a hot water bottle. Dirty snow melted from the grips of her wellies and ran across the tiled floor, and she stared at the puddles of grey water, too knackered to work out at first how they had got there.

"Bollocks," she said, kicking off the boots and toeing them back toward the doormat. Dragging the mop in one hand, she put the kettle on the stove with the other and sparked up the gas.

Although lunch had been half a sandwich, and nerves had made her skip breakfast altogether, cooking anything for her supper seemed like a waste of time when she was planning to fall straight into bed. Nibbling on a biscuit while the kettle boiled, she took out her phone to check her messages. Having bypassed two texts, she hovered over an e-mail from her boss, scared to death of opening it, its empty header an ominous sign. As the kettle began to whistle, she slid it from the stove and jabbed her finger on the e-mail, most of her attention fixed on avoiding the steam and extinguishing the gas. By the time she was finished with the kettle, the message hadn't gone away, but the trembling in her hands had stopped.

As was customary, Detective Inspector Eleanor Stanhope hadn't beaten around the bush: *See me in my office, 7:30 a.m., regarding the Mulligan case.*

Sanne had been expecting the summons—the EDSOP grapevine was lively, and very little passed Eleanor by—but that didn't assuage the dread that sent black dots spiralling across her eyes. She closed the e-mail and scooped the remnants of her biscuit into the bin. The phone lay on the counter like a portent while she screwed the top onto her hot water bottle. It would be so simple to break its jinx, to pick it up and read the unopened texts, but she knew that would make everything worse. Clutching the heated bottle to her chest, she turned out the kitchen light and walked upstairs in the dark.

Megan Fielding shivered as a pair of cold feet inched their way up her legs and came to rest between her thighs. The mattress dipped and rocked gently, and Meg opened her eyes in the half light as chilled but nimble fingers unfastened the buttons on her pyjama top and grazed across her torso. The press of warm lips against her throat made her shiver again.

"Is it still snowing out there?" she asked, not really caring one way or another, as the fingers circled her breast.

"No, but everything's frozen."

"Including you."

"Including me. This helps, though."

Meg chuckled. "I'll bet it does, Dr. Woodall." She pulled Emily closer and kissed her nose. "How did you get on with your asthmatic?"

"He died." Emily put a finger over Meg's lips. "Shh, no work."

"No work." Meg nodded and then sucked in her breath as Emily pushed a hand beneath the elastic of her pyjama bottoms. "Jesus Christ."

"Funnily enough," Emily murmured, "I'm much warmer now."

Meg sighed, every bone in her body seeming to melt into the bedding. "I'm very happy to be of assistance," she said.

Chapter Two

Meg woke to the smell of cinnamon and to a soft kiss on her cheek. She smiled, rolling over in layers of quilt that twisted around her legs and reminded her that she had never put her pyjamas back on.

"Morning." Emily set a mug of tea on the bedside table and held out a plate of raisin toast. She was dressed for work, having somehow managed to shower and make breakfast without disturbing Meg.

"Morning." Meg sat up and tugged the quilt until it covered her naked chest. "You spoil me, y'know. I'm used to fending for myself."

Emily perched on the edge of the bed. Her hand carried a faint scent of perfume as she ran her fingers through Meg's hair. "I like spoiling you. Indulge me."

Meg bit into a slice of toast, remembering to swallow before she spoke. "Consider yourself indulged. Shit, is that the time?"

"Afraid so." Smoothing the wrinkles from her shirt, Emily headed into the small en-suite bathroom, where Meg heard her run the tap and begin to clean her teeth. Then the door closed, muting the sounds, and Meg pushed the mug aside, running her hand along the top of the cabinet in a futile search for her phone. Light flooded the bedroom as the door opened again, and she changed course, picking up her tea, but Emily was already stooping by the bedside.

"I must've knocked it off with the mug," she said, passing the mobile to Meg. "I didn't hear anything from it last night. Did you?"

"No." Meg sipped the tea, aiming for nonchalance and apparently falling short, since Emily stayed on her knees and put a reassuring hand on Meg's thigh.

"I'm sure she's okay, but why don't you call her if you're worried?"

"I might," Meg said, knowing she probably wouldn't. "It's just difficult, you know, with all this."

"With us."

"Yeah, with us." The phrase felt weird: not unpleasant or wrong, just strange. "You better get going. The roads will be a disaster if it's snowed."

Emily accepted the change of subject gracefully. "There's no snow, but I need to be in early anyway. I'll see you at handover." She gave Meg a kiss flavoured with mouthwash. "Are you staying here today?"

"I'm not sure. I might head home, check whether the pipes have frozen and swap some clothes over. Was there something you needed me to do?"

"Oh, no. I didn't know whether to try to nip back here for lunch, that's all." Emily adjusted a clip and checked her hair in the mirror. She ran a finger over a smudge of lipstick, rubbing until she was satisfied with the result. Intrigued by the ritual, Meg attempted to spot the difference when Emily turned around, but nothing seemed to have changed. She still looked fresh and lovely, and she was regarding Meg with such a wanton gleam that it made Meg want to call in sick for the both of them.

Laughing, Emily shook her head and held up a finger in warning. "I'm going to go now," she said. "Before you get us into trouble."

Meg waved her off with a piece of toast, scattering crumbs on the quilt.

"The Hoover's in the cupboard next to the kitchen," Emily called over her shoulder.

"Yeah, yeah." Meg licked her finger and used it to dab up the crumbs, her phone still gripped in her other fist. She waited for the rattle of Emily's key in the lock before flipping open the protective leather casing. There were no new messages, no missed calls or e-mails. “Fucking hell, San,” she whispered.

She debated sending Sanne another text, something cheerful and irrelevant that would be easy to respond to, but nothing she thought of seemed right. She wondered at what point they had stopped being able simply to chat. She pulled her knees up and wrapped her arms around them, the phone dropping unnoticed to the bedding. Somewhere outside, a siren wailed, its two-tone horn blasting off the buildings and fading away almost immediately. In the flat next door, Christa marked six a.m. by switching on a blender and turning up her television to compensate. Meg put her hands over her ears, breathed through her nose, and did her utmost to tune it all out.

Sanne stood by her kitchen window and gazed out onto frosted pastures and hills whose summits gleamed white beneath the moon. Bearing the weather in mind, she had set her alarm for earlier than usual, but there had been no new snow overnight, so she’d had extra time to sweat through the first shirt she had put on and almost throw up her breakfast into the toilet. She hated being in trouble, and she was under no illusions regarding her upcoming meeting with Eleanor. It made her feel eight years old again, hemmed into a corner by a clique of girls in the year above who didn’t understand exactly why she was their target, just that she was odd enough for them to single her out. She knew that the circumstances were completely different, that this time she deserved whatever was coming, but it didn’t lessen the panicky sensation fluttering in her stomach or the urge to draw the curtains, lock the doors, and hide beneath her bed with a blanket over her head.

The idea of trying to squeeze in among the junk stored under her bed brought a smile to her face. She stacked her breakfast dishes and rubbed her eyes with her fingertips, and five minutes later, she was out of the door, bundled up against the subzero temperature and cracking the ice on the hens’ water trough.

"Morning, girls." In the torchlight, she spied the rooster snuggled in the corner of the coop, his flock surrounding him. "Morning, Git Face."

They had plenty of food left, so she started the engine on her Land Rover and kept her fingers crossed until she was sure that it wouldn't cut out. Although a thick layer of frost covered the windows, the heater performed a small miracle by coming on when she turned the dial. Opting to stay in the warmth and let the windows thaw slowly, she dug out her mobile and finally read Meg's messages, the first wishing her good luck in court and the second asking her how she had got on.

I fucked everything up and I'm in deep shit, was what she wanted to say, but that would only make Meg worry and try to phone her. *Everything's fine, don't you be fretting*, she typed. *Say hello to Emily.* It was a long time before she pressed *send.*

❖

Meg ate her second piece of toast sitting on the floor by the living room's patio doors. Neither the bedroom nor the kitchen had a window, but from this vantage point she could watch the sky lighten as the sun began to rise. The shadowy outlines of nearby apartment blocks gradually became solid shapes, while the orange streetlamps arcing over the bypass blinked off in a random order. The window overlooked the courtyard of the complex, whose residents were striding through it in a steady procession, their schedules governed by a nine-to-five workday and the vagaries of public transport.

Crunching her toast, Meg strained to see the hills that surrounded the city, a sudden claustrophobia making her push the doors open. She was three floors up, and the wind rushed into the room, carrying with it a waft of diesel fumes and frying bacon. Scowling, she slammed the doors shut again and took her plate into the kitchen. Emily's apartment was only four miles from Sheffield Royal Hospital, so convenient for work that Meg often stayed over during a run of shifts. It was a routine they had fallen into, but Meg had never been a city girl, and five months down the line she could feel the walls closing in around her.

She rinsed her plate and mug, splashing suds onto the floor, heedless of the mess she was making. As she turned around, a flash of silver caught her eye, and she picked up the small parcel Emily had left on the table. She unfastened the ribbon binding it, and the paper unravelled to reveal a box of chocolate truffles with a note resting on top: *No reason. I just like making you smile. Em x*

Meg laughed and shook her head, her bad mood falling away. Back at her spot by the patio doors, she shoved the biggest chocolate into her mouth and settled against the sofa to watch the city wake up.

❖

Anxiety washed over Sanne the instant she stepped into the office. Her palms were already sweaty, and damp patches beneath her armpits were making her replacement shirt stick to her. Duncan Carlyle sniggered as she walked past his desk, but she stared directly ahead, resisting the impulse to kick him in the shin and focusing her attention on Eleanor's office door. It was shut, but she could see someone moving behind its frosted glass.

"She said to send you straight in."

Sanne spun around to face Fred Aspinall. He was close enough to touch her, although she hadn't heard him approach. One of the thick files balanced across his arms slipped, sending a cascade of paper to the floor, and he swore, attempting to keep the pile under control while bending to retrieve the escapees.

Sanne put a hand on his shoulder. "I've got it, Fred." She crouched in his stead, both knees clicking loudly.

"Bloody hell, yours are worse than mine." At fifty-six, and with a considerable paunch, Fred wasn't renowned for his athleticism, but he succeeded in making Sanne smile.

"Fell runner's knees. Occupational hazard." She stood and gave him the papers. "You, on the other hand, look positively spry. What's your secret?" She had heard rumours about a new lady love for the triple divorcee, and the blush that spread to the tips of his ears told her there was truth behind the gossip.

He seemed on the verge of answering but snapped his teeth together instead and nodded over her shoulder. "You better get in there."

When Sanne looked up, she saw Eleanor's door was ajar. "Fuck," she whispered. "Wish me luck, will you?"

"Be over before you know it." He winced. "Your bollocking, not your career, love."

"Yeah, I hope you're right. Only one way to find out."

She crossed the short remaining distance and knocked on the door. Eleanor's response was a curt and immediate, "Come in."

Sanne stopped in front of the desk with her hands fisted by her sides. "You wanted to see me, ma'am." She managed to keep her voice steady, but there was no way she could unclench her fingers.

Eleanor gave a single nod. "Before we begin, do you want a Federation representative present?"

"I'd prefer not to, ma'am." Sanne had already decided against contacting a rep. She trusted Eleanor to be fair, whether or not an independent witness was present. It might be naive, but the fewer people involved, the better, as far as she was concerned.

Eleanor ticked a box on a pre-printed form. "I spoke to Margaret Harris at some length last night," she said. She paused for Sanne to acknowledge the name of the prosecution barrister assigned to the Mulligan case. "It was late, and she was obviously tired, so I'll make allowances for that, but she was not at all happy with you, Detective Jensen."

Sanne flinched at the use of her official title. It was a tactic that Eleanor rarely resorted to. "No, ma'am, I don't imagine she was."

"'Lacklustre,' 'hesitant,' and 'barely convincing' were just a few of her more polite phrases. She wanted me to throw the book at you, and I must admit that after listening to her tirade for more than an hour, I am tempted to abide by her demands."

"Yes, ma'am." For a fleeting second, Sanne wanted the same, to have it all done with so she could go home and stop pretending that she could function. Digging her fingernails into her palms, she let the sharp pain excise that notion. It took all her willpower, but she met and held Eleanor's gaze. "I can only apologise. I don't have any excuses, and I know I let everyone down. It won't happen again."

Eleanor leaned forward and considered Sanne in the manner of a scientist scrutinising an unusual specimen. "What the hell is going on with you? You look like death warmed over, your most recent case reports are all substandard, and you're going to pieces on the witness stand. Is it the Cotter case? Some delayed posttraumatic reaction?"

Sanne stiffened at the name, but she refused to use Billy Cotter as an excuse for her behaviour, easy as that would have been. "No, ma'am. It's not that."

"Because I can arrange counselling if necessary."

"No, thank you."

"Are you and Nelson having problems?"

"No." Sanne shook her head emphatically. "Definitely not."

Eleanor pushed her glasses to her forehead and folded her arms. "Which leaves me with family, finances, or the death of a beloved pet."

It was only the hint of a reprieve, but Sanne took heart from it.

"It's sort of a family thing, boss." She left it at that, hoping Eleanor wouldn't pry, wouldn't force her to reveal that she felt as if her life had slowly broken into pieces over the last five months. She didn't need to voice the admission to know how pathetic it would sound, and she resolved to get a fucking grip on herself, if she managed to leave the office with a job.

"Anything you need support with?" Eleanor asked, sounding less like a detective inspector now and more like a boss who knew a fair bit about Sanne's background.

"No, but thank you." Sanne's fingers ached as she straightened them. She wondered whether her nails had drawn blood.

"You've always been an asset to this team, but I won't hesitate to transfer you out if you become a liability." Eleanor dropped her glasses back into place and made a note on the file in front of her. "You're on a three-month improvement notice. If there are no further issues after that time, the notice will be removed from your records."

"Yes, ma'am," Sanne said, both relieved and mortified.

Eleanor nodded. "You're dismissed. Shut the door on your way out."

Chapter Three

It would have been so simple for Sanne to lock herself in the bathroom, to stay there until most of her colleagues had left the office on fieldwork assignments and she could face the rest. She didn't, though. She hadn't earned her position as the only woman on Eleanor's team, and its youngest member, by being a coward. Sticking to her usual route, she headed straight back to her desk, which gave Carlyle another opportunity to grin at her and earned her encouraging nods from Fred and George.

A mug of tea was waiting on her mouse mat, steaming hot, with a pair of chocolate digestives beside it. Nelson had judged the timing of her bollocking to perfection. He let her take a couple of mouthfuls of tea and start in on the biscuits before he spoke.

"How'd it go?"

"I'm still here." She adjusted her grip on the digestive, where the chocolate was melting in her sweaty fingers. "Three-month improvement warning. I expected worse."

Nelson was watching her carefully. They had worked together for almost two years, and he was adept at gauging her moods. "Still feel like crap, though, don't you?"

She nodded, and felt less crappy for having admitted it. "I wish she'd yelled at me. I'd rather deal with that than with quiet disappointment."

He smiled in recognition. "Took the mum route, did she? My mum scarcely raised her voice, but she could set me on a guilt trip for a month."

"I think they must all go to some sort of course," Sanne said. "Mine would never shout at us. She just had this way of making us feel awful for days after we'd done something wrong, whereas my dad would throw a tantrum, belt us one, and then go to the pub and forget all about it."

"That was probably down to the cider, San."

"Aye. One of the few advantages to having an alky for a parent." She sucked the chocolate from her fingers and used the cleanest to switch her computer on. "Right. Roberts and Hussein. Are you still okay with Burgess and Harrison?"

Her crisp return to their open cases made Nelson grin. "I should be able to get mine off to the CPS by this afternoon, and then I can take one of yours off your hands."

She was already double-clicking her first file. "Fabulous. I'm almost done with Roberts. If you get a spare hour, how about you read my summary through and I'll crack on with Hussein?"

Nelson licked the nib of his pen in readiness. "I love it when you organise me," he said.

❖

Sanne was midway through reading an interview transcript and tapping notes into a second document when she heard the footsteps approaching. She didn't need to look up to know who was behind her. It wasn't the shadow falling across her desk that gave him away—Duncan Carlyle was of average build, with a nondescript profile—but he wore the same pungent aftershave every day, and every day it made her want to stick her head in a bucket. He had obviously waited until Nelson had gone to fetch a late lunch, leaving her alone. She braced herself for the inevitable diatribe, for him to tell her that she'd have been bumped back into uniform if he'd had his way, and that it was only a matter of time before she fucked up again and made Eleanor regret giving her a second chance. Carlyle had been sullen and vindictive prior to the Cotter case, but his bitterness had ramped up to a whole new level in the aftermath.

"Hey, Sarge," she said, a polite greeting intended as damage limitation. When he didn't answer, she minimised her notes to prevent him reading over her shoulder. His proximity was making her nervous, so she rolled her chair sideward, widening the gap between them and allowing her to make eye contact. She only saw the file as he dropped it onto her keyboard.

"You're up," he said.

She shook her head, reaching to pass the file back. "No, Scotty and Jay just closed theirs. We already have four open."

He shrugged, and a smile elongated the feeble moustache he had been growing since November. Something pink, possibly a crumb of jammy toast, was stuck to the edge closer to Sanne.

"As of"—he made a show of checking his watch—"forty minutes ago, Scotty and Jay are helping me with a special project. Which means that you're up. Dead smack rat in Malory Park. Enjoy."

"Right." She straightened the file. She couldn't argue with him. He would already have agreed to the allocation with Eleanor, so her only option was to play him at his own game by refusing to react. "No problem, Sarge. We'll get right out there."

Her heart sank even as she forced brightness into her words. No one would give a shit about another dead heroin addict. There would be no cooperative witnesses and no media interest, the motive would trace back to the drugs, and securing a conviction would be next to impossible. The assignment was the equivalent of Carlyle giving her a rope and kicking her toward the gallows. She wondered whether she'd be able to keep her head out of the noose. On the plus side, she had to admit that even a small chance of pissing on his chips was attractive. She touched the side of her face.

"Got a bit of something in your 'tache, Sarge."

He frowned and dabbed at the offending crumb, catching it on his finger and then floundering because he had nowhere to wipe it. As his face turned scarlet, he shoved his hand into his trouser pocket and strode away, almost colliding with Nelson in the narrow aisle between the desks.

"Sanne Jensen, have you been upsetting the sarge again?"

Nelson placed a paper bag in front of her, and she handed him the file in an unfair exchange. One look at its cover sheet told him everything he needed to know.

"Sorry, mate," she said.

"Don't be. It's not your fault he's an arse." Nelson picked up the lunch bags again. "Come on. We can picnic at Malory. I've heard it's lovely in the winter."

"You heard wrong," she said, and caught the coat that he threw at her.

❖

"Third left off Balan. Second right, first right." Sanne traced the route with her finger, the map dog-eared by years of similar treatment. "No, second right, then second right," she corrected herself, spotting another tiny street leading off the feeder road.

"I hate this place," Nelson muttered. He indicated before switching lanes, preparing to leave the bypass and turn into Malory Park. The sign for the council estate was a pock-holed, graffiti-strewn remnant that might as well have borne the legend: *Abandon All Hope, Ye Who Enter Here*.

Built six miles outside the city centre and encircled by concrete flyovers that seemed designed to trap its residents within its confines, Malory was a pit of crime and poverty, where Sheffield Council housed its least desirable citizens just to keep them away from everyone else. Sanne had grown up on a similar sinkhole estate, but compared to Malory, Halshaw's residents had been model citizens, their houses almost palatial. Despite the efforts of community projects and social workers and schools in special measures, most of the kids raised on Malory stayed on Malory, and the cycle of alcohol, heroin, underage pregnancy, and chronic unemployment rarely got broken.

In a rush to get to a crime scene reported more than three hours ago, Nelson and Sanne had eaten their lunch en route, and Sanne's egg sandwich sat uneasily in her stomach as Nelson drove around Balan, the largest of the estate's circular roads.

"Third left," she said, aware that he had the memory of a goldfish when it came to directions.

"What is it we're after, again?"

"Twenty-six B Pellinore Walk. According to the file, it's an upstairs flat."

She wiped the steam from her window, squinting through a mist of freezing rain to the houses beyond the slick pavements. Several were boarded up, bearing notices declaring that everything of value had been removed. Their doors had been smashed open anyway by enterprising or destitute residents distrustful of authority. A tiny proportion of the occupied houses were in a reasonable condition—their gardens not too overgrown, clean net curtains behind their barred windows—but most were verging on ruin, with a desperate air that made Sanne gnaw on the skin at the side of her thumb.

"Three…four…" Nelson straightened fingers on the wheel as he counted. "Five, oh, and there's six."

Sanne rolled her eyes. "Six sofas, or six mattresses?"

"Both. I thought I'd go for the record. Ah, seven."

Wrecked furniture dumped in front gardens was as ubiquitous on this estate as the pairs of muddy trainers tied together at the laces and launched over the telephone wires. It was easy to understand why: people either had no transport to get to the tip or couldn't be bothered trying to keep up appearances, and the council levied a charge for removing large items. Sanne remembered a tattered sofa sitting in her mum's back garden one glorious summer while she and Meg made it into dens, battered each other with the cushions, and used it as an impromptu trampoline. Her mum had eventually chopped it into pieces small enough to carry, and given Sanne and her two siblings fifty pence each to carry it bit by bit to the local dump. Though she had left it in the garden for a while, she would never have kept it out the front where anyone walking past could have seen it.

"There's your eighth." Sanne pointed out a mattress and caught a glimpse of movement around a hole where the springs had burst forth. "Ooh, do you get a bonus if it's rat-infested?"

"I'm not sure, but I think I should."

"I'll let it count for double. Are you happy now?"

He beamed at her, his target surpassed. "Delirious."

She shook her head in despair. "Meanwhile, back with our dead chap. Take your first right. That's Pellinore, and the evens are on, let's see, your side."

She counted down for him, stopping when she spotted the Crime Scene Investigation van outside the address. Rain hit her full in the face as she got out of the car. She bowed her head and hurried across to 26B. Blue-and-white crime scene tape fluttered around the tiny paved area where the wheelie bins were stored, one loose end of ribbon taking flight in the wind. A young officer, soaked through and visibly miserable, nodded at them as they approached. They entered their collar numbers and the time into his log and signed their names.

"SOCO still up there?" Nelson asked.

"Yeah, but I think they're almost done. First on scene is at Twenty-two A, with the bloke who called it in." The officer wiped a drip from his nose. "SOCO are waiting for you," he added in a tone verging on petulant.

Having both spent countless hours on similar thankless assignments, neither Sanne nor Nelson commented on his insubordination. Possibly grateful for the reprieve, he held the door to the flat open and then shut it again behind them.

"Bulb's gone," a male voice called down almost at once, pre-empting any attempt to switch on a light. "We left you some clobber by the stairs."

Panning around with his Maglite, Nelson located Tyvek suits, booties, gloves, and masks. Sanne donned her outfit in record time. In the close confines of the entrance, even the air felt mucky. Avoiding a trail of crushed beer cans and what looked like ingrained dog shit, she led the way upstairs and through a single door that opened into the living room.

In lieu of curtains, someone had covered the window with thick black paint. Even with her own torch, it took a moment for Sanne's eyes to adjust, and her sense of smell rushed in to compensate. She put a hand to her face, pressing her mask inward to shut out the stink of faeces, rotting dog food, and clotted blood.

"Jesus Christ," Nelson said, sweat beading on his brow.

"We're in the bedroom," the voice called. "Tread carefully."

Sanne looked down, noting the mess of foil wraps and needle-topped syringes glittering at her feet. There was only one piece of furniture in the room: a sofa with a single, mismatched cushion. On its arm, a Jif lemon balanced beside an overflowing ashtray.

"Desperate times," she said, tipping the plastic lemon with a gloved finger. She would balk at putting the juice on her pancakes, never mind mainlining the stuff, but addicts used it as a handy though dangerous substitute for pure citric acid.

"It can make you go blind, you know," Nelson said as they tiptoed through the detritus.

"Yeah? No wonder! It tastes vile."

His mask twitched, and the shape of his eyes told her he was smiling. "From injecting it, not eating it, you pillock. I Googled the finer points after we took that lad in from Halshaw. Remember him?"

"Gap-toothed Brian with the manky leg ulcers? How could I forget?"

She made a beeline out of the room, relieved to see a bare but functioning light bulb in the hallway, not that it did anything to improve the ambience. A short strip of uncarpeted concrete led to a kitchen comprising a grease-covered oven and a bin stacked high with polystyrene takeaway boxes, a bathroom with a suite that might once have been eggshell blue, and a bedroom, from which a blond man poked his head.

"Kept the place nice, didn't he?" The Scene of Crime Officer shook their hands in turn. "Ted Ulverston, Senior SOCO. We're not far from finishing up in here. I never thought I'd be glad to get outside and breathe the Malory air."

Sanne knew the feeling. As she stepped into the bedroom, the stench became even more pronounced, the air stifling. An electric heater still emanated warmth, having only just been unplugged, and a grotesquely bloated and discoloured body lay before it.

"Vic's name is Andrew Culver, thirty-five years old. First officer in here found a tattoo on his right forearm and got a hit when she ran it through the PNC." Ulverston stooped and tapped the ink stretched taut across the swollen limb, leaving a trickle of brown fluid in his wake. "Three stab wounds to the chest, one to the abdomen, and one to the neck that severed the right common carotid. Weapon is a serrated blade approximately three inches in diameter, and the wound tracks are deep. We'll know more after the PM, but I think it's safe to say that our perp is one pissed-off individual."

"Any idea how long he's been there?" Nelson asked.

"It's tricky to say, because the rate of decomp has been accelerated by the fire. He's come out of rigor, though, so at least forty-eight hours."

Nelson grunted in assent. Sanne crouched by the body, trying to see past the decomposition. Blood had sprayed across the walls in gradually diminishing arcs, suggesting that the wound to Culver's carotid had been one of the first inflicted. She imagined him raising his hands to try to stem the flow and leaving himself defenceless as his assailant continued to hack at him. His jeans and shirt were stretched taut across his distended belly, but their original size implied a man of slight build, which would fit in with chronic drug abuse. He probably hadn't put up much of a fight.

"Did he live here?" she asked. She pushed back to her feet, restoring some distance between herself and the black tongue lolling from Culver's mouth. The bedroom was as Spartan as the living room, with a mattress taking up much of the floor space and a solitary comb sitting atop a cardboard crisp box. The price sticker still on the soles of his fake leather shoes revealed they'd been a bargain at £3.99, while a bin bag seemed to function as an improvised wardrobe, although he hadn't had enough clothing to fill it.

"According to the first officer, Culver's been renting the flat for eighteen months," Ulverston said, standing up with Sanne. "I think she's already spoken to the landlord to confirm that."

"Right. I'll have a word with her." Tired of playing catch-up, Sanne put out a radio call to summon the officer back to the flat. Half listening to the affirmative response, she walked into the hallway and waited for Nelson to join her. "Front door's the only way in, and there are no signs of forced entry."

"I'm guessing people around here lock everything up," he said.

She nodded, not mentioning that she habitually secured her own doors and windows even though she lived in the middle of nowhere.

"The door had a security chain and a peephole. If we can establish that Culver normally used them, it would narrow our suspects down to someone he knew and let in."

"It's unlikely to be random, San," Nelson said, returning to the living room. "I can't see it being a burglary gone bad."

"Me neither. I'm just trying to keep an open mind." She sighed, and the warmth of her breath moistened her mask. "What would a burglar have pinched, though?"

There were no marks or depressions in the grimy carpet to suggest that a television or other electronic goods had recently been removed, and the odds of Culver owning anything of value seemed slim. He must have existed hand-to-mouth, or in his case hand-to-vein, his benefits exchanged for the best hit he could find and just enough food to keep him ticking over. Surrounding a boarded-up space where a fireplace would have been, a wooden mantelpiece—the landlord's one concession to homeliness—stood bare. Culver had amassed no keepsakes or ornaments. Were it not for his body in the next room, the flat would have appeared abandoned.

"Could've just pinched his stash, I suppose," Sanne said. "We've seen people killed for less." She wasn't convinced, though. The violence meted out seemed too extreme somehow, too personal, not the result of a scrappy fight between two desperate users.

"True," Nelson said, but he sounded equally sceptical. He toed an empty metal bowl near the corner of the sofa. "I wonder where the dog is."

"Scarpered, stolen, or taken in by the bloke at Twenty-two A. Hopefully, the latter." Sanne scribbled on her pad, adding the final touches to a sketch of the living room. "There aren't any signs of a struggle, are there? I mean, it's hard to tell when there's so little furniture, but nothing's scuffed or knocked over in here, and it was the same in the bedroom."

"No. Adds more credence to the theory that Culver knew the perp and was taken by surprise."

"Aye," Sanne said over her shoulder. Her sketch complete, she was busy opening the kitchen units. "Hey, I found his filing cabinet." She set the drawer on the countertop and riffled through the assorted paperwork. "He was three months behind in his rent, so the landlord needs looking at. Methadone prescriptions, gas bill and leccy bill, both well in the red…" Her summary trailed off as she lifted a set of photographs from the bottom of the pile. Two dated in the early eighties were small and faded. Both featured typical family scenes: a young boy riding a donkey on Blackpool beach, and the same lad playing football in a back garden. More recent photos were of an elderly couple—annotated *Mam and Dad, silver wedding*—and a thirty-something woman with a pretty smile. She returned to the beach shot.

"Think he might be our vic?" Nelson said, looking over her shoulder.

"Most likely. The age is about right." The boy on the donkey was laughing, the sky behind him a cloudless blue. "Poor sod."

"Makes you wonder where it all went wrong." Nelson rustled the set of evidence bags he'd stolen from SOCO's pile. "Anyway, we need to start bagging and tagging, or we're going to be here all night."

"I wouldn't bet on that. Other than the paperwork, I've found a spoon, a fork, and a knife."

"A serrated, blood-caked knife about three inches in diameter?" he asked, hope shining in his eyes.

She displayed an implement that might have cut through butter on a good day. "Not as such, no."

"Bugger."

"I do admire your optimism, though. It's one of your finest assets." She took half the bags from him and sealed up the cutlery just in case. "Meet you in the bedroom?"

He laughed. "Can't refuse an offer like that, can I?"

"Not seen you for a while, love."

Arthur Grimshaw's gravelly voice made Meg pause at her front door, key half turned, her truffle-sticky thumb still in her mouth. Arthur lived next door but one, and was perennially cheerful despite his metastatic throat cancer and a prognosis he had outlived by reaching Christmas.

"Hey, Arthur. I've been staying in the city quite a bit." She prodded at the icy step with her boot, hoping he would leave it at that.

"Got yourself a new lady-friend, have you?" Showing no inclination to leave it at that, he wandered up the drive toward her. "What happened to the little one? Sanney?"

"Sann-er." Meg made the correction without thinking. "And we were never a couple, Arthur. Well, not really. It's hard to explain." She kicked the step with more force. Her relationship with Sanne baffled them both. They had never been able to decide what, if anything, was going on between them, so defining it in terms that her elderly neighbour might understand wasn't going to happen.

Fortunately, Arthur seemed to sense her discomfort. He blew on his hands to warm them and then tipped his hat at her. "Just so long as you're happy," he said, and gave a phlegmy whistle to bring his dog to heel.

"I am. Thanks." She returned his wave. "Give my best to Flo."

He continued to whistle as he wandered back out to the street, the melody altering in pitch and volume without ever becoming recognisable, the dog beginning to yap along with it. The sound stopped abruptly when Meg closed the front door behind her. She stood in the darkened hallway, breathing in the familiar smells of home and then wrinkling her nose at the odour of something forgotten and now decaying.

"Bollocks."

Two mummified bananas and a furry pear-shaped blob had turned her fruit bowl into a biology experiment. She disposed of them in the compost bin and reluctantly added the withered bouquet of roses that had occupied pride of place on the kitchen table. The card fell from the vase as she lifted it, and the note inside—short and charming, in fountain-penned handwriting improbably neat for a doctor—made her smile as she reread it.

Meg hadn't lied to Arthur. She really was happy, and she was as shocked as anyone by that. One last-minute, half-jokey date two weeks after returning from a holiday in Greece had led to another, less jokey one, and then a third involving flowers, champagne, and a candlelit dinner. Midway through rinsing out the fruit bowl, Meg shook her head and her smile widened. Emily Woodall had literally romanced the pants off her, and she had surprised herself by enjoying every minute of it.

Tucking the card into her wallet for safekeeping, she returned to more mundane matters. She fished out her list and spread it on the table, putting a big tick through *Chuck out rotten stuff* and skipping to the next item: *Underwear*. Although she and Emily were a similar size, Emily favoured frills and lace, so sharing wasn't an option, not that Emily seemed particularly inclined to swap their clothing around. It was subtle differences like that that always gave Meg pause, forcing her to bite her tongue on a comparison: "Sanne would steal my knickers on a whim" or "San's got a sweater of mine that she's had for so long, she's convinced she bought it," harmless details that now seemed dangerously loaded. Her friendship with Sanne had become a minefield, to the extent that she hardly dared mention her at all, although Emily often asked after her. At times, Meg felt as if she had lost a vital part of herself—the easy references and conversational shortcuts, the years of growing up together, and the shared memories—but Sanne had put herself at such a distance in the last few months that Meg was no longer sure how to breach the gap or whether Sanne even wanted her to.

Holding up a well-worn bra, Meg tried to remember whether it was hers. She packed it into her overnight bag regardless, having not yet reached the stage of parcelling up all Sanne's belongings and leaving them on her doorstep. The phone rang and cut off again within seconds, but the sound reminded her to check its messages. With half an ear, she listened to a double-glazing salesman, two hang-ups, and a dental reminder, and she was contemplating deleting them all when the last message stopped her in the middle of the bedroom floor. Bundled socks dropped from her slack hands as she recognised her brother's voice. She ran to the machine, stumbling over the clothing, but when she tried to replay the message she got the dentist instead. She hit *next*, jabbing the button with painful force.

"I've just been to Mum's," Luke said, even that simple sentence sounding like a warning. "We need to talk. I'll be in touch."

The machine dated the call as two days ago, and he hadn't phoned back since. Meg listened to the recording again, picking out street sounds: car horns, the rumble of engines, a merry laugh. He had probably used a telephone box, which left her no way of pinpointing his location or contacting him. She huddled on the edge of the bed, her arms wrapped around her torso as if to ward off a blow. She had no idea how he had found her number, but if he had that then he undoubtedly knew her address.

"Fuck," she whispered.

Her first instinct was to call Sanne.

Chapter Four

Sitting on the very edge of a sofa that carried a distinct whiff of urine, Sanne watched smoke curl up from Kevin Hopkins's cigarette. It had taken him four attempts to light it, and his hand was still trembling so violently that he was in danger of extinguishing it again. He sucked on the filter, sending a flare of orange to the tip, and aimed the smoke toward the ceiling.

"Sorry, miss," he said. "I forgot what you asked me."

"That's okay, Kevin." She kept her voice low and reassuring. From the officer's account, Hopkins had spent most of the afternoon crying or throwing up. They weren't treating him as a suspect; according to a discharge note from Sheffield Royal, he had been hospitalised with cellulitis for the last five days. "You'd just said you had a key to Mr. Culver's, sorry, Andy's flat. I asked what prompted you to let yourself in there this morning."

He nodded and knocked ash into a mug. "Buster."

She patted the head of the dog whose chin had been resting on her knee for the past forty minutes. "What about Buster?"

"I could hear her barking and carrying on. She went mental when I knocked on the door, and Andy would always yell at her if she did that, only he didn't." Hopkins stifled a sob by drawing on his cigarette, and then blew his nose on a wet tissue. "I thought he'd gone under on the smack—he'd stopped breathing once before—and the chain was off the door, so I went in, and I found…I found him all black and swelled up like that."

Buster whined at the sound of Hopkins's distress, and Sanne scratched the dog's ears while she waited for Hopkins to settle. She felt her phone vibrate with an incoming call, before the voicemail cut it off.

"Can you remember when you last saw Andy?" she asked, once Hopkins had regained his composure.

"What day is it today?"

"Thursday."

His fingers tapped on the chair as he counted out the week. Blisters and open sores on his skeletal arms spoke of a lively heroin addiction, so any timeline he provided would be sketchy at best.

"Maybe last Friday," he said. "It were the day before I went in with my bad legs."

She watched Nelson scribble a note. He had taken a back seat in the interview, letting her develop a rapport while recording the salient points for her. The more Hopkins perceived the interview as an informal chat, the more forthcoming he was likely to be.

"And how did Andy seem to you?" At Hopkins's blank look, she expanded the question. "His mood, I mean. Was he his normal self, or did you notice anything different about him? Did he tell you that he was worried or scared about anything?"

Hopkins took a mouthful from the mug he had shaken ash into, grimaced at the taste, and took another. "I think he was normal. Happy, even. Said things were looking up."

"Did he tell you why?"

"He might've, but we shared a tenner's worth." He opened his hands in apology. "Don't remember nothing after that, miss."

"That's okay. You've been very helpful."

Hopkins had already provided a list of Culver's friends and associates, although Sanne doubted it was comprehensive. Culver's parents had both died recently, leaving him with no immediate family in the area. Single for six months since the smiling woman in the kitchen photograph had broken his heart by calling off their engagement, he had loved his dog, hadn't gone out much, and had always used the security chain and peephole.

Still clenching the cigarette between his teeth, Hopkins staggered into the kitchen, where Sanne heard him open and close the microwave. He came back proffering a wad of notes.

"For Andy's funeral," he said, dropping the money in her lap when she was too slow to accept it. "They'll bury him like shit, otherwise."

Looking down, she estimated his donation ran to almost a hundred pounds. "I can't take this. I'm not going to be involved in organising the funeral." She tried to return the notes, but he waved her off.

"Pass it on for me, then. I'd sort it myself if I could." His face crumpled and he began to cry again, so she folded the money into an evidence bag and put it in her pocket.

"I'll make sure the Co-op get this. I promise," she said.

He wiped his nose on his hand and then wiped his hand on his trousers. "I appreciate that, miss."

She nodded at Nelson, who stood to leave. "If you think of anything else, give me a call on this number." She set her card on the arm of the sofa and patted Buster's head in farewell.

"You'll find who done this, won't you?" Hopkins said as they reached the door.

"We'll do our best," she said, and watched his expression shift from expectant to despondent as he read between the lines.

He nodded, resigned to the inevitable. "Thanks anyway, miss."

❖

Stiffened by multiple layers of paint, the bolts on the back door grated as Meg shoved them into place. This was the first time she had ever used them. One of the reasons she had chosen to live in Rowlee was the sense of safety that the tiny village afforded her, and although the kidnapping case over the summer had made her more circumspect in those first shell-shocked months of its aftermath, keeping her doors locked had seemed enough of a precaution.

She took her frustration out on the lower bolt, slamming it across and kicking its metal handle until it lay flush against the door. Luke had never been to Rowlee. They had met occasionally, at his behest, but Meg had always insisted those meetings took place on neutral ground, a cafe in Manchester that gave no hint as to her home address and where there would be plenty of witnesses. He would cadge money and a fry-up, berate her for not getting in touch with their dad, and then vanish into the crowd. She hadn't seen him for three years—a gap suggestive of a jail sentence—but one hint of a threat from him and she was triple-locking her doors and jumping at the slightest sound.

Determined not to be hounded from her own home, and with time to kill before her shift, she brewed a pot of tea and took it into the living room. Sweeping out the fireplace seemed too much like hard work, so she draped a rug over her knees and curled on the sofa with her mug. Her mobile rang the instant the tea touched her lips, the hot liquid splashing onto her chin as she jumped.

"Fucking hell!" She wiped her face dry and snatched up the phone. Confident that it was one number Luke wouldn't have, she answered the call without hesitation, hoping it was Sanne. The voice on the line dashed that hope instantly.

"Ms. Fielding? It's Clara, from Rainscroft."

"Hi, Clara. Everything okay?" Meg couldn't remember ever having spoken to the woman before. The staff at Rainscroft Nursing Home were in a constant state of flux, with new faces replaced by even newer ones on an almost weekly basis.

"Well, there's been a bit of an incident," Clara said, in the singsong tone traditionally used with toddlers.

"What kind of incident? Is my mum all right?"

As Clara cleared her throat, prevaricating, Meg could hear someone singing a sea shanty in the background. A door shut, silencing the chorus mid-sentence.

"A man came to visit her," Clara said.

Mouthing a litany of curses, Meg closed her eyes. "Did he give his name?" she asked, once she was certain she wouldn't swear down the phone.

"Yes, he did. He said he was Mrs. Fielding's son Lucas, and she did seem to recognise him when we took him to her room, but a few minutes later, we heard her shouting for help, and, well, he…"

"He *what*?" Meg wanted to reach down the connection and shake the answer out. With the phone wedged between her ear and shoulder, she grabbed her keys, listening to Clara stuttering something about bruising and a policy of phoning an ambulance. "Cancel the ambulance. I'm on my way over," she said, and cut Clara off before the excuses could start.

❖

Meg threw her wet coat on an empty hook and scribbled her name in the Rainscroft visitors' book. On the line above, Luke had signed in at 3:50 p.m. He hadn't signed out again, and he had managed to misspell his own surname.

"You stupid piece of shit," she muttered.

Seven years older than Meg and as thick as two short planks, Luke had spent most of his schooldays smoking pot and drinking lager on the back field. After failing the two GCSEs he had bothered to turn up for, he had been employed by their dad as a plumber's apprentice, until his first spell in prison had squandered that opportunity as well. Not long after his release, their dad had ditched the family to live with a seventeen-year-old in London, and that was about the point where everything had gone to hell.

"Meg? Thank you for getting here so quickly."

Meg dropped the pen back into its holder and shook Rosalind Cairn's outstretched hand. A stout, bustling woman, Ros had managed Rainscroft for twenty-three years and knew everything there was to know about the residents in her care. Her unwavering dedication was a key reason Meg had chosen to place her mum there.

"What happened, Ros?" Meg followed her down the main corridor, falling into step in the central lounge, where they dodged tottering old women and Zimmer frames and a lone man wielding his walking stick like a fencing sword.

"Careful, Frank, you'll have someone's eye out," Ros said and turned to Meg. "I'm not sure what happened, love. Clara left your brother alone with your mum for about fifteen minutes. She went back when she heard screaming and she found your mum with a number of minor injuries."

"Jesus," Meg whispered. "Where was Luke?"

"He pushed past Clara in the doorway and left before anyone could stop him." Ros held her hands wide apart in a gesture of helplessness. "He's a big lad, and we have a lot of vulnerable residents."

"I know." Meg's brother took after their dad in a number of ways: drinking, gambling, womanising, and making effective use of the brute force that came from being six foot three and overweight. She had learned at an early age not to argue with him.

Stopping outside her mum's room, she ran her fingers through her hair, making an effort to compose herself. Through the half-open door, she could hear her mum repeating the same refrain: "No, no, no, that's bad. No, no, no."

"Hey, Mum." Meg went straight over to her and knelt by the side of her chair. "Shh, it's okay, it's Meg. Let me take a look at you."

Her mum blinked when Meg touched her, the chant now inaudible, although her lips still formed the words. She didn't seem to recognise Meg, but neither did she pull away.

"Could you get me a bowl of warm water and a flannel, please?" Meg asked Ros through gritted teeth. Luke had gripped her mum's forearms so tightly that he had torn her skin. Bruises encircled her wrists, and his attempts to wrench off her wedding and eternity rings had left further gouges on her fingers. As Meg carefully palpated for fractures, her mum began to cry.

"All finished now. I'm sorry, love." Meg smoothed back her mum's hair, kissed her forehead, and dried her face with a handkerchief. "I'll get you cleaned up, and we'll have a cup of tea and a biscuit. How does that sound?"

Too distraught for any kind of comfort, her mum stuffed the corner of her hanky into her mouth and took up her chant again.

"He was asking about the house," Ros said, entering quietly and setting down water and a first aid kit. "Tahir overheard him from the corridor. He wanted to know where the money from selling her house was."

"Right." Meg dampened the cloth and scrubbed at the dried blood on her mum's arms. Devoting her attention to the task stopped her from smashing the bowl and raging against the stupidity of her brother and the senselessness of what he had done. There was no money. After early-onset dementia left her mum incapable of living independently, Meg had been forced to sell the family home to pay for the care in Rainscroft, but the going rate for houses on Halshaw estate was less than half the national average, and at £650 a week, Rainscroft's fees had soon sucked up the proceeds. Meg was now supplementing a paltry state contribution with her own wages to try to keep her mum in a decent facility where the surroundings and routine were familiar. If Luke had come back to the area to collect his inheritance, he was going to be very disappointed.

"Almost done," Meg said, watching her mum wince and clack her false teeth. "Do you want chocolate biscuits or would you prefer custard creams?"

Her mum remained silent as Meg wrapped a bandage around her wrist. Once her injuries were hidden from view, some of the distress eased from her expression. "Custard," she said, patting the back of Meg's hand.

Meg secured the bandage with a piece of tape and kissed her mum's cheek. "Excellent choice."

❖

In a bus shelter on Avalon Road, Sanne used Nelson as a sneaky windbreak while she consulted notes she'd gleaned from a late afternoon of door-to-door enquiries.

"Twenty-six A has spent the last week on a bender, thanks to Universal Credit paying him all his benefits in one fell swoop," she said, summarising the first entry. "He can't afford his rent now, and he might have to mug a granny if he wants to eat, but he reckons it was worth it."

Nelson shook sleet from his hair. The sky was already dark, and the temperature had dropped close to freezing. "I'm guessing he didn't hear his neighbour being stabbed in a violent frenzy, then?"

"You are correct. I'm not sure he even knew he had a neighbour. Twenty-seven A is eighty-six, slightly demented, and very deaf. She didn't see or hear anything either, but on the plus side she does make a decent brew. Twenty-seven B is empty. Its previous tenant is currently serving time for GBH in Strangeways." She closed her notebook. "How did you get on?"

"One elderly lady touched my face, made the sign of the cross, and gave me a KitKat. I had a 'fuck off, you fucking nigger scum' from Twenty-eight B—he might need revisiting—and the nineteen-year-old with three toddlers at Twenty-nine A just sighed and said that all she *ever* hears is screaming. She did see Culver in the corner shop on Monday morning, though. He bought chocolate and Rizlas, and loaned her twenty pence when she was short at the till."

Sanne did a quick mental calculation. "That'd definitely put Hopkins in the clear. He was an inpatient by then. When we get to the office, I'll phone the Royal and double-check the dates of his admission." Stomping her feet to try to restore some circulation, she looked out at a post office with bricked-up windows, and a Bargain Booze whose blue lights were drawing a steady, shambling parade of customers. "Time to head back? We could start chasing down a few of the names Hopkins gave us and set up some—"

"Detective Jensen!"

The enthusiasm in the hail made Nelson snigger. Sanne kicked his boot and turned toward the approaching officer. PC Zoe Turner, one of three constables working overtime to help canvass the estate, was the officer who had responded to Hopkins's 999 call. Looking past Nelson, she fixed her attention on Sanne.

"I might have a witness," she said. She paused to catch her breath and patted her hair self-consciously. "There's a chap at the corner of Pellinore and Avalon who remembers seeing a dark-coloured van parked up on Pellinore on Monday night. He'd never seen it before, and he's not seen it since."

"Did he get the reg?" Sanne asked, and felt a twinge of guilt when Zoe's face fell.

"No, but it was a Vauxhall Combo, navy blue or black."

"That's great." Sanne jotted down the information and smiled at Zoe. In the background she could hear Nelson briefing the other officers over the radio. "I think we're going to call it a day. When you've written up your interview notes and your statement from this afternoon, you can e-mail them to me at this address." She handed her card to Zoe, who studied it carefully before slipping it into her pocketbook.

"Can I call you if I think of something after I've submitted my paperwork?"

Although the question sounded innocent, the accompanying glint in Zoe's eye was anything but. Pushing six foot, with long blond hair and a full figure, she reminded Sanne of a Valkyrie, or at the very least someone more suited to a Scandinavian name than Sanne herself. The intensity of her focus was a little unnerving.

Sanne took a step back and bumped arses with Nelson. "Sorry," she muttered. Then, to Zoe, "Call me or e-mail, whichever's easiest. Thanks for all your hard work today."

"My pleasure."

Sanne raised a hand in farewell, as Nelson stifled a laugh.

"Don't say a word," Sanne warned him, once Zoe was well out of earshot.

In an elaborate mime, Nelson locked his lips and threw the key over his shoulder.

"Tosspot," she said, and ignored the note he held up that read: *She proper fancies you!*

He screwed up the note and unlocked the car. "Am I allowed to speak now?"

Busy wrestling her phone from an inside pocket, Sanne narrowed her eyes. "About case-related matters, yes. About lascivious police constables who are much taller than I am, no."

"Okay, fine." He pulled away from the kerb but hesitated at the first junction. "Damn. Left or right?"

"Left," she said, without looking. She had just noticed a missed call from Meg, time-stamped earlier that afternoon. Indicating another left turn to Nelson, she accessed her voicemail and keyed in the code. When Meg's message finally began, the sound of her voice sent butterflies swirling into Sanne's stomach even before she registered the message's content.

"Shit." She lowered the phone and stared at its call log. Meg had phoned her more than five hours ago. She hit "return call" immediately, oblivious to the months that had passed without regular contact and to the reasons for her self-imposed isolation, but Meg's phone rang out and flicked to voicemail.

"Meg, it's me," Sanne said. "I only just got your message. Phone me as soon as you can, okay? No matter what time it is." She hung up but kept hold of the phone.

"Everything all right?" Nelson asked.

Sanne shook her head. Everything was far from all right.

Chapter Five

With a sandwich clamped between her teeth, and her scrubs top midway over her head, Meg kicked open the door of the staffroom and stumbled in the approximate direction of her locker.

"Here, let me get that."

She felt Emily's hands tug at the scrubs and came blinking into the glare of the overheads like a cantankerous newborn. She had missed the shift handover by almost an hour and had wanted a couple of quiet minutes alone to finish her supper before anyone saw her.

"You didn't have to wait for me," she said.

"I was late off myself." Emily kissed Meg's cheek, avoiding the sandwich. "How's your mum?"

Meg swallowed her mouthful and retrieved the remaining portion of her makeshift meal. "She's okay, just a few lumps and bruises. The staff are going to keep a close eye on her."

"Shame they weren't doing that before she fell."

"Yeah." Turning to her locker, Meg busied herself trying to remember her code. The lie had come easily enough in her brief call to Emily earlier, but maintaining it was less straightforward when she had to look her in the eye.

"One nine eight two," Emily said. "You went for super-cryptic and used the year of your birth."

"So I did." Meg entered the code and hunted down her stethoscope and medical formulary. Her phone started to ring as she slid it into her trouser pocket.

"Are you not going to answer that? It might be Rainscroft."

Meg glanced at the caller ID: Sanne. "Unknown number. I'm not really in the mood for a solar panels sales pitch." The phone stopped vibrating as it switched to voicemail. "Hell, I better get out there or Donovan will have my arse."

"Tell him I saw it first." Emily pulled her into a hug. "Try to stop your F2s admitting everything to my ward, will you? It's full to bursting, and we're all rather stressed."

"Damn these people for getting sick!" Meg kissed her and then wiped off a transferred smear of mayo. "Sorry about that. I'll head home tonight, save disturbing you when I finish here." She made the suggestion lightly but saw Emily frown.

"You're on again tomorrow, so it'd be much easier for you to stay at mine. I don't mind if you wake me."

Unable to tell Emily that she needed to be at home in case her criminally deranged brother decided to pay a visit and smash the place up, Meg just plastered on a smile and nodded her accord. "Okay. I'll see you later, then."

Appeased, Emily shooed her out of the staffroom. Meg jogged past a row of offices and entered an A&E verging on collapse. In the corridor, five ambulance crews waited in a queue for beds, a couple of them playing on their phones while their patients dozed on stretchers, and the remainder administering drugs and fluids to patients who clearly ought to have been in cubicles. The Hospital Arrival Screen showed another three ambulances en route, and as Meg walked toward the nurses' station, the Bat Phone rang again. She answered it, grabbing a Magic Marker in lieu of a pen. The dispatcher relayed the details in an apologetic tone.

"Twenty-two-year-old," Meg repeated. "Anaphylaxis, systolic of sixty, wheezy, with airway oedema. Got it. ETA?" She'd run out of room on the paper, so wrote "15" on her palm. "Cheers for that." She saw Liz approaching with an armload of linen and waved the paper at her. An experienced A&E nurse, Liz rarely allowed the pressure to affect her, but even she looked fraught. By contrast, Meg relished the chaos, grateful for the distraction it provided.

"Welcome to hell," Liz said, scanning the information and then turning Meg's hand over to check the ETA. "Buggeration. We need to shift someone out of Resus."

"I'm supposed to be in there with you. Is anyone well enough for Majors?"

Exasperation coloured Liz's cheeks as she shook her head. "We've got an MI waiting for transfer, but all the ambulances are snared up in the corridor. Donovan yelled at their control an hour ago, but she just yelled back and refused to give us a deflection, even though St. Margaret's is half-empty."

Meg followed Liz down the line of curtained bays in Resus. As well as the heart attack victim, there were two elderly patients clearly at death's door, and an obese woman in the end bed who was relying on a CPAP machine to do most of her breathing for her. A lone and painfully young doctor regarded Meg like the second coming as she approached.

"Well, fuck me," she muttered, pulling on a pair of gloves. "What a fucking disaster."

"Mr. Johnson keeps having runs of VT," the junior said, too panicked for introductions.

"Righto." She noted the name and designation on his ID badge. He was an F2, one year away from becoming a registered doctor. "Can you hold down the fort for another five minutes, Asif?" His Adam's apple went into a noticeable spasm, but he nodded. "Good man. I'll be right back. Liz, break out the usual for the anaphylaxis, will you?"

She left Resus and headed for the mass of green uniforms still lining the corridor. "Okay, lads and lasses," she called, and the ambulance staff fell quiet. "Anyone finishing in the next hour?"

One crew raised their hands, but their patient looked too poorly for Meg to ship into the waiting room, so they were fine to queue for a cubicle. Starting at the head of the line, she began to assess the other patients in turn, quickly bypassing two before stopping at a third, more promising one. She pulled the paramedic aside.

"What've you got?"

He sighed. "Nineteen-year-old, vomiting for three hours. Says she feels faint."

The patient was engrossed in her phone, probably updating Facebook to tell everyone how critically ill she was.

"Obs okay?" Meg asked.

"They're all perfect." He displayed his paperwork for Meg.

"Grand." She beamed at him. "Stick her in a chair and put her in the farthest corner of the waiting room. Hopefully, people will steer clear of her if she starts puking. Then how do you fancy bluing an unstable MI over to the cath labs?"

The paramedic's eyes lit up, and Meg knew she had him. He must be a new recruit, fresh out of university and keen to practice his skills.

"How unstable?" he said.

"Tendency to go into VT, so he could be a tricky one. He's in the first Resus bay."

In his excitement, the lad had forgotten a salient point, and his face fell as it dawned on him. "Uh, Doc, I don't think it works like that. We have to go through control, and they might not authorise the transfer."

"You leave it to me." Meg clapped his shoulder. "I'll see you in there."

While passing through Majors, she had already spied her next target, and she honed in on him before he could do a runner.

"Are you our ambulance liaison?" She held out a hand and managed not to wince at the sweatiness of his. "I'm Meg Fielding, one of the A&E consultants. I've just commandeered Alpha three nine six for a transfer."

"You've what?" The man's face turned scarlet as his blood pressure rose. Meg quietly hoped he wouldn't pop something vital, because she really didn't have a bed for him. "You can't just *commandeer* one of our ambulances! We have jobs outstanding!"

A flurry of movement in the corner of the department caught Meg's eye. She saw Richard Donovan, the Senior Consultant, beginning to close in.

"See that ETA?" Meg tapped the arrivals screen. "In approximately seven minutes I'm getting an anaphylactic patient who could die in the back of the ambulance if I can't clear a space in Resus. Meanwhile, I have an MI waiting to ship out to the cath lab and a vehicle ready to do the transfer. None of us would be up shit creek if your lot had granted the deflection we requested, and I'd be willing to tell the press as much, should they come nosing around looking for someone to blame."

"Is there a problem, Dr. Fielding?" Donovan's question cut across the liaison's enraged intake of breath.

"I don't know," Meg said, and turned back to the liaison. "Is there?"

"No," he spluttered. "No, I'll clear everything with the resource manager."

"Thank you." Meg turned to Donovan. "Sorry I was late."

Donovan nodded, still eyeing her suspiciously as he tried to fathom what had just transpired. "I heard your mother had an accident."

"She had a fall, but she's all right. Minor injuries," she said, before adding the only thing Donovan would care about, "I'll work the hour back."

"Fine. Stay on tonight," he told her, already walking away.

"Prick," she muttered, but she was feeling too smug to inject any real venom into the insult. Her next patient's bed was sorted, the heart attack might yet make it to the catheter lab, and she still had four minutes to spare.

❖

"Okay, great. Thanks for your help."

Sanne hung up the office phone, keeping one eye on her mobile. The fact that Meg hadn't returned her call didn't necessarily mean anything awful had happened. She was probably with Emily, or at work. In the months since they had last spoken properly, Sanne had lost track of Meg's shifts. The A&E at Sheffield Royal was rarely out of the headlines these days, thanks to a bed crisis following the downgrade of a neighbouring A&E, and if Meg was on duty, she was likely to be swamped.

Stacking all these reasons into a logical pile had helped Sanne get through the last few hours. She couldn't afford to lose her focus, not when she had Eleanor watching her like a hawk and Carlyle waiting to pounce the moment she took a wrong step.

"Hopkins's alibi is solid," she said as Nelson cracked his knuckles in sequence. "The hospital confirmed he was admitted to the Medical Assessment Unit on Saturday evening and discharged this morning. Visiting Culver must have been one of the first things he did when he got out, the poor sod."

"You're a soft touch, Sanne Jensen," Nelson said without malice. A stranger might have expected her to loathe addicts of all types, but she'd always had a peculiar affinity for those dependent on heroin.

She tossed a pen at him and held up her mouse mat as a shield when he readied himself to launch it back. Neither of them noticed Eleanor standing behind Sanne until she cleared her throat.

"Evening, boss." Nelson converted his throwing motion into an ear-scratching.

Eleanor gave a slight shake of her head but withheld comment. "I've taken a look at your files on Roberts and Harrison, and they're fine for the CPS. Am I to understand that Burgess is also ready to submit?"

"Just added the finishing touches to it," Nelson said.

"Good." Eleanor pulled up a chair and sank into it. She never complained of fatigue, but it was written in the lines of her face and the blue-black shadows beneath her eyes. "How did it go at Malory?"

"About as well as could be expected," Sanne said, appreciating Nelson's tact in leaving her to respond. If she didn't speak to Eleanor now, the lingering nerves from the morning would multiply a hundredfold overnight. "You've seen the photos? Right. So, the lad who found him—good friend and key holder—has an airtight alibi. There were no signs of forced entry, and nothing obvious was taken from the flat, although we can't rule out a missing stash. We'll have unis back on the estate tomorrow, and we're trying to trace a dark-coloured Vauxhall Combo van spotted close to the address on Monday night. One of the known associates Hopkins mentioned was a lad called Liam Burrows. Apparently, Culver had had issues with him about dealing. The mobile number Hopkins gave us has been disconnected, but Burrows has a record as long as your arm, so he's one we'll be keeping an eye out for."

"Has the PM been scheduled?"

"Yes, tomorrow at eight. We also have an interview with"—Sanne consulted her list—"Natalie Acre, Culver's ex. His landlord might come in, too, if he can find the time. Culver was behind in his rent, but the chap's already provided an alibi."

"Worth talking to anyway," Eleanor said. "Did the press bite?"

"They nibbled. The *Sheffield Post* ran a small sidebar tonight that included the number for the incident line, and the free paper might mention it, unless another dog falls through the ice at Endcliffe Park, in which case we've got no chance."

"Best we could hope for, given the vic."

"Imagine what our solve rate would be if they were all clean-living, middle-to-upper-class types leaving behind a grieving yet photogenic family." Nelson's tone was so dry that Sanne feared for the welfare of the potted plant on her desk.

"Well, you sound as if you're on the right lines." Eleanor supported the small of her back as she stood. "I doubt I can spare anyone to assist, but I'll let you know if that changes."

Sanne waited until Eleanor had almost reached her office. "Did I forget anything?" she whispered to Nelson.

"Nope, you were very thorough." He smiled softly at her as she eased her grip on her mouse mat. "Come on. I'll make you a brew."

❖

"I don't want…to die." The young woman was wheezing at the midpoint of each sentence. "I've…got kids. Don't let…me die."

Meg straightened the nebuliser the woman was grappling with and caught her hand. "You're not going to die, Chloe. Any minute now, all those drugs I've given you are going to kick in and you'll feel fabulous." She reconsidered. "Well, maybe not fabulous, but definitely less crappy."

Adjusting the flow of the IV, she watched the numbers on the monitor climb down from critical to borderline stable, and allowed herself to relax. Despite her assurances, she knew Chloe had been peri-arrest on her arrival in Resus. Although Meg was adept at hiding her panic face from patients, she preferred not to have her control of it tested so thoroughly.

"Good girl," she said. "You're doing really well."

Chloe's teeth began to chatter, but she was calming, her breathing becoming less laboured.

Meg tucked a blanket under her chin and squeezed her hand. "Better?"

Chloe nodded.

"You going to stay away from your mate's codeine from now on?" Meg asked. A more vigorous nod made her smile. "Excellent."

She watched Chloe's eyes close as the medication took hold, and for a second she felt as exhausted as Chloe looked. She swayed, grabbing the bed's railing, as Liz came into the bay with a fresh bag of fluid in her hand.

"You all right?" Liz asked.

"I'm fine," she said with little conviction.

"Anything I can do?"

Meg stared at the monitor, where Chloe's baseline obs were all within normal range. "Can you cover for me for five minutes? I really need to make a phone call."

"Of course I can. Make mine a white coffee, one sugar, when you come back."

"Deal."

Poking her head out of Resus, Meg checked the corridor. At the far end, a paramedic was marching a bloodstained drunk toward the waiting room, but the coast was otherwise clear. Meg made it to the ambulance bay without anyone noticing her, and slinked into the shadows behind the store of oxygen cylinders, where a littering of cigarette butts showed a blatant disregard for health and safety in any form. Lacking time to second-guess herself, she selected Sanne's number from her mobile's directory.

The phone only rang once before Sanne answered.

"Hey," Meg said.

"Hey yourself."

Meg could hear the smile in Sanne's voice and wondered whether she was feeling the same rush of relief and happiness and regret. She leaned against the cold bricks and tried not to cry.

"You still there?" Sanne asked, sounding worried now.

"Yep, still here. Sorry I didn't call earlier. Everything's gone to shit at the Royal, as usual."

"I suspected as much. I've spent the afternoon at Malory, knee-deep in a decomp."

"Oh, how lovely."

"It was joyous." Sanne sighed, and her voice dropped, signalling the end of the small talk. "Meg, what the hell is going on? What's Luke up to?"

The bluntness of the questions made Meg close her eyes in gratitude. She didn't have to explain or fudge the truth. She could answer, and Sanne would understand implicitly.

"He's looking for money from the house, and he hurt Mum," she whispered. "He's an arsehole, a fucking *arsehole*, and if I knew where he was I'd go round there and tear him apart." She banged her head back on the bricks, a sting of pain tempering some of her anger and setting her ears ringing.

She dimly heard Sanne ask what time she finished work and gave her a rough guess that would probably be wrong.

"I'll meet you in the ambulance bay," Sanne said. "Promise me you won't do anything daft before then."

"Can I do something daft afterward?" Meg asked, but her rush of fury had dissipated, leaving her with only a headache to show for it.

Sanne ignored the bait. "Ambulance bay, about one-ish," she said. "Don't worry if you're late. I'll wait till you're done."

❖

Sanne checked her watch for the fourth time in twenty minutes. In front of her car, an ambulance pulled away from the bay, its blues coming on as it immediately copped for another job. It was 1:30 a.m. on a Friday morning, but there were three ambulances parked beneath the canopy, their crews still busy in A&E, and every vehicle she had seen leave had gone out with its blues on, heading for another emergency. No one seemed to sleep anymore. There was no longer a lull in the witching hours when the city rested and those on the front line got a chance to regroup and take a break. Someone somewhere was always drunk, or getting smacked, or going online to find out whether that muscular ache in their chest could be something more sinister.

Sanne shook her head in the darkness. Her own chest had given her some twinges when she had arrived at the hospital. She wondered whether it was trepidation at seeing Meg or a reaction to being back beneath the ambulance canopy for the first time since last summer. Most likely, she supposed, it was a combination of the two.

When the A&E entrance swung open, she gave it only half a glance, sure that another crew would wander out, plastic cups of cadged brews cradled in their hands like precious trophies. Instead it was Meg, who paused to scan the crowd of vehicles, recognised Sanne's, and hurried across to it. The passenger door opened seconds later, bringing in a blast of cold air and then Meg, before Sanne had a chance to fret or panic or realise that her pulse rate had shot back through the roof.

"Bloody hell, it's nippy out there," Meg said. "So say my nips."

Sanne laughed at the familiar joke, forgetting her nerves and pre-planned greetings, as Meg had no doubt intended. She started the engine and nosed past the ambulances. "Don't know about you," she said, "but I could murder a kebab."

❖

Abdul's on Croft Street wasn't much to look at from the outside, but its reputation as one of Sheffield's best takeaways was well deserved. It also had a small cafe area for those who weren't minded to stagger home through the sleet eating from a paper wrap. The local pubs had emptied hours earlier, so there was a table free for Meg and Sanne to pile high with lamb and chicken shish kebabs, chips, and glasses of mango lassi. They swapped halves of the kebabs without negotiation, and tucked in for a few silent, satisfied minutes.

"How's your mum?" Sanne asked, once her stomach no longer felt as if it were digesting itself.

Meg dabbed her lips with a napkin, which made a change from wiping her face on her sleeve. "She's okay. I spoke to Ros a few hours ago, and she said she was in bed and settled. Luke doesn't have a fucking clue how much that place costs or how far gone Mum is now. When he couldn't get her to tell him where the money was, he tried to yank her rings right off her fingers, the bastard."

"Jesus. Did you call the police?"

"No, I just called you. What good would reporting it do? My mum was the only witness, and she's not capable of making a complaint. I don't know where he is, so it's not as if you could get someone to go round and smack some sense into him."

Sanne almost choked on a chip. "I don't think we're allowed to do that anymore. I'm pretty sure the brass frown on it. And I can't PNC him—sorry, that's the police national computer—not without making it official. I'd get my arse handed to me." She hesitated, not wanting to reveal she was already walking a fine line at work, because Meg would want to know why. "I can put out some feelers, though. See if any of the patrol officers have heard he's back in the area, and then nip around for a chat if we track him down. Do you think he's been in prison again?"

Meg shrugged. "It's possible. He's been out of the loop for three years, which is a good indicator. Either that or he's pissed someone off and had to keep his head down."

"He should be easy enough to find if he's out on licence," Sanne said, wondering whether her new best friend from the Malory case would be willing to do her a favour and what she might want in return. "Leave it with me. And try not to worry, okay?"

That seemed to be good enough for Meg, who bit into her kebab with renewed vigour. Sanne made a chip butty with a piece of pitta, dipped it in ketchup, and took a gleeful bite.

"I like your hair," she said at length, using her improvised sandwich to outline Meg's new style. It was longer than she had ever seen it, and Meg had used a plethora of clips and kirby grips to wrestle it under control. Nothing else seemed to have changed, though. Meg hadn't taken to wearing makeup or designer clothes, and after her initial attempt with the napkin, she now seemed content to leave grease smeared around her mouth.

"Yeah?" She stole a chip from Sanne's fingers. "It's a pain in the arse, really, but Em seems to prefer it. Come summer, I'm having it all chopped off again."

Sanne squirted more ketchup on her chips. "How is Em?" she asked, trying to keep things casual. The nickname felt too familiar for someone she hardly knew, but it was her own fault that they weren't better acquainted.

"She's fine. Tired, like the rest of us. She finished Ortho last month and moved to Medical Assessment. Our shifts clash more often than not, but it's nice when we're together. We get on well." Meg paused to mop up yoghurt dressing, taking her time about it, her eyes on the plate. "I didn't mean for it to happen, San, any of it, and I really didn't want to lose you." Sauce slopped across the table as she gesticulated with the pitta bread. "God, I've made such a fucking mess of everything."

Sanne passed her another napkin, and Meg looked at it in confusion before noticing the splashes of sauce.

"I meant us, not the bloody table," she said.

"We're not a mess," Sanne said. "And you've not lost me. I'm where I always was."

Meg gave her a look, the one that said "don't bullshit me" with a mere arch of her eyebrow. "Sanne Jensen, you are slipperier than a fish to get hold of on the phone, and you always have an excuse not to visit. After the first couple of months, I got to the point where I stopped trying so damn hard. If you were mad at me, I wanted to be mad at you too."

The smell of fat and meat began to turn Sanne's stomach. She pushed her plate away and brought her lassi closer. "I wasn't mad at you. I was never mad at you. I just didn't want to be the dog in the manger."

"The dog in the what, now?"

"The manger. My mum always used to say it. You know, when you don't want something yourself, but you sit in it anyway, just to stop anyone else from having it."

"Huh." Meg sucked on her straw and then spoke around the end of it. "So I'm the manger?"

"Yeah, sort of."

"And you were afraid of sitting in me? Am I getting this right?"

"You're skirting the crux of it." Sanne knew when Meg had worked it out, because her face fell.

"So you really didn't want me?" she asked quietly.

"I don't think I knew what I wanted," Sanne said, hating herself for telling the truth, even though she knew Meg would have caught a lie. "I never know what I want till I've fucked it up."

Behind the counter, the grill sizzled, sending up a cloud of aromatic smoke as the chef threw something on it and called out to the deliveryman in Urdu. Meg waited out the brief influx of noise, her eyes locked on Sanne's.

"Made a bit of a bugger of things, didn't we?" she said when the men quietened.

Sanne shook her head vehemently. "No, don't say that. Whatever was going on with us, it was always going to end, Meg. If it'd been perfect, we would never have kept dating other people."

Meg mulled this over, stirring her lassi. "I suppose not," she said, but her words were laced with uncertainty.

"What did Emily say about Luke?" Sanne asked, trying to steer the conversation into less choppy water. She saw Meg wince and begin to pick at the chipped Formica on the tabletop. "Oh for fuck's sake, have you not told her?"

"No." When Meg looked up again, tears were brimming in her eyes. "Can we get out of here, please?"

❖

Outside, snow had started to fall, a flurry of pellet-like flakes that left a crunchy layer on the pavement. Meg used a scraped-up handful to clean the grease from her fingers and cool her cheeks. At the crossroads, she looked to Sanne for guidance before choosing at random, heading down a tree-lined street whose huge detached houses were now split into flats and hostels. A front door slammed, and a man shouted abuse in a language that might have been Polish as he careened up the road ahead of them. Meg slowed her pace to keep him at a distance and turned to Sanne.

"Do you remember when you came out, San?"

Sanne nodded, her hazel eyes sombre in the intermittent light from the streetlamps. "Yeah. I think that's the most scared I've ever been." She paused, and Meg assumed she was factoring in the night Billy Cotter had tried to murder her. Her breath escaped in staggered clouds of white as she shivered. "I was a good few years before you, wasn't I? I begged my mum not to tell my dad, and she promised me she wouldn't, so Michael tried to blackmail my pocket money out of me for a month and then told him anyway."

"The little shit." Meg brushed snow off a low wall and pulled Sanne's coat sleeve until she sat beside her.

"Don't have much luck with brothers, do we?" Sanne said.

"That's putting it mildly." Shrugging forward to keep herself warm, Meg tucked her hands into her pockets. "I can't forget the look on my mum's face when I finally plucked up the courage to tell her. I barely recognised her. Her lips went into this thin furious line, and I didn't know whether she was going to cry or batter me. She did both, in the end, but I never want to see that look again, San. Not ever."

"If you're worrying about Emily, I think she might already know you're gay, love," Sanne said gently, but her knees were drawn up to her chest, her arms wrapped around them protectively, and Meg suspected she had worked out the real issue.

"I've told her a lot about me," Meg said. "She knows I grew up on Halshaw and that I paid my way through uni by working on the market. She knows about Mum, and how little is left of my wage once Rainscroft and my mortgage and student loans have been taken out of it." Meg felt Sanne's cold hand slip into hers and squeezed the fingers tight. "I'm not ashamed of any of that—I never have been—but I don't know how to tell her that my dad buggered off to London with a girl just out of secondary school, or that Luke smacked me and Mum around for years and neither of us could do a thing to stop him."

The breath she took seemed to stick in her throat. She hadn't spoken that truth aloud since that summer's day spent sunbathing with Sanne on the back field. She couldn't remember how old they had been—eleven, or maybe twelve?—just the scents of freshly cut grass and lemonade, and that Sanne had seen her wince as she lay down. Back then, it hadn't been a big deal. Sanne's dad regularly clouted her too, and after listening to Meg's whispered confession, she had kept the secret without question. Once she reached adulthood, Meg understood that it should have been a big deal, that even if your dad left, your brother wasn't supposed to black your eye or punch you so hard that you pissed blood. Her teachers had ignored the bruises, though, and the prospect of being taken into care had terrified her into silence. Luke, for his part, had eventually learned how not to leave a mark.

Meg stared up at the blizzard swirling beneath the streetlamp, each flake drifting to the pavement in the end, like a singed moth giving in to gravity. Right then, she knew the feeling.

"You were the only one I ever told, San," she said. "And it's not been an issue for so long now that I never thought I'd have to tell anyone else. It'd be like coming out all over again. Emily's from Harrogate, for fuck's sake!"

Sanne gave a shocked gasp, hand on heart, mouth agape. "Oh good Lord, not *Harrogate*! What's a scrubber like you doing with a posh girl like that?" She nudged Meg hard enough to rock her sideways, letting her know how daft she was being.

Meg covered her face with her hands. "Sod off," she mumbled. "I'm being serious here."

"I know." Sanne pulled Meg's hands down and waited until she looked at her. "And I get it, love. It's not like I wear a Team Halshaw T-shirt to work, is it?"

"I suppose not." Meg licked snow from her lips, its chill a welcome balm for her dry mouth. "I'm not sure which would be worse: Em wondering what the hell she's got herself into, or her viewing me as a pity project. She can be a bit of a bleeding heart at times."

"How long's she been in the job?"

"Almost two years."

Sanne grinned. "Plenty of time yet for her to turn into a cynical old bugger like you."

Meg smiled too, but she didn't share Sanne's conviction. Her tendency toward misanthropy was one of the few things she and Emily argued about, and Emily seemed determined not to develop the bleak outlook of so many public sector workers. There were occasions when her refusal to acknowledge the bad in anyone got right on Meg's wick.

"Anyway." Meg pushed to her feet and held out a hand to Sanne. "Enough about me. How's everyone at Eds Up?"

Uncertainty flickered in Sanne's eyes, but she covered it well by standing and stomping snow from her boots. "By the sound of it, we're in the same boat as your lot. Overworked, stressed, tired out, and underpaid." She set off walking in the wrong direction, turning only when Meg pulled her round.

"'Tis the season." Meg kept hold of Sanne's sleeve for a moment before releasing it and falling into step beside her. "What did you cop for in Malory Park?"

"Heroin addict stabbed multiple times, vicious even for Malory. Serrated blade about so big." Sanne held her thumb and index finger apart.

Meg gave a low whistle. "Nasty. Any verdict on the Mulligan case?"

Sanne shook her head, her teeth gnawing at her bottom lip. Sensing a sore point, Meg studied her properly. Even half-hidden in a bulky jacket, it was obvious she had lost weight; her cheeks were pinched, her jaw more defined. Dark smudges covered the puffy skin beneath her eyes, and her lips were chapped and peeling. Her usual mop of wavy hair, the bane of her life, had been cropped in a manner suggesting utility rather than fashion. It made her look smaller, and she was only five foot four on a good day. The contrast with post-Greek holiday Sanne couldn't have been more pronounced.

"Oh, oh!" she said suddenly, mischief brightening her eyes. "You'll never guess what Keeley's done."

Heartened by her enthusiasm, Meg played along. "Sweet Christ almighty, did your sister get a job?"

Sanne laughed. "Close, but no cigar."

"She won the lottery and is now living in a pink palace with a gilt-edged, oversized trampoline for each of her many kids?"

"Not quite, but keep going on the kid theme."

The penny dropped with a noticeable thud. "Oh. Fuck. Off," Meg said. "I thought you'd told her to get a different hobby."

"I did. Unfortunately, I also gave her thirty quid to go on a hot date with Wayne."

Meg stopped dead and yanked Sanne to a halt. "This is *your* fault? You funded the conception of baby number"—she paused to count on her fingers—"six?"

"It's baby number five, and yes, I am completely to blame, because apparently my sister can't resist Wayne's charms when he's gone and got her drunk on Asti Spumante."

"Aw, who said romance was dead?" Meg rubbed her hands. "So, when's the due date? I need time to open a book."

"Tenth of March." Sanne gave her a perplexed look. "Open what book?"

"The Great Baby Name Bet, of course. I wonder what odds I should put down for Kai. We've had a few Kais in A&E of late." She hurried after Sanne, who was making a show of setting off without her. "Too avant-garde? How about Kermit? Kelly? Kelly's nice. You can't go wrong with the classics."

By the time she caught up with Sanne, they were both out of breath and laughing. With her cheeks pink from exertion, Sanne no longer looked as if the world were beating down on her.

"We should do this more often," Meg said.

"What? Sneak out to eat kebabs in the wee hours and then hare around the streets while the city sleeps?"

Meg kissed her forehead. "Yes, exactly that."

Chapter Six

There was little dignity in post mortems: the body laid out naked on the slab, with every external imperfection on show and all its internal faults waiting to be discovered beneath the glare of the lights. As a rule, Sanne tended to avoid them, the transcribed reports giving her more than enough detail and making her presence at the actual dissection redundant. Nor did she feel the urge to prove that she could reach the end of one without puking or keeling over. At thirteen years old she'd had to wade barefoot through approximately half her dad's blood volume, and there hadn't been much left to be squeamish about after that. However, having a spare set of clothes in the boot of her car and no desire to drive home at four in the morning, she'd decided to stay in Sheffield overnight and had volunteered to get a jump on the official report by observing the examination of Andrew Culver's body. Still shouldering a significant amount of guilt over the Mulligan trial, she was glad to take one for the team, and Nelson had all but climbed down the phone line to kiss her.

"The stomach is almost empty," the pathologist said, enunciating clearly for the benefit of his Dictaphone. "A small amount of liquid mixed with blood, which is undoubtedly a result of the wound to the oesophagus."

She watched him pour the meagre contents into a measuring jug before beginning to prise the layers of the stomach apart. The stab wound to Culver's neck was so savage that it had bisected his trachea and oesophagus, making the cause of death a combination of exsanguination and suffocation. The lack of significant haemorrhage from his other injuries indicated that the neck wound had occurred first and swiftly proven fatal.

"Stomach is intact and healthy, aside from an area of erosion consistent with gastric ulceration." The pathologist paused the tape to address Sanne. "I'm just about done here, Detective. Toxicology will take three to four days, although I don't expect it to show much to get excited about. Was there anything else you needed?"

"No, thank you," she said. "I appreciate you letting me observe."

She looked from her notepad to the pathologist's assistant, who covered up the lower half of Culver's body and started to close the Y incision that split the torso. His part in the proceedings concluded, the pathologist stripped off his blood-slickened gloves and gown, and nodded to Sanne as she left the room.

The tang of viscera and decomposition followed her into the corridor, but it became more tolerable by degrees as she walked past the labs and through an office space where someone had overcompensated with plug-in floral deodorisers. The chemicals instantly made Sanne sneeze. She put a hand to her nose and held her breath until she made it out to the brick-walled bay where the private ambulances parked.

She had assumed the PM would take up most of the morning, but it had finished early, gifting her a small window of opportunity to make good on her promise to Meg. The bay was empty, the only noise coming from a crisp packet dancing around in the wind. She fished out her phone and then found the scrap of paper on which she had scribbled Zoe Turner's contact information. An approaching vehicle made her hesitate, but it continued past, removing her last excuse to procrastinate. Muttering a curse, she dialled Zoe's number before she changed her mind.

❖

Sanne never fidgeted when she was nervous; she just fell back on her habit of counting things. After ten minutes waiting in a fancy patisserie that she had often drooled over but never actually entered, she knew there were fifteen types of coffee on the menu, eight flavours of syrup, and twelve varieties of cake, and that the couple seated to her right had said "oh golly" three times apiece. The cafe's owners favoured subtle lighting and shades of blue: pleasant in sunshine, no doubt, but dingy on an overcast winter's morning that was threatening more snow. The murkiness made Sanne feel illicit, as if she had arranged a clandestine meeting in a location where she and her contact wouldn't be identified. In reality, Zoe had suggested the place for its excellent pastries, not that that did much to dispel Sanne's jitters.

She rechecked her watch and then her phone, making sure no one at work had missed her yet or tried to find her at the morgue and discovered the PM had concluded half an hour previously. That scenario made her fingers twitch, and she misjudged the size of her saucer, hitting its edge with her teacup just as the bell above the door tinkled and Zoe walked in. Spotting Sanne in the gloom, she waved and headed for the counter. Sanne watched her hang up her coat, chatting easily with the man in front of her and then flirting with the barista. By the time Zoe made her way to the table, Sanne had counted most of the stripes on the curtains.

"You have got to try one of these," Zoe said by way of greeting. She set down a plate with two iced apricot pastries and took the seat opposite Sanne, her thin woollen sweater clinging to her curves and outlining well-toned arms as she stirred sugar into her coffee. She was so tall that she blocked out what little light the window let through, leaving Sanne to guess where her teacup was. A sudden spark of flame made Sanne inch back and blink in confusion, and then curse herself for an idiot when she realised it was just Zoe's lighter. The wick of the tabletop burner kindled, and the table slowly brightened.

"There, that's better," Zoe said, the mellow glow catching her smile. "I got snared up in traffic. Have you been waiting long?"

"No." Sanne cleared her throat. "No, not long. Do you live near here?"

"Yep, I'm renting up on Ecclesall Road. Convenient for work and great for getting into the city." She nudged the plate closer to Sanne. "Aren't you hungry?"

Sanne had forgotten the pastries were even there. She picked one up and took a bite. "Oh, that's really good," she mumbled, the buttery sweetness revitalising an appetite that had been quashed by her early morning rendezvous with the pathologist.

"Told you so." Zoe's gaze never left hers. "I was glad you called. What can I do to help?"

Kicking herself for letting her professionalism slip, Sanne wiped her fingers clean and passed Zoe a handwritten sheet with Luke Fielding's details, description, and usual stomping grounds.

"This bloke is back in the area, and I'm trying to find out where he's staying. I've spoken to the parole office, but he's not one of theirs, he's not tagged. I was hoping that you and anyone discreet enough on your shift could keep an eye out for him, maybe ask around the usual haunts."

"Unofficially?"

"Yes, unofficially." She didn't want to betray Meg's confidence by saying much, but it seemed wrong to expect assistance and offer nothing in return. Even so, she chose her words carefully. "He's my best friend's brother, and he's causing trouble for her family. She doesn't want to make a big song and dance about it, so I said I'd see if I could have a word with him."

"Gotcha." Zoe nodded, folding the paper in two before slipping it into her wallet. "I'll put the word out, Detective." She gave a crisp salute that left her with icing in her hair.

"Uh, you've got a bit of something here." Sanne rubbed the side of her own head.

Laughing, Zoe swiped at the blob and took her time licking her finger clean. Sanne didn't know where to look, and she inadvertently solved the quandary by inhaling a flake of pastry that made her cough until her eyes blurred.

Zoe slid a glass of water toward her. "Here. You okay?" she said, sounding more amused than concerned.

"I'm fine." Sanne had gulped half the water, and her throat was still in spasm as she answered.

"I better get going. I should be on shift, but I blagged an hour off for a dentist's appointment after you phoned." Zoe smiled, showing her teeth. "Do they look shiny?"

"Very," Sanne said. They were shiny, and they were quite possibly bleached.

"Enjoy your pastry." Zoe winked at her. "I'll be in touch."

Pretending to busy herself with the teapot, Sanne surreptitiously watched Zoe collect her coat and blow a kiss at the barista as she left. The teapot lid chimed as it fell back into place.

"You owe me big time, Meg Fielding," Sanne muttered. She wrapped her pastry—along with the one Zoe hadn't touched—in a napkin, hoping they might sweeten Nelson's mood when she confessed about the morning's moonlighting. After casting a furtive glance around, she sneaked the leftovers into her bag, ignoring the disdainful look a thirty-something businesswoman shot in her direction. The woman barely had room for her oversized cup of coffee on a table where an iPad, iPhone, and laptop were all clamouring for her attention, while her suit probably cost more than Sanne made in a month. Not that Sanne gave a damn. She patted her bag and left with her head held high. She was her mother's daughter, and if there was one thing Teresa Jensen had instilled in her eldest child, it was the principle of waste not, want not.

With the patio doors flung wide open and snow blowing onto the carpet, Meg paced across the small apartment's living room. Eight steps took her to the kitchen counter. When she turned round, eight more brought her back to the balcony's threshold. Clasping the metal railing, she looked over the balcony's edge at a rectangular patch in the courtyard that contained the only visible greenery amid the expanse of concrete paving. Snow melted in her hair as she rocked back on her heels. She wanted to visit her mum and then go home, but Emily was still at the gym, and apparently it was bad form to leave without saying good-bye.

Her foot tapping out a brusque staccato, Meg checked her watch again. Planning a schedule to suit someone else was fast becoming a pain in the arse. There was too much she needed to do before her shift for her to be waiting around, but the last time that she had just written a note and headed out, Emily had spent the evening in a sulk. Holding that thought, Meg dropped onto one of the patio chairs and stared at the grey clouds tumbling across the sky. At what point had she started to rearrange her life like this? She had stayed at the flat the previous night because it was easier than having an argument about it, but Emily wasn't at home now to stop her leaving.

"Fuck it," she muttered, but just as she grabbed her bag off the sofa, the front door opened. She stuck her head into the hallway, curtailing Emily's efforts to keep quiet. "Hey, I'm awake."

"Hey, you. Good morning." Emily kissed her, the touch light at first and then more demanding.

Meg closed her eyes as Emily's hands slipped beneath her sweater and cupped her breasts. "Em, I can't. I don't have ti—"

Another kiss silenced her protest, and a rush of adrenaline made her lightheaded. Emily was a very good kisser, all soft lips and sure tongue, and Meg had proven herself useless at offering up any kind of resistance, especially when caught unawares. Splayed against the wall for support, she spread her legs as Emily dropped to her knees. Trailing a line of kisses down Meg's torso, Emily tugged Meg's trousers and underwear down.

"Sorry, what were you saying?" Emily asked.

"Nothing," Meg whispered. She panted when Emily pushed the tip of a finger inside her. "I didn't say a word."

Emily smiled and flicked out her tongue, her hand surging upward with force enough to make Meg gasp. "Excellent answer," she said.

❖

"You were late home this morning." Emily nibbled the skin just above Meg's belly button and then tilted her head so that Meg could see her face. "Did Donovan make you stay on?"

"No." Meg sat up and reached for her T-shirt, feeling too naked for the conversation they were about to have. "No, I met Sanne, and we went for something to eat."

"Oh." That was all Emily said, but every muscle in her body seemed to have frozen, and she kept hold of the breath she had drawn in.

"She phoned me toward the end of my shift." Even as Meg spoke, she could feel the pit she'd been digging for herself grow wider and deeper, but she couldn't bear to go back and try to fill it in. "She's having some problems at work and wanted to chat." That at least was true. Sanne might not have said as much, but something had definitely been troubling her.

"Is she all right?"

"Better now, I think."

"It's good that you've finally seen her," Emily said, her eyes fixed at a halfway point on the bed's headrest. She sounded genuine, but she was still wound tighter than a spring, her limbs rigid. Meg stroked a hand through her hair.

"It was just a kebab and a catch-up, Em."

"It's fine. I don't mind." Emily began patting the bed to track down her clothes. "I woke up at half three and you weren't here, so I was worried, that's all."

"I would've sent a text, but I didn't want to disturb you."

Pausing in the middle of pulling on her jeans, Emily leaned over and kissed Meg's nose. "Next time, disturb me."

"No problem. Will do," Meg agreed readily, but being chastised like a child made her want to kick back against the censure. "I'm going to see my mum and then head home for a while."

Emily wrenched the curtains open, though Meg was still only wearing a T-shirt. "I told Holly we'd meet her for lunch. I've rearranged my shift so that I'm doing a twilight as well, and she's coming all the way from Harrogate."

Meg nodded slowly. "But I already have plans."

"Can't you change them? Please? For me? You could wear that lovely blue shirt."

"No." It came out blunter than she had intended, but she knew how adept Emily was at getting her own way. "I'm sorry, Em, but I've told Rainscroft that I'm coming in, and I need to go home."

Disappointment and anger passed across Emily's face before she managed to neutralise her expression. "You're staying here tonight, though, aren't you?"

"I'm not sure." That all depended on what Meg found at her house. "Probably, but don't wait at the hospital for me, okay?"

It seemed to have dawned on Emily that she wasn't going to win this one. She smiled brightly and forced cheer into her voice. "Just remember to text me."

Meg smiled back, relieved to have stood her ground, and drew a solemn cross over her heart. "If I make a move, you'll be the first to know about it."

CHAPTER SEVEN

"San? San! Check this out!"

Waylaid, Sanne stopped in the middle of the office and watched open-mouthed as Fred performed a series of dance-like manoeuvres. Either that, or he was suffering from some kind of waking seizure—in all honesty it was difficult to tell. At the desk opposite, Fred's partner, George, thumped his head onto his mouse mat and began to emit a strained noise that might have been laughter. Having finished his display with a flourish of finger snapping in lieu of castanets, Fred beamed at Sanne.

"Am I getting good at this or what?"

Sidestepping the obvious response, she gave an enthusiastic round of applause that made him blush. "I never knew you could dance," she said.

"He can't, the big lummock," George muttered around his sleeve.

Sanne diplomatically ignored him. "What was it?" She hazarded a guess based on the invisible castanets. "Flamenco?"

"Salsa," Fred said. He mopped his brow with a polka-dotted handkerchief. "I've been going to evening classes."

"Really? Good for you. They're working a treat, mate." She eyed his waistline. "Have you lost a bit of weight too?"

"Aye, two pounds, but Martha's bringing a ginger cake this week, so I'll probably put it all back on again."

"Martha, eh?" Light began to dawn for Sanne, helped along by George crossing his eyes and thudding his head back onto the desk.

"Five to one," Fred said with unadulterated glee. "You should try it, San."

"Huh?"

"That's the ratio of women to men. I've got as much rhythm as a day-old corpse, but they can't get enough of me. It's bloody brilliant." He twirled Sanne around, tripped over his feet, and sat on his desk as if he'd meant to do that all along.

"I'll bet you there's a few lezzies there," he said, still out of puff. "There's this couple with short hair and a right lot of tattoos. I danced with one of 'em once, but she scared the shite out of me."

"Those damn butches." She patted his shoulder sympathetically, somehow keeping a straight face. "They can be pretty mean."

"I'll say!" Fred seemed to be on the verge of elaborating, but his phone rang and interrupted him. "Speaking. Yep. Aw, bollocks. When?"

Sanne pushed a pad toward him and recognised the address he scribbled down as a street on the outskirts of Malory.

"We've got one," he said to George when he'd hung up. "Murder most foul."

George levered himself from his chair with a grimace and several clicks of his spine. "Anything exciting?"

"Stabbing. Some poor sod who was minding his own gas-huffing business found the vic on a patch of wasteland."

"Lovely."

Sanne waved them off, grateful that Carlyle hadn't tried to ditch this one on her and Nelson as well. "You boys have fun, now."

Ignoring George's obscene gesture, she returned to her desk. "Fred reckons I should take up salsa," she said to Nelson.

Nelson raised an eyebrow. "Is that what he was doing over there? I thought he was having a stroke."

Sanne's chuckle turned into a full-blown fit of the giggles.

"White men of a certain age should not attempt to dance," Nelson said, his tone so serious it set her off again.

"Oh fuck." She wiped her eyes and tried to remember what she had been doing before Fred accosted her. "Okay, Natalie Acre in twenty minutes." The name sobered her; although Natalie had broken up with Andrew Culver six months previously, she'd sounded devastated when Sanne phoned her. "Are we both interviewing her?"

Nelson rattled his pen between his teeth, considering. "You take it, if you want. I'll see if I can chase down Mr. Burrows and type up my notes from the landlord, such as they are."

It was meant as a vote of confidence, and Sanne accepted it graciously. "Cheers, mate."

"I know the circumstances weren't ideal, but you should meet up with Meg more often," Nelson said quietly, as if he'd been unsure whether to broach the topic. "She's good for you."

Sanne couldn't argue with him. She had been in a buoyant mood all day, able to focus on her work and make progress despite her lack of sleep.

"It was great to see her," she said, but then held up a finger in warning. "Don't you go and bloody tell her that, though. Her head's big enough as it is."

The East Derbyshire force had done well out of the recent government project to update, amalgamate, and centralise police stations. Awarded enough funding for a new four-storey building, it had relocated its HQ and administrative services there and remembered, somewhat as an afterthought, that its Special Ops department also needed a home. Tagged on at the back, the EDSOP offices were nevertheless modern and well equipped, with the added bonus of views over rolling fields.

Adjacent to the main open-plan office were two interview rooms. Interview One, with its dull grey walls, one-way mirror, institutional furniture, and general air of claustrophobia, was used for suspects, uncooperative witnesses, and anyone else who might fall beneath the umbrella term *arsehole*. Interview Two had a more homely feel, its comfortable chairs and decor sharing a warm colour scheme, with a window to soften the effect of the overhead lighting. It was designed to ease answers from the bereaved or the victims of crime, and it was into this room that Sanne escorted Natalie Acre.

"Can I get you something to drink?" she asked. "Tea? Coffee?"

Natalie shook her head and sat in the chair that Sanne indicated. She crossed her legs but uncrossed them again when her skirt rode up, her movements stilted and self-conscious. A smell of cigarette smoke lingered on her clothing, and she didn't seem to know what to do with her hands now that she had nothing with which to occupy them. Slim, of average height, with red-rimmed eyes and dirty-blond hair tied back in a ponytail, she looked like an adult version of most of the girls Sanne had gone to school with. She had previous convictions for Class A drugs possession and shoplifting, but nothing in recent years.

"Thank you for coming in," Sanne said, once Natalie had settled and the recorder was running. "I appreciate how difficult this must be for you."

Natalie blotted tears with a tissue, careful to avoid her mascara. "I couldn't believe it when I heard. Still can't." Her accent was pure Sheffield, and grief thickened it even further.

"We spoke to Kevin Hopkins, who said that you and Andrew had been engaged for a while."

"Yes, almost a year. Andy proposed at the Dog and Duck just before the bingo." Her smile was a watered-down version of her carefree grin in Culver's photo. "He never bought me a ring, but I didn't mind."

Sanne jotted a note and stayed silent, waiting to see whether Natalie would clam up without regular prompts.

"I broke it off about six months back," she said, appearing keen to fill the gap. "He kept promising he'd get clean—he even went on methadone—but after a couple of weeks, he was selling his prescriptions. We stayed in touch, though. His parents are both dead, and he didn't really have any friends."

"He and Hopkins seemed close," Sanne said, remembering the tattered fistful of money that Hopkins had given her.

Natalie's lips narrowed, and a flush mottled the skin of her throat. "Oh, they were close. Who do you think gave Andy the idea of selling his scripts?"

"Right." Sanne paused as Natalie smoothed her skirt again, her palms leaving damp patches on the cloth. Hopkins was obviously a sore subject, but Sanne had to stick with it for now.

"Hopkins hinted that things might have been improving for Andy, that he had seemed happy shortly before his death. Do you have any idea why that might have been? Did Andy tell you anything similar?"

"No, nothing," Natalie said. "But then most of what Kev says is utter crap." She winced at her choice of phrasing. "Sorry."

Sanne waved away the apology. "When did you and Andy last speak?"

"Maybe three, four weeks ago? We'd check in every now and again, you know? Text, call. Mostly text."

"Can you think of anyone who might have wanted to hurt him? Was there someone he was afraid of, or in trouble with?"

Natalie rapped a manicured finger on the arm of her chair, the sound sharp and overly loud in the small room. Her eyes were lowered to the carpet. She opened her mouth to speak and closed it again.

"Natalie, this interview is confidential," Sanne said. "You have my word on that."

Natalie took a deep breath. "Andy had a fight about five weeks back. He was at the Mission Cross, and Liam set into him. Gave him a right good kicking."

The name made Sanne lean in closer. She didn't believe in coincidences, and this was the second time a "Liam" had been mentioned in connection with Culver.

"Would that be Liam Burrows?"

"Yeah, the nasty little prick. He lives with his mam up on Phelot Walk, unless she's booted him out again."

"Thanks, Natalie, that's great." Sanne skimmed her notes, a scrawled mess scattered with asterisks and underlined words. "Is there anything else you can think of that might be helpful?"

Natalie sat back, her face more relaxed now she sensed the interview was coming to an end. "Will there be a press conference? One of those public appeals? I could speak at one if you needed me to. If you thought it would help."

"It's very good of you to offer. We'll let you know if we arrange one."

"Thanks." Natalie's smile fell well short of her eyes. If she had seen the negligible newspaper coverage of Culver's murder, she must have known how unlikely a press conference was. She stood, straightened her skirt, and accepted the card Sanne gave her.

"If you do think of anything, no matter how small, please get in touch." Sanne shook her hand. "Thank you for your time. You know you can claim your travelling expenses, don't you?"

Natalie nodded. "I hope you catch him. Andy didn't deserve to die like that."

"No, he didn't." Sanne hadn't known him, but no one deserved that kind of fate. She escorted Natalie to the lobby, willing the lift to hurry so she could get back to her desk, start pulling her notes together, and tell Nelson they had their first potential suspect. When the lift finally swished open at the ground floor, Natalie hit the button to hold the doors.

"Will you keep me updated, Detective? I know I'm not family, but I was the closest thing Andy had."

"I'll call if anything develops. We've got your contact details."

That seemed to be good enough for Natalie. She dropped her hand and allowed the doors to close. Sanne stabbed her finger on the fourth button, cursing the lift for taking its time and wishing she'd just run up the stairs.

Meg knew something was wrong the instant she opened her front door. The wind that had bitten at her cheeks on the way from her car was still whistling around her once she'd stepped into the hallway, and a repetitive knocking was coming from the kitchen. Standing with her back to the door, she listened hard, trying to separate the natural creaks of an old house in winter weather from noises that weren't so natural. She heard nothing, no footsteps, no voices, no obvious movements, but that didn't necessarily mean she was alone.

With her pulse pounding like a snare drum, she grabbed one of the hiking poles propped by her shoe rack. Brandishing it pointed end uppermost, she stomped toward the kitchen, thumping her boots on the wooden floor to give the impression that someone far larger was approaching. The draught caught the kitchen door as she pushed it, swinging it back until it banged into the wall, giving her an expansive view of the carnage beyond.

"You fucking shithead," she whispered.

She slammed the pole against the tiles, hard enough to jar her arm and send tingles through the nerves in her wrist. Someone had smashed the window closest to the patio and proceeded to wreck her kitchen. It didn't take a genius to work out the culprit's identity. Only her brother would be stupid enough to make himself a sandwich and leave half of it uneaten beside an empty bottle of beer.

She poked the bread with her finger, testing its staleness. It felt as if it had been sitting there for a few hours, while the bottle, stolen from her fridge, was at room temperature and free of condensation. There were no visible fingerprints on the glass, but a lab would have a field day with the DNA left around the bottle's rim. Although Luke's actions displayed a complete disregard for criminal forensics, Meg knew that arrogance also played a part. She had never reported him to the authorities before, so he must suppose himself untouchable by now.

Turning full circle, she viewed the damage he had wrought: the drawers emptied and discarded on the floor, the crockery shattered on the tiles, her favourite mug in pieces next to the sink. The blind, rocking in the breeze above the smashed window, was the source of the knocking she had heard. She left the mess in situ and went into her living room, where a similar sight greeted her. Upstairs, her bedroom had borne the brunt of Luke's wanton destruction, little there remaining intact. She had taken her wallet with her, but £50 was missing from her underwear drawer, along with her Kindle and a gold chain bequeathed by her gran. She was surprised Luke hadn't rolled around in her bed like a dog, to tag his handiwork.

Perching on the edge of her windowsill, she rubbed her face and tried to wait out the rage. It took some doing, but the shaking in her legs finally stilled, and her heart no longer felt as if it were pummelling through her breastbone. She picked up her house phone, put the batteries back in the handset, and slid the cover into place. It peeped a cheerful melody to celebrate its resurrection, setting her teeth on edge. Waiting impatiently for its icons to appear, she mulled over what she was about to do and realised that she had no intention of talking herself out of it. That she'd never reported Luke's past abuse had nothing to do with misplaced family loyalty and everything to do with a child's instinct for self-preservation. She shrugged, her fingers already dialling. She wasn't a child anymore, but her mum might as well be, and Luke had threatened them both.

The call was answered quickly, the new non-emergency police number still being underused by a general public accustomed to dialling 999.

"Hello. Police. How can I help?"

"Hello," Meg said with estimable calm. "I'd like to report a burglary."

Nineteen Phelot Walk was accessed via a garden overgrown with knee-high grass and dandelions, among which rusted beer cans lay like flotsam. Mud oozed beneath Sanne's boots as she avoided a bulging bin bag and slid along the edge of a puddle. Nelson grabbed her arm to steady her, and she threw him a grateful smile.

"Hope we don't get invited in for tea and cakes," he muttered.

Sanne hesitated, about to knock on the front door. "I hope we don't get invited in at all," she said before thumping on the reinforced glass in a no-nonsense manner.

When no answer came, Nelson followed up by bellowing, "Police!" through the letterbox. Seconds later, a shuffle of movement in the hallway and a yell of, "Hold your fucking horses!" announced the imminent arrival of a middle-aged woman. The door cracked open just enough for her to glare at her unexpected guests.

"What now?" she snapped.

"Are you Mrs. Glenda Burrows?" Sanne asked, holding out her ID. She couldn't see enough of the woman to match her with the mugshot from the PNC. Fifty-six-year-old Glenda's impressive criminal career had included long jail terms for dealing and a particularly devious scam that preyed on the elderly.

The door opened a little farther, allowing the smell of the woman's unwashed body sweating out days' worth of alcohol to hit Sanne full in the face, an odour so replete with sense memories that it made her reel. For the second time in as many minutes, she felt Nelson's hand supporting her, and she managed not to let her revulsion show.

"Are you Glenda Burrows?" She pushed the door with her foot, prompting the woman to wrench it open.

"Yeah." Glenda folded her arms across her grubby dressing gown. "What of it?"

Nelson stepped forward, and Glenda eyed him with open disdain. "We're looking for Liam, Mrs. Burrows," he said. "We were told he's been staying with you."

"Well, you were told wrong." She spoke in Sanne's direction, apparently viewing her as the lesser of two evils. "I turfed him out more than a month since. That toerag would nick anything that weren't nailed down. *You* can come in and check if you want."

The distinct emphasis placed Sanne firmly in the firing line, and she heard Nelson's muffled snort. As they didn't have a warrant, the invitation was too good an opportunity to pass up, though, so she followed Glenda into the living room, where Glenda popped the top off a can of super-strength lager and slumped into the nearest armchair.

"Cheers," she said, raising the can and taking a long drink. "Don't mind if I sit this one out, do ya?"

"Not at all." Sanne took Glenda's belch as her cue to move into the kitchen. Accustomed by now to the foul atmosphere, she cast a swift glance at a week's worth of pots stacked in the sink, and opened the three cupboards that still had doors attached. Aside from a loaf of bread and a tin of mushy peas, the larder was empty.

She stuck her head through into the living room. "Where's your back door key?"

"How the fuck should I know?" Well into her second can, Glenda was beginning to slur her speech. "There's only rats and shite out there."

"Lovely." Sanne buzzed Nelson on her radio. "Your mission, should you choose to accept it, is to go round the back and have a toot in the yard."

"Great," he said. "No, really. There's nothing I'd rather do."

Sanne grinned. "Glenda says to watch out for rats and shite."

"I will be sure to do that. How are you getting on in there?"

She started up the stairs as she answered. "Well, I'll be wiping my feet on the way out, and there's no sign of the elusive Master Burrows. I'm just about to check under the beds. Wish me luck."

"You need me to come in?" he asked, suddenly serious.

"No, I'm okay." She paused on the landing, fumbling for a light switch. An energy-saving bulb came on overhead, and the shadows that had surrounded her slowly faded. "I'm fine," she said with more assurance. "Meet me out front when you're done."

A cursory inspection cleared the bathroom. There was nowhere to hide, and she had no desire to cross its threshold. The furniture in the spare bedroom comprised an empty chest of drawers and a single mattress, whereas Glenda's own bedroom actually boasted a bed and a wardrobe, each flanked by towers of tattered Mills and Boons. Sanne traced her finger across a cover, revealing a muscled male and a swooning bride beneath the layer of dust. The clash between fantasy and reality couldn't have been more pronounced.

There were more books stacked under the bed, propping up the sagging springs and leaving no space for anyone to conceal themselves. A mounting urge to get back outside gave Sanne the impetus to yank open the wardrobe, her haste making the hangers clank against the rail, shredding what remained of her courage. She slammed the door, taking a shaky breath. Nobody was lurking ready to smash in her skull, she reassured herself, and there was no corpse bleeding into the floor. There was just a mangy bedroom and a woman downstairs who wasn't willing to kill to protect her son.

"All clear, Nelson," she said into her radio.

"Copy that. Yard's clear as well. I'll see you in a minute."

She found Glenda snoring on the sofa, beer resting on her chest, a cigarette burning close to her fingertips. Crouching beside her, Sanne pinched out the cigarette and dropped it into a crowded ashtray. She shook Glenda's shoulder, watching as Glenda instinctively reached for her can.

"Who the fuck are you?" Glenda squinted harder. "Oh, didn't find him hiding in me knicker drawer, then?"

"No." Sanne stood, restoring a safe distance between herself and Glenda's breath. "So where does Liam go when you kick him out?"

Glenda finished her beer and tapped the last cigarette from a crumpled packet. Sanne tossed her a lighter that left a greasy residue on her fingers.

"Now and again he gets a bed at the Mission Cross, but mostly he goes down by the canal with the rest of the smack rats."

"Any idea where?"

"Cadmer Bridge? Cadbury Br—Oh, I don't fucking know."

Fortunately, Sanne did. "Cadman Bridge?"

Glenda nodded through her cloud of smoke. "Bingo."

"Don't suppose you have a current mobile number for him?"

"You don't suppose right."

"Thank you," Sanne said, trying not to inhale too deeply. "You've been very helpful."

"Yeah, whatever." Glenda spoke around her cigarette, her expression suddenly thoughtful. "Hey, what did the shithead do this time?"

"I couldn't possibly say." Sanne placed her card on the arm of the sofa, and then changed her mind and propped it by a four-pack of lager where Glenda was more likely to see it. "If he drops round for a cuppa, ask him to give me a call, will you?"

She left without waiting for the predictable response. Nelson met her at the front door, the apprehension easing from his face when he saw she was in one piece.

"According to Ma Burrows, Liam could be at the Mission Cross or hanging with his buddies by Cadman Bridge," she said as they navigated back out to the street.

"Cadman Bridge? Jesus, I'm not going there in the dark."

Sanne looked up, as if out of a daze, to see the deep blue-black of a winter evening. She hadn't realised how late it was. "How about we head for the Mission?" she said. "If he's there, all well and good. If he's not, we can try the canal first thing tomorrow."

Nelson gave her a thumbs-up and ducked into the car. She Googled the address they needed, as he sat shivering and waiting for the windscreen to defrost.

"How long till it's summer again?" he asked through chattering teeth.

Sanne took her time calculating. "Maybe six months, more likely seven up here, and we've hardly even had a winter yet, you nesh bugger."

"I beg to differ." He pointed to the dashboard display that registered the temperature as minus three degrees. "And I can't help being nesh. My people are used to warmer climes."

She laughed. "Warmer climes, my arse. You were born in Manchester!"

He turned the heater up another notch and pulled away from the kerb. "I'm sure my Caribbean blood's thinner than yours. I think they proved it scientifically on the telly."

"You're a pillock. You know that, don't you? What happened to those passion killers your mum got you for Christmas? Did Abeni chuck them in the bin?" She patted his leg, trying to detect an extra layer.

The car jerked as he rolled up his trousers enough to display his thermal long johns.

"Oh, sweet Jesus," Sanne said. "Those are hideous."

He changed gear without adjusting his clothing. "They're cosy, though, and snug in all the right places."

She put her hands over her ears. "Enough, I've heard enough. Turn right at the roundabout, left at the first lights, and please, if you value our partnership, put your bloody legs away."

CHAPTER EIGHT

Sanne wasn't sure what she'd been expecting the Mission Cross to look like: perhaps a church or at least a building bearing some kind of religious iconography. Instead, it occupied a mid-sized unit on an industrial estate half a mile from Malory Park, a building so nondescript that Nelson drove past it twice before Sanne noticed the sign.

"Very cloak and dagger," he said, pulling into a parking space and switching off the ignition.

Craning her neck, Sanne watched as the front door of the shelter swung open and a young woman in a coat too short for the weather tried to corral two small children and a pram while carrying three bulging plastic bags. "I guess those who need it know where it is," she murmured.

Nelson shook his head in obvious dismay. "How's she going to get home?"

"She'll walk," Sanne said. "Some folk'd rather come to these places when it's dark."

Nelson murmured his understanding. She didn't need to tell him that that was what her own mum had done on the rare but—for Teresa Jensen—mortifying occasions when the money had run out completely and a food bank had been her only way of providing for her kids. She had walked there and back under cover of night, refusing even to take the bus in case someone saw her and guessed where she'd been.

As Nelson and Sanne got out of the car, the young woman hurried by with her head lowered, the pram now full of bags, leaving the children struggling to match her pace. Sanne's feet ached in sympathy. She hoped they didn't have far to go, but she knew that the offer of a lift home wouldn't be appreciated.

"Come on. Let's get this done." She gave Nelson's sleeve a gentle tug to prevent him intervening, and after a moment's hesitation, he followed her lead.

Although the front door was unlocked, it led only into a vestibule, the actual entrance being controlled by a security system. Posters covered the walls—helplines for victims of domestic abuse and forced marriage, with text in English and Urdu; support groups for people struggling with substance abuse; and assistance for job seekers or those confused by recent changes to their benefits. As Sanne pocketed a leaflet about subsidised childcare, intending to pass it to Keeley, a voice sounded through a tinny speaker. Nelson had apparently buzzed for access while she'd been busy reading.

"I suppose that'd be Daniel," the voice said, and the speaker transmitted a reluctant sigh. "Push the door and I'll come fetch you."

"I asked for the manager," Nelson told Sanne.

They had just stepped into the main building when a plump, middle-aged woman walked toward them wiping her hands on a grimy apron. Either she wasn't fond of the police or she didn't consider her hands clean enough, because she didn't offer one in greeting. She acknowledged Nelson's introductions with an inclination of her head and studied their ID badges in turn. Her apron had *Pauline* stitched on it in red cotton, but she didn't confirm her name.

"Daniel's in the kitchen," she said, leading them along a corridor where the smell of cooking gradually became stronger. "You couldn't have come at a worse time."

Teatime, Sanne realised. Tea was 5:30 p.m. sharp in the Jensen household, and the Mission canteen evidently adhered to a similar schedule. The rattle of crockery and cutlery and a hubbub of voices greeted them as they entered. It took mere seconds for their presence to register, and the diners—a mishmash of no-fixed-abodes, young families, and others not so easy to categorise—quietened, their eyes dropping to their plates as they tried to avoid being singled out.

"I think we've been rumbled," Nelson said in an undertone.

"Yeah? Whatever gave you that idea?" Sanne paused in her scanning of the room to waggle her fingers at a toddler shovelling mash and gravy into his mouth. He giggled and shook his spoon, splattering the table with food.

The numerous avoidance strategies made it difficult to see everyone's face, and Sanne had just conceded defeat when a man turned around, waving her and Nelson over. Dressed in jeans and a shabby sweater, he stood out only by virtue of being clean-shaven and having a tidy haircut. After pausing to speak to an elderly woman, he came to meet Sanne and Nelson halfway across the floor.

"Daniel Horst," he said, shaking both of their hands. His smile was genuine, if tired. "How can I help?"

Aware of multiple ears pricking up around them, Sanne kept her voice low. "Is there somewhere we can talk that's a little more private?"

Daniel glanced at the serving hatch, where a queue still waited.

"Ten minutes, max," Sanne said.

His shoulders dropped in acquiescence. "We can go to the office."

The office was locked, an understandable precaution. Daniel produced a bunch of keys and selected a blue-capped one. Once inside, he flicked on the light to reveal a room crammed with value-label food and household goods. Stacks of toilet rolls covered the desk, and both of the chairs were loaded with tins of baked beans.

He started to move a box but then realised he had nowhere to put it. "We just had a delivery from one of the supermarkets. Some of them donate damaged items or food nearing its sell-by date. This has been a good week, hence…" He gestured at the disarray.

"It's okay," Sanne said. "We won't keep you for long. We're looking for Liam Burrows, and his mum told us he stays here on occasion."

"Ah, Liam." Daniel shook his head in regret. "I've not seen him since December, when we had to sanction him." His eyes widened as if he'd made a connection. "Does this have something to do with Andy?"

Nelson sidestepped a direct answer. "We heard that he and Andrew Culver had a fight here. Did that prompt the sanction?"

"Yes, I'm afraid so." Daniel touched the cross around his neck in a subconscious gesture. "The argument had started outside, something to do with Andy short-changing Liam on a deal. They were allowed in on the proviso that they remained apart, but Liam provoked a fight in the dining hall. There were several families in there at the time, so we had no option but to issue him with a temporary ban."

"And he's not been back since?" Sanne asked.

"Once, just after Christmas. I gave him a sandwich and a hot drink." Daniel's already flushed face turned a deeper shade of scarlet. "He's not a bad lad, Detective. He's just taken a bad path."

"Like Andrew Culver?" Nelson said.

"Similar, yes, except that Andy made several attempts to get clean. He even volunteered with us for a couple of weeks when we were working on a community allotment." Daniel reached behind a box and took a framed photograph from the wall. He handed it to Sanne.

"When was this taken?" she asked. It was raining in the photo, but no one seemed to mind. The ten or so volunteers were all wearing muddy waterproofs and grinning. She recognised Culver and Natalie Acre among them.

"May, I think, last year."

"Is there anyone else who might have borne a grudge against Culver?"

Daniel shook his head. "Not that I can think of. He was a quiet lad, used to come in for a meal every now and again. We'd chat about football if he wasn't too strung out." He moved to Sanne's side and tapped the photograph. "Have you spoken to Natalie? She and Andy broke up not long after this, but she's probably the closest thing he has to a next of kin."

"We spoke earlier today." Sanne passed the photo to Nelson. "When you saw Liam in December, did he tell you where he'd been staying?"

A sigh preceded Daniel's response. "'Here and there,' which usually means out by the canal. He was dishevelled, filthy. I let him use the shower after he'd eaten. My wife says I'm too much of a pushover, but someone has to try, haven't they?"

"Aye."

Nelson returned the photo to its hook. "We'll let you get back to it," he said.

As Daniel escorted them to the entrance, the canteen door swung back and forth, latecomers rushing in and others drifting back out into the cold.

"Are mealtimes always this busy?" Sanne asked.

"Always, and it's getting worse," Daniel said. "Job cuts, punitive benefit sanctions, the bedroom tax. They might be popular with the voters, but they're driving people out of their homes and into poverty. We're seeing more families, more people who actually have jobs and still can't make ends meet." He didn't sound like a party political broadcast, merely someone who had to deal with the fallout on a daily basis. "We're affiliated with a local church, but we don't shout about that in case it puts people off coming to us for help."

Sanne nodded. That explained the building's anonymous façade, although she was sure Keeley would happily listen to any sermon if it came with free nappies.

"We appreciate you sparing the time," she said at the door.

"I hope you find him," Daniel said. "Liam, and whoever killed Andy." He turned away before they could offer any hollow promises or parting pleasantries. Leaving them to navigate the icy car park, he went to greet a girl whose toes were poking through one of her shoes.

"Our perp and Liam Burrows could be one and the same," Nelson said, rubbing his hands together to warm them. "Burrows is our sole person of interest so far. Maybe Culver tried another sour deal, but this time Liam was packing more than his fists."

"Sounds plausible," Sanne said. "Shall we head to the canal early doors, when we've more chance of catching everyone in bed?"

He grinned at her across the car roof. "You've got yourself a date. Are you ready to call it a night?"

"God, yes." The very mention of going home made her aware of how tired she was. Andrew Culver's post mortem felt like days ago, and she hadn't slept much the night before.

As she opened the car door, her phone started to ring. Seeing Meg's name, she paused to answer.

"Hey, what's up?"

"He broke into my house," Meg said, her voice sounding odd and distant. "And he wrecked everything."

Sanne placed her hand on the car bonnet, focusing on the sting of frost beneath her palm in an effort to keep calm. "Have you called the police?"

"Yes, SOCO just left." A sob rattled out of Meg as she paused. "I think he might come back," she whispered.

"Sit tight, love," Sanne said. "I'll be there in about an hour."

Sanne made it to Meg's in seventy minutes. Factoring in the persistent sleet and a diversion to her own cottage to throw some food at the chickens and collect a change of clothes, it was possibly a new land speed record. Meg's front door remained obstinately shut until Sanne shouted through the letterbox, and the first things she saw were the hammer and rolling pin positioned on the second stair.

"Hey," she said.

"Hey." Meg tried to smile but made a mess of it, grimacing instead. When Sanne reached out to tuck a stray piece of hair back into its clip, Meg's bottom lip began to tremble, and she leaned forward to rest her head on Sanne's shoulder.

"You didn't need to come," she said.

"Yeah, yeah." Sanne rubbed Meg's back, trying to ease some of the tension in the muscles. She guessed Meg had been sitting on the stairs for hours, armed to the teeth, as she waited for her brother. "What did the police say?"

"Not much." Meg pulled away and returned to her perch. Sanne moved the makeshift weapons and joined her.

"Did you tell them about Luke?"

Meg nodded. "The officer said he'd speak to the staff at Rainscroft, but there've been a few burglaries in the village the last month or so, and he seemed convinced this was related. SOCO are going to run a DNA sample—Luke helped himself to a sandwich—but that'll take a few weeks. They didn't find any obvious prints, so I suppose he had the sense to wear gloves."

"How much of a wreck are we talking?"

In lieu of an answer, Meg stood and led Sanne to the kitchen, stopping just over the threshold.

"Bloody hell," Sanne whispered. "Every room?"

"Pretty much." Glass crunched beneath Meg's trainers as she crossed the tiles. "I don't know where to start. I was supposed to be on shift an hour ago, but I managed to swap onto a full night, so I've got till eight."

"Can't you call in for emergency leave?" Sanne was still trying to make sense of the scene in front of her. Anyone worth their investigative salt would have seen this was more than a simple burglary. Luke had lashed out like a spiteful child, hell-bent on teaching Meg a lesson.

"I was late in yesterday, so I'm already on Donovan's shit list," Meg said. "No doubt I'll be on Emily's as well. I've not told her anything yet."

"Right then, that's where we start." Sanne handed her the phone and picked up a dustpan and brush. "You call Emily. You don't have to tell her all the gruesome details, but you need to tell her something. I'll get cracking in here, and I'll sleep over tonight while you're at work. How does that sound?"

Meg sagged against the closest kitchen unit. "That sounds great. But don't you have someplace you'd rather be?"

"Yes, of course." Sanne made a shooing motion with the brush. "I had a hot date with my sofa and a tin of soup. Now go phone Em, before I phone her for you."

"Okay, I'm gone." Meg dodged around the dustpan. "Bin bags are in the second drawer down."

❖

Meg took the phone upstairs, where she played for time by clearing a space on her bed and folding all of her discarded clothing into neat piles. Finally, having run out of excuses to delay, she sat cross-legged on her quilt as she dialled Emily's number. Emily had phoned every twenty minutes since the start of the twilight shift that Meg hadn't turned up for, and she answered immediately.

"Meg? Where the hell are you?" She sounded pissed off, which was understandable given Meg's radio silence.

"I'm still at home. I got burgled, so I changed onto a night shift."

Meg heard Emily's sharp intake of breath as anger switched to concern. "You what? Jesus! Are you okay?"

"I'm fine. The house is trashed, but they didn't take much." Meg stared at her reflection in the mirror as she rattled off another lie. "The police said there's been a spate of break-ins since Christmas, that they always get a run of them this time of year."

"God, that's so horrible. Do you want me to come over?"

"No, there's no need." Realising she'd answered too quickly, she tried to explain. "By the time you got here, I'd be heading into work anyway. I'm going to tidy what I can and then set off."

"You poor thing." Emily covered the phone to reply to someone in the background and then came back on the line. "I'll come down and see you when I can, okay?"

"Okay," Meg said, feeling as if she'd dodged a bullet. "I'll see you then."

Downstairs, she was greeted by the smell of frying garlic, making her stomach rumble and her mouth start to water.

"I'm starving, and I'm guessing you've not eaten either," Sanne said, spotting her lurking by the door.

A large pan of pasta sat on the hob, and Sanne was busy sprinkling herbs into a pot of tomato sauce. In addition to preparing the food, she had swept the floor and cleared the countertops of debris. Meg went over to the stove, wondering what else Sanne had found that was still edible.

"You know that salami's been open for about six weeks, don't you?" she asked.

Sanne shrugged. "I cut the end off it, and the rest seemed fine. I'm not surprised Luke left half his sandwich. The cheese he'd used was a month out of date."

"I hope he gets listeria." Meg strained the pasta and looked around for something to serve it in.

"Voila," Sanne said, setting two mismatched Tupperware tubs in front of her.

"Really? Is this what we've been reduced to?" Meg shrugged. "Oh, what the hell. It'll taste exactly the same."

"That's the spirit." Sanne wiped a cloth over the table, removing remnants of fingerprint dust, before they sat down.

"I told Emily I'd been burgled," Meg said, pre-empting the inevitable question. "I don't think she needs to know anything else."

Sanne stabbed a piece of pasta in a non-committal fashion, keeping her counsel. If it was one of her interrogation techniques, it worked; Meg duly felt obliged to fill the gap.

"I don't want to tell her about Luke. Not if I don't have to."

"Mmhm." Sanne chewed deliberately. "Did you tell her I was here?"

"No, I didn't." Defeated, Meg dropped her fork into her tub. "I'm fucking everything up, aren't I?"

"You do seem to be making things difficult for yourself," Sanne said, with the tact of a consummate diplomat. "But you've got your reasons, and I can see why you'd want to keep Emily out of this." She put the fork back into Meg's hand. "Eat your tea, or you'll be keeling over on your patients later."

Meg took another mouthful, but it seemed an age before she could swallow it. "Luke's really lost the plot this time," she said quietly. "If he could do all this, what the fuck is he going to do next?"

"We're looking for him, Meg. Officially and unofficially." Sanne squeezed Meg's fingers. "We'll find him."

Meg kept hold of Sanne's hand, her own suddenly cool and clammy. "He'll probably find me first," she said.

Chapter Nine

On Meg's computer, alarm clock icons were blinking beside the names of eight patients, and as if that wasn't warning enough, the names were now highlighted in red.

"Donovan's on the warpath," Liz muttered, injecting antibiotics into a small IV bag. "And he's got someone in a fancy suit with him."

"Breach manager." Meg clicked the mouse to discharge a patient with her left hand while she filled out a drugs chart with her right. "It *is* a nice suit, isn't it?"

Liz appeared to consider that as she untangled the IV tubing, a task so familiar she could do it blindfolded. "Can Ms. Fancy Knickers magic beds out of her arse?"

Meg chuckled. "Not according to my little flashing clocks, no."

"Well, that's what they get for downgrading County." It was a refrain so popular that staff were threatening to get it printed on T-shirts. Government targets stated that ninety-five percent of patients attending A&E should be seen within four hours, a figure that had been barely achievable even before the Royal had become the only A&E in Sheffield. Add the pressure of a particularly harsh winter, and it was the perfect recipe for a bed crisis.

Meg shoved her steth into her pocket and studied the board, not in the mood to handle any kind of crisis. "Is Asif dealing with Four?"

"Yep, slowly but surely." Liz came alongside her. "Cubicle Six is an intoxicated fall, these are for Two, and the rest are stuck here or in the corridor until the lady in the swanky suit works a miracle."

"I'll take Six." Meg wrote her initials by his name. "Tell me honestly, Liz, do you think I'd look good in a suit like that?"

Liz's hoot of laughter followed Meg into the cubicle, where her patient was sprawled on the bed, drooling bloody saliva and vomit onto the sheet.

"For fuck's sake," she muttered.

Roger Clemens was smartly dressed and old enough to know better. According to the ambulance paperwork, his nose was probably broken and there was a two-inch laceration hidden somewhere under his thatch of black hair.

Standing with one foot each side of a puddle of vomit, Meg pulled on a pair of gloves and shook his shoulder. "Mr. Clemens? My name's Dr. Fielding. I need to take a look at you and sort your head out, if you could just wake up for me, okay?"

Roger snored and blew out a spit bubble. Meg envied his oblivion, if not his incontinence.

"Mr. Clemens? Roger?" She raised her voice and shook him again, to no avail. Concerned that the severity of his head injury might have been underestimated, she set her pen against his nail bed and applied mild pressure.

The effect was instantaneous. Swearing incoherently, he gripped her wrist and twisted it hard enough to make her gasp. She tried to pull away, but that only made him clamp down harder, so she resorted to a technique half-remembered from training, using her free hand to push at the base of his damaged nose. That worked. He let out a howl and released her, pawing at the injured part as the tears streaming down his face mingled with snot and fresh blood.

"Call yourself a doctor? You broke my fucking nose!" His yell came out wet and nasal, and smothered by his hands.

Cradling her throbbing wrist, Meg watched as he took aim and spat at her. At three a.m., it was the final straw of a particularly lousy day. Without saying a word, she pulled back the curtain and walked out.

❖

Tucked into a corner of the staffroom, Meg was trying to open an icepack with her teeth when she felt a kiss on the top of her head. She swivelled around to find Emily smiling at her.

"God, it's like a zoo out there. I thought you might appreciate a pick-me-up." Emily's smile vanished and her voice trailed away when she saw what Meg was wrestling with. She abandoned the two chocolate muffins on the table and extracted the pack from Meg's mouth. "Is this for you? What happened?"

Too weary and sore to couch the truth, Meg motioned toward her arm. "Drunk bloke didn't take kindly to being woken up," she said. Ugly, finger-shaped bruises already encircled her wrist, and rotating it made her feel sick. She closed her eyes in relief as Emily laid the icepack against it, a relief that lasted until Emily spoke again.

"Did you provoke him?"

Meg snapped her eyes open. Emily was watching her intently, as if to gauge the honesty of her answer.

"Thanks for the vote of confidence," Meg said.

Emily's hands went up in surrender, a gesture she habitually made when she realised that she had stepped out of line but didn't really regret it. "I know you can go in all guns blazing at times, that's all."

Meg moved her arm away as Emily reached for it, and the pain that shot through her wrist fuelled the anger in her reply. "He had a head injury, and he didn't respond to voice, so I tried a pen on his nail. That's when he grabbed me. The fucker had been playing possum all along."

Emily frowned. "What makes you think that?"

"Because he knew I was a doctor rather than a nurse, which means he'd heard me introduce myself when I first walked in there. I didn't go looking for trouble, Em. I've been doing this a long time, and I'm not stupid."

"I know you're not," Emily said, but she looked piqued by the unsubtle reference to her own inexperience, and she changed the subject quickly. "Have you had it X-rayed?"

"No."

"Have you even reported it?" Her voice had risen a pitch.

"I warned the doc who took over the patient from me."

"But you've not done anything officially?" She huffed in exasperation. "This is how they get away with it, Meg. This is why people think it's okay to assault medical staff."

It wasn't okay, Meg knew that, but she didn't have the time to write up an incident report, file a complaint, and give a statement to the police. All she wanted was to get to the end of her shift and go home to lick her wounds in peace. "I don't need a lecture, Em," she said.

The strain in her tone made Emily relent. She touched the fingertips of Meg's bad hand. "Have you taken anything?"

"Diclofenac. It should kick in soon."

"You could have a fracture in there."

Meg carefully flexed her wrist. "It's just a sprain," she said, once she was certain she could speak without throwing up. She slipped the icepack into a carrier bag to keep it incognito and forced herself to stand. "I should get back out there. No one's had a break tonight."

"You should be going home."

Meg paused in her efforts to wrap the bag around her wrist. "Home sort of looks like a bomb's hit it. I'm probably better off here."

The reminder made Emily wince. "Heck. With all this, I'd forgotten the break-in. You sleep at mine when you're finished, and I'll go round and start tidying."

Meg's imagination rapidly conjured a scenario in which Emily walked in on Sanne's one-woman slumber party: a slapstick comedy, except that no one was laughing and Meg wound up with a lot of explaining to do.

"I got some of it sorted this afternoon, and I'll do the rest tomorrow." She cupped Emily's chin and kissed her, cutting off any chance of a protest. "Thanks for the offer, though, and for the muffin."

Emily smiled. "Poor thing, you've not had a good day, have you?"

Meg shook her head and said nothing. Emily scarcely knew the half of it.

❖

It had snowed overnight: not enough to impact on Sanne's commute from Meg's, but enough to make the towpath of the Sheffield and Tinsley canal precarious underfoot. The cold air was irritating Sanne's nose and making her sneeze. She snuffled into a tissue and nodded her thanks when Nelson blessed her.

"I checked the FWIN first thing this morning," she said, folding the tissue away. "No updates. No mention of Luke being sighted or, better still, arrested. I managed to get everything at Meg's cleaned up, but he'd not left her a plate to eat off." She paused to squint at a bridge number. "Cadman Bridge should be the next one down."

"Why didn't her neighbours hear anything?" Nelson asked. He had halted, too, and he set off again as she did, their footsteps crunching in synch on the frozen layer of snow. It was a good question, and it made Sanne glad to have confided in him. He was guaranteed to pick up on the salient points, some of which she might have overlooked. This one, however, had a simple answer.

"She's in an end terrace. The couple next door were at work, and next door but one are both hard of hearing. Luke might've been waiting for her and run out of patience." Thinking about this possibility sent a chill straight through Sanne. She shoved her hands in her pockets and tried not to shiver too noticeably. Luke had always been impetuous, and it was that trait, coupled with his temper, that made him so unpredictable. If Sanne had her way, Meg would be staying at Emily's until he was apprehended, but she suspected Meg might have something to say about that.

"Bloody hell, San, I'd forgotten how grim it is down here."

Nelson's voice broke across her train of thought. She looked around at the derelict mills crowding both sides of the canal, their brickwork sprouting ferns, weeds, and even the odd buddleia. Back at Victoria Quays—the city's canal basin—a programme of regeneration had created an attractive centre for tourists and locals alike, but the budget obviously hadn't stretched this far.

"Cadman Bridge is Grade II listed," she said. She smiled at Nelson's incredulity. "I was reading about it on the way here. It's one of only two original 1819 bridges on the canal."

His gaze took in the bridge and its wider surroundings. "I'm guessing the folk who live round here didn't choose it for its architectural appeal."

They stopped at a rough construct of cardboard and plywood, examining it long enough to check that it housed only a pile of blankets and two empty cider bottles. Tucked off the towpath in a clump of hawthorn, it was the first sign of inhabitation since the narrowboats moored at the basin.

"Let's hope its owner got a bed at a shelter for the night," Sanne said. The forecast had predicted a low of minus five degrees, but it had been minus eight when she'd set out that morning.

Having worked local beats as uniformed officers, they knew that many of the rough sleepers congregated around the disused mills and warehouses that had once been the backbone of a thriving industrial area. With the slow death of manufacturing, the companies had disbanded, initially one by one and then en masse, and the drive to convert the abandoned buildings into deluxe apartments had been confined to the city centre.

"Let's try that mill over there first and see if someone will be kind enough to point us in the right direction," Nelson said.

Sanne arched an eyebrow at him. "By 'kind enough,' I'm assuming you mean hungry or cold enough."

He rustled a bag full of sandwiches, chocolate, and crisps. If those failed as incentives, they would resort to Sanne's collection of sweaters, gloves, and woolly hats taken from a box of long-unclaimed lost property. She had drawn the line at his suggestion of a couple of six-packs.

The mill's main entrance had been secured with a metal grille in a half-hearted and vain attempt to deter trespassers. Most of the ground-floor windows were shattered, and the rear door hung on a single disintegrating hinge. Nelson shone his torch through the gap and then stepped aside.

"Ladies first," he said, and lit up his grin with his Maglite.

"You'll be sorry if I go arse over tit straight through the floorboards," Sanne said, but she ducked beneath the rotting wood and inched her way inside. To her relief, the floor was solid concrete, strewn with litter of every imaginable form.

"Far left," she whispered to Nelson, once he had squeezed through the gap. "You see it?"

Taking care to shine her torch obliquely, she indicated a pair of boots sticking out of a cardboard lean-to. The boots came with legs attached.

"Is quarter to seven too early for a house call?" Nelson muttered as they approached. "I never know what's polite in these situations."

"I think we're okay. I doubt he has to get up for work." She gave a trio of discarded condoms a wide berth, trying not to consider what would lead anyone to have sex in such a place. As she and Nelson closed in on the shelter, a loud, sloppy snore reverberated through the Kellogg's cereal and Walkers crisp boxes, and she realised that their silent approach had been a little over-cautious.

"After you," she told Nelson. Even from a distance, the smell of their quarry was making her eyes tear.

He scowled at her and nudged the disembodied legs with the tip of his boot. "Rise and shine! We've brought breakfast!"

"And hats and gloves," Sanne added.

The boxes shook as the legs drew out of range. "What the fuck? Fuck off!"

Nelson and Sanne exchanged a surprised look. Neither had expected the occupant to be female. Seconds later, a man's voice berated her for stealing the last of the cider, and the presence of the condoms suddenly made more sense.

Using his best conciliatory tone, Nelson tried again. "Hey, we're just trying to find someone, and we'd appreciate your help."

A shuffling noise suggested someone was sitting up. "Coppers or God-botherers?" the man asked.

"Coppers," Sanne said, uncertain which would cause the least offence.

The woman groaned and stuck her head into view. "You really got food?"

Sanne angled the light so she could see the woman. Barely out of her teens, she was scrawny and filthy, with skin broken down by drug abuse. Without speaking, Nelson opened his bag and held out a selection of everything he'd brought.

At the sound of packets tearing, the man also put in an appearance. Just as dishevelled as his partner, he was older, jaundiced, and definitely not Liam Burrows.

"Got any beer?" he asked around a mouthful of ham sandwich. Nelson threw Sanne an *I told you so* look as she offered the man a thick sweater instead.

"We're looking for Liam Burrows," she said, showing them a recent mugshot.

The woman gestured expansively with her Mars bar. "I seen him once or twice, but not in here." She looked at the man, as if to check it was okay for her to act as an informant. He shrugged and bit into the second half of his sandwich. "Go past the Dickinson warehouse," she told Sanne. "There's a smaller one on the left."

"It's on the right," the man said.

"Oh, yeah, on the right. Got blue boarding and one of those wavy roofs. I seen him go in there before."

"Have you seen him recently?" Sanne asked.

The woman nodded and counted to five on her fingers. "Three days back." She grinned in triumph, displaying blackened teeth.

"That's great, thanks." Sanne added gloves and hats to their new ensemble. "You two know there are shelters you can try, don't you?"

The man nodded, and the woman ran an affectionate hand over his unshaven chin. "Most of them make us split up," she said. "We like it fine in here."

There wasn't much Sanne could say to that, and in any case the couple were already tucking themselves back into their sleeping bags. She left more sandwiches by their feet and turned away.

"Each to their own," Nelson said, but he sounded as troubled as she felt.

"Aye." When she glanced back, the boxes had been swallowed up by the darkness. "There but by the grace, though, eh?"

Outside, the dawn was grey and watery, yet bright enough to make her shield her eyes, and Nelson spotted the Dickinson building before she did. They identified the other warehouse by its roof, its blue paintwork having peeled away to reveal the wooden slats beneath. The owner—or whoever utilised it illicitly—had nailed down the obvious access points with a fair amount of determination, and it was only by wading among the nettles at its rear that Sanne found a section of board that was wedged into place so as to appear fitted but that was loose enough to remove. She and Nelson had to light the way for each other to climb through, but once their vision had adjusted, the slivers of daylight piercing the cracked woodwork were enough to see by.

Sanne took a few cautious steps away from the wall and paused to take stock. The single-storey warehouse had an open-plan layout, the flooring so long neglected that it had reverted to hard-packed dirt. It was immediately apparent that someone was living there. To her left, run-off from the roof was dripping into a lop-sided bathtub, beside which a plastic mug and plate were stacked. An area in the right-hand corner showed recent signs of being used as a toilet, and ashes were still glowing in a central fire pit. Following the logical organisation of the space, she focused on the corner farthest from the toilet, where a double mattress lay swathed in blankets.

Nelson held up a single finger, indicating one body beneath the mound of bedding. She nodded, and they split, approaching from both sides and with as little noise as possible. They were less than five feet away when the blankets parted and a man launched himself forward like a sprinter off the blocks. He didn't pause when he saw them, but aimed straight for Sanne, knocked her flying, and hurtled for the exit.

"What the—? *Stop! Police!*"

From her prone position, the sound of Nelson giving chase drowned out the rattle of the breath she was trying to pull into her lungs. She struggled to her hands and knees, intent on helping but managing only to lean there and wheeze. By the time her diaphragm stopped rebelling, two sets of footsteps—one pounding and one more of a scuffle—were heading toward her.

"San? You okay?" With his hand still wrapped in her assailant's collar, Nelson knelt at her side, provoking a yelp of protest as the lad was dragged down with him.

She nodded and then remembered that actual speech would be more convincing.

"I'm fine," she said, letting him pull her to her feet. Something in her left knee ached, and her palm had been sliced by a piece of glass, but overall it was her pride that had suffered the most damage.

"Look who I found." Nelson jerked the cloth in his fist, encouraging the lad to lift his head.

"Oh. Hey, Liam." Sanne waved the hand that wasn't oozing blood.

Liam Burrows attempted to glare at her, but his deer-in-headlights countenance undermined the effect. He was smaller than she was, with the slight build and elfin features suggestive of foetal alcohol syndrome.

"I didn't do nothin'," he muttered, his thick Yorkshire accent making his words run together like porridge. "I were just havin' a kip."

"You assaulted a police officer," Nelson said.

"Didn't know you was police."

"You didn't give us a chance to tell you."

Leaving Nelson to debate the finer points of Liam's behaviour, Sanne pulled on a pair of latex gloves and shook out his bedding, one stinking blanket at a time. A hairbrush, spare socks, a fork, and half a box of matches fell to the floor. None of the clothing she found bore any stains that looked like blood, and he didn't appear to be in possession of a knife with a serrated three-inch blade. Running the length of his bed was a crude wooden shelf upon which he had laid out a porcelain dog, a postcard of Anfield stadium, and a chipped, obviously well-loved collection of Matchbox cars. She spun the wheels of a Porsche, attempting to reconcile the lad who had tried to make this place into a home with the one whose criminal record showed such a fondness for violence. Enlightenment proved elusive, however, so she set the car back in place and rejoined Nelson.

"Anything?" he asked.

Shaking her head, she turned to Liam. "Come in with us and answer some questions, and I'll forget you knocked me on my arse."

Liam stared at her, presumably working out the pros and cons. It took him a while. "So you're not nicking me," he said at length.

"No. We'll question you under caution, but you're not under arrest. 'Course, that could change if you don't cooperate." She took off her gloves, making sure that he saw the blood smeared across one of them.

He bit a piece of chapped skin off his lip. "Okay, I'll come with you, miss." He was already wearing multiple layers, but he grabbed his coat and shrugged into it.

"Have you had anything to eat today?" she asked, as they headed for the exit.

"Naw, not yet. I had a Pot Noodle day before yesterday."

She handed him a sandwich, a bag of crisps, and a Twix, and his face lit up like a kid on Christmas morning.

"Yeah, yeah, I know," she said to Nelson. "I'm a soft touch."

"A soft touch who's up to date with her tetanus, I hope." He lifted her hand to examine her palm.

She tolerated his scrutiny for a few seconds. "Now who's being soft? It's just a scratch."

Walking beside her, Liam finished his sandwich and burped his appreciation. "'Scuse, miss," he said around a mouthful of Twix.

Nelson shook his head in despair and delved into his bag. "Splendid, there's two left for us. Cheese and pickle, or sausage and egg?" He held both sandwiches up to Sanne.

She laughed. "You even have to ask?"

"I was hoping you might've gone veggie overnight."

"Fat chance of that, mate. We're not all sandal-wearing, *Guardian*-reading, muesli-eating meat-haters."

"Damn," he said with feeling, and relinquished the sausage and egg.

CHAPTER TEN

The EDSOP detectives worked a shift pattern that vaguely resembled a regular nine to five week, except that overtime was commonplace and paid back as days in lieu, rarely taken. Given the current caseload, Sanne wasn't surprised to see Mike Hallet, George, and Fred at their desks at eight fifteen on a Saturday morning.

"Hey, San," Fred called. "What the devil happened to you?"

"Nelson and I took a stroll down by the canal." She rooted in her desk for her bag of toiletries, keen to rectify her "dragged through a hedge backward" look. "Ran into a suspect. Well, he ran into me. You know how it is."

"Brute," he said, coming across to survey the damage.

George followed swiftly on Fred's heels, toting the first aid kit from the kitchen. "Aw, San, you're only a little 'un." Without waiting for her consent, he ushered her into his chair and doctored her palm with wipes, antiseptic cream, and a generous application of gauze. Aware that both men meant well, she suffered the attention without complaint, taking the opportunity to nosy through the photographs on George's desk.

"This your vic?" she asked over the rip of Micropore tape.

"Yep." Fred separated one of the images out for her. "Nasty, eh?"

The photo was a grisly shot taken at the initial crime scene of a young white male, his eyes half-lidded and clouded. Sequential photographs from the post mortem detailed six narrow stab wounds to his chest and abdomen. Sanne pulled up the first one again and studied his face.

"We're still trying to ID him," Fred said. "PM says he's a chronic alcoholic, probably homeless, but his prints gave us nothing."

"Huh," she murmured, and then realised George had asked her a question. "Sorry, what?"

He tapped the bandage on her hand. "I said, 'How's that?'"

"Oh, it's great. Thanks." She indicated the photo. "Do you mind if I keep hold of this? Just for an hour or so."

George frowned. "Why? Do you recognise him?"

"I'm not sure." She pushed his chair back. "But I might know someone who does."

Her intention to get cleaned up forgotten, she headed straight for Interview One, where Liam sat surrounded by sandwich packaging, his hands wrapped around a plastic cup of coffee. Nelson was leaning against the wall in front of him.

"Ready to get started?" Sanne slipped the photo beneath the file Nelson had left on the table, and they both took their seats.

"He declined legal representation in favour of a tuna butty," Nelson murmured.

"Super." She made the necessary introductions for the benefit of the recording and reminded Liam that he was being questioned under caution. "Liam, have you any idea why we've brought you in here today?"

He took a slurp of coffee, thoroughly at home with the proceedings. "'Cos of my mum? She's always saying I've pinched stuff when I've not."

"Okay, no, it's got nothing to do with your mum. We wanted to talk to you about Andrew Culver."

He gave her a blank look, his brow knotted, his tongue poking out. She knew foetal alcohol syndrome caused developmental delay, so she decided to keep things as simple as possible for him. She showed him the photograph they had issued to the media, not that the press had ever bothered to use it. Liam's expression altered from confusion to concern, every step of his thought process clearly signposted.

"He started it," he muttered into his cup.

"He started what?" Nelson—who could hear a pin drop across a footy field—asked, even as Sanne was still working out what Liam had said.

"At the Mish. He started the scrap. I were just minding my own, and he started it."

"Andrew Culver was found murdered on Thursday, Liam," Nelson said. "And we have two witnesses naming you as someone who might have wanted to hurt him."

Liam's mouth flapped open and closed again. In desperation, he looked from Nelson to Sanne, as if expecting her to assume the role of good cop. Instead, she swapped the image of Culver for two of his body.

"Did you do this, Liam?" she asked.

He shook his head, spraying spit onto the table. "No, miss, no! I didn't even know he were dead!"

Unswayed by his vehemence, she continued to push. "One of those witnesses stated that you started the fight with Andrew, that you were banned from the Mission Cross as a result."

"It weren't my fault. He ripped me off on a bag. People always do it, 'cos they think I'm a retard."

"So you got angry?" Nelson said.

"Yeah, I got angry. I punched his face in, and Mr. Horst chucked me out." Liam's nostrils flared as he spoke, and his fists were clenched on the table. "That were ages ago, though. Before Christmas."

"When was the last time you saw Andrew?"

He grinned suddenly, unable to repress his triumph. "When he were on the floor, snivelling like a little girl." Too late, he realised what he'd said and made a hasty clarification. "When I'd punched him! Because I never killed him!"

Despite his previous convictions and his history with the victim, Sanne believed him, and one glance at Nelson told her they were on the same page.

"Can you drive, Liam?" she asked, thinking of the van seen on Pellinore around the time of the murder.

He shook his head with obvious regret. "Couldn't afford it, miss."

"Do you remember where you were earlier this week? Between Monday and Thursday?"

The blank look was back in place. "Sort of."

That was better than Sanne had expected. "Because it would really help you and us if we could piece that together. Anywhere you went, anyone who might have seen you. Could you try to write that down, if we get you another brew and something else to eat?"

He nodded, spurred on by the offer.

"One final thing," she said, reaching for the photo she had taken from George's file. "Do you recognise this man?"

His jaw tightened as he worked out what he was looking at. He was silent for a long moment.

"It's Jonesy," he said finally. "Marcus Jones. He used to go down the Mish, and I see him round the Bridge sometimes. He's all right, is Jonesy. He buys me chips." The tension in his jaw slackened into a tremor. "Is he dead too, miss?"

"Aye, I'm afraid so." Sanne took the photo back. "How about I get you that brew and a pen and paper?"

Nelson followed her into the corridor, shutting the interview room door. "Dare I ask?" he said.

"Probably not." She gave him the photo and paced across the corridor. "That's the vic from Fred and George's latest case. I thought I'd seen his face before, and Burrows just confirmed it. This lad was in the photograph Daniel Horst showed us at the Mission. Do you remember? The allotment one?"

"Oh, bloody hell. You're thinking our case and this one are related?"

"I think it's a possibility. There are obvious differences—weapon, location of the body, even location of the wounds—but the profile of the two vics is almost identical, and they were both in that photo, so they knew each other, and then there's the severity of the violence…" She took a breath and committed herself. "Yes. I think we could be looking at the same perp for both murders."

Nelson groaned, but his eyes were bright with excitement. "Reckon it might be Liam?" he asked, but he was testing her, playing devil's advocate.

"I doubt it. He likes a good scrap, but nothing in his priors suggests he's working his way up to multiple murder, and his reactions in there seemed solid. He might be useful as a witness, though, if he can draw up a list of mutual associates for Culver and Jones."

Nelson held up a hand. "Easy there, tiger. Let's take this one step at a time."

Sanne could always count on Nelson for sensible advice. She leaned forward and set her hands on her knees. She felt as if she'd run a marathon, her pulse going like the clappers and her head spinning.

"Shall we speak to George and Fred first?" she asked.

"Definitely. They might have a suspect in mind who's entirely unconnected to Culver."

"And if they don't?"

Nelson slapped her on the back. "If they don't, then you get to ruin the boss's weekend."

❖

Fred and George, it transpired, had very little to go on, and Sanne's tentative identification of their victim was greeted by a sloppy kiss on her cheek and the sharing out of a packet of Jaffa Cakes.

"It could just be a coincidence," Sanne murmured. She nibbled the sponge around the edge of the cake, leaving the orange jelly centre until last. The photos from the two post mortems were spread across Fred's desk, and Nelson and George were reading each other's case files. She, meanwhile, was attempting to construct a timeline.

"Andrew Culver was last seen Monday morning. Time of death was tricky to pin down, but we think he may've been murdered that night or early on Tuesday. Nelson, what's Jones's estimated TOD?"

Nelson flicked back a couple of pages and scanned the PM report. "Approximately thirty-six hours prior to him being found, so"—he let out a low whistle—"Wednesday night. Crikey."

"Two in three days," George said. He usually felt the cold, but his jacket was already discarded over the back of his chair, and he began loosening his tie. "Bloody hell, it's Saturday. Should we be expecting another body? Someone should tell the boss."

"Whoa, hang on a second," Sanne said. "Don't we need more to go on before we contact the boss? I mean, if she was here then perhaps we could mention it, but it's Saturday. We'd better be damn sure of our facts before we involve her."

There were thoughtful nods from the three men, none of whom seemed keen to pick up the phone and make that call.

"So, we keep brainstorming," Nelson said, his decisive tone a balm on Sanne's fraying nerves. "Try to confirm the ID on the second vic, pin down anything that connects him to ours, identify common and uncommon features."

"Did you request CCTV of the area?" Sanne asked George.

He stopped wrestling with the top button on his shirt and opened a folder on his computer. She recognised the file names as areas local to the murder scene, the majority of them around shopping precincts and bus stops.

"The recordings were sent through late last night, but we've only had time to look at three of them," he said. "Quality is iffy at best. The most interesting thing we've seen so far is a shag behind a Biffa bin."

"Classy," she said. "It might be worth going over them again to check if a dark-coloured Vauxhall Combo van shows up at any point. We have a note of one parked close to our scene on Monday night. It's about the best lead we've got."

"Righto." Fred licked chocolate off his fingers with the air of one prepared to get stuck in.

"San, do you want to see how Mr. Burrows is getting on?" Nelson asked.

She nodded, snagging the remaining Jaffa Cakes. "Incentive," she said, in answer to Fred's shocked reaction. "Nelson, if you can't find a next of kin for Jones, Daniel Horst might be able to provide a more reliable ID."

"Good thinking."

"Yeah, I'm full of great ideas." She kept her voice light, but she was beginning to wonder what the hell she had set into motion less than a week into her three-month improvement notice. Her suggestion that Sheffield harboured a multiple murderer had set half the department off on what was likely to be a wild goose chase. In terms of career enhancement, it probably wasn't what Eleanor had had in mind.

❖

Meg woke up ten minutes before her alarm with a thick head, her fingers curled around the hammer she had taken to bed. Had her mouth not been gummed shut, she would have cursed the world and everyone in it, but she settled instead for bashing the mattress a couple of times. She was due back at work in less than three hours, a killer turnaround that was the result of her shift-swap. Sleep deprivation and rotating shift patterns were things she had grown accustomed to over the years, but the stress of the last two days was gnawing at her, and she barely had the energy to drag herself upright.

She was debating whether to sacrifice food for more sleep when a bang from downstairs made the decision for her. She shot out of bed, grabbing the hammer and getting her legs caught in the sheets. The combination of a head rush and the bedding almost put her on the floor. Having waited out the dizziness, she kicked free from the cotton and tiptoed across the carpet. The bedroom door creaked open, the rest of the house falling silent as if holding its breath. Three steps took her onto the landing, where she could hear what sounded like the rhythmic swish of a potato peeler. As the scent of spicy cooking began to waft up to her, the knot in her guts loosened slightly.

"Em? Is that you?" she shouted from a safe distance, still clutching the hammer and within easy reach of the phone in her bedroom.

"It's me," Emily called back. "Sorry, I dropped the lid from a jar. Did I wake you?"

Meg stashed the hammer behind the laundry basket and forced her trembling legs to take the stairs at a trot. They were almost steady by the time she entered the kitchen.

"Crikey, you've been busy."

The kitchen was spotless, apart from the unit where Emily had been preparing vegetables. A new set of crockery sat by the kettle, and a tea bag waited in a replica of Meg's favourite mug.

"Where on earth did you find this?" Weariness forgotten, Meg laughed and flicked the kettle on.

"What? Oh, the mug? It was just hanging on the rack."

A pan on the hob began to spit out orange gloop. Turning away to adjust the heat, Emily missed Meg biting her tongue and mouthing the word "bollocks." The mug's original incarnation had been a Christmas gift from Sanne, who had apparently bought a replacement and left it for Meg to find. Meg assumed she had purchased the crockery on the same trip.

"It's a good thing you managed to get to the supermarket last night." The pan crisis dealt with, Emily ushered Meg into a chair and set a bowl of homemade muesli in front of her. Fresh milk, sliced fruit, and yoghurt were arranged neatly on the table.

Meg gave her best noncommittal smile, eyeing the seeds and nuts and hoping that Sanne had loaded her fridge with bacon and eggs. "This all looks great," she said.

By anyone's standards, Emily was an excellent cook. She just preferred not to cook meat. Given that Meg's repertoire amounted to eggy bread, Super Noodle surprise (the surprise came if she didn't boil them dry), and a passable fry-up, she had been eating an unprecedented amount of vegetables and lentils over the last five months. Even now, the thought of her illicit late-night kebab left her drooling into her bowl.

Emily brought Meg's mug of tea over to the table and sat down. "I made sweet potato curry for your supper. Just give it three minutes in the microwave." She helped herself to cereal. "How's the wrist?"

"Not too bad if I don't move it." Meg spoke through a mouthful, but swallowed when she saw Emily grimace. "Sorry."

She rolled up her pyjama sleeve and displayed her arm. The bruises had deepened overnight, mottling her skin with lines of livid purple. It had been years since she last had to choose an outfit to cover bruising, but fortunately she tended to wear a long-sleeved T-shirt beneath her scrubs top in winter.

"Oh, sweetheart," Emily whispered. She ran a careful finger over the swollen skin.

Meg hitched her chair closer and pulled Emily into a hug. "Hey, I'm fine. These things happen. Come on. Don't get all upset."

Emily sniffled. "He should go to prison for doing that."

"He probably wouldn't even get a fine, Em." She used her thumb to wipe Emily's tears away. "He'd hire a good lawyer, who'd argue that I startled him or that the head injury made him confused. He'd be clean-shaven and contrite, dressed in his best suit, and I'd walk straight into court off a night shift, forget my own name, and accidentally say 'fuck' in front of the judge."

Emily laughed softly, her breath a warm tickle on Meg's neck.

Encouraged, Meg continued, "They'd end up fining me for contempt and awarding him compensation."

"Most likely." Emily's voice was still quiet, but she'd stopped crying. "How many times have you been hurt like this?"

"Three," Meg said. For the purposes of this conversation, three was all she was going to admit to. "One bloke had just come out of a seizure, though, so that couldn't be helped."

"And the other?" Emily sat up ramrod straight, as if to steel herself.

"Twenty-year-old who wasn't happy that his drunk girlfriend had been kept waiting for almost half an hour. He walked round to Majors and punched the first medic he found. He pleaded guilty to common assault and spent a couple of months in jail. He's come back in with a broken leg since then, but he didn't recognise me."

Emily crinkled her nose and pushed her mug of tea away as if its smell was making her queasy. Her A&E rotation had lasted four months, and she'd already told Meg she had no desire to return to emergency medicine. Her ultimate goal was general practice in a village surgery, somewhere pleasant and rural where housewives came for regular doses of antidepressants and anyone seriously ill could be referred on to the hospital. It sounded like Meg's worst nightmare, but there was certainly money in it. Emily's mum had been a GP for most of her career and had retired at fifty to spend her days playing golf or heading off to far-flung parts. It was a fair bet that none of her patients had ever smacked her.

"How can you be so blasé about it?" Emily asked.

Meg readjusted her sleeve and wrapped her cold fingers around her mug. "I think you just get used to it."

The man made no attempt to disguise what he was doing. He opened his trousers, took aim, gave it a shake when he'd finished, and tidied himself away again. Two minutes and forty seconds later, he caught the number fourteen bus. The remaining five minutes of film recorded the wanderings of a dog, far better mannered than most of the people with whom he was sharing his brief flush of fame, and then the grey fuzz indicating a full tape.

Sanne rocked back on her chair, waiting out the end of the file before closing it down and adding it to her *Watched* folder. There were six files there now, all capturing Malory Park's finest going about their nocturnal business, and all completely useless to the investigation.

"There are only two shops in Sheffield that stock knives similar to the one used to kill Andrew Culver." Nelson turned his monitor so Sanne could see the website for Streetz Emporium, a shop located in the trendy Hartfield Quarter, where small independent businesses flourished away from the high city centre rates. The page, headed *Shit Kickers*, categorised its weaponry according to "Fear Factor." In the top corner, a knife with a savage serrated blade and an ornate handle scored ten out of ten.

"Definitely worth sending a couple of unis round for a visit," she said, "if only to piss the proprietors off."

Nelson chuckled. "The murder weapons were probably purchased online, but you never know, we might get lucky. How are you doing over there?"

"Nil for six." She stood and stretched her back, her muscles stiff and sore from sitting still for hours. She'd been looking forward to a run, but it was already dark, so that wasn't going to happen. "I've learned that the number fourteen bus is reasonably punctual, that White Ace cider appears to be the Malory Park cheap booze of choice, and that The Frying Pickets outsells Trawlers chippy by about two to one."

"That'll be down to its fabulous name."

"Quite possibly. Did you get hold of Daniel at the Mission?"

"Not yet. A woman who may or may not have been Pauline said he was out on the estate delivering food and clothing. She didn't know when he'd be back. George is still in with Liam Burrows, trying to dig out a next of kin for Marcus Jones and helping firm up Burrows's alibi. 'Asleep in the warehouse' and 'wasted out back of Bashir's Kebabs' are unlikely to convince the boss of his innocence."

Halfway toward touching her toes, Sanne shivered. "Please don't mention the boss. If she gets wind of this and it turns out to be noth—"

Nelson held up a hand to cut her off. "No one will say a word, and pooling resources for the afternoon hasn't done us any harm."

Her fingers grazed her boots, the motion a pleasant pull on her back. "True, but she'll think I got all giddy and jumped the gun, trying to be flash."

"Yes, because everyone knows you're nothing but a glory hound."

"Oh aye." She straightened up and reached for their mugs. "I love seeing my face plastered all over the papers and having reporters stake out my cottage."

He gave her a sympathetic smile. "Well, this one is unlikely to make the front page. It's probably just a falling out between smackheads and nothing to do with Jones."

The sound of a toppling chair made them both look around. Fred was rapidly bearing down on their desks, his hands beckoning them over.

"Got something!" he yelled. "Come and take a look!"

Sanne glowered at Nelson. "You and your big mouth," she muttered.

Fred had rewound the CCTV file. For almost a minute, Sanne stared at the edge of a shopping precinct, the camera clipping the side of a Raja Brothers convenience store and the road that ran to the right of it.

"This is from Wednesday night, one of the closest cameras to our scene. Just keep watching." Fred's feet played out a tap dance as the seconds ticked by. "There!"

He paused the tape, prompting Sanne and Nelson to lean forward in unison. The time stamp in the corner of the screen read 23:27, just above the image of a dark-coloured mid-sized van.

"Is that the same make and model?" Nelson asked.

Fred maximised a website displaying a Vauxhall Combo and pulled the video file adjacent to it. "I'd say they're a match." He beamed at Sanne and pushed his phone toward her.

"Buggeration," she said.

Chapter Eleven

Sanne turned a deaf ear to Fred humming a funeral dirge and ignored Nelson's enquiry as to what she'd order for her last supper. Despite their teasing, they were showing a lot of faith in her, and she wasn't going to let herself or her team down by contacting Eleanor before she felt adequately prepared.

"Did I miss anything?" she asked Nelson as he returned her notes.

"Spot on," he said. "Use the phone in Interview Two if you want some privacy."

"I will. Cheers, Nelson."

Interview Two was empty and quiet, a sodden tissue and a lipstick-smeared coffee cup all that remained of its last guest. Sanne shut the door and perched on the chair closest to the phone. Then she dialled Eleanor's number from memory and began to count the rings. The call was answered after two with a terse "DI Stanhope."

Sanne dug her nails into the chair's upholstery. "Boss, it's Sanne. Sorry to disturb you at the weekend."

The voices in the background—one older male, a television, two lads arguing—faded, and she heard Eleanor shut a door.

"What's the problem?" Eleanor didn't seem at all irritated by the disruption of her day off. She expected her team to be available around the clock, and she led by example. If anything, she sounded curious.

"Boss, this murder at Malory Park that Nelson and I were assigned to, we think it might be connected to the one George and Fred are working."

There was a shuffle as if Eleanor had moved something, and then a rustle of cloth as she sat down. "Go on."

Although Eleanor pitched her tone halfway between a command and a request, the assertion of her authority had the incongruous effect of making Sanne feel calmer. With only the barest of glances at her notepad, she detailed the similarities and inconsistencies between the two murders, and the appearance of what was potentially the same vehicle close to both scenes. Eleanor listened without interrupting, and when Sanne had finished, the line remained so quiet that she checked the phone to make sure they were still connected.

"So you have the Mission Cross, the van sightings, the victim profile, and the manner of death," Eleanor said eventually.

"Yes, ma'am. Those are the common factors."

"No motive?"

"Not as yet, ma'am."

"No witnesses?"

"No, ma'am." Sanne could feel sweat trickling into her bra.

"And Nelson, Fred, and George are in agreement with you on this?"

The inference was clear: Sanne had made the call, therefore ownership of the initial theory must be hers.

"Yes, ma'am. They're all on board."

"Is it snowing over there?"

"Uh…" The question left Sanne completely wrong-footed. She peered through the window and then in desperation opened it and stuck out her hand. "No, I don't think so."

"Excellent. I'll be with you in about an hour."

"Right." Sanne stood to attention, and then remembered that no one was there to see her, and felt stupid. "Apologies for wrecking your Saturday evening."

Eleanor's laugh was short and dry. "The lads can't decide which horror film to watch, and Doug is falling asleep in his popcorn. Coming in to work is no hardship."

She disconnected the call, and Sanne dropped the receiver back into its cradle as if it were a live snake whose jaws were closing in on her fingers. Outside the room, Nelson and Fred greeted her with pensive expressions.

"Well?" Fred asked.

"She'll be here in an hour."

Nelson grinned and touched his knuckles to her jaw. He knew that Eleanor wouldn't be making the trip if Sanne had fucked up.

"Nice one, mate," he said.

❖

Eleanor was no idiot. She arrived bearing two bulging bags of fish and chips, along with fresh milk for brews. On the downside, she had also summoned Carlyle to her impromptu tea party.

"Uh oh." George waggled a piece of battered fish as Carlyle approached the desks they were picnicking around. "Have we dragged you away from a hot date, Sarge?"

Dressed in a designer suit and gleaming shoes that tapped like high heels when he walked, Carlyle had evidently had plans for the evening. Gel darkened his ginger hair, and his aftershave was so strong that it almost put Sanne off her chips. Taking a seat next to Eleanor, he sulked into his mug of coffee and refused to engage with his subordinates. Eleanor passed him the file she'd finished reading and opened Marcus Jones's instead.

"I think the Mission Cross is our first obvious port of call," she said, once the plates were cleared and she'd familiarised herself with the case details. "Whether or not the two deaths are related, both vics had that place in common, which means all the regular attendees and staff need interviewing in depth and their alibis verifying."

Nelson turned a page on his notepad and tracked a finger down the lines. "I thought we might be paying the shelter another visit, so I did a spot of research when I phoned. Sunday lunch is their busiest meal, which is very convenient for our purposes. After that, Monday and Friday evenings are the best attended."

"We need to move on this before word gets around," Eleanor said. "Tomorrow's lunch would be ideal. Where are we up to with Burrows?"

Sanne handed her a typed summary. "His whereabouts for most of the last week are largely unverifiable. He spends much of his time alone or with people whose names he doesn't know. All the same, I'm pretty certain he's not our man for this." Afraid she might have spoken out of turn, she glanced at Nelson and George, but both men nodded their agreement.

Carlyle set down his mug with enough force to make it thud. "What did he do, Jensen, bat his eyelids at you and tell you a sob story about how wicked his daddy is?"

"No, Sarge," she said, holding his gaze. "I don't think he mentioned his daddy. His sob story was all about his evil, drunken mum."

"Where is he now?" Eleanor asked, before Carlyle could respond.

"Taking a nap in Interview One," George said.

"Good. Let's leave him there if he's comfortable. The later we release him, the better our chances at the shelter. I'm going to pull Scotty and Jay in to help with the interviews tomorrow, and I'll co-opt a few unis for the preliminaries as well."

Sanne raised an eyebrow, but Carlyle said nothing about the supposed "special project" to which he had assigned Scotty and Jay. Not that she cared overly much. If the case turned out to be a multiple murder, then he'd done her a favour by shoving it onto her workload, although his self-satisfied smile told her he'd not fathomed that.

Someone had been playing hangman on the front sheet of the flipchart that Eleanor dragged over to the desks. She tutted at a misspelling, tore the sheet off, and tossed it into the bin.

"I'm not taking this any further up the chain of command until we've been to the Mission," she said. "If—and it's a big if—the DCI accepts that the cases are connected, he'll want to involve the press, and I can think of no surer way of sending every Malory Park scrote bag scurrying for cover. So, let's make a to-do list, shall we?"

An hour later, the flipchart was down to its final page, the milk had run out, and Sanne's right leg had developed an uncontrollable twitch. While it was good to see everything broken down and itemised, nothing of any real significance had arisen during the discussion, and frustration had left everyone short-tempered and fidgety.

"Okay, I think it's time we called it a night." Eleanor sounded as disillusioned as everyone looked. "Be here for a briefing tomorrow at nine, and we'll travel to the Mission in convoy."

Sanne stifled a groan as she massaged the pins and needles from her thigh. The rumble of furniture being rearranged covered the sound of someone kicking her chair. Startled, she turned to find Carlyle watching her, his head tilted slightly, as if she were a scientific curiosity he couldn't decide whether to pin under his microscope or crush beneath his shoe.

"I don't know how you do it, Jensen," he said, his voice lowered to ensure it didn't carry. "You snap your fingers and the boss comes running every damn time."

She stood up, which didn't exactly put her on his level but made her feel less vulnerable all the same. "If you have a problem with any of this, Sarge, you need to speak to the boss, not me."

"You know what? I *do* have a problem. I don't like wasting my weekend because you mistook a bunch of coincidences for genuine leads."

She could feel heat prickling her face and fought to keep her voice steady. The sole aim of any bully was to provoke a reaction. "I think you should be having this conversation with the boss, Sarge," she repeated. From the corner of her eye, she saw Nelson starting toward them, and she shook her head once to ward him off.

"Yeah, I might pass on that," Carlyle said. "You set this ball rolling, Jensen, so why would I want to stop it?" He collected his jacket and strode past her, careful not to make contact but coming close enough to force her back a step.

"Arsehole," she muttered, as he passed Eleanor's office without pausing.

Nelson approached once the coast was clear. "What did he want?"

"Oh, just to let me know that he's looking forward to seeing me fall flat on my face."

"That was good of him." Nelson handed her her bag, and they began to walk toward the lift. "I always find those kinds of chats highly motivational."

She frowned. "You do? He makes me want to punch him in the head."

"You've got to think outside the box, San. Carlyle sets a standard for everyone."

The lift pinged and its doors swept open.

"Yeah," she said. "The better you do your job, the more you piss him off." She thought about that for a second, and her face brightened as the penny dropped.

Nelson started to laugh. "See what I mean?" he said. "Brilliant motivation."

❖

The shoulder returned to its socket with an audible click, a success lost on its owner, who had drunk enough whiskey to sedate an elephant and hadn't needed to be anaesthetised.

Meg stepped forward, more concerned about Asif, the F2 performing the reduction, than his insensible patient. Wan-faced at the bedside, he was swallowing rapidly.

"Good job," she said. "Distal pulse is fine, and her hand is well perfused. So, collar and cuff, X-ray, and then it's just a case of sobering her up and arranging an outpatient appointment. What would you have tried had the Kocher's method failed?"

"Modified Milch," he answered promptly, far more confident in theory than he was in practice. "Then Hippocratic as a last resort."

"Excellent. Always remember to take your shoes off before that one, though."

He smiled, the colour returning to his cheeks. "Thanks for your help, Dr. Fielding."

"Meg," she reminded him, although her attempts at informality were proving futile. She felt her phone vibrate and checked the text: Sanne, *Give me a ring when you can.* She poked her head between the shock room curtains and looked around the rest of the Resus bays. Three were empty, and Liz was chatting to the patient in the fourth.

"Will you be all right in here for a few minutes?" she asked Asif.

He nodded, too busy wrestling with the padded sling to glance up.

"I'll be in the ambulance bay if you need me. If Donovan needs me, tell him I've nipped to the loo."

A lone ambulance stood in the bay, its crew hiding behind it to sneak a cigarette. Meg shuddered as an icy gust of wind hit her, her numb fingers fumbling with the phone.

"Sit in the back, Doc," a familiar voice called. "The heater should still be on."

Through the cloud of smoke, Meg recognised Kathy, a paramedic with a knack of attracting bad or just plain weird jobs. The last time Meg had seen her, she'd been attempting to resuscitate a fifty-year-old who'd expired while dressed as Father Christmas.

"Bloody hell. If I'd known you were on, I'd have booked the night off."

Kathy all but choked on her cigarette. "Likewise! I only turn into a shit-magnet when you're working. We just brought in a bloke who'd tried to ice skate on a pond, only he didn't have any skates."

"Or enough ice," her mate chipped in.

Halfway up the ambulance steps, Meg stopped and grinned. "Well, you know how the saying goes: We can't fix stupid, we can only sedate it."

"They should stick that on a sign above the main entrance," Kathy said, and took a long drag on her cigarette.

After shutting out the cold and the smoke, Meg chose the back seat and dialled Sanne's number.

Sanne answered through a mouthful of something. "Hphm. Sorry. Hello."

"Hello yourself. What's that you're eating?"

"Chocolate HobNob. Eleanor bought chippy for us all, so I'm having dessert."

Meg nestled down in the seat, propping her feet on the stretcher frame. "Are you working weekends now?"

"Yeah." There was a pause, as if Sanne was deciding how much to divulge. "Our Malory Park stabbing might be linked to another. I drew the short straw and had to call the boss in."

"You drew the straw or the connection?" Meg asked, detecting the conflict in Sanne's voice.

"Both. It's all been quite stressful."

The understatement made Meg smile. "I can imagine."

"Anyway." Sanne was straight back to business. "Enough about me, I wanted to see how you were."

"I'm fine. It's all gone quiet on the Luke front. And I loved my mug. Thank you."

"I bet you loved the bacon more."

The mere mention of the thick cut, smoky slices she had found in her fridge set Meg's mouth watering. "You know me too well, Sanne Jensen."

"You are easy to please," Sanne said, and quickly covered her accidental innuendo with ostentatious crunching.

Meg held the phone away from her ear so Sanne wouldn't hear her laughing. When she put it back, Sanne was telling her something about a "Fwin."

"You checked the what now?"

"The Force Wide Incident Number. It's a unique reference attached to a reported incident. I've looked at the one assigned to your break-in, but there's been no movement on it."

Meg nodded, unsurprised. "Any luck with the unofficial side of things?"

"Not yet, but then I only put the word out yesterday."

"Don't worry, San." She could hear footsteps, interspersed with the occasional bang, and imagined Sanne pacing across her kitchen, kicking out at unfortunate items of furniture. "You've got enough on your plate as it is."

"You just keep in touch." Sanne's voice was quiet and intense. "Promise me?"

"I promise."

The ambulance doors slammed as Kathy and her mate got into the cab. Seconds later, a high-pitched beeping was drowned out by a tirade of colourful curses.

"I've got to go," Meg said as the engine started. "I'll speak to you soon."

"Okay. Have a good shift."

Meg thought of the spare beds in her Resus, of Donovan safely sequestered in Minors, and of the breach manager's absence. "It's been nice so far," she said, climbing back down into the chill of the ambulance bay. "Long may it continue."

❖

"Henoch-Schönlein purpura," Meg said, and stuck out her tongue as Liz pulled a face. "What? It affects the small arteries in the kidneys, skin, and GI tract."

Liz shook her head and continued to sort through the supplies in the shock room. "I knew I shouldn't have played this with a bloody doctor. What letter are we up to? I…I…Influenza."

"Jackson-Weiss syndrome."

"Oh, shut up!"

Laughing, Meg caught the suture pack that Liz hurled at her and tucked it in a drawer. Before Liz could throw anything else, the shrill chime of the Bat Phone signalled an abrupt end to the game. Meg snatched up the receiver and found the pen she had stuck in her hair. The dispatcher relayed rapid-fire details, his urgency raising goose pimples on Meg's neck. Having read the first line over Meg's shoulder, Liz yelled for Asif and reached for another phone.

"How long?" she asked as Meg hung up.

"Six minutes. Four wounds to central chest and abdo. He's bleeding out. Fast bleep Cardiothoracic." Meg knelt by the blood fridge and began to gather bags of O-negative. "Asif, prep for bilateral chest drains. Have you done one unsupervised yet?"

He shook his head, and she tried very hard not to swear.

"Well, this may be a first for you. Let's get the thoracotomy tray ready for the cardiothoracic chaps. Hopefully, they'll be here to help us out, if it comes to that."

"Is he intubated?" Liz, ever the pragmatist, was adjusting the settings on the vent.

"No, still breathing, but I think we'll be needing this." Meg opened the sterile airway pack. "Can you get hold of Anaesthetics as well?"

"Already did. Sahil's on his way down. I've paged Donovan, but he's on a break somewhere."

Meg smiled, grateful for competent backup. "Y'know, it's not true what they say about you."

"Some of it is."

Meg almost knocked Sahil off his feet as the sound of approaching sirens sent her dashing to the door. "Adult male, multiple central stab wounds, GCS nine and dropping," she told him. "Vent's good to go."

He saluted and hurried past her into the shock room. Right on cue, an ambulance streaked into the bay, its lights still blazing.

"I might've guessed," Meg muttered, recognising Kathy's mate, his uniform and forearms now covered in blood. Grim-faced, he worked the ramp mechanism as Kathy unhooked an IV bag and gave Meg a single distraught glance.

"He's peri-arrest," she said. "Brady at forty, can't get a systolic. Half his fucking guts were hanging out when we got there. Police are right behind us."

Meg nodded, taking in the failing heart rate on the monitor, the stertorous breaths, and the blood soaking the dressings and dripping onto the floor. The man's eyes were open but unseeing, his skin a waxy, jaundiced colour. His right hand flexed as if reaching for something and then fell limp against the stretcher.

"Shock room's ready," she said. She held up the fluid and squeezed the bag, trying not to trip over the stretcher as she ran alongside it. The instant it bumped the hospital bed, she nodded to Kathy, who began her handover as the team rolled and checked the man's body.

"Unknown male, found in the street by a passerby. Stab wounds to left and right upper chest, and two to the lower abdomen, with evidence of massive blood loss. Breath sounds are poor. I wrapped his bowel in a wet dressing." Kathy faltered, checking the scribbles on the back of her glove to see what she'd omitted.

"How much fluid has he had?" Meg prompted her gently.

"That bag will make it two litres." Kathy had started to move with more purpose, helping to attach leads and unravel tubing. "Do you want us to stick around?"

"That'd be great." Meg turned to Liz. "Any word from cardio?"

"No, not yet."

"Fucking hell."

One of the stab wounds was just below the heart and angled upward, and the man was on the verge of cardiac arrest. In Meg's book, he ticked most of the boxes indicating an emergency thoracotomy. On the monitor, the heart rate slowed to twenty-eight, stamping out her indecision. She tore open a set of defib pads and slapped them into place.

"Asif, get a drain in on the right. Sahil, can you give him a hand once you've intubated? Liz, you're with me on thoracotomy duty. Can someone start compressions? He's doing fuck-all with a rate that poor."

Kathy stepped up to the mark, but the monitor screeched before she could get her hands into position. "VF!" she called.

"Everyone clear?" Meg hit the shock button. Two hundred joules fired through the man's chest, jerking his limbs and sending him straight into asystole.

"Go," she told Kathy, who started to pump the chest in smooth, hard compressions. "First adrenaline's in."

She opened the left chest wall, parting skin and fat with a scalpel and then hacking through the intercostal muscles with scissors. Without warning, blood sloshed out onto the floor, a warm, lurid wave that splattered her legs and trainers. Sahil muttered something in Urdu that was probably a prayer as Meg shoved the rib retractors into place and cranked them open, ignoring the pain that shot through her bad wrist. A vertical cut across the pericardial sac sent more blood pouring into the chest cavity and revealed the damage to the heart: a jagged wound in the thick muscle of the left ventricle.

"Jesus," she whispered, astounded that the man had lived long enough to reach the hospital. "Not a hope in hell."

Nevertheless, she covered the wound with her finger and began to squeeze the heart between her hands, counting out a rhythm in her head as she watched fresh blood race through the IV lines.

"If anyone finds a bleeder, suture it or stick something on it," she said. "Asif, how're you doing?"

"Drain's in." He looked across the patient at her, his eyes wide. "Almost a litre out already."

"Aw, shit. Are we getting any volume into him at all?"

"No," Asif said, as Sahil shook his head. "Nothing."

Meg quickly considered her options. "Okay, one last try. Asif, come and take over this for me. I'm going to stitch this lac, so keep it nice and smooth."

Although she'd never put sutures directly into myocardium before, it wasn't as if she could make anything worse. She worked fast, tying off large, clumsy stitches that succeeded in plugging the hole and holding together under the stress of the direct massage. It took nine to keep the laceration closed, and when she had finished, absolutely nothing happened. Whenever Asif paused, the line went flat on the monitor, and the transfusions continued to pour in blood that failed to get anywhere near the heart. When the sixth adrenaline had gone in, Meg checked the clock on the wall: they had been working on the man for half an hour. She wiped sweat from her forehead with the back of her arm.

"Everyone in agreement?" she asked. She didn't need to say anything else. There were nods all around. "Right then, I'm going to call it. Time of death, eleven thirty-seven p.m. Thank you all. I'm sure his family will appreciate your efforts. Just leave everything as it is until I've spoken to the police."

The air left the tube with a reluctant sigh as Sahil disconnected the vent. He touched the bloodstained cross hanging from the man's necklace, his lips moving soundlessly, and Meg turned away to grant him privacy. She was tearing off her apron when multiple footsteps approached the shock room and the curtain surrounding the cubicle was yanked aside.

"You've already stopped?" Donovan—red-faced and visibly fuming—stated the obvious through clenched teeth. Two surgeons stood either side of him, staring at the carnage on the bed. Meg wondered whether they'd been exchanging golfing anecdotes in the corridor while she'd been splitting the man's ribcage.

"Yes," she said, daring him to take issue with her decision after he'd ignored an urgent request for assistance. "His entire blood volume is either in his chest or on the floor."

Donovan grunted and surveyed the body, evaluating Meg's interventions from the airway down to the open-heart surgery. Apparently finding nothing to criticise, he grunted again and left the room with the surgeons close behind him.

Meg shut the curtain and stared at the blood clotting on the tiles until her eyes blurred and she felt less like screaming. Once she had regained her composure, she took the time to study the man's body.

"You poor bastard," she whispered.

His slackened features were free from pain or distress, and Sahil had closed his eyes with tape, but there was no denying the brutality of his death or of the attempts to resuscitate him.

"Do we know his name?" she asked Kathy.

"No. The police did a quick check of his pockets before we set off. No wallet or phone, and he was too far gone to speak."

Meg used the markings along an endotracheal tube to gauge the size of the wound on his right chest. A troubling suspicion began to take shape as she noted the wound's ragged edge.

"Where did you find him?"

Kathy consulted the paperwork she was completing retrospectively. "Top end of Balan, on Malory."

"Shit." Meg had really wanted to be wrong about this. She ripped off her soiled gloves and hoped that Sanne hadn't planned on getting a full night's sleep.

❖

Sanne had dozed off to the sound of sleet hitting her bedroom window, an incessant beat that sent her into a restless dream. When the phone woke her an hour later, snow was falling, silent flurries of white that were ghosting past the glass and had already covered her car and driveway. Half-dazed, she had to stumble toward the ringtone until she remembered which bookcase she had left her mobile on. Calls at this time of the night were never good news, and she felt a fresh surge of panic on seeing Meg's name.

"Meg? Are you okay?"

"Hey, sorry, did I wake you?"

"No. Yes. It doesn't matter." Sanne sat on the carpet, pre-empting an undignified topple onto it. "What's wrong?"

"There's nothing wrong with me," Meg reassured her quickly. "We've just had a stabbing brought in: male, late thirties, found with multiple wounds on Balan Road. Wounds were deep, nasty, approximately three inches wide, and showed signs of being made with a serrated blade. I thought you might appreciate a heads-up."

"Bloody hell." Still on the floor, Sanne dragged open a drawer and began to grab clothes. She wriggled out of her pyjama bottoms, any remnants of sleep obliterated. "What's his prognosis?"

"He died, San. About ten minutes ago. The police are here, but there's no sign of anyone from your lot." Meg's words were running into each other, and she sounded exhausted.

"Has he been identified?"

"Not yet. He had nothing with him."

Sanne fought the urge to tell Meg to get a hot drink, sit down, and put her feet up. "Tatts? Scars? Anything our computer might get a hit on?" Her keys in one hand and a sweater in the other, she ran into the bathroom with the phone trapped against her shoulder.

"No. He's about six foot, short dark hair, clean-shaven, wedding ring. He doesn't look like your typical Malory scrote, if you know what I mean."

The keys clattered into the sink as Sanne lost her grip on them. "Was he wearing any other jewellery?"

"A crucifix on a chain. No, wait, it was one of those plain crosses without the little Jesus on it."

"Fuck," Sanne whispered. She closed her eyes and heard Meg call to her as if from a great distance. "I think his name is Daniel Horst," she said.

CHAPTER TWELVE

Nelson lived closer to the hospital than Sanne did, and he was waiting for her in the A&E corridor. Her wet boots squeaked on the lino as she ran toward him. It had taken her over an hour to get through the snow on the Snake Pass.

"Is it him?" she asked. Her phone had registered three missed calls during her journey, each cut off by the weather and the lousy reception in the hills.

Nelson caught her sleeve, preventing her from heading into Resus.

"He's been moved to the Viewing Room, San." He kept his grip on her, even though she'd stopped. "You were right," he said quietly. "His wife Adele just identified him."

"Damn it. What the fuck is going on with this case, Nelson? Why kill Daniel?"

"I don't know, but the boss has spoken to the brass, and they've already called a press conference."

Farther down the corridor, the door to the Viewing Room opened and Eleanor escorted a woman out. Adele Horst was petite, smartly dressed, and heavily pregnant. Her head bowed low with grief, she allowed Eleanor to guide her to the Relatives' Room and into the care of a uniformed officer.

"The baby's due in four weeks," Nelson said. "Adele thought Daniel was working late at the shelter. Meanwhile, the people there thought he'd got caught up late on the streets and just gone home afterward. Apparently, he got mugged a few months back, and ever since then he's emptied his pockets before going onto the estate."

"Someone knew who he was. This can't have been random." Sanne heard the rise in her voice but could do nothing to temper it.

Nelson, by contrast, had had time to process everything, and he answered calmly. "I doubt it was random, but most people on Malory probably knew him, which gives us a massive pool of suspects."

Hearing the rapid tap of high heels, they turned to meet Eleanor together, subconsciously presenting her with a united front.

"So much for keeping this under the radar," she said by way of greeting, and then continued without pause for breath, "SOCO are still at the scene, and we've gathered the CCTV from the surrounding area. This one was different again: main road, more public, and a passerby found Horst within minutes."

"Escalation or opportunism?" Sanne asked.

Eleanor threw up her hands. "Your guess is as good as mine. And without a motive, guessing is all we're fit for. The PM is scheduled for first thing in the morning, which should give us an idea whether the same weapon was used for Culver and Horst. The cynic in me says that Horst got himself involved with something through the Mission, maybe drugs—dealing or supplying—so we'll need to check his bank records for any irregularities."

Sanne nodded, taking everything on board, though her instincts contradicted Eleanor's. Having met Daniel, she would bet her eye teeth that his finances were spotless. "What about the Mission?" she asked. "Are we still holding off until morning?"

"No, word has already travelled fast, and we have officers there now with Fred and George. Most of the sober patrons are up and about, and a few of the staff members have come in as well. There are murmurs about a candlelit vigil being arranged before the evening meal. Hopefully, it'll be well attended, and we can round people up after it." Eleanor sighed. "Respectfully, of course. If we go barging in, all we'll do is make people resentful. For now, we have the passerby and Adele Horst to interview, and we need kid gloves on for those as well, which is why I'm assigning them to the two of you."

Sanne looked over Eleanor's shoulder at Meg entering the Relatives' Room. "Will Mrs. Horst speak at the press conference?"

"Yes, she's agreed to make a public appeal first thing in the morning."

Silence followed Eleanor's response, but Sanne suspected they were all thinking the same thing: after the press had paid scant attention to two coldblooded murders, a third had finally given them their perfect photogenic widow.

❖

The door creaked as it opened. For a second or two, harsh light and the everyday chatter of the A&E flooded into the Viewing Room, shattering the peace and making Sanne blink.

"I thought I might find you here," Meg said. She stepped inside and shut the door, restoring the sense of sanctity evoked by low-wattage lamps and by the selection of religious texts carefully arranged on a coffee table.

"I have to interview his wife," Sanne said. "It seemed wrong to do that without seeing him first."

The police officer in the corridor hadn't questioned her request to view Daniel Horst's body, but merely asked her to sign an evidence log. In the section headed *Reason*, she had scribbled something about "wound comparison," leaving it borderline illegible. It was the best she could come up with at short notice.

"You can't tell, can you?" she said, as Meg came to stand beside her. "You can't really tell how bad it is."

"Did you look?" Meg asked, and winced when Sanne nodded.

The body lay in a forensic bag, but someone had carefully covered that with a sheet to give an illusion of sleep. Daniel's face was unmarred and slack, his eyes almost shut. The only thing to ruin the effect was the thick odour of clotted blood.

"I had to explain to his wife what had happened to him." Meg's voice bore an unfamiliar tremor. "And I told her what we, what *I'd* done, but when she identified him she saw him like this."

"How is she?"

Meg dragged her gaze away from the body. "She's not good, but she wants to get it over with. You're probably better staying here and using the Rellies' Room. She's had a couple of twinges in the last hour, so I'm going to refer her to Antenatal Assessment once you're done."

"That's fine. It shouldn't take long."

"I did my best for him, San." Meg stumbled backward as she spoke, her legs hitting the table and sending a Bible onto the floor. She sat down in its place, her body seeming to fold in on itself. "Why is everything so fucking shit?" she whispered. "'Your husband's been stabbed to death and, oh, by the way, I've just hacked up his body trying to restart his heart. When's your first baby due again?'"

Sanne nudged Meg with her knee and squeezed onto the table, stacking the remaining books to make space. When Meg leaned into her, the smell of herbal shampoo overpowered that of blood. Sanne took hold of Meg's hand and felt her tense briefly before relaxing again.

"Would you do anything differently if you had the time over?" Sanne asked.

"No." Meg drew the word out and then huffed a small almost laugh. "Maybe I'd go in at the correct rib. I didn't even count the bloody things, just guessed and cut. I'm sure the coroner will have something to say about it."

Sanne smoothed a wet strand of hair away from Meg's cheek. Meg had obviously showered and changed in preparation for talking to Adele Horst, and limp curls were falling from misplaced clips. "Did you get where you needed to be?"

"Yes."

"Well then, I doubt the coroner will mark you down for being out a rib or two."

That prompted a rough chuckle and a kiss on Sanne's cheek.

"We should get back to work." Meg made no move to do anything of the sort.

"Yes, we should."

"Or we could hide in here a while longer."

Sanne thought of the pending interview and the sleepless night ahead of her, and she tightened her grip on Meg's hand. "One more minute," she said.

❖

"Some days he'll go out at five in the morning and I won't see him again until midnight. He doesn't wear a watch, so he'll just lose track. We joke about it, but he's promised to cut back a little once the baby is born."

Adele Horst stopped suddenly, her monologue snapping to an end as if something had sparked out the power. She looked at Sanne, her lips forming a mute "oh." Like Daniel, she had a habit of touching the cross around her neck when she was upset, and her grip on it now was so tight that it whitened the skin on her knuckles. For twenty minutes she had managed to answer Sanne's questions, but she had referred to Daniel in the present tense throughout, and Sanne had been dreading the moment she realised this.

"Oh God," she whispered. "Oh God, he's really gone, isn't he?" She lowered her hands to the bulge of her abdomen as tears dripped off her nose. When Sanne passed her a tissue, she didn't seem to know what to do with it.

"Do you want to stop?" Sanne asked.

Adele shook her head. "Please, carry on. I'll be okay."

Sanne glanced at her notes, saw the word *Motive* underlined in thick black pen and wished that she wasn't so rubbish at rock, paper, scissors. Her ineptitude meant that Nelson was currently back at HQ interviewing the passerby while she had to quiz a shell-shocked widow about the finances of her late husband. The smell of instant coffee mingled with Adele's perfume, exacerbating the headache that was nagging at Sanne's left temple. Promising herself a dose of paracetamol later, she swallowed half a glass of water and pushed on with her next question. To her surprise, Adele answered it with firm precision.

"No, absolutely not. He made a pittance at the shelter, and he's useless with money." She paused before correcting herself in a pained tone. "He *was* useless. I took care of all our finances, and his wage went into a joint account. I would know if anything had changed."

"What about unusual purchases? Perhaps an item for the baby that he shouldn't have been able to afford?"

A slight, wistful smile curved Adele's lips. "He's spent seven months making furniture from salvaged wood: a crib, a changing table, cabinets, even toys. I work in corporate law, so my salary covers all our essentials. Daniel's job was more of a calling. He would never have become involved in anything untoward."

"I'm sorry. I don't mean to cause offence. It's just that we have to explore every possible avenue." Sanne felt even worse when Adele nodded her understanding. She turned the page on her notebook to cue her next question and took heart from its being largely blank. "Did he ever mention having problems at the Mission or on the estate? Had anyone threatened him recently?"

"If there were fights or arguments at the Mission, they tended to be among the clients, with the staff acting as peacemakers," Adele said. "Daniel was careful what he told me, especially after he got mugged, but he wouldn't have held back anything serious."

"Did the police find out who attacked him?"

"Two lads from the estate. I think they were twelve years old. They broke his jaw, but he refused to press charges." She began to cry again, fresh tears following the tracks of old ones, her grief so overwhelming that Sanne could hardly bear to witness it. "He was my whole life. What am I supposed to do now he's gone?"

There were endless platitudes that Sanne could have used, all banal, trite, and ultimately meaningless. She didn't think Adele was the type to take comfort from them.

"I don't know. I can't even imagine," she said. She tried, though, tried to imagine her life carrying on without Meg, with no chance of ever hearing her voice again or seeing her face, but she couldn't conceive of that depth of loss. Adele choked on a sob, her entire body shaking with the effort of holding in her misery.

Sanne quietly noted the end of the interview and clicked off the tape.

CHAPTER THIRTEEN

The spikes attached to Sanne's trainers bit into the snow, creating bursts of spindrift as she increased her pace. The stiffness in her muscles eased, replaced by a fluid warmth that made her body hum with energy, and what had seemed like a stupid, impulsive idea mere minutes ago began to make perfect sense.

After uploading the interview with Adele Horst to the case file, Sanne had managed three hours of sleep, fragmented by nightmares and a long period of staring at a patch of moonlight on her bedroom wall while conflicting hypotheses buzzed around her brain. Rather than count down to her alarm, she had given up and thrown on her winter running gear. It had still been dark when she stepped outside, the sunrise just a smudge of purple bleeding into the black, but a head torch provided plenty of light, and even a short run would be better than staying in bed. As she rounded a corner, the east wind hit her full pelt, forcing freezing air into her lungs and blowing away any remaining sluggishness. She coughed and then laughed, the noise startling a stoat, which hurtled beneath the snow-covered heather.

"Sorry," she whispered as she passed its hiding place.

At the halfway point, she checked her watch, calculating the time she needed to leave for the Mission and factoring in a shower, breakfast, and the hike to the lay-by where she had left her Land Rover. The candlelit vigil wasn't scheduled until four p.m., but interviews and door-to-door enquiries were to take place throughout the day, and the overtime had been thrown open in order to draft uniforms and additional manpower onto the case. With the media now bandying around terms like "serial killer" and "spree killer"—one step away from tagging the culprit with a sensational nickname—the brass were disinclined to leave anything to chance.

Excitement lengthened Sanne's stride, and she completed the route at a sprint, switching off her torch as lilac ate into the edges of the darkness and the hills became more distinct. The media fervour held no appeal for her, and her only current ambition was to keep her place on the EDSOP team, but any detective who didn't get a kick out of being involved in a major manhunt was probably in the wrong job.

Her rooster squawked as she jogged past the chicken coop.

"Shut it, you," she said. "Today is going to be a good day."

❖

Emily handed Meg a steaming mug and snuggled next to her on the sofa, tucking a blanket over them both. Meg raised the mug and gave it a dubious sniff. Coffee, cream, and something unidentifiable but spicy lurked in the brew.

"Old family recipe," Emily said. "My granny swore by it. I thought it might perk you up enough to go for a walk later."

Meg's first sip burned her mouth, warmed her throat, and curled a pleasant heat into her belly. Her lips and tongue tingled when she spoke. "What the hell have you put in this?"

Emily laughed. "It's your basic Irish coffee with a dab of chilli powder. Did I mention that my gran was a bit eccentric?"

"Well, if ever any proof were needed…" Meg left the sentence hanging and reached for the television remote. On the rolling news channel, Eleanor was guiding Adele Horst into the centre chair of the press conference desk. Information about the murders dominated the banner streaming beneath the picture, and a hotline number flashed up at regular intervals.

"I can't believe the police kept this quiet until now," Emily said. "What on earth were they thinking?"

Meg had slept badly, and a combination of alcohol and lassitude allowed her to answer without biting Emily's head off. "It's not like they had a choice. The press didn't give a shit about the first two victims. Dead drug addicts don't sell papers." She gestured at the screen, where Adele was speaking about her husband with calm dignity. "Dead, clean living, religious types, on the other hand, make ideal front page material."

The sofa creaked as Emily sat up. "Surely there's more to it than that."

"There really isn't. Just your basic edict that smackheads and their like have it coming." Meg swallowed another mouthful of coffee, welcoming its fiery aftertaste. "I don't make the rules, Em."

"No, but you don't seem bothered by them either."

"Maybe because I grew up with them," Meg said quietly. "And they've not been rewritten since then."

She watched the camera linger on Adele as a caption reminded the viewers exactly how advanced her pregnancy was. In the top corner of the screen, a rotating series of photographs showed her wedding day, a visit to the Mission, and a holiday snap taken somewhere exotic. Once Eleanor began to field questions, a family liaison officer ushered Adele from the room, providing an opportunity to show images of the other two victims, but the bulletin switched to a sports round-up within thirty seconds. Emily rested her chin on Meg's shoulder.

"You're probably right," Emily said. "I just wish your outlook was slightly less cynical, at times."

Meg slid an arm around her. "Do you worry about me, or worry you might turn into me?"

"A bit of both, but mainly the former." Meg felt Emily's chest heave as if she were preparing to plunge into deep water. "You know, it might do you good to get out of A&E for a while."

Meg was shaking her head before Emily finished speaking. "I love emergency medicine. I don't want to do anything else."

"How about another hospital, then? One in a different area?"

"You mean a better area."

"Yes! A better area, where you don't get punched or hurt and you don't come home so damn bitter about everything."

The latter point burrowed beneath Meg's skin like a thorn. "I don't mean to be a bad person," she said.

"You're not a bad person." Emily nestled closer, her hands warm and soft on Meg's face. "I shouldn't have said anything. I'm sorry."

The bell was well and truly rung, though, and Meg curled into a ball on the sofa, feeling too pummelled to offer the reassurance Emily sought.

"I'm sorry," Emily repeated. She kissed Meg's cheek, her shoulder, anywhere she could reach. "I didn't mean it. I'm sorry."

Niamh Shelton didn't seem able to spell her first name. She swapped the *m* with the *h* and then changed them back again, her cheeks growing pinker by the second.

"It's a pretty name," Sanne said, drawing the statement paper toward her. "I think most people go with m-h. What do you reckon?" She blocked the letters out on the header and displayed them for Niamh's approval.

Niamh stuffed the end of her ponytail in her mouth and nodded sagely in agreement. A twenty-five-year-old regular at the Mission, with a record for assault and battery, she matched a hastily devised "person of interest" profile, which meant that her interview fell to an EDSOP detective. She was Sanne's fourth such interviewee that morning, each being asked a standard set of questions to ascertain whether they warranted a more in-depth cross-examination. Meanwhile, uniformed officers were speaking to everyone else who had arrived at the shelter for breakfast. After the slow start typical of a Sunday morning, the Malory grapevine had evidently kicked up a gear, with the promise of gruesome gossip and the presence of the media outweighing any concerns about being nabbed by the police.

As the shelter comprised only two dorm rooms stuffed with bunk beds plus two offices stuffed with supplies, every table in the canteen had been co-opted for the taking of statements. Utilising one of the offices as an administrative base, Eleanor had turned a blind eye to the bacon grease, egg yolk, and ketchup smeared across the submitted paperwork. Full bellies and the promise of top-ups on mugs of tea had loosened the tongue of even the most reticent interviewees.

"Bit like speed dating, innit?" Niamh smiled and waved at a toothless man on the next table. "The Dog and Duck used to do it on a Tuesday night, but it got so that the same three blokes and Nelly Adams were the only ones turning up, and Nelly's in her seventies. He with you, that black fella?"

Struggling to decipher Niamh's rapid speech, Sanne was slow to acknowledge the abrupt change in topic. She followed Niamh's longing gaze, caught Nelson's perplexed expression, and smothered a laugh.

"Yes, he's with us," she said. "And very happily married."

Niamh sighed. "All the good ones are," she said, sounding far older than her years.

"Aye, it's terrible." Sanne tapped the paper in front of her. "Can you account for your whereabouts last night, Niamh?"

Niamh frowned, distracted by her newfound crush. "Of course I can count. I'm not thick. I went to school till I were thirteen."

"*Ac*-count," Sanne said. "Oh, never mind. Just tell me where you were last night and who you were with."

"At Sheila's, watching *Dirty Dancing* with my mam."

"I'll need their telephone numbers."

"Sheila's my mam's new girlfriend. She knows all the songs." Niamh fiddled with her mobile and then held it out for Sanne to copy the numbers from. "We were a bit tipsy and having a right good laugh, and then Ace came in and said that Dan had been stabbed."

"Who's Ace?" The detail immediately caught Sanne's attention, though Niamh didn't appear to realise she had said anything of significance.

"Paul Barber, Sheila's ex-husband. We call him Ace after his favourite cider. They're still mates, but she's a lesbian now."

Sanne paused her pen in mid-flow, deciding that wasn't a salient point. "Can you remember at what time Paul told you about Daniel?"

Niamh chewed her hair contemplatively. "About five past eleven. Reese was bugging us to put *Match of the Day* on."

Sanne riffled through her case notes until she found the details of the 999 call. The ambulance had been phoned at 11:02 p.m., which meant that Paul Barber had known about the attack within minutes. "Are you sure about the time you've just given me?" she asked.

"Really sure."

"Did Paul mention how he'd found out about Daniel?"

The chewing slowed and then stopped. "Huh. No, he didn't."

"Did the two men know each other at all?" Sanne tried to keep her tone casual, but Niamh was shaking her head, wary of having disclosed something likely to cause her trouble.

"No, I don't think so. I don't know, but I don't think so."

"And yet Paul told you it was Daniel who had been stabbed."

It took almost a full minute for Niamh to catch up with Sanne's logic. "Aw fuck," she said. "I should've stayed in bed. I've got such a fucking hangover."

"How did Paul know Daniel?" Sanne asked.

Niamh swapped her soggy hair for a false fingernail. "Food bank, free meals, same as everyone knew him. And he didn't kill him. He was right upset last night."

"Were his clothes bloody?"

"No! He didn't touch him. There was a bloke already there trying to help."

"Did Paul see what happened?"

"No, but he heard yelling, and he saw Daniel with his guts all out."

Sanne nodded, recording everything in a hotchpotch personal shorthand. The nature of Daniel's injuries wasn't widely known, so even if Paul Barber hadn't murdered him, he had at least been close to the scene and then fled without coming forward as a witness.

"Have you got Paul's address and phone number?"

The mobile came out again, and Niamh glanced around furtively before reeling off a number. "You didn't get that from me," she said.

"Right." Sanne capped her pen. "I'm sure Daniel's family will appreciate your help."

Niamh gave her a dubious look, but her mood rallied as she continued to scrutinise Sanne's face. "Y'know, you really don't look Swedish."

Sanne smiled. "I'm not Swedish."

"Or Danish."

"I'm not Danish either."

Niamh paused to take a mental trip through Europe. "Dutch?"

"Born and bred in England. I'm named after something in Norway that my mum loved, and my dad just happened to be a Jensen." It was half the truth, but as much information as Sanne was willing to give a complete stranger.

To Niamh's credit, she didn't push for the whole story. She twirled her hair around her fingers and glanced pointedly at her watch. "Are we finished? My mam said she'd do my makeup before the vigil in case I get on the telly."

"We're finished," Sanne said. "Thank you very much for your time."

She watched Niamh sashay close to Nelson's table, realise neither man was paying her any attention, and make a beeline for the door. As soon as Nelson's interview wrapped, Sanne slipped into the newly vacated seat opposite him.

"I hope you're having more luck than I am," he said, flicking a baked bean off his latest statement before draining a mug of coffee. "Mine have been a bunch of numpties whose alibis feature being drunk in public houses, being drunk in their own houses, or"—he curled his fingers into air quotes—"'shagging my mate's wife, Tina.' Most of them knew Daniel, a couple also knew Andrew Culver, and one was a friend of Marcus Jones, but no one has admitted to knowing all three."

Sanne pinched Nelson's notes and scanned through them. "It's unlikely anyone is going to admit to that."

"Yeah, the potential for subterfuge had crossed my mind."

"I got one incoherent lad who smelled so strongly of dope that he gave me the munchies, and two who alibied each other. My last, however, accidentally let slip the name of a potential witness."

"Oh, nice one." Nelson grinned. "Don't tell the boss it was an accident, though. Tell her you prised the information out of a hostile interviewee using the full extent of your detective skills."

Sanne batted him with his paperwork. "I think I'll just give her the name, eh?"

She pushed to her feet as a lanky teenager in a knock-off Adidas tracksuit strode toward their table. Then the bubble he was blowing in his chewing gum popped all over his face, and he had to stop to scrape off the mess. Nelson looked at Sanne and mouthed the words "Don't leave me."

She laughed. "Hang in there, mate. Only another five hours until the vigil, when we get to start this all over again."

Fresh snow, dotted with bird tracks, layered the frozen pond in Endcliffe Park. Here and there, Meg could see where kids had lobbed stones to breach the fragile surface, but the overall effect was still picturesque. Squinting as the sun broke through a gap in the clouds, she tugged Emily to a stop, rustling the bag of bread she had brought.

"You know that's bad for them, don't you?" Emily said, though her admonishment lacked any real edge.

Undeterred, Meg launched a handful of torn crusts onto the pond, stepping back to admire the ensuing spectacle of ducks ice-skating between Canada geese.

"Nice bit of Warburtons never did no one any harm," she called over her shoulder, dropping in a double-negative to further yank Emily's chain.

Wisely omitting the grammar lesson, Emily waited for the bread to be demolished and then held out a mitten-clad hand. Meg finished scolding the bossiest goose and jogged over to plant a kiss on Emily's cold nose. Feeding the ducks was one of life's simple pleasures, and it never failed to put her in a good mood.

"Fancy a scone at the cafe?" she asked.

"Sounds lovely."

Emily snuggled close as they walked alongside the pond, her attentiveness reminding Meg that the ducks weren't the only ones treading carefully. Emily had been solicitous to a fault since breakfast, and Meg, buoyed by fresh snow on her day off, had not returned to the subject of the morning's discussion.

They paused next to the playground to watch shrieking children on sledges and tea trays and bin bags hurtle down a small hill, and when they set off again everyone they passed said good morning. Even the city looked attractive in the watery sunlight, the snow giving the harsh lines and dull shades of its architecture a transient makeover. Although Meg had no desire to live in Sheffield full-time, on this particular morning, she could see its appeal.

"Meg?"

A shake of her arm suggested that Emily had been trying to get her attention for a while.

"Mm? Sorry, what's up?"

"My mum phoned while you were in the shower." Emily spoke quickly, her eyes on the path ahead. "She invited us over for supper tomorrow. I told her a tentative yes, but that I'd check with you first."

"Aren't you working tomorrow?" Meg asked, in a blatant attempt to stall. A supper invitation from Emily's mum was never just for an evening meal, it was a late-afternoon summons to Harrogate for drinks and polite chat before the food finally hit the table around eight. Escape would come no earlier than midnight, which was a long time for Meg to deflect enquiries about her family background and be on her best behaviour.

"Yes, but I'll be finished by one." There was a note of pleading in Emily's voice. When her mother said "jump," Emily felt obliged to ask "How high? And can I get you anything while I'm up there?"

Meg understood the desire to appease and keep the peace better than Emily might imagine. She squeezed Emily's hand.

"Supper sounds fine," she said, and laughed as Emily smothered her face with kisses.

❖

The vigil for the three murdered men had arranged itself into a natural hierarchy of mourners: bereaved family members at the front of the car park, friends and well-wishers in the next row, and those who were there to rubberneck or get on the telly crowded at the back. A mass of flowers and messages of condolence surrounded the entrance to the Mission, some of them tied to the railings, ready to be homed in on by the cameras. Hundreds of flames flickered in the keen breeze, gloved hands cradling the candles to form a protective shell and keep fingers warm. The cloudless sky had made the temperature drop sharply, and from her vantage point, Sanne could hear the surreptitious shuffle of feet as the cold began to bite.

On the other side of the temporary stage, Nelson caught her eye briefly before returning his attention to the proceedings. Several more EDSOP detectives and officers in plain clothes were scattered through the crowd, eavesdropping on murmured conversations and trying to separate gossip and rumour from fact. Within the press enclosure, strategically positioned police photographers would attempt to record the face of everyone present. Several people were already familiar to Sanne. Adele Horst and Kevin Hopkins had both shaken her hand, and Liam Burrows—released without charge after his nap in Interview One had inadvertently provided him with an alibi—had grinned at her before remembering that he was supposed to be upset.

As the majority of people bowed their heads in prayer, Sanne studied those closest to her: an elderly male, a young couple hand in hand, an even younger mum holding a sleeping baby. Sanne knew that the killer could be within touching distance, hiding in plain sight, either for fear his absence would be noticed or because he was twisted enough to get a thrill out of witnessing the misery he had wrought. Sticking her hands in her pockets, she blew out a frustrated breath. Previous cases had repeatedly proven the pattern of offender behaviour, but hardly anything about this case made sense, so applying conventional wisdom was pointless. For someone who preferred order and the proper application of rules, these murders, lacking both motive and a consistent MO, seemed designed to provoke.

Once the final speaker had thanked everyone for their support, the gathering broke apart, and a ripple of hushed voices gradually rose in volume, as if a dam had ruptured to release an hour's worth of grief and tension. People drifted toward the Mission or the press or into the unlit recesses of the car park, where officers rounded them up and escorted them back for interview.

Steeling herself to return to the canteen, Sanne froze as she heard her name being called. She recognised the voice immediately, giving her time to brace for impact.

"Hey, Zoe."

Zoe gave her a surreptitious wave. "Hiya. Big case, eh? Rumour has it that you spotted a link even before Horst's death."

Sanne shrugged, vowing never again to underestimate the scuttlebutt at HQ. "I couldn't possibly comment."

Zoe's smile made her eyes sparkle in the remaining candlelight. "You are modest to a fault, Detective. Anyway, our sarge asked us to fetch Paul Barber in for questioning. He's a bit worse for wear, but he's waiting for you in the canteen."

"Define 'worse for wear.'"

"Drunk to the point of slurring, but cogent enough if you speak to him in words of less than two syllables."

"Ah, right. Did he give you any trouble?"

Zoe raised an eyebrow. "I could snap him over my knee."

Sanne declined to pass comment on that either. She had no doubt it was true. They set off for the canteen, avoiding the press, who had free rein of the car park now that the vigil was over. Natalie Acre, neatly clad in a charcoal suit, nodded at Sanne and wiped her eyes with a handkerchief before returning her attention to her interview with a local news reporter, while representatives from the BBC, ITV, and Sky News swarmed around Adele Horst.

"Fucking vultures," Zoe muttered.

Sanne said nothing, the kneejerk part of her that agreed with Zoe neutralised by the necessary evil of keeping the press on board. At the steps, they passed the woman who might have been Pauline kneeling in silent prayer before an icon of the Virgin Mary. Too drab for the cameras, she had been overlooked by the media feeding frenzy. She crossed herself as Sanne walked by, rosary beads moving through her fingers, her gaze fixed and remote. No one came to comfort her. She might as well have been invisible.

The entrance to the Mission stood open, but Sanne stopped in the vestibule, mindful of the large police presence in the main building. "Have you had any luck with Luke Fielding?" she asked.

Zoe shook her head. "Nothing as yet. I've put the word out to my shift and a few others I trust, but we've all drawn a blank. Has he bothered your friend since?"

"No." At least, Sanne didn't think he had.

"Maybe he got out of Dodge. He probably knows we're after him by now."

Sanne wasn't sure if that was a good or a bad thing, but she appreciated Zoe's efforts regardless. "Thank you," she said.

"Any time."

Although there was nothing overly flirtatious in her answer, everything about Zoe seemed geared toward making Sanne trip over her own feet. She started walking again, putting on a spurt of pace, but Zoe easily kept up with her until they reached the canteen.

"Third table along. Bald head, black sweater." Zoe pointed Sanne in the right direction.

"Got him. Cheers."

They drew a simultaneous breath to speak, Sanne deferring to Zoe, who kept it simple.

"I'll see you later."

That much Sanne could deal with. "Yep, see you later."

She turned a blind eye to the single-fingered response Zoe flashed at a wolf-whistler, and took the seat in front of Paul Barber, who, oblivious to the commotion around him, was asleep in his chair. A small, fat man, he had a cider-enhanced belly with the same firmness of liver failure that Sanne had seen in her dad before the diuretics kicked in. His snores wheezed in and out, the overheads highlighting a tinge of jaundice and a spiderweb of broken veins on his cheeks. The smell of him—stale alcohol oozing out of every pore, and an acetone stink on his breath—made her push her chair as far away from the table as was practicable.

"Mr. Barber?"

He came awake in pronounced stages, his body jolting as he tried to remember where he was.

"The fuck?"

His chair slid sideward with a squeal of metal on tile, but he couldn't create enough of a gap for his girth. The exertion made his nostrils flare, like a bull whose plans to stampede had been thwarted by a technicality.

"Hey, settle down." Sanne only had to raise her voice slightly to stop his flailing. "You're at the Mission Cross. The police brought you here because of Daniel Horst's murder."

He swiped a stained sleeve across the drool on his chin. "You police?"

"Detective Jensen." Sanne shook his hand without grimacing, a minor triumph. "I need to ask you some questions about what you saw last night."

His nod set his double chin quivering. "Heard more than I saw."

"Okay then." She tried not to let her eagerness show. From the transcript of Nelson's interview, she knew that their only other witness, the passerby, had happened upon Daniel on his way home from the pub, and had neither seen nor heard anything of significance. "Let's go back a bit first. Take me through what you did from around ten p.m. onward."

Barber looked at her as if she had asked him to explain Pythagoras' theorem, so she employed the full extent of her imagination and came up with two suggestions. "Were you at home? Or did you go out to the pub?"

"I watched telly and drank a few cans," Paul said with halting remembrance. "*X-Factor* or some shite like that."

"Can anyone verify this?" He stared at her until she clarified. "Was anyone with you while you were watching the telly?"

"Oh, no. Sheila left me. She reckons she's a lezzer now."

"Right. What happened next?"

"I ran out of booze, so I went to the corner shop to get some more."

"And this corner shop would be?"

"Patel's, on Top Balan precinct. He's a reasonable bloke. Keeps his prices down."

Sanne made a note to request the security tape from Patel's. One good thing about the high crime rate on Malory was the proliferation of cameras in the local shops.

"What happened then, Paul?" She kept her prompt gentle. Barber's jaundiced face had paled, and sweat was beading his forehead.

"I came out onto the precinct, thought maybe I'd get some chippy, and that's when I heard the noise."

"Can you describe that noise for me?"

"Horrible," he whispered. "Like a rabbit with its leg in a trap. Then it cut off." He snapped his fingers. "And there was this yell, reminded me of a footy fan on the terraces."

"What, like a cheer or something?" Sanne asked, appalled.

"Yeah, a bloke gave a cheer, and then I heard running, and everything went quiet."

"Can you remember in which direction the person ran?"

"Away from me." Barber frowned, deep in concentration. "Toward the school, I think."

"Did any kind of vehicle pass you?"

"No, nothing."

Sanne nodded, wishing she had a map handy on which to plot the roads and possible means of egress. Although far from perfect, Barber's testimony would narrow down locations for fingertip searches.

"Tell me what you did next."

"I crept over the road. I didn't know where Dan was at first, but another bloke had already found him and was on his phone, shouting for help."

"Did you speak to this bloke at all?"

"No. I saw Dan on the pavement. He weren't moving and there was blood and guts everywhere, and I didn't want to be there no more, so I went to our Sheila's."

"Is there anything else that you remember, Paul?"

He shrank back, and Sanne could practically see the shutters coming down. "Just that noise. Just that fucking noise."

She clicked her pen closed and set it on the table. "Sit tight," she said. "I'll fetch you a brew."

Chapter Fourteen

Snowflakes still melting in her hair, Sanne squeezed into the space Nelson had saved for her atop an empty desk, and accidentally elbowed Fred's ribs in the process.

"Bloody hell," he hissed, rubbing the offended part. "Was that your elbow or a pickaxe? You need to get some meat on your bones, San."

"I'll eat more pies, I promise," she said, taking care to wrestle out her notebook without inflicting further damage.

Pen readied and notes in hand, she felt able to relax a little. She hated being late, her stress further amplified by the scheduling of a full departmental briefing during which she had been asked to report on Paul Barber's statement.

"Roads bad?" Nelson said.

"Yeah. I set off early, but it took me ages just to get over the Snake. After that, it was mostly idiots driving at ten miles an hour because there's an inch of snow on the pavements."

He chuckled. "I got your text. I was all ready to stand in for you. Did you happen to catch the news this morning?"

She shook her head. "I spent the drive practising for this and swearing at morons. What did I miss?"

"Oh, not much." A smile began to spread over his face. "Just Trevor Mulligan guilty of first degree murder."

"You're shitting me," she said, far more loudly than she had intended. Several people turned to look in her direction, but she didn't care. If there had been enough space, she would've thrown her arms around Nelson. "Unanimous verdict?"

"Yep. Came in late yesterday evening."

Sanne felt like a ton weight had just been rolled off her. She would never have forgiven herself had her shaky testimony wrecked the prosecution's case. "Thank fuck for that. When's the sentencing?"

"Later today. He'll get life. No doubt about it."

"I hope they throw away the bloody key," she muttered, watching Eleanor and Carlyle take up positions at the front of the room.

"I'm sure they will."

"Good morning, everyone." Eleanor's voice easily carried over the diminishing murmurs of conversation. "I appreciate you coming in for such an ungodly hour. This is where we're at, as of thirty minutes ago." She flicked the lights off and opened a PowerPoint presentation, the first slide a well-lit image of Daniel Horst's blood spilled on the pavement.

"The post mortem on Horst has confirmed that a similar, most probably identical, weapon was used in his and Andrew Culver's murders. Attempts to cast the wound tracks failed due to decomposition in Culver's case and resuscitative attempts in Horst's, but the knife we're looking for resembles this one." She clicked to a slide depicting a large, curved blade. "None of the three PMs have identified any trace evidence from the perp, which could indicate a degree of forensic sophistication. That the perp had kit with him on Saturday night—at the very least, gloves and the knife—implies the attack on Horst was planned rather than random. If he's used the same blade twice, then it's something he's hung on to and it's likely still to be in his possession, so keep your eyes peeled during house-to-house. This lad might be clever, but he's taking more and more risks, which means he's going to make a mistake at some point." She turned to Carlyle. "Sergeant?"

Carlyle nodded and stepped forward, his silhouette looming over the screen until he remembered to avoid the light.

"So far, the only link between the three vics is the Mission Cross, and none of the interviewees yesterday described the men as anything other than passing acquaintances. Horst's finances were completely clean, but we still have officers cross-referencing phone records to try to identify any overlap of contacts." He paused, licked his thumb, and flipped to a new page in his file. Having glanced over the notes, he snapped the file shut. "I'll be supervising further interviews at the shelter throughout the day. We're expecting stragglers will keep turning up, and a round-the-clock police presence has been agreed for the next week. Police visibility here and on Malory Park is crucial. There is understandable fear among residents, and we need to ensure that people can see us doing our job. While there is nothing to suggest that we may be a target, stab vests are to be worn at all times if you're out on the streets." He eyeballed the mass of detectives and officers until he spotted Sanne. "Before we let you all get on, Detective Jensen has some information from a new witness."

At his cue, Sanne slid off the desk and made her way to the front. Carlyle switched on the main lights without warning her, leaving her blinking as she tried to focus on her notes.

"Cheers, Sarge," she said, her sarcasm softened by a smile in his direction. "Morning, everyone. Last night, I interviewed Paul Barber, a local man who'd just come out of a shop on Top Balan precinct as the attack on Daniel Horst took place. While parts of his testimony were vague and he didn't actually see anything, he remembered hearing a male give a celebratory yell." She paused to let that sink in, gauging reactions ranging from shock to disgust. "Moments later, Barber stated that someone ran in the direction of Malory Park Primary School. We're assuming that someone was our perp."

She retrieved the remote that Carlyle had left on the table and clicked onto the next slide: a road map of the area immediately around the crime scene. She circled the murder site with the remote's pointer.

"This is where Horst was found, and this"—she plotted a path past the school—"is the most probable route for the perp. These streets will be the focus of a fingertip search, and house-to-house will also concentrate on this area. We're particularly interested in any sightings of the perp as he fled, or of a dark-coloured—black or navy—Vauxhall Combo van that was spotted close to the first two crime scenes. An example of the make and model is in your briefing pack. The CCTV outside the school has been offline for the past week, but one of the traffic cameras leading out to the bypass is ANPR-enabled, so we're hoping to get something from that when its footage is analysed."

Feeling absurdly proud that she'd managed to get through her section of the briefing without her voice quavering, she scanned her notes to ensure she'd covered everything. On the verge of heading back to her seat, she paused as she spotted a raised hand.

"Uh, go ahead," she said, unsure as to whether she should be taking questions.

A detective drafted in from Domestic Violence cleared his throat. "This bloke, Barber. What did he mean by a yell? Was he able to elaborate?"

"He said it sounded like a football fan cheering." Sanne's long commute had given her ample time to mull over this detail. "I suppose that could imply a thrill element to the murders. Each one becoming bolder, more public, and then, in the case of Daniel Horst, involving a victim with a higher social status who is more likely to garner attention." She halted her conjecture as numerous debates broke out in the group. "Shit," she whispered, the curse inaudible beneath the growing babble of voices.

It took Eleanor's return to the front to quieten the room. "Assignments have been posted," she said. "Briefing packs are with Sergeant Carlyle. Vests and ID badges at all times, and no one but the media department is authorised to speak to the press. Thank you."

Sanne remained in place, feeling like prey in the thrall of a predator, until the room emptied and Eleanor approached her.

"That was an interesting bit of supposition."

Sanne winced. "Sorry, boss. I was thinking aloud, and then I wasn't thinking at all."

"It might have been better discussed in private before you decided to share with the group."

"I know." The only way Sanne could have been more mortified was if she'd accidentally made her presentation in her underwear.

"Having said that, the idea has crossed my mind more than once, and it's not entirely without merit." Eleanor dropped a pile of files into Sanne's arms and nodded in the direction of her office. She waited until they were in the corridor before she spoke again. "If we're lacking a motive, maybe it's because there is no motive."

"Someone killing for kicks?" Sanne nudged the office door open with her backside. "It's about the only thing that makes sense. Our perp has escalated from a private dwelling to wasteland and now to a main road, and from two vics no one cared about to a man well regarded on the estate."

Eleanor nodded. "If it's publicity he's after, he's got it. Did you see the papers this morning? They've taken to calling him the 'Sheffield Slasher.'"

"Christ."

"Precisely. A bona fide sociopath on the loose on our patch." Eleanor sat down with such force that her chair skidded back. "That's just what we bloody well need."

❖

"If it's any consolation, it's an obvious theory, San." Nelson stopped to check the keys in his hand and then headed farther to the left. "There's only so long you can search for a motive before you start to think that there might not be one."

"I know," Sanne said, tagging after him. "And the boss wasn't really pissed off. I just wish I hadn't blurted it out like that."

"It raised a few eyebrows. You're not exactly renowned for improvising."

Sanne didn't consider that an insult, but neither was it entirely accurate. "Except when it comes to scrapping with old ladies who're trying to murder me with a tyre iron."

"Okay, yeah, there was that one time," Nelson conceded.

"See? See?" She wagged a finger at him. "I can improvise just fine. Now where's this bloody car?"

"A-Eight."

She glanced round and steered Nelson to the right. Most of the bays were empty, and snow was falling fast to cover the tarmac.

"This is forecast to last most of the day." She opened her mouth, trying to catch flakes on her tongue. "I'll probably get stuck halfway home and have to sleep in my car."

"You don't sound too bothered by that." Nelson double-clicked the fob, and the indicators on a Vauxhall Astra flashed as it unlocked.

"I packed a sleeping bag, spare clothes, and a Thermos. I'll be fine."

Holding open the passenger door, Nelson gave her a little bow as she climbed in. "And here's me saying you can't improvise."

The roads leading away from HQ were a nightmare of stationary traffic and nervous snow drivers.

"Did the boss authorise lights and sirens for this?" Nelson asked.

"Nope." Sanne propped her feet on the dash and ripped the top off a packet of custard creams.

"It's going to take us all day to get over to Malory."

"Yep." She offered him a biscuit.

"Let's hope the Sheffield Slasher is a fair-weather type, eh?" he said through a mouthful of crumbs.

Sanne gazed at the fields rapidly turning white beneath the storm. "Aye," she said. "Let's hope so."

"Why do you *do* that? You bloody stupid birds!"

Meg hooted the horn and skidded around a pair of ducks who had chosen to snooze in the snow in the middle of the road. The ducks, notorious for napping on the access road to Rowlee village, didn't twitch a feather as she drove past. Approaching the welcome sign, she turned the radio off and opened her window. All she could hear now was a robin singing in a nearby hedgerow. Even the car's engine sounded muffled. Coming home to this was worth the slog from Sheffield along the freshly ploughed Snake Pass. She had told

Emily she was going to pick up a smart shirt for that afternoon's soiree in Harrogate, but her reasons were even simpler than that: she wanted to see the hills and her village in the snow, and to spend the morning away from the city.

She waved to Arthur Grimshaw as she fishtailed onto her driveway, taking her time pulling on her gloves until she saw that he was safely home. Once his door closed, she grabbed her keys and stomped her feet into the drift her tyres had created, instantly reminded of pitched snowball battles with Sanne and Keeley, and of rolling massive snowmen on the back field. They had never had a sledge, only a shared metal tea tray, cadged from Sanne's mum because it had two handles and could fly downhill faster than shit off a shovel.

Remembering a ten-year-old Sanne using that exact phrase in front of her mum, Meg laughed and unlocked her front door, shoving it over the mail and local newspaper on her mat. She kicked off her boots, slung her coat on the banister, and went straight to the kitchen for a bacon butty. Eyes fixed on the fridge, she didn't see Luke until he moved, pushing off the countertop to stand just beyond her reach.

"What the fuck?" Too shocked to do anything but stare at him, she gripped the door jamb to steady herself.

"Hey, sis," he said, as if breaking into her house for the second time was perfectly normal behaviour.

"How did you get in?" Now she knew he was there, she could smell things and see things that she hadn't noticed before: a trace of cigarette smoke and fried food, a pan used and left full of congealing fat on her stove, and a small gap around the board covering the window that he had smashed. The glaziers weren't due to repair it until Wednesday.

He jerked his chin at the wood, and a faint smile of pride at a job well done crept onto his face. "Needed more nails in it."

"Right." She flinched as he took a step toward her, and he reacted immediately, raising his hands in conciliation and coming no closer. He had gained weight, his bulk straining the seams of a shirt and trousers that no longer fitted him. Unshaven, with tatty, oil-slick hair, he smelled dirty, and in a moment of barely tempered hysteria she thought how typical it was that he had raided her food but hadn't bothered to use her shower.

"I just wanted to see you, Meg. I wanted to talk to you," he said, his voice thin and nasal. She had heard that whine before, usually pre-empting a demand for money.

"You hurt Mum, and you wrecked my house," she said. "Fucking hell, Luke, you tried to steal the wedding ring off her finger. Do you really think I want to sit down and have a chat with you?"

"I were desperate." His bottom lip curled into a pout. "I'd been inside for a few months, and I thought this bloke would forget I owed him, but he were straight on me as soon as I come out. I've been trying to hide, but I know he'll find me."

"How much do you owe?" She did a quick calculation. She could afford fifteen hundred at a push, which would be money well spent if it got rid of him.

"Twenty grand," he said.

She closed her eyes in despair. "Twenty thousand pounds? What the hell did you do with that? Fly to the Caribbean? Buy a flashy car?"

"I owed someone else," he snapped. "Some bent fuck who jacked up the interest. He threatened me, Meg, proper scared me. I didn't know what to do."

"So you took out another loan to pay off the first?"

His fist hammered on the counter, making her jump. "You got a better fucking idea? Huh? Come on then. Let's hear it."

She said nothing, her eyes flickering to the block of knives beside the kettle, and the drawer beneath that where she kept her rolling pin. With an obvious effort, Luke calmed his breathing and unclenched his fingers.

"I needed help, Meg, and when I went to Mum's and Mrs. Baxter told me you'd sold the house, I knew you'd have the money. And some of that money, well, it's mine, isn't it? So I just want what's mine, that's all." He made it sound so reasonable, his face all doe-eyes and a big smile, but the smile disappeared as Meg shook her head.

"There's no money, Luke. The house wasn't worth much, and Mum's care home costs a fortune. The money ran out months ago."

"You're lying." He delivered his verdict in a neutral tone, as if he hadn't quite decided which way this would play out.

She inched away as he moved forward, her options now limited to running for the front door.

"You're lying." He took another step, forcing her to retreat again. "And you set the cops on me."

Meg's stomach lurched as Luke adjusted his stance, his knees bending slightly. She knew the signs, knew that she didn't have much time, and she was breathing so fast that her fingers were starting to tingle.

"I haven't spoken to the police," she said, willing him to believe her.

"Liar!" he yelled, spittle flying from his lips. "The cops are looking everywhere! I got friends, you stupid bitch. They tell me stuff. I can't get into the hostels or the shelters, and it's your fucking fault!"

On the word "fault," she bolted, turning and sprinting down the hallway, but her fingers had only grazed the door handle when a tug on her shirt sent her flying. She collided with the wall, the thud of her head on the plaster leaving her too dazed to resist as he grabbed her again. With both hands wrapped around her collar, he hauled her into the kitchen and slammed her back against the sink. She felt her ribs crack on impact, and all the air seemed to leave her in a rush.

"Stop," she gasped. "Luke, please."

He snarled and punched her, splitting the skin on her cheek. Her head lolled to the side, and then she was falling, her legs collapsing as he dropped her. Curling into a ball, she dimly sensed him step over her and leave the kitchen. It didn't take him long to find the keys in her coat pocket. He shut the front door quietly behind him and started her car. Terrified that he would return to drag her out with him, she sobbed when she heard him drive away instead. Blood filled her mouth, frothing and bubbling with every breath she snatched, and when she tried to straighten, pain arched through her torso, keeping her in a foetal position.

"Oh God," she whispered.

He had hurt her before, but not like this, never anything like this, and she had no way to get help. Her mobile was in her coat pocket, her house phone out of reach on the countertop, and her immediate neighbours both worked late. The blood running down her throat made her retch, and she vomited a stream of crimson onto the floor. Panting against the pain, she swiped a clumsy hand at the mess and then pounded the tiles with her fist. Luke had her keys. He could come back any time he wanted.

"Fuck that," she said. "Fuck that."

She reached behind herself and managed to open the nearest cupboard, knocking plastic bottles of ketchup and HP sauce onto the floor, until her fingers closed around a glass pasta jar. Fusilli skittered across the tiles when she smashed the glass, and the exertion made her vomit again, her vision failing her as she dry-heaved. Leaning her head on the cold tiles, she wrapped her fingers around the base of the jar and waited for the sickness to pass. A solitary beam of sunlight sparkled on the jagged edges of her weapon and threw rainbows across the floor. She watched the colours with unfocused eyes and wondered how long it would be before Emily got worried enough to come looking for her.

Chapter Fifteen

The snow might have been playing havoc with the fingertip searches, but it had certainly livened up Sanne's day of house-to-house enquiries. Two of the local schools were closed, leaving kids to run riot on the estate, and she and Nelson had already found themselves caught in several snowball fights. Despite all attempts to bait them, however, they behaved with the dignity and composure befitting police officers—that was, until an ambush left them soaked and prompted covert but effective retaliation. The group of ten-year-olds now shadowing their every move thought they were the best thing since sliced bread.

"It's good for community relations," Nelson said, proving the accuracy of his aim by taking out a shrieking kid from twenty feet. "And Carlyle did say that we needed to be visible."

Sanne flicked snow out of her ear and ducked a missile, which splattered on the wall behind her. "I'm not sure this was what he had in mind."

"Miss! Miss!" a scrawny kid with no front teeth yelled as he ran toward her. Assuming he was referring to the snowball, she ignored him until he tugged on her coat.

"Oh, hey, what's up?" she asked.

"Are you really bobbies?" Beaming at her, he selected a toffee from a large paper bag and shoved it into his mouth, a habit that explained the gaps in his teeth.

"Yes, we're really bobbies." She watched Nelson unleash a barrage from his stronghold behind a hedge. "Although you'd be forgiven for thinking otherwise."

"Eh?" The lad obviously didn't have a clue what she'd just said. "Where's your cuffs, then?"

Sanne mimicked his haughty pose. "What if that's a secret?"

He eyed her for a few seconds. "I'll give you a toffee if you tell me."

Toffee choosing was a serious business, and she took her time about it, rejecting liquorice and fudge in favour of a caramel with a white swirl.

"Them's my favourites," he declared proudly, as if she had passed some unspoken test.

"Okay then, a deal's a deal." She unfastened her coat and opened it wide enough to reveal her stab vest. Her cuffs, CS gas, notebook, and radio were all clipped in place.

"Oh, cool. You're like Batman or something."

She nodded, not well enough versed in the gadgetry of superheroes to know whether Batman really carried CS gas.

"Have you got a gun?" he asked.

"No."

"Why not? Bobbies have them on the telly."

"American telly, maybe. Most of us over here don't carry guns."

"What about a Taser?" He mimicked an electric shock, his thin arms shaking as he giggled.

"No, I'm not trained to use one."

"You're a rubbish bobby."

His disappointment was palpable, so she tried to give him a new angle to consider. "Well, I'm a detective, which means that we look at clues and evidence and then we catch the really bad people."

He picked his nose, deep in thought. "Danny Horst used to give us toffees," he said, wiping his finger on his trousers. "He were nice."

"Yes, he was."

"You're all right 'n' all."

She smiled. "Thank you."

"Pow!" he said. "Like in Batman." He nodded, apparently expecting her to be pleased, which she might have been if she'd had any idea what he was talking about.

"I'm sorry. You've lost me."

He raised his eyes heavenward. "My granny reckoned you were looking for a blue van. She sleeps at the back, but my room's at the front. P-O-W," he said, as Sanne stared at him, dumbfounded. "Them's the last three letters of its number plate."

❖

Sanne and Nelson played no part in tracking the van from the partial plate, but Eleanor had promised to keep them updated, and her phone call made them abandon their doorstep interview mid-question and race back to the car.

"Steven Rudd, thirty-eight years old, lives at fifteen North Bank, Parson Cross, and is the registered keeper of a navy blue Vauxhall Combo, registration Bravo X-ray zero six Papa Oscar Whiskey." Eleanor spoke clearly, aware that Sanne had put her call through to hands-free. "No priors. The officers working to trace the van were processing by profile fit and then alphabetically, so although Rudd is on their list, he's not been interviewed yet. He's lived in the area for about eighteen months and—saving the best for last—he has visited the Mission Cross on occasion. He didn't ring many bells with the staff, though. A couple remembered him as being unemployed and a hard drinker, but pleasant enough."

"What's the plan, boss?" Nelson asked. Far from being tired after his snowball escapades, he was almost bouncing in the driver's seat.

"Tactical Aid are on their way to North Bank with a warrant." Eleanor sounded more cheerful than she had in weeks. "I will see you there in half an hour. Silent approach, but blues are authorised en route."

Nelson whooped and drowned out the hum of the dial tone by revving the engine. He grinned at Sanne. "Want to go play with the boys in big boots?"

"Best offer I've had all day." She laughed as he hit the sirens and four kids pelted the car in an honorary salute. "Left at the roundabout," she said, just in case he'd forgotten.

They travelled for a while without speaking, Nelson focusing on the roads, now icy after the snow had turned to sleet, and Sanne busy plotting a route to North Bank that would circumvent the early rush hour traffic.

"Penny for them," he said at length, drawing her attention away from the window and the graffiti-covered concrete of the bypass.

She propped her feet on the dash, placing her boots precisely in the prints she had left there that morning. If anyone but Nelson had asked the question, she would probably have lied.

"I was thinking how random stuff is at times," she said. "I mean, what are the odds of us meeting that lad through an illicit snowball fight? Any other day he'd have been at school, and if we'd not played along, he'd never have trusted us enough to come forward."

"Luck and little things," Nelson said. "We depend on those all the time. The brass would never want us to admit it, but sometimes we just fluke this detective lark."

She put a hand to her chest, feigning astonishment. "I thought we were all intuitive and brilliant."

"Well, we're that too." He slowed for a red light, glancing at her as he hung back and waited for two lanes of traffic to part for him. "You got Billy Cotter bang to rights, didn't you?"

"Aye," she said, trying to quell any overt reaction to the name. "But maybe that was down to luck as well."

"No way, San." Nelson's eyes were back on the road, but she felt as if they were still drilling through her. "I don't give a damn what that note in your file says. You're the best EDSOP partner I've had."

Her cheeks suddenly felt hot, and she bowed her head, bashful as ever about accepting praise. Nelson was in his eighth year on the squad, and he'd had three previous partners.

"No truth to the rumour that you're trading me in for Fred, then?" She directed the question at her toes.

"I have to admit the salsa dancing does give him a certain appeal." He switched the siren from whoop to wail and hit eighty in the outside lane. "But I think I'll stick with you for now."

❖

Funnelled between two blocks of flats, the wind howled along the walkway of North Bank, prompting Sanne to pull on her woolly hat and sidle closer to Nelson. She blew on her hands and rubbed them together, her fingers already too frozen for gloves to be of any benefit. Six doors down, the Tactical Aid Unit were approaching flat number fifteen in as stealthy a manner as eight men in full body armour could manage. Several residents were watching from the opposite block, but most of them merely checked that trouble wasn't heading in their direction and shut their doors against the cold.

"Bet you a quid he's not home," she whispered to Nelson.

"No bet," he whispered back.

The blue van was conspicuous by its absence in the car park, a fact that hadn't gone unnoticed by Eleanor, who stood conferring with Carlyle and looking decidedly less chipper. Two storeys below, an ambulance was waiting on standby, a sensible precaution given the nature of the murders for which Steven Rudd was now the prime suspect. No one was needed to cover a rear exit. The flats were one way in, one way out.

"Police! Mr. Rudd, open the door!" the TAU sergeant bellowed, hammering on a glazed partition. "Police! Open up!"

The perfunctory warning taken care of, he moved aside, allowing another officer to step forward, enforcer ram in his hands. The officer drew back the sixteen kilograms of hardened steel and battered it against the door, the impact sending a shockwave through the UPVC and rattling the neighbours' windows. Having located a weak point, he focused a barrage of hits around the area. Someone in the next flat turned up their television, a section of the doorframe flew six feet down the aisle, and three teenagers hanging off a balcony cheered as the door finally imploded.

Further yells of "Police!" accompanied the team's entrance, and Sanne fixed her eyes on the now-empty walkway, counting beneath her breath as seconds and then minutes passed. The sergeant was the first to reappear, a solitary shake of his head delivering his verdict.

"Fucking hell," Eleanor muttered. It wasn't as if the news was unexpected, and EDSOP hadn't been idle in the interim. Alerts had already been posted, and attempts to track Rudd's family and known associates were underway, but hopes of a speedy resolution were nevertheless dashed. She nodded in acknowledgement and turned to her three detectives. "Okay. Nelson and Sanne, top-to-bottom search. Flag anything that might point to another possible address: garage, allotment, obliging mate, et cetera. Carlyle and I will start talking to the neighbours. We'll see you in there."

As Sanne unwrapped a Tyvek suit, the wind caught at it, whipping its legs out like a drunk performing the can-can. She wrestled it under control, keen to get to work.

"Tell me honestly, San, do these things make me look weird?" Nelson asked, as she swapped her hat for the suit's hood. She took a moment to appraise him. His six-foot-plus, well-built physique was swaddled in white material that clung in all the wrong places but made his arse sag.

"Honestly?" she said, and waited for his nod. "You look like the abominable snowman's handsome younger brother."

He shook out a pair of gloves. "I don't know how to take that."

"Backhanded compliment," she suggested.

She turned side-on to squeeze past the muscle-bound TAU lads filing out of the flat. Nelson, with no chance of doing likewise, caught up with her in the living room.

"We've been in worse," she said, and he murmured his agreement.

A large leather sofa dominated the relatively tidy room, the focal point being a wall-mounted flat-screen television that was surrounded by neat stacks of DVDs, mainly horror and action films interspersed with the occasional incongruous romcom.

"Stick or twist?" he asked.

"Stick." She gave the reply without needing to think. She had uncovered enough nasty surprises during recent bedroom searches to last her a lifetime. Her phone buzzed as Nelson left her, but she couldn't remember in which layer of clothing she had hidden it, so she let it go to voicemail and headed instead for a mismatched cherry wood cabinet in the far corner of the room. An old-fashioned piece of furniture, probably bought on the cheap or supplied by a landlord, it wobbled as she opened it, and a three-legged china dog keeled over onto its nose.

"Bugger." Her gloves left smudges in a thin layer of dust as she righted the dog. Satisfied that he wasn't going anywhere, she dropped to her knees and began to sort through the paperwork crammed onto the cabinet's shelf.

Twenty minutes of skim-reading and categorising told her a lot about Steven Rudd's life. A pile of repeat prescriptions and hospital discharge notes spoke of recent ill health, with well-documented treatment for high blood pressure and depression. The overflowing ashtray and empty whiskey bottle by the arm of the sofa implied that his doctors' advice to stop smoking and drinking had fallen on deaf ears. His bill payments were sporadic and often late, leading to frequent disconnection of his utilities, while missed appointments at the job centre had seen his benefits cut by sanctions.

Spotting patterns was something Sanne thrived on. She set aside three notifications of reductions to his Jobseeker's Allowance, along with a handwritten response pleading for the decision to be overturned, in which he cited eighteen months of obediently jumping through every hoop the job centre had set for him. The letter, dated two days before Andrew Culver's murder, had been signed but obviously not posted. Meanwhile, a shopping receipt from the Friday after Marcus Jones's death mainly comprised alcohol and cigarettes.

Ignoring another call to her mobile, Sanne delved into the first drawer, finding a stash of thiamine and vitamin B—mainstay treatments for alcoholism which she recognised from her dad's prescriptions—plus several old boxes of painkillers, and leaflets from local takeaways. Her stomach growled at the gaudy images of kebabs and curries. It was past teatime, and a packet of crisps had made for a meagre lunch.

"San! Come and take a look at this!"

At Nelson's yell, she abandoned the leaflet atop her miscellaneous junk pile and ran back out into the hallway. "Which room?" she called.

"Bedroom. Last on the left."

He met her in the doorway, holding up a pair of jeans liberally decorated with dark-red splotches.

"Oh, hey, did you hit the jackpot, mate?" She touched a gloved finger to the cloth, feeling the rigidity of the stains. A familiar metallic-sweet smell confirmed that it was blood.

"He'd shoved them behind the immersion heater in the airing cupboard," he said. "There's something else there, but it's stuck."

"There might be a pair for each murder. Half his wardrobe could be stuffed in there by now."

"True. I'll give the boss and SOCO a shout. How've you been getting on?"

"Okay. No smoking gun so far, but anecdotal evidence of someone slowly letting things slip." She picked up a framed photograph from the dresser, its glass bearing a large crack across it, distorting the image of a proud-looking man holding a newborn baby. "Is this him?"

"Yep." Nelson pointed toward a paper envelope, the type used to mail out photographs before everyone had switched to digital. "Two kids and a wife in those, but there's no sign of them ever staying here. Mind you, Rudd doesn't seem native to these parts either."

"He certainly doesn't." Sanne paused at a picture taken in the back garden of a detached house, in which Rudd—handsome and tanned in a smart suit—toasted the camera with a glass of wine. She looked around his bedroom, at the curtains that failed to meet in the middle, the dirty sheets strewn on the threadbare mattress, and the two soggy condoms tossed onto the carpet.

"A couple of drinks at lunch, a couple more when he gets in, stressful job. Maybe he overstretches himself on an expensive house and car." She gave the envelope back to Nelson, who took up the story.

"He loses his job to the booze and can't meet his mortgage payments. His wife gets sick of him or trades him in for someone who can pay the bills. She jumps ship with the kids, and he gets rehomed in North Bank."

"Where he snaps?" Sanne said, not confident enough to phrase it as a statement. "He's taking antidepressants, but I've not found anything to suggest he's prone to violent psychotic episodes."

Nelson rustled the evidence bag into which he'd placed the pair of jeans. "I think I might have."

"Yeah," she said. The bloodstained clothing certainly lent the scenario credence. "Who'd have thought the Sheffield Slasher was once a respectable middle-class dad?"

Nelson rummaged in his suit for his radio. "It takes all sorts. Although these days, those sorts are more likely to take their kids for a drive off a cliff, just to punish the ex."

Sanne shuddered. They hadn't yet found any contact information for Rudd's family, and the urge to check on their well-being was an ache she had no immediate way to soothe.

"It'll be the first thing the boss does," Nelson said, following her train of thought. "At least we know who we're looking for now. That's a heck of a lot more than we started out with this morning."

"I better get back to it," Sanne said, somewhat reassured. "Before SOCO get here and chase us off with a big stick."

"I thought I'd leave the airing cupboard to them. It was full of spiderwebs."

"Probably wise. Take the kitchen instead. Knowing your luck, you'll find the murder weapon stashed in the bread bin."

"Or in the corn flakes." He grinned, willing her to get the joke. "Y'know, because he's a serial, *cereal*…"

She groaned as she walked away. "Oh God, that's terrible. Promise me one thing, Nelson," she called over her shoulder.

She could hear him laughing even as he answered.

"What?"

"Never give up your day job."

❖

"Courtesy of Mrs. Gaskell at number eleven." Eleanor proffered the tray until everyone had taken a mug. "She took a shine to Sergeant Carlyle."

Sanne turned her mug to avoid its chipped rim and took a grateful sip. As predicted, SOCO had requested space to work, leaving her and Nelson no option but to meet Eleanor back on the walkway, where icy rain was now blasting over the railing and soaking their feet.

"Let's keep it short and sweet," Eleanor said. "We can discuss the finer points at HQ when my face has thawed."

Nelson took the initiative. "SOCO have just fished out a coat to go with the jeans, both covered in what appears to be blood. They couldn't see anything else in the cupboard, and the rest of the bedroom and kitchen were clear. The only other significant find was two used condoms." He swallowed a mouthful of coffee to hide his grimace. "They, uh, appear to have seen recent action, but we've not found anything to indicate who Rudd's been sleeping with or whether he's currently in a relationship."

"Neighbours haven't noticed anyone," Eleanor said. "But it could've been a late-night hookup, or a prostitute. Mrs. Gaskell goes to bed at nine fifty on the dot, before the ten o'clock news can give her nightmares."

"Have Rudd's family been contacted?" Sanne asked. A small writing pad found tucked between the sofa cushions had listed their address and phone number.

"Yes, they're safe and well in"—Eleanor checked her notes—"Horsforth, Leeds. George and Fred are on their way to interview the ex-wife, but she claims not to have spoken to Rudd for more than six months. Apparently, his e-mails and phone calls just stopped, and he missed the birthday of their youngest son. She described him as 'charming but temperamental.' He lost his job after an investigation into financial irregularities, started hitting the bottle, and became less charming, more temperamental."

"It'd be interesting to put together a timeline and see if there are any other triggers for what's happened." Sanne toed the bag of paperwork she had set by the front door. "I've only been able to go through about half of that so far."

"Right, good. Add it to your to-do list." Eleanor retrieved the tray and gave it to Carlyle. "Let's head to HQ for a quick summary briefing and find out what everyone else has been doing while we've been freezing our arses off here."

Interpreting that as a dismissal, Sanne led the way to the car, her numb feet making her tread heavy. She clasped her hands across her rumbling belly.

Nelson laughed. "Whoa, San, are you okay?"

"No, I'm bloody starving. Do you fancy grabbing a curry or something? My treat."

"Can I have bhajis with mine?"

She tapped her pocket, jingling the loose change in it. "Yes, I'm sure the budget will stretch to bhajis."

He gave a contented sigh. "San, if I wasn't married and you weren't gay, we'd be perfect for each other."

The thought of food seemed to spur him on. He outpaced her and clicked the fob to unlock the car the instant it came into view. He'd started the engine and was flashing the headlights at her when her phone rang again.

"Crap," she muttered. As she hadn't recognised the number on her missed call log, she hadn't bothered listening to her voicemail, reassured that it wasn't Meg trying to contact her. That same mobile number was calling now. She jabbed a finger to accept it, expecting to be hijacked by a nuisance sales pitch. "Hello?"

"Sanne? It's Emily Woodall."

The name failed to register at first, its significance buried beneath the snap of irritation and the clink of cutlery in the background. Emily didn't wait for a response, though, and her next question scared Sanne so much that she almost dropped the phone.

"Is Meg with you?" Emily phrased it as an accusation, the verbal equivalent of someone stomping their feet.

Sanne didn't give a shit about the insinuation. She was too busy trying to remember what time Emily had first called. It must have been hours ago, just as Sanne had gone into Steven Rudd's flat.

"Jesus Christ," she whispered. Then, louder and rapid-fire, "Meg's not with me. I'm at work. When did you last see her? Is she not answering her phone?" She forced herself to pause, to give Emily a chance to reply.

"No. She sent me a text this morning to say that she was going home to pick up a shirt—we were supposed to be having supper with my family—but she didn't meet me after I'd finished my shift, and she's been ignoring my calls, so I drove to Harrogate on my own."

"Had you argued?" It wasn't really Sanne's place to ask, but she was trying to be logical, to think like a detective and not like a terrified best friend.

"No, but I suppose I should've expected this. It's typical of her. She wasn't keen to come here, and if she doesn't want to do something, she doesn't do it. No one in A&E has seen her, and she told me that the two of you had been in touch recently." She left the implication hanging, as if to provoke a denial.

Sanne was already running for the car. "Will you phone me if you hear from her?" She yanked the car door open, barely acknowledging Emily's answer before she hung up.

"What's wrong?" Nelson asked, as she dialled Meg's home number.

"I'm not sure." She counted the rings until the answer phone clicked on. "Meg, give me a call when you get this. It doesn't matter if you wake me up." Her voice began to shake, as some subconscious part of her accepted that Meg wasn't going to phone. "Shit. I'm coming over, Meg, okay?"

She set her mobile on her knee where she could keep an eye on its screen, and met Nelson's concerned gaze. "Emily doesn't know where Meg is. She hasn't answered her phone since this morning."

"Have they had a fight?"

Sanne shook her head. "No. Meg said she was heading home for something, and Emily just left her to it because she doesn't have a fucking clue what's been going on with Luke. God, I need to—can you get me back to my car?"

He pulled onto the main road, accelerating beyond the speed limit. "You'll miss the briefing," he reminded her gently.

"I know. I'll speak to the boss in the morning." Her career was way down the list of her current priorities. She glanced at the dash, willing him to go faster.

"Do you want to send a patrol round?"

"No." She had considered but discounted that option. "There's every chance it could be a false alarm. Emily sounded pissed off, so she might not have told me everything." She began to feel calmer as she rationalised aloud, almost able to convince herself that it would turn out to be a lovers' tiff. "I've got a key for Meg's house. She wouldn't appreciate a giddy officer kicking her door in."

He slammed the brakes on for a red light, too far away to jump it as he had the last two. "Do you want me to come with you?"

"No, but thanks. Just try to cover for me at the briefing, if you can. Don't worry. I'll be fine." She managed a weak smile and beat down the doubts threatening to overwhelm her. "I'll find her and bollock her, and everything'll be fine."

CHAPTER SIXTEEN

The Snake Pass was light on traffic and clear of snow, but Sanne cursed every pitch-black bend and steep climb that devoured all of her hard-fought speed and reduced her Land Rover to a crawl. Even though it was cold in the car, sweat was trickling down her back, and she couldn't seem to catch her breath.

Far from easing, her panic intensified once she hit the final descent and passed the Rowlee two-mile marker. Meg's house was no more than five minutes away, and on an ordinary visit Sanne would have given her three rings at that point to tell her to put the kettle on. Instead she was sobbing as she turned onto the road, her legs shaking so hard that she ground a gear and almost stalled the car. Most of the houses in the terrace had lights glowing behind closed curtains, their residents settled in for the night, but Meg's house was in complete darkness, the curtains open and the driveway empty. Sanne pulled into the space where Meg's car should've been, terror boiling up in her again. If Meg wasn't here, where the hell was she?

As Sanne got out of the car, the nip of frost and the smoke from a neighbour's chimney irritated her throat. She coughed, the sound loud and grating in the otherwise peaceful street, but none of the curtains so much as twitched. With no idea what she was about to walk into, she threw open the back of the Land Rover and ransacked its puncture repair kit, bypassing the jack and a lightweight spanner for a far heftier wrench. With the cold burn of the metal against her palm and the CS gas readied on her harness, she unlocked Meg's front door.

"Meg?" she called from the welcome mat, her hand slapping at the wall until she hit the light switch. The low-energy bulb came on slowly, giving her eyes time to adjust. The first thing she noticed was Meg's coat slung over the banister, and then the boots that Meg always wore when it snowed.

"Fuck." Leaving the door wide open, she took a wary step into the hall. "Meg?"

She raised the wrench, her body rigid with tension as she listened for the slightest hint of movement, but it wasn't movement that she heard. It was Meg's voice, thin and breathy.

"San?"

Sanne sprinted toward the kitchen, but then stopped and pushed the door carefully, uncertain of Meg's exact whereabouts. The light from the hallway was enough for her to distinguish a motionless form in the middle of the floor.

"Christ," she hissed.

Congealed blood and streaks of vomit covered the tiles close to where Meg lay surrounded by shards of glass. The arm Meg was using to shield her eyes trembled as she shivered. There was a draught coming from somewhere, and the room was frigid. Leaving the wrench on the kitchen table, Sanne tiptoed around the debris and dropped to her knees beside Meg. When she lowered Meg's hand, the damage she revealed made her feel sick.

"Hey." She touched Meg's face, avoiding the laceration that had left a wide split in her cheek. Meg's skin was slick with cold sweat, and she was breathing in quick, shallow gasps. Sanne jumped at a sudden crack of glass, but it came from the base of a broken pasta jar that Meg had just loosened her grip on.

"Open your eyes for me, love. Come on. I've left the light off."

The chivvying worked. Although Meg moaned, she complied, squinting painfully at Sanne. "Sorry," she whispered. "I tried. Couldn't get up."

Sanne used her sleeve to dry Meg's tears and then shrugged out of her coat. "Here. Let's get you a bit warmer." She tucked the coat around Meg, her common sense overriding the part of her that just wanted to curl up by Meg's side. "Where else are you hurt?"

Meg licked her chapped lips, her voice hoarse. "My back, ribs, I think. I hit the sink."

"Luke?"

She nodded. "He was waiting when I got home. He took my car."

"Have you been like this all day?" The thought horrified Sanne, as did remembering every stupid thing she had done since that morning—the snowball fights, chatting to the kid with the toffees, joking with Nelson—while Meg had been lying here bleeding and scared half to death.

"Mm." Meg barely shaped the sound, but the hint of a smile tugged at her lips. "You took your bloody time getting here."

Sanne gave a slightly crazed laugh. "I really didn't. I broke a lot of speed limits." She squeezed Meg's hand. "Painkillers still in your bathroom cabinet?"

"Yeah. Bring me a bucket load."

"I won't be a minute." She scrambled to her feet. "Don't go anywhere."

"Ha. Ha." Meg flipped Sanne a lethargic but recognisable bird.

Having shut the front door on her way to the stairs, Sanne doubled back to fasten its security chain. In the bathroom, she filled her pockets with tablet boxes as she phoned the police control room, gave her collar number, and requested backup.

"Twenty-five minutes," the dispatcher promised her. "The ambulance should be there sooner."

Steeling herself for a battle with Meg about the latter, she thanked the dispatcher and then stopped on the stairs to send Emily a brief text: *Found Meg, she's okay. Will call when I can*. Cryptic wasn't exactly Sanne's style, but as she didn't know what else to say, sticking to the basics seemed the safest option.

"You still awake?" she asked Meg as she entered the kitchen.

This time around, Meg's single-finger salute was a thumbs-up. Through half-lidded eyes, she tracked Sanne fetching a bottle of water from the fridge and emptying the pills from her pockets.

"Can you sit up?" Sanne asked.

"Don't think so."

"Can you take these without choking on them?"

"Probably. What've we got?"

Sanne reeled off the names from the packets.

"Not tramadol," Meg said. "They make me sick. Co-codamol and Brufen should be okay."

"Right." Sanne set the tablets between Meg's lips one by one and angled the water for her. "Sip it. We want these to stay down."

As if on cue, Meg clamped her mouth shut, her nostrils flaring, but the nausea seemed to pass, and she relaxed visibly when Sanne pulled a cushion from one of the kitchen stools and eased it under her head.

"Better?"

"Mmhm."

"Those pills should kick in soon."

"Hope so." Meg cast her hand about until Sanne took it. "Did Em send you?"

Given the circumstances, Sanne decided it was acceptable to hedge the truth. "She phoned me when she couldn't get hold of you."

"She went to Harrogate, didn't she?" Meg said, apparently not fooled. She chanced a couple of deeper breaths but groaned as the pain folded her in on herself.

"Shh." Sanne circled her thumb on Meg's palm. "It doesn't matter."

"I didn't stand her up."

"No, you didn't." She dampened the corner of a tea towel with the leftover water and used it to staunch the fresh blood seeping from Meg's cheek. She knew she should be documenting the scene or asking Meg for more specifics about what had happened, but she couldn't bring herself to do anything other than sit on the tiles and cling to Meg's hand.

"San?"

"What, love?"

Meg answered so quietly that Sanne had to lean close to hear her. "I've wet myself."

Even though Sanne felt like kicking something, or more precisely *someone*, her only outward reaction was to nod. "Don't worry. I'll help you get changed."

"Before the cavalry barge in here?"

Sanne smiled. Meg might be concussed, but she wasn't stupid. "Just as soon as you get your arse off this floor."

"Yep, any minute now."

Meg could feel the codeine working its way into her system, blunting the edge of the pain. Sanne's hand was still wrapped around hers, its warmth like a lifeline after hours spent in agony.

She had shouted at first, banging a pan against the tiles until her voice and then her strength deserted her. Subsequent attempts to move toward the cord for the phone had induced nausea, and she had lost consciousness at some point, waking up again in the dark. The fear had been bearable. As the hours had passed, it became ever more unlikely that Luke would return. The loss of control and sheer sense of helplessness, however, had been far more difficult to come to terms with. The sole saving grace of a thoroughly shitty day was Sanne rather than Emily being the one who found her, and Meg almost welcomed the headache that stopped her working through the ramifications of that.

"Okay," she said with as much conviction as she could muster. "Shall we give it a go?"

"On three?"

"No, just—" When she started to push with her feet, Sanne got the message and eased her into a sitting position. Meg groaned as the room began to spin, the kitchen cupboards disappearing and the ceiling dipping in to take their place. The leg she had been lying on felt numb and useless, and pins and needles raced along her right arm. Gagging, she tasted bile and then unceremoniously vomited onto her lap.

"Shit." She leaned forward, coming up against something solid and familiar. "Sorry," she muttered into Sanne's shoulder. "Did I puke on you?"

"No, and stop apologising." Sanne wiped Meg's mouth with the tea towel. "We've got half the job done."

"Let's do the other half before I chicken out."

"Are you sure?"

Meg nodded, spurred on by the imminent prospect of police and paramedics knocking on the door.

Sanne didn't argue, despite her obvious misgivings. She simply took most of Meg's weight and ensured that she wouldn't fall back down. "You're not going to manage the stairs," she said, pulling one of the kitchen chairs closer. "Sit here and I'll get you some clothes."

Meg sat, obedient only because she loathed fainting.

"Meg?" Sanne tilted Meg's chin.

"Mm?"

"Are you going to pass out?"

"Nope."

"I'll be two minutes," Sanne said. Then, in an undertone, "Less if I hear a thud."

Forcing her eyes wide, Meg co-opted one of Sanne's tricks and began to count.

❖

Sanne put the bowl of water on the kitchen table and rolled up her sleeves. Meg was still brushing her teeth, the scratch of the bristles attesting to the force being used. With the central heating on full, a hint of colour had returned to her cheeks, and she'd loosened her death-grip on the chair.

"You'll have no enamel left," Sanne warned her.

Toothpaste frothed at Meg's lips as she answered. "So long as there's no vomit left either."

After another minute of frantic scrubbing, she surrendered the brush into Sanne's waiting hand. Sanne reluctantly held up her mobile phone.

"I need to take some pictures before you wash that blood off." She had been dreading this, hating that she needed to treat Meg like a victim, but Meg merely signalled her consent by raising her head and staring at the far wall.

"I'd rather you do it than someone I don't know," she said.

She followed Sanne's instructions to the letter, with the air of shell-shocked acceptance that Sanne had seen so many times in cases of domestic violence. For her own part, Sanne concentrated on the technicalities: the clarity and detail of the composition, the choice of background, the lighting, flash or no flash. Although juries could be swayed by a smart defence lawyer, it was difficult to argue against vivid photographic evidence of a defendant's brutality, and more than anything, she wanted Luke in prison and away from Meg. With that goal at the forefront of her mind, she steadied the camera and repositioned Meg with the seasoned detachment of a crime scene photographer, a strategy that worked right up to the moment that Meg took off her shirt and displayed the injury to her back. Deep purple bruising spread across half of her torso, flaring out from an obvious point of impact where blood had gathered and darkened to form an ugly, swollen line.

"Jesus fucking Christ." Sanne dropped the phone on the countertop and walked away, her anger an easier refuge than her grief. "If Luke was here, I'd string him up by his fucking bollocks."

"Is it that bad?" Meg's attempt to look over her shoulder was thwarted by the pain. "Damn, yeah, it feels pretty bad."

Meg's curse brought Sanne hurrying back to her side. "Hey, stay still, you pillock." For want of a better idea, Sanne gritted her teeth and snapped a picture.

Meg studied the image carefully. "Nice haematoma. If it wasn't on me, I'd be rather impressed by it."

The droll verdict tempered Sanne's foul mood. She kissed Meg's forehead and retrieved the flannel soaking in the bowl.

"How about we get you ready for your guests, eh?"

❖

Meg's first "guest" turned out to be Kathy on the rapid response ambulance car, who did a creditable job of disguising her reaction when she recognised her patient. Meg had managed to walk into the living room, where she sat drowsing in front of a blazing fire as Kathy assessed her.

After scribbling a note on her glove, Kathy pushed her glasses onto her head. "You need to go to the hospital."

Meg blinked, and the rest of the room muscled its way back in. "No, I'm fine here. I can—"

Kathy was having none of it. Her raised hand cut Meg off. "Your blood pressure is low, you're dehydrated and still vomiting, and you're not tolerating oral meds. You have a head injury, so you need neuro obs, and your face needs stitching." She folded her arms. "Stop being such an awkward sod."

Meg turned to Sanne. "I don't want to go to the Royal." It came out more like a plea than the demand she'd intended.

"That's okay," Sanne said, perched on the arm of the sofa. "You're sort of halfway between the Royal and Manchester Central, anyway."

Meg hadn't finished bargaining. "No ambulance," she said. She trusted Kathy to maintain her confidence, but the more people involved, the more likely it was that tongues would wag.

"Planning on walking?" Kathy subjected her to the kind of look usually reserved for combative drunks and libidinous old men.

Sanne intervened before Meg could think of a suitable response. "It's not a problem, I can take her. We can go as soon as the police arrive to secure the house." Always the peacemaker, she sounded like she was mediating with a hostile witness.

"Bloody doctors. You've not got the sense you were born with," Kathy said. More cars pulled onto the street, and she opened the curtains a crack. "Here are the police now."

"They can take a statement at the hospital," Sanne told Meg. "You're not in any fit state to be giving one at the moment."

"Okay." Meg felt as if she was sinking, the pull on her heavy and implacable. "Okay. I'm just so tired."

"I know you are, love." There was nothing but raw affection in Sanne's voice, and her whole face lit up when she smiled. "But you'll be fine."

Meg wanted more than anything to believe her.

❖

"Oi, take a deep breath." Sanne prodded Meg's leg as an alarm sounded on the monitor. Two broken ribs, combined with a dose of morphine, were causing her oxygen levels to dip. She rumpled her nose in objection but succeeded in hitting ninety-five percent, and the noise ceased.

"Just mute the bloody thing or it'll go off all night," she told Sanne.

Sanne propped her feet on a second chair. "Not if I keep poking you."

"Sadist." Meg yawned, wincing as the stitches in her cheek pulled. "You don't have to stay, San."

"I know, but I think I might all the same."

Outside the cubicle, someone shouted for help, and a baby began to wail. The A&E waiting room had been packed with people who appeared neither very ill nor injured, and the triage nurse had prioritised Meg, taking her straight through to Majors.

"Same shit, different city," Meg muttered, before heading off on another tangent. "God, what am I going to tell Em?"

"The truth?" Sanne glanced at her mobile. Emily had replied to her earlier text but not yet phoned. "Your colleagues might believe that you slipped on the ice, but Emily's going to see your back at some point, and even an idiot would smell a rat with that pattern of injuries."

Meg picked at the tape on her IV for a few seconds. "Is it too late to call her?"

"No, it's only just midnight, and I doubt she'll be asleep, anyway."

The alarm set off beeping again, and Meg took a breath without prompting, but she must have overdone it because the pain knocked her back into her pillow and left her as white as the bedding.

Sanne unclawed Meg's fingers from the sheets, encircling them loosely until Meg was able to look up again. "Do you want me to phone her?" she asked.

Meg nodded. "I know I need to speak to her, but I can't think properly." A certain amount of frustration coloured her words, but she seemed too exhausted to be embarrassed.

Sanne tapped the screen on her mobile and found its signal wavering at one bar. "Crap. I think I'll have to go outside. Will you behave yourself for five minutes and keep that monitor happy?"

"Yep. No more alarms, I promise."

"I won't be long." Sanne moved the emergency buzzer and a glass of water within easy reach. She knew she was fussing, but she couldn't help herself.

"Five minutes, San," Meg reminded her. "The sky will not fall."

"I know." Sanne hesitated by the end of the bed. "Do you want the lights off?"

"Please."

She flipped the switch to leave Meg in the glow of the monitor.

"Tell Em not to worry," Meg said, as Sanne opened the cubicle door.

Sanne had no reply to that. If Emily was so concerned, she thought, why hadn't she bothered to phone?

❖

Manchester Central's ambulance bay was strewn with the detritus of a bleak January night. Students freshly returned to university clustered in groups around intoxicated friends with minor wounds, their shabby-chic designer outfits a contrast to the authentic shabbiness of the city's less affluent residents. Drunks and addicts dragged IV stands behind them as they smoked in coveted sheltered spots, or threw up or coughed up or did both simultaneously. Ambulances manoeuvred around the bay with their reversal warnings blaring, and people continued to stagger behind them, oblivious to the danger.

Circumnavigating a man sitting in a puddle and drinking vodka, Sanne headed for the hospital's main entrance, where the smell of curry from the takeaways around the corner overpowered that of cigarettes. Her phone buzzed as the improved reception delivered multiple texts from Nelson. She had messaged him before leaving Meg's, and his replies had obviously backed up.

Hot on the heels of a kneejerk: *Bloody hell, hope she's okay. Shout if you need me*, was a rather more measured: *Don't fret about the briefing, nothing new to report. Full departmental scheduled for 6:30 a.m. See you there?*

She replied in the affirmative, even though he was probably in bed by now, and then found Emily's number. Nerves skittered through her belly, but she reminded herself that she was doing this for Meg and took the plunge. Emily answered within the first few rings, an accompanying tinkle of crystal and laughter quickly silenced by the closing of a door.

"Sanne? Where's Meg? What the hell is going on?"

It was difficult to tell whether she was afraid or indignant, and Sanne, suspecting a combination of the two, decided to come straight to the point. "She's in the A&E at Manchester Central. We got here about three hours ago."

"Jesus." All the fight left Emily's tone, while the scrape of furniture and a soft thud suggested she had abruptly sat down. "What happened? Did she have an accident?"

"No. The same man who broke into her house attacked her this morning." Sanne relayed the information she had mentally rehearsed, sticking to the facts but omitting the finer points. Meg could fill in the gaps later. "She has a couple of broken ribs, eight stitches in her cheek, and a concussion. They're admitting her overnight for observation."

"Oh my God, who was he? Why would he do that?" Emily paused as another detail hit home. "You said it happened this morning?"

"Yes. She'd been trying to reach the phone all day." Sanne raised her head, watching a cloud swallow the brightness of the moon, and ignoring the muffled sob at the end of the line. She found it hard to sympathise with Emily's distress. Meg would have been found hours earlier, had Emily not assumed the worst of her.

"I didn't know," Emily said. "How could I have known that?"

"You couldn't have." Sanne scuffed her heel against the wall, cross with herself for capitulating, but suspecting she had made her point nevertheless. "It's no one's fault, Emily."

Emily snuffled and then blew her nose. "Did you tell Meg what I said about her coming here?"

"No." The question rankled. Sanne had had better things to do in the last few hours than try to cause trouble. She checked her watch. "Look, I've got to get back to her. Are you driving over?"

"I can't. I've had a drink." Emily let the confession hang for a moment as if in penance. "Will you tell her I'll see her first thing in the morning?"

Surprise blunted Sanne's answer. "Yep, will do."

"Give her my love."

Sanne made a perfunctory farewell, hung up, and dialled another number.

"Hiya," she said as the call connected. "Sorry it's so late, Mum, but I need a really big favour."

❖

The light from a well-aimed pen torch almost blinded Meg. It wasn't the first time it had happened, and she decided to cooperate in an effort to hurry the process along.

"It's Tuesday. My friend here is Detective Sanne Jensen, who should be at home in bed, and that idiot Cameron is still running the country." It was only when she surveyed her surroundings that her bravado wavered. "Huh. Did I get moved?"

Curtains had been drawn around her bed, and she could no longer hear the ubiquitous white noise of the A&E, only the fizz of a nebuliser and the soft snore of a nearby patient.

"You're on the A&E ward." The nurse slid her torch back into the pocket of her tunic. "Behave yourself and I'll get you both a cup of tea."

Meg waited for her footsteps to fade before squeezing Sanne's hand.

"Hey."

Sanne returned the gentle pressure. "Hey yourself. How are you feeling?"

"Not too bad. Have you managed any sleep?"

"Probably more than you." Sanne indicated her reclining chair and the blankets covering it. "I've slept on worse." She had an ability to nod off no matter the circumstances, a talent that Meg had always envied.

"What time is it?" Meg asked. A second chair sat by her bed, but there was no indication that anyone had used it.

"Just gone three." Sanne must have followed Meg's train of thought, because she suddenly seemed to find something interesting on the overbed table. "She said she'll be here first thing, that she couldn't drive because she'd had a drink."

"Oh. Right." Meg chewed on that one for a while, unsure why she was so disappointed. Harrogate was miles away, and it was unreasonable to have expected Emily to drop everything and rush to her side in the middle of the night. But still… "I suppose a taxi was out of the question. I mean, it would've cost a small fortune."

"About ninety, ninety-five quid," Sanne answered absently, and then blushed.

Meg laughed, a proper belly laugh that made her feel brighter despite the throbbing in her face. "Sanne Jensen, you've been Googling!"

"No! I just—" Sanne rubbed her cheeks as if trying to account for the heat there. "Okay, yes, I Googled. It's ninety bloody quid, though, and times are hard. You can get a lot for that these days."

"Twenty chippy teas," Meg said after a quick calculation on her fingers.

Sanne deliberated. "Slap-up meal for four at the Red Lion, now it's gone all gastro-pub."

"Loads of chocolate, and I mean really nice chocolate." Meg grinned. "You notice how food is always at the forefront?"

"Decent running shoes," Sanne said. "Books, books, and a few more books."

"Emily likes designer perfume and clothes." Meg tried to sound nonchalant, but the truth was that Emily had money to burn even on a junior doctor's salary—her parents saw to that—and she'd think nothing of spending twice the amount they were discussing on treating herself.

"I think you're worth ninety-five quid," Sanne said quietly. "Y'know, if it was me needing to get here, I'd pay it." She straightened Meg's blanket and then sat down and rearranged her own. She didn't speak for a few minutes, and Meg was wondering whether she'd fallen asleep, when her voice drifted up again. "Hell, Meg, I'd even tip the driver."

CHAPTER SEVENTEEN

Sanne was accustomed to functioning on minimal sleep, but things still felt off-kilter when she walked into HQ at 6:00 a.m., her hair wet from the hospital shower, her clothes a mixture of her own spares and those pilfered from Meg. Although she returned the smile of the officer on the front desk, she didn't hear what he said to her, and the ping of the arriving lift startled her so badly that she took a step back and then pressed the button for the wrong floor.

"Bollocks," she muttered.

Grateful to have the lift to herself, she glanced at its mirrored wall and flattened a wayward tuft of hair, wincing at the darkened skin beneath her eyes. Her less than auspicious start to the morning got even worse when the doors opened and she stumbled out in front of Eleanor.

"Sanne. Just the person I wanted to see."

And that was that. No time to prepare, no chance for a nerve-settling confab with Nelson. She could do nothing but follow Eleanor into her office and shut the door at her request.

"You look like death warmed over." Unusually for Eleanor, she stayed in front of her desk. Leaning her backside against it and folding her arms, she eyeballed Sanne. "You missed the briefing last night."

"Yes, ma'am, I'm sorry. I—" Sanne took a breath, poised to launch into an explanation, but Eleanor cut in.

"How is Dr. Fielding?"

Sanne's mouth dropped open, her brain too scrambled to work out how Eleanor might have learned what had happened. The grapevine was fast, but it wasn't that fast, and she was sure Nelson wouldn't have said anything.

"You were the reporting officer," Eleanor reminded her. "As such, the file, while strictly within the remit of Domestic Violence, was also sent to me. I've just read your statement."

"Oh, of course." Sanne felt like banging her head on the wall, if only to knock some sense in. "Sorry, boss. Meg's all right. Well, she's sore and grumpy and probably not telling me the half of it, but the doc said she was lucky, relatively speaking."

"Yes, I saw the photographs. Is she being interviewed today?"

Sanne nodded. "When Detective Fraser came to see her last night, he decided that she wasn't coherent enough to make a statement. She identified Luke—her brother—as her assailant, though, so DV have somewhere to start."

Eleanor leaned across to retrieve a Post-it from her desk. "I've spoken to Fraser this morning," she said. "Fortunately, he's also an early riser, and he's going to keep me in the loop. He thinks Dr. Fielding's car might be their best bet, and he plans to contact all the local dealers and auction houses first thing."

"Thank you, ma'am." Tired and vulnerable enough for Eleanor's concern to make her feel weepy, Sanne tried for a stoical approach, which didn't fool Eleanor in the slightest.

"Are you fit to work today, Sanne?"

"I'll be fine. I slept at the hospital."

"Excellent." Eleanor nodded at the clock on the wall. "You've got twenty minutes or so. I would suggest a strong brew and some breakfast."

"That does sound good."

Sanne had turned to leave, her hand on the door, when Eleanor spoke again.

"Detective Fraser was impressed, given the circumstances. He said the scene was well-preserved and your photographs were comprehensive. That can't have been easy."

"No, it wasn't." A tremor ran through Sanne's fingers, and she lowered her arm out of sight. "Everything was such a mess."

"I can imagine," Eleanor said quietly. She went to sit behind her desk. "I'll see you at half past. Go and get that brew."

❖

Meg could hear herself gulping for air even as she began to wake from her nightmare. The unguarded movement sent pain lancing through her back, and a monitor's alarm drowned out the strange clack-clack sound that had infiltrated her dreams.

"Shh, Meg. You're in the hospital. You're safe."

Meg struggled to place the voice, but the soothing touch that went with it, one finger circling her palm over and over, was oddly familiar. She silenced the monitor with a couple of expansive breaths and opened her eyes.

"I thought it was you." Her smile was broad enough to tug on her sutures. "What on earth are you doing here?"

Teresa Jensen set her knitting aside and stood to kiss Meg's forehead. Beyond the curtains, the lights were still dimmed, but the ward was beginning to stir. "Sanne had to go to work early, and she didn't want you to be on your own. She asked if I'd take second watch until your Emily gets here."

"She didn't need to do that." Meg caught Teresa's hand and held it tightly. "Thank you for giving in to her madness, though."

Teresa chuckled, deepening the wrinkles on her face. "I jumped at the chance. It's been months since I've clapped eyes on you, Megan Fielding." She poured Meg a fresh glass of water. "How are you feeling?"

"Not too bad." Meg touched her cheek self-consciously. "How does it look?"

"Honestly?" Teresa shook her head. "It looks terrible, love. I'd tan your brother's hide if I got my hands on him. He always was a bloody thug, that one."

"I know," Meg said. Teresa had put witch hazel on enough of Meg's bruises to speak from experience.

"Not that our John was a prince or anything," Teresa continued. "He wouldn't think twice about belting us. But he can barely lift his pint pot now, and there was always something just plain nasty about Luke."

"I don't think he'll be getting a Christmas card." Meg tried for levity, but she was tired and hurting everywhere, and she couldn't remember when her own mum had last been able to comfort her. When Teresa sat on the bed and held out her arms, Meg tucked herself into them.

"You and Sanne, always such little soldiers," Teresa murmured into Meg's hair. "She scared the life out of me last year, and here you are doing the same all over again. I have enough grey hairs already." She guided Meg back to the pillow and mopped up a stray tear with a tissue. "There. Better now?"

Meg nodded, and Teresa, seeming to know exactly the right thing to do, retook her seat and her knitting. Meg watched her fingers begin to work, the needles knocking together to produce the clacking sound that Meg had heard in her sleep. It brought back memories of wet Sunday afternoons at Sanne's house, crowded around the gas fire while her dad was at the pub: Teresa in one chair, a pile of wool gradually being transformed into a sweater or a cardigan for whichever of her children needed it the most, and the scent of a roast dinner making everyone's mouth water.

"It's for Keeley's newest," Teresa said, raising the knitting so that Meg could see the bonnet taking shape. "She's sure it's a girl, but I went for yellow just in case. Boy or girl, it'll be a winter babe, so it'll need a few hats."

"Sanne told me Keeley was pregnant. Not long to go, is there?"

"About six weeks. She's usually early, though. She's had so many now that a good sharp sneeze might be enough to birth this one."

The idea set Meg off laughing, and she ended up curling on her side to ease the pressure on her back.

"I don't know where I went wrong with her. She's not got a lick of sense," Teresa said. Her hands moved quickly as she spoke, the ball of wool disappearing before Meg's eyes with hypnotic inevitability. "Kiera's a bright little thing, though. I'm hoping she takes after her aunt, not her mum. Sanne's the only one of my three who ever had any gumption."

"Sanne has gumption in spades," Meg said. The fondness in her voice brought the needles to a standstill, and Teresa lowered the bonnet into her lap.

"I'm glad you two are back in touch. Sanne wouldn't say anything to me, but I could see she missed you."

"I missed her too." The admission cost Meg nothing. It was the simple truth, and it felt good to speak it aloud.

"Yes. Well." Teresa busied herself with her knitting again, clearly reluctant to interfere. She moved onto a safer subject instead. "How's your mum? It's been a while since I've had the chance to visit her."

"She's much the same. She seems to like the home, and they're really—"

The curtain pulled back without warning, and Emily stepped into the gap, her arms full of flowers. Meg saw horror flicker across her face as she saw the extent of the injuries, but then she noticed Teresa, and confusion made her hesitate on the threshold.

Meg beckoned her forward. "Em, this is Sanne's mum, Teresa."

"Oh, hello." Juggling the bouquet awkwardly, Emily shook Teresa's hand.

"Lovely to meet you. Those are beautiful flowers," Teresa said, already starting to collect her belongings. She stooped to kiss Meg's cheek. "Don't be a stranger, you promise me?"

"I promise." Meg held onto Teresa's hand, running her thumb over the calloused skin, unwilling to let her leave. "Wait. How are you getting home?"

"Taxi," Teresa said, a shake of her head cutting off Meg's anticipated offer. "Sanne gave me plenty of money. She said it was 'cheap at half the price.' I've no idea what she meant by that, but she seemed to think you might."

Meg smiled, paying no heed to Emily's miffed expression. "I know exactly what she meant. Thank you for being my second watch."

"Any time, love." Teresa gently extricated her hand and picked up her bag. "I'll see you soon." She wagged a stern finger at Meg.

"Aye, see you soon."

Emily took her time setting down the flowers, waiting until she was sure Teresa had gone before she crossed the tiny bay to give Meg a kiss. She cupped Meg's chin in both hands.

"I'm so sorry. I got here as soon as I could." Her hands were cold against Meg's swollen face, and her gaze fell away as she spoke. "God, you poor thing. What on earth happened? Sanne didn't tell me much."

Too weak to provoke an argument, Meg adopted Emily's tactic of evasion. "A man attacked me and stole my car. The police are looking for him."

"Do they know who he is?"

"Yes. They're coming back for a statement this afternoon. San gave them your address, if that's okay?"

That perked Emily right up. She smiled broadly, her voice slightly too loud as she answered. "Of course that's okay. You're not going anywhere near your house until the police have arrested this idiot. I spoke to the nurse on the way in. She thinks you'll be discharged after the morning rounds and will just need someone to stay with you for a day or two."

Meg nodded, although the thought of going back to Emily's flat was a miserable one. She didn't want to be mollycoddled by a girlfriend with a guilty conscience, who would eventually realise—if she hadn't already—that Meg knew far more than she was saying.

Emily moved to the closest chair, the one not swaddled in blankets, and eyed the plates and cups on the overbed table. "Was Sanne here all night?"

"Yes. Her mum swapped in when she left." Meg massaged her temple. The constant sense of walking on eggshells was turning her headache into a migraine. Waves of homesickness assailed her, a longing not for her own home but for Sanne and Teresa and everything familiar that came with them. She felt like she had when she was eight years old, sore from an appendectomy and utterly bewildered by her first stay in hospital.

"You can go back to sleep if you want to," Emily said, her fingers brushing through Meg's hair. "We can talk about everything properly when we get home."

The latter prospect wasn't at all restful, but Meg took advantage of Emily's suggestion anyway and closed her eyes.

❖

Sanne slotted the receipt for Steven Rudd's weekly shop into a date-ordered pile of similar receipts, all from the same local supermarket and none totalling more than fifteen pounds. He bought his alcohol from the precinct, a walk rather than a bus ride away, and most weeks he spent far more on that than on food. She had been fishing through the minutiae of his life all morning: his overdue bills, his shopping lists scrawled in a shaky hand, the hard-core pornography secreted away between the pages of a television guide, his appointments at Drug Alcohol Services, and the unsent letters to his children. With half a bag still to go through, she was rapidly running out of space on her desk.

"Right, you. Time to take a break." Nelson dropped a grease-proofed parcel in front of her.

"Crikey, I didn't know it was that late." Determined not to lose her focus after the briefing, she had thrown herself into her task, and although she'd kept an eye on her mobile, she had only sent one text. Meg's reply had confirmed her release from the hospital and that she was on her way to Emily's, and she had signed off with: *Thank you for your mum.*

"It's only half eleven, but I factored in our early start." Nelson gestured at her desk. "Find anything exciting?"

Sanne shook her head, her mouth stuffed with prawn mayo and salad. She made a noise that he correctly translated as "How about you?"

"I spent an hour at the Mission, where the staff couldn't remember Rudd having any particular friends or even acquaintances," he said. "He went in for a meal every now and again, perhaps more so in the past couple of months when his debts started to mount. I did find a member of the kitchen staff who seemed to have a slight crush on him, though. She told me that, like most of Malory's hardened drinkers, his local's the Dog and Duck, but the landlord there hasn't seen him for about six weeks."

Sanne swallowed, wiping a smear of mayo off her chin. "That'd fit with his home alcohol consumption. Judging by his receipts, it's increased quite a bit since mid-December."

"He might be buying for two, if he's hooked up with someone. Like tends to call to like."

"Not always."

His dark skin flushed darker. "No, sorry. Not always." He chewed the last of his sandwich and licked his fingers. "Have you heard from Meg?"

"Aye, she's out of hospital and Emily's taking her home, but that was a few hours ago."

"And how many times have you checked the FWIN?"

"I'm sure I don't know what you're talking about." Sanne didn't even try to sound convincing. "Okay, twice," she admitted. "No word from any of the car dealerships. No updates or developments."

"They'll find him. He doesn't stand a chance after what he's done."

It was probably true, but nothing was happening quickly enough for Sanne. She screwed up her sandwich wrapper. "I better get back to the grind. Are you in or out this afternoon?"

"In. It's bloody cold out there. I think I'm reviewing the CCTV from Rudd's precinct. Actually, I should check that with the Ginger Whinger."

Sanne laughed. "That's hair-ist."

"I'm not hair-ist! I'll have you know that some of my very best friends are redheads."

"Just not the sarge."

"Exactly."

He walked off like a man on his way to execution, his shoulders low and his tread heavy, leaving her to delve back into her last bag of Rudd's amassed paperwork. Whatever else Rudd might be, he wasn't a keen recycler.

"Here, San. You look like you need this more than I do."

She glanced up from a handful of Mission Cross advice leaflets to find Fred proffering a slice of cake. Word about Meg had obviously got around, because George and Scotty had been plying her with brews all morning.

"Martha made it, so it's guaranteed to be delicious," he said.

She shook her head, touched by his generosity. When he was between wives, cake was the love of Fred's life. "Oh, Fred, I couldn't do that to you. I've just had my lunch, and I'm fine, really."

He pulled a chair over and sat down. "How about we share?"

She accepted half the slice, munching it as Fred rummaged among the leaflets she had been sorting.

"Self-help sort of bloke, is he?" He held up a leaflet on smoking cessation, peering at it closely in lieu of putting his glasses on.

"Huh," Sanne murmured. "Fred, can I see that one?" The leaflet had black type on a red background, difficult to read, but a name and number written on the back had caught her attention. "Bloody hellfire." She double-clicked the case file on her desktop and scrolled through until she found the main contacts list. Fred leaned over to see what she was doing, scattering crumbs as he moved.

"Bingo," she said, tapping a fingernail on the name at the top of the list.

"Natalie Acre? The ex-bird of the first vic? What about her?"

She flipped the leaflet around so he could see the name *NAT* written in thin ballpoint, and watched him compare the mobile number with the one on the screen.

"Well, bugger me," he said.

"Precisely. She has a definite link to one victim and a potential link to our main suspect. We'll need to—"

"San!"

Her head shot up at Nelson's excited yell. He was waving at her from the opposite side of the office, where a small group of detectives was gathered around Carlyle's desk. Eleanor already had her coat on, and Carlyle was reaching for his. Sanne and Fred hurried over to join them.

“They’ve found the van,” Nelson whispered, as Eleanor raised a hand for quiet.

“Okay, rendezvous point is the corner of Alain Road and Bedivere Mount,” Eleanor said. “The van was dumped on the wasteland that borders the canal and stretches right out to the start of the bypass, and there’s no sign of Rudd. It’s a hell of an area to search, and we don’t have much daylight left, so wrap up warm, vests on, and use blues en route, please.”

The group dispersed in haste, most heading to the locker room. It was only when Sanne got back to her desk that she realised the leaflet was still in her hand. She shoved it into her pocket and grabbed her coat.

CHAPTER EIGHTEEN

Brittle flakes blew into Sanne's eyes as she checked Nelson's position and took a couple of strides closer to him. With the light failing and snow beginning to fall in earnest, the team was working to a buddy system, keeping each other within sight and earshot while listening out for updates from command. The expanse of wasteland was covered in brambles, nettles, and unexpected ditches, and Sanne could hear cursing at intervals as people stumbled and tripped over unseen obstacles. New homes had once been planned for the site, but the money had eventually gone elsewhere, and Malory's kids and addicts now had free rein over the area.

No attempt had been made to hide Rudd's van. It had merely been driven until a rut claimed a front tyre, and then it had been abandoned. Although the weather and a convenient bramble thicket concealed it from passing traffic, officers assigned to a local search had soon spotted it.

A prickly strand of bramble attached itself to Sanne's trousers and wrapped around her boot. She stopped and used her stick to unravel the stem, casting it aside and then stamping on a remaining tendril. Her legs felt leaden, her toes numb in her boots, and she'd lost her grip on her stick countless times. Now that the adrenaline of the drive and the initial fear of ambush had faded, her lack of sleep at Meg's bedside was starting to tell on her. Promises of a long bath and a warm bed were just about keeping her on her feet, but it was her unspoken responsibility for the safety of Nelson to her left and Scotty to her right that was forcing her to stay alert. She tapped her stick on a rusted beer can, pushing it aside to check the ground beneath it. Hearing the metallic clink, Nelson looked across, but she shook her head at him and moved on. No smoking gun uncovered, just decades' worth of litter that would never biodegrade.

The wind almost swallowed the sudden vibration of her mobile. She pulled off her glove with her teeth and took the phone from her pocket. Hopes that it might be Meg faded as Zoe's name appeared.

"Shit." She watched the phone buzz, the noise like a wasp on a windowpane, and then steeled herself and accepted the call. "Hey, Zoe."

"Hallo!" Zoe—obviously not knee-deep in nettles in the middle of a blizzard—sounded full of beans. "Did you have any plans for the evening?"

Sanne lifted her hat from her ear, sure she must have misheard. "Did I what? I'm sorry. What did you say?"

Zoe laughed. "Tonight, this evening, are you busy?"

"I'm in the middle of a case, Zoe. Of course I'm busy."

"Ah, right." Zoe's playful tone became serious. "It's just that I have something on your friend's brother, and I was wondering if you could meet for a quick drink to discuss it."

Sanne rested her forehead on her stick and counted to ten. She didn't want to go. She knew she would, of course, but she really didn't want to. If she were being honest, she was mystified as to what Zoe saw in her. Everything about them seemed worlds apart, and the most plausible theory might be that Zoe simply liked a challenge.

"Can you not tell me over the phone?" she asked.

"No, it's something I need to show you."

Ten yards ahead of Sanne, Nelson hesitated and turned back. She waved at him, letting him know she was all right. "Okay, I can probably be with you by eight," she said, when Nelson had walked on. "I'll text you if anything changes."

"Great. Do you know the Bay Horse on Suffolk Street?"

"Yep, I know it. I'll see you there." Sanne ended the call and tugged her hat back down as Nelson jogged over.

"Everything okay?"

"Just fabulous," she said. "I have a date with the Valkyrie tonight at eight."

He whistled and bumped his stick against hers. "How did she manage to wangle that?"

"She dangled a carrot in the form of Luke Fielding."

"Ah." Nelson winced in sympathy. "So basically she has you over a barrel."

"Yeah, that's about the size of it. I just wanted to go home and have a bath, Nelson."

He slung a comforting arm around her shoulders, and she leaned into him. "Grin and bear it, San. Guzzle a lemonade, listen to what she has to say, and you'll be home by ten."

"God, I hope so. If it helps Meg, it'll be worth it."

"That's the spirit." He released her and turned her in the right direction. "Come on. If we get as far as that patch of crap over there, I have a KitKat with your name on it."

❖

Detective Fraser had a habit of licking his pen nib, and a tongue speckled with black ink. Sitting on Emily's couch with a long-finished mug of coffee, he patiently talked Meg through the events of the previous day and transcribed her answers into statement form.

"I'm not sure what time Sanne found me," she said, trying again to find a position that didn't make her want to cry, and settling for one that was tolerable. "It'd been dark for a while, but I'd lost track. It was late, I think."

"And Detective Jensen—Sanne—she has her own key for your house?"

"Yes, she's had one for years. She usually knocks if I'm there, though. She hates just letting herself in."

That detail made Fraser smile. He was older than Meg's dad, with grey, thinning hair, and eyes that missed nothing. "Lucky for you she broke her own rule."

Meg nodded. “I was very glad to see her.” She glanced around as Emily ducked her head into the room.

“We’re almost finished,” Fraser told Emily. She had taken herself off to the shops as soon as he’d arrived, and a rustle of bags suggested she’d had a fruitful outing. He waited for her to close the door again. “Sanne’s statement details everything I need from that point onward. Are you happy for me to incorporate that into yours?”

“Yes, that’s fine.” Meg could feel sweat gathering at her hairline. She stared out the window as Fraser resumed writing. It was snowing again, a small drift collecting on the balcony and the skyline disappearing amid streaks of white. All at once, the room felt too hot and too small, and she pushed at the blanket covering her knees.

“Meg?”

Fraser’s voice made her jump, although he hadn’t raised it.

“Can I just…?” She pointed to the patio doors, and he understood at once, giving her an arm to lean on and walking with her across the floor. As she stepped outside in her slippered feet, raising her heated face to the snow, the breath she took seemed to loosen her lungs.

Fraser stayed beside her, his hand wrapping around the balcony’s railing a safe distance from hers. “I know you’re a doctor and that you’ll probably have access to all of this anyway,” he said, “but if you need someone to speak to, I can give you the relevant contact numbers.”

“Thank you. I appreciate the offer, but I’ll manage.” She listened to the patter of snow hitting the concrete and tried to imagine talking to a complete stranger about what had happened, when she couldn’t even bring herself to tell Emily.

Two inches of snow in less than an hour had transformed the derelict patch of land into a pleasant field of gentle slopes and glittering foliage. The clouds cleared as dusk gave way to true night, a large low moon providing better visibility than the daylight. The weather would play havoc with Sanne's journey home, but she still couldn't resist the lure of a good snowfall: the scrunch of it beneath her boots, the giddy glee of something so different from the usual murk and drizzle of a northern English winter. The hills would be at their most spectacular, and the city streets, even on estates like Halshaw and Malory, would look clean for once. Halfway to the middle of nowhere, her breath puffing out in mint-scented clouds from the humbug warming her throat, she was sorry to hear the call from command ordering everyone back to the rendezvous point. Nothing useful had been found in the hours they had spent out there, but the repetitive forward-prod-uncover-recover routine had worked to take her mind off everything but her colleagues' well-being and the placement of her own feet.

Turning back made her stumble, her legs too accustomed to a slow onward plod. She dug her stick deep for balance and waited for Nelson to join her.

"I have officially out-frozen the capabilities of my long johns," he announced with all the gravitas of a BBC news reporter. A layer of snow had stuck to his wiry curls, giving him an impromptu cap. "You look cosy. What's your secret?"

Sanne took his arm and set off toward the closest pavement. "Layers, mate. Lots and lots of layers. Also, you need a hat that's not made out of ice."

He batted at his hair, but more snow quickly began to fill the gap he made. "Reckon Carlyle will share his brolly with me?" he asked as they neared the shivering group of searchers reconvened by the roadside.

"I doubt it," Sanne said, releasing his arm once she felt the firmness of concrete beneath the snow. "The sarge has never struck me as the sharing type."

Carlyle wasn't even sharing his umbrella with Eleanor, who stood nearby, gauging how many of the team were yet to arrive. Seemingly satisfied, she lowered her hood.

"I'm going to keep this brief," she said. "I know you're all cold and knackered, and it's getting late. So in a nutshell, go home, and be back at HQ tomorrow at six for assignments. Most of you will either be out here again or farther along the canal to continue searching the buildings and warehouses we're in the process of obtaining warrants for. The forecast is for more of the same, so don't turn up dressed for the office. And thank you for your efforts today."

The group broke apart with a flurry of hails and shouts, arranging transport home or to cars left at HQ. Sanne checked her watch: twenty past seven. Given the state of the roads, she would have to go straight into the city if she wanted to meet Zoe.

"Keep the pool car," Nelson said quietly. "I can get a lift back to HQ with Scotty."

"Would you mind?" Sanne peered around to see who might be listening. Protocol dictated that the car be returned at the end of a shift. "I think I'll miss her otherwise."

"Of course not." He brushed a snowflake off her nose and held out the keys. "Good luck."

"Thanks. I have a horrible feeling that I'm going to need it."

He hurried off to catch Scotty, leaving her to scrape the snow from the car and then sit hugging herself as the windows defrosted. The cold draught from the heater made her nose run, so she delved into her pocket for a tissue, pulling out the Mission Cross leaflet along with it. Still unable to see a thing through the windscreen, she made a snap decision and dialled the number on the back of the leaflet. Her pulse galloped as she waited for the call to connect. She didn't have a clue what she was going to say, and it was almost a relief when she heard the automated message: "This number has not been recognised." She lowered the phone and double-checked what she'd dialled, but the number was right, and she knew it matched the one listed for Natalie in the case contacts. She half-considered phoning Eleanor, but was loath to until she'd dug a little deeper, something she would do as soon as she got into the office the next morning.

Spurred on by her plan, she wiped the last of the mist from the windows and pulled out onto the road. She reached Sheffield's city centre with two minutes to spare and threw a handful of change into the first available parking meter. Leaving the ignition running, she adjusted the rearview mirror and gave her hair a quick once-over.

Her hat hadn't done her any favours. What it hadn't flattened, it had pushed into wild tufts, while windburn had chapped her lips and left her face scarlet.

"Oh, fuck it." She switched off the ignition and plunged the car into darkness.

Suffolk Street was lively with happy hour-seeking office workers, no doubt making the snow their excuse for staying out late and going home drunk. A pair of women, tottering along in high heels and dresses that barely covered their arses, shrieked as they clutched at each other for support and begged Sanne to lend them her boots. One of them blew her a kiss when she declined, but she was doing them a favour really. After a day in the field, her boots were so disgusting that the smell of them alone would probably suffice to keep Zoe at a safe distance.

The doorman at the Bay Horse looked at her askance, as if permitting entry to such a downtrodden ruffian would be bad for business. He stepped aside just as she was about to pull her ID on him, his grudging "Good evening" aimed at the floor.

"Thank you. Good evening," she said with perfect diction, her head held high. She was used to people making snap judgements about her, and it always amused her to confound their expectations.

The Bay Horse had the façade of a traditional pub and the interior of an upmarket wine bar, its open-plan design forcing most of its customers to gather around floor-to-ceiling concrete pillars while gazing enviously at the lucky few who had managed to secure a booth. The lighting was minimal and tinged with red, giving it the ambience of an over-populated bordello. As Sanne walked past a speaker, she could feel the deafening bass beating against her sternum.

Starting at the near end, she scanned each face in turn, the dingy lighting forcing her to venture farther into the crowd. Everyone seemed to be taller than her, their cheeks pink with alcohol and the strain of shouted conversations. She was on the verge of turning tail and making a run for it when she heard Zoe's voice. Zoe was sitting in one of the smaller booths, an intimate curve of leather seating around a circular table. Three pint glasses and a shot glass already sat empty in front of her, and she swayed slightly as she stood to greet Sanne. The kiss-blowing girls on the street would probably have rejected her blue satin dress on the grounds of indecency.

"Hi!" She left the booth to kiss Sanne's cheek, a warm waft of beer on her breath. "What can I get you?"

"Something soft, please. Apple juice?"

Zoe passed no comment, her broad shoulders merely rising in an elegant shrug as she headed for the bar. Sanne wriggled into the booth, edging away from Zoe's spot and taking off her coat before anyone could stage a coup. Although her instincts were screaming at her to find out what Zoe knew and then scarper, she didn't want to appear rude. If Zoe had discovered something useful about Luke, then the least Sanne could do was take the time to have a drink with her.

"Here you go." The booth wasn't designed for a graceful entrance, but Zoe somehow managed one, handing Sanne a tall glass of sparkling apple complete with straw and cocktail umbrella.

"Sorry, I should've got these." Sanne patted her coat, searching for her wallet.

Zoe waved the offer down and clinked her glass against Sanne's. "My pleasure. It's really good to see you."

As if given permission, Sanne sucked up a quarter of her juice, but her mouth was dry again the second she released the straw. "I didn't mean to leave you waiting. I got stuck at work, and the main roads were worse than I'd expected."

"Oh, don't worry. I had the day off, so I came in to the shops." Zoe indicated a heap of bags stashed beneath the table. "I usually head here to unwind when I've finished. The chap on the door is a good mate of mine."

"I nearly didn't get past him. I don't think I'm compliant with the dress code." Sanne's heart sank as she looked again at the bags by her feet. There was little likelihood of Zoe having obtained any information while busy on a shopping spree. Sanne swirled the straw in her glass, trying not to betray herself by stabbing it into the ice cubes. "Zoe?" she said.

Even with the music pounding, Zoe must have heard the warning note in Sanne's voice, because her lips curled into a rueful pout. "Okay, it's a fair cop. You got me," she said. "I wanted to see you, and I couldn't think of any other way."

Sanne pushed her glass aside. "You lied about Luke just to bring me here?"

"It worked, didn't it?" Zoe grinned, her teeth a flash of brilliance in the crimson gloom. She leaned across and brushed her fingers down Sanne's cheek. "Come on. I didn't mean any harm by it. I'd be flattered if I were you."

Sanne flinched away, more annoyed at herself than anything. She really should have seen this coming. "I don't have time for this, Zoe. I've got so much to do, with the case and everything. I have to go." She had gathered her coat and inched to the end of the seat when Zoe caught her arm.

"You can't even finish your drink?"

Sanne shook her off. "No, I'm sorry. I wouldn't have come if I'd known." She managed to get out of the booth and headed for the exit. The racket from the bar left her ears ringing, and she didn't realise anyone was behind her until she turned onto the side street where she'd left her car.

"Sanne!"

She kept walking, but Zoe overtook her and blocked her path.

"What the hell is wrong with you?" Zoe used her height to full advantage, forcing Sanne onto her back foot. "Why are you being so fucking uptight?"

Sanne raised her head to meet Zoe's furious gaze. "Maybe because I spent last night in the hospital with Meg." She was too disheartened to be angry, and her measured tone was in direct contrast to Zoe's indignation. "Her brother beat the shit out of her, broke her ribs, split open her face. I want the bastard off the streets where he can't hurt her again, and I thought you might be able to help me with that."

"Jesus Christ." Zoe threw up her hands. "How the fuck was I supposed to know?"

"You weren't. You just have really shitty timing." Sanne tried to smile, opting for placation over provocation. "I didn't intend for this to be a date, Zoe."

The look Zoe gave her would have curdled milk. "I guess it's true what they all say about you, that you're a fucking frigid bitch."

"I'm going to assume that's the drink talking." Sanne wasn't about to start slinging insults on the street, no matter how much Zoe might be spoiling for a fight. She walked past Zoe, giving her a wide berth and slapping away her grasping hand. She refused to run, but Zoe must have thought better of following, and within seconds, the only thing Sanne could hear was her own shuddering breaths. When she reached the car, she unlocked it and then chanced a look behind her. The entire street was deserted, the scene that had played out there already seeming like a surreal dream.

More snow started to fall as she got into the car, but she was so jittery that she didn't even think about going home. Instead, she pulled out of the bay and turned in the direction of HQ.

Chapter Nineteen

The EDSOP office was empty, even Eleanor having apparently taken her own advice and gone home for the night. The overhead lights flickered on with an irritated burr as Sanne disturbed their sensor. Intimidated, she tiptoed to her desk, where she shoved a bag of hastily bought essentials into her drawer and turned on her computer. It took its time loading up, giving her the opportunity to check her phone for texts: *All Fine. Detective Fraser took my statement, and I look like I've been smacked with a brick. Love Meg.* And one from Nelson, too: *If you need me to fake an emergency for you, just let me know.*

Deciding that the whole sordid story with Zoe was too complicated to tell Nelson in a text message, she sent a brief reply to Meg and stashed her phone away. With a fresh pad of paper in front of her, she opened the case file and began to scroll through it. There was nothing new in the forensics or interview files, and none of the day's CCTV analysis had noted anything of significance. Unsure what she was looking for, she clicked into the media folder and scrolled through scanned copies of the photographs she had found in Andrew Culver's kitchen drawer. She paused at the Mission allotment photo. On the back row of the shot, Andrew Culver stood with his arm around Natalie Acre, while Marcus Jones and Daniel Horst crouched in the row in front of them.

"Oh, bollocks."

Sanne bit down hard on her pen. She had forgotten that Natalie had been there that day. Every time she'd viewed the image, she'd focused on the three men, all of whom were now dead and all of whom had obviously been known to Natalie. Up until that point, Sanne had harboured major doubts, sure that she was wrong, that Steven Rudd having Natalie's number was nothing more than a coincidence, but those doubts evaporated as she stared at the picture. Could Natalie have lined the victims up for Rudd? Were they a kind of Bonnie and Clyde team? If so, what could Natalie have gained from the murders? Sexual gratification? Drugs or alcohol as incentive?

Sanne filled the first page of her pad with bullet-pointed questions and flipped over to a clean sheet. She fished out the transcript of Natalie's interview and read it once to re-familiarise herself with the details, and then again with a more sceptical eye. A casual mention of the Dog and Duck pub—recently identified as Rudd's local—got bullet-pointed and underlined, as did Natalie's claim that she hadn't spoken to Culver for three to four weeks prior to his death, a claim that the officer tasked with analysing the comms hadn't verified. On a roll now, Sanne began to see patterns emerge: Culver's enthusiasm about things "looking up," along with the newly purchased shoes that he had died in. He might not have unchained his door for Rudd, but if Natalie had arranged a date and knocked first, Rudd would have had no problems gaining entry. A quick check in the comms section of the case file gave her Culver's mobile phone record. She leaned back from the screen, her eyes flicking between Natalie's phone number, copied out in large print, and the list of calls.

"Don't you have a home to go to?"

Sanne's reaction to the unexpected interruption was a literal kneejerk. She leapt so far off her chair that her knees bashed the underside of the desk.

"Shit!" She looked up at Eleanor, unable to conceal anything with her in such close proximity. The best she could hope for was deflection. "What are you doing here so late?"

"Press conference. The brass had the bright idea of offering a reward for any information leading directly to Rudd's arrest."

"That should liven up the days of our hotline people." Sanne slid her hand toward the mouse but froze when Eleanor picked up her notes and began to read them.

"My thoughts exactly," Eleanor murmured, now scrutinising the computer screen. "Hmm, why did Ms. Acre call our first vic three times in the days leading to his murder?"

"She did? Ah, I knew it!" Curiosity and a surge of excitement made Sanne forget that she was trying to be evasive. "I was just checking that."

Eleanor took the mouse and highlighted the phone calls. "Here you go. These are all from her phone number."

Sanne chewed a piece of skin off her bottom lip. "She knew all three vics, boss, and I think she's been in contact with Steven Rudd. He has that same number written here." She handed Eleanor the Mission Cross leaflet. "And they both go to the same pub."

"Fucking hell." Eleanor snatched the leaflet. "When did you figure this out?"

"Just now. I found the leaflet this afternoon, but with the search I didn't have a chance to look into it. She hasn't got any violent priors and she volunteered herself for interview, so to all intents she was treated like a bereaved family member."

"Did you record the interview?"

"Audio only, ma'am."

"And I assume you've tried her mobile."

"Yes. It's been disconnected."

"Home address?"

"Nine Rian Walk."

Eleanor checked her watch. "Get everything together and written up for a warrant. I'll see if TAU can assist with a dawn raid."

"Right, boss." Sanne didn't move. "Are you sure?"

"The question is, Sanne, are *you* sure?" Eleanor pulled a chair closer and sat down, swivelling the Mission leaflet so it was facing Sanne. "You found this lead hours ago, yet you said nothing. You should have told me straight away, instead of wasting the afternoon slogging through a crap-hole in the snow. Maybe then I wouldn't have to go cap-in-hand to the TAU sarge, begging for a last-minute loan of his team."

Sanne stayed silent. She had no excuses to offer, and knowing that she had squandered even more time with Zoe only made matters worse.

"Look, you're an excellent detective," Eleanor continued in a slightly softer tone. "You're bright, perceptive, but you need to have the courage of your convictions. You'll have to grow bigger balls than any of the blokes if you're going to get anywhere in this job." She paused and waited until Sanne looked at her. "So, are you sure?"

"Yes," Sanne said. "Yes. I think Acre is involved. I think she's setting up the victims for Rudd."

Eleanor nodded. "Good. Get that paperwork sorted."

❖

"I hope you catch him. Andy didn't deserve to die like that."

Reaching across Sanne, Eleanor paused the audio file.

"Jesus, she's cold." She leaned back in her chair. "If she singled Culver out for Rudd, she may as well have stuck the knife into his chest herself. And then to come in here and give this level of performance…" She shook her head in disbelief and tossed her pen onto her notes.

Sanne knew exactly how she felt. They had listened to the interview twice, and if Natalie Acre had been lying, the ease with which she'd done so was as impressive as it was disturbing. During the first run-through, Sanne had been on tenterhooks, waiting for the moment Acre would give herself away, for the misplaced word or off-key intonation that would blow a hole in her charade, something that Sanne had missed because she'd been too soft-hearted, too readily hoodwinked. But there had been nothing, just a woman who sounded sincere in her desire to assist the investigation.

"The only thing I can see in retrospect is her request to be involved in a press conference. That might point to a notoriety angle." Eleanor skipped back to the beginning of the file. "Plus, her readiness to name Liam Burrows as a potential suspect helped to keep our focus elsewhere."

"Five minutes of fame can't be all she's getting out of this," Sanne said, trying to tune out the misgivings that were beginning to re-form. "I've seen her interviewed for a couple of local news reports and I think the *Sheffield Post* ran a piece on her, but she's not been front-page material."

"It probably all boils down to sex. Male-female teams such as this are often formed around an element of sexual thrall. The gender choice here is unusual—the victims are more commonly children or women—but maybe that's an added perk for Acre. She could be using Rudd to settle scores on her behalf." Eleanor set her glasses beside her pen. Another sixteen-hour day had left her eyes reddened. "Sometimes I wonder what this world's coming to."

The computer desktop faded as its standby mode took over, sending the office into darkness. Sanne fought to suppress a yawn. "Do you want a brew, boss?"

"No, thank you. I'm going to go home. Are you stranded in the city?"

"Yeah, I think so. The Snake was closed last time I checked the BBC travel site." Sanne opened her drawer to reveal her Asda bag. "I did a bit of shopping on the way over here, though."

Eleanor smiled. "I've had to do that a few times myself. I can vouch for the sofa in Interview Two, if you want to save on a hotel room."

"Cheers." Sanne still had a sleeping bag in her car, along with freshly purchased clothing and no inclination to drive back into the city centre.

"Try to set an alarm." Eleanor pulled her jacket on. "Sergeant Carlyle has a tendency to come in early."

"Oh, I'll definitely be awake before that."

Eleanor laughed at her decisive accord. "Night, Sanne."

This time Sanne did yawn. "G'night, boss."

❖

Wrapped up in her sleeping bag, with her coat slung on top for extra warmth, Sanne was dozing when her phone rang. She answered it before her eyes had focused, and smiled when she heard Meg's voice.

"Sorry, did I wake you?"

Sanne rolled onto her back. "No, I wasn't asleep. Are you okay?"

"Yeah." Meg's speech sounded thick, as if the swelling to her face had stiffened her mouth. "I evicted myself to the spare room. I couldn't get comfy, and my wiggling was disturbing Em. She's on an early tomorrow."

"Are you taking your painkillers?"

"Yes, Mum."

"I only nag with the best of intentions, because I know what you're like." Sanne shuffled down, tucking her free hand back beneath the covers. The sofa might have come recommended, but the heating had gone off hours ago. "I'm glad you called."

"You are?" There was a rare note of uncertainty in Meg's question. She didn't usually seek reassurance, which gave Sanne an idea of how badly Luke's assault must have affected her.

"Of course I am. I wanted to ring you, but I didn't know what to do for the best." Sanne closed her eyes and swallowed against the lump in her throat. For almost nineteen hours, she had been trying not to think about Meg. She had handed Meg's care over to Emily that morning and clapped a lid back on all the emotions rekindled by the previous night. Her fraught day had been a bonus in that respect, but after less than a minute on the phone, that lid had sprung an impressive leak and she was on the verge of blubbing.

"Ringing me is always for the best, San," Meg said softly. "I never got round to talking to Em, anyway."

"You didn't? Why ever not?"

"Because for once she chose not to push, and then the afternoon got taken up by Detective Fraser, but mostly because I'm a terrible coward who faked sleeping in the gaps."

"How long do you think she's giving you?"

"Probably till she finishes work tomorrow." Meg lowered her voice to a whisper. "God, my back hurts."

Sanne heard the metallic crinkle of pills being popped from their strip, and two pronounced gulps as Meg washed them down. "I should let you get some actual sleep," she said. A shuffling noise and a series of groans told her that Meg was changing position.

"Mm. Will you stay on till these tablets knock me out?"

"I'll stay on for as long as you like."

"Thank you. So, what are you wearing?" Meg managed to sound serious right until she started to laugh.

"A sweater, my socks, and a sleeping bag."

"What? I thought you were in bed. Where the hell are you?"

"They closed the Snake, so I'm on the sofa in one of our interview rooms. I might opt for a hotel if I'm still stranded tomorrow. I have a spring sticking up my bum."

"Nice," Meg drawled. "Remember that summer with your mum's old sofa? You need to make a den, right now."

Sanne laughed. "I don't have any spare blankets or garden canes, or clothes pegs for that matter."

"Excuses, excuses. That was the best summer ever." Meg yawned. "I can't keep my eyes open."

"So close them."

"You're full of good ideas."

"Are they closed?"

"Mmhm."

"Okay then."

"Can I phone you back if I need to?"

"Of course you can."

"Any time?"

"Yes, any time." Sanne listened as Meg's breathing slowed and deepened. "Sweet dreams, love," she said, and clicked off the phone.

CHAPTER TWENTY

Sanne had taken a shower and stashed her sleeping bag beneath her desk long before anyone came into the office. Arriving ahead of the crowd, Carlyle helped himself to coffee and microwave porridge and asked Sanne to help him set up the briefing room.

"One on each chair. If there aren't enough, people will have to share," he said, dropping a pile of stapled notes into her waiting arms.

A large photograph of Natalie Acre dominated the front page of the notes. Sanne flicked through the rest of the summary to find a short list of known associates and a précis on male-female serial killing teams that appeared to have been cobbled together from the Internet. Noticing that she had stopped to read, Carlyle placed a remote control beside his laptop and walked over to her.

"I didn't have much warning," he said, for once sounding flustered rather than defensive. "Acre wasn't home when the TAU went round there this morning, and the boss got called away to a press conference. I had a few old studies on the likes of Hindley and Brady, but I went online for some of the more recent examples."

"No harm in that, Sarge." Sanne resumed her task. "You can't write a dissertation in two hours."

He nodded but didn't answer, returning to the laptop and bowing his head until the shadows swallowed his expression. When she'd reached the last chair, Sanne looked at him for further instruction, but he continued to type and made no attempt to waylay her as she left the room. She found Nelson at their desk, meltwater from his snowy hair dripping down his face as the steam from his coffee caused a sudden thaw.

"Morning." She handed him a wad of tissues. "Still bad out there?"

He scowled, blotting at his hair. "Worse. How did you get in so early?"

"I never left."

"Ah." He waggled his eyebrows at her. "And what happened with Zoe?"

"Not much, really." Sanne nudged her phone behind a stack of files and out of his sight. She had lost count of the number of apologetic texts Zoe had sent her, but they were still arriving at regular intervals.

"No?"

"Nope."

"Why are you shredding that tissue, then?"

"Aw, crap." There was makeshift confetti scattered across her desk. She collected the tiny pieces into her palm and watched them flutter into the bin. Recalling the events of the previous night still caused a prickle of humiliation. When she finally answered, she couldn't meet Nelson's eyes. "It was all a ruse, that stuff about Luke. She didn't have anything on him, and I wasn't in the mood to play games, so I left."

"And, what? She just held the door for you?"

Sanne realised she had picked up another tissue. She forced herself to put it back in its box and wrapped one hand around the other to keep them still. "No, she followed me into the street, and I think her exact words were 'you're a fucking frigid bitch.'"

Nelson folded his arms, his dark eyes set with disapproval. "Are you all right?"

"I'll live. I came back here, where Eleanor told me I needed to grow a pair and I told her that Natalie Acre is somehow connected to Rudd. The TAU did a pre-dawn raid on Acre's house this morning, but she wasn't there."

"Bloody hell!" The hinges on Nelson's chair squeaked as he swung backward. "You don't half get up to some mischief when I leave you alone. Natalie Acre, eh? Where on earth did she come from?"

"Rudd had her phone number, and—" Sanne stopped short as people began to file into the briefing room. "Come on. We're being summoned. I'm sure Carlyle will fill in the blanks for you."

"Can't wait." Nelson sounded genuinely intrigued. He bagged them seats close to the front and leafed through the notes that Sanne had distributed. As he reached the last page, he poked his nose over the top. "These don't seem up to Carlyle's usual standard. What did he do, copy and paste from Wikipedia?"

Burying her head in her file, Sanne stifled a laugh and said nothing.

❖

"Not what I imagined." Sanne squinted through the falling snow at a terraced house, its neat garden surrounded by a recently trimmed privet hedge. The front gate sat on both hinges, and clean venetian blinds hung at the bay windows. The entire street was tidy and quiet, the empty parking spaces suggesting that many of its residents were at work.

"Shall we?" Nelson stepped out of the car, his coat fastened high beneath his chin. Sanne met him at the gate, and they stomped the snow from their boots as he rang the front door bell.

Natalie Acre's father had requested a late morning interview due to a run of night shifts starting that evening. He opened the door promptly and shook their hands without checking their ID badges. He was middle-aged, with a smooth-shaven head and a rounded belly, and his smart shirt and matching tie were so crisp that they looked fresh from the packet.

"Wilfred Acre, but I go by Wilf. Come in out of the cold and we'll try to get to the bottom of all this." The spotless carpeted hallway he led them down made Sanne want to take off her boots. "This is my wife, Barbara," he said as they entered the living room. "And our son, Benjamin."

Sitting prim and bolt upright against a support of several cushions, Barbara Acre nodded at her guests. A crutch was propped by the sofa, and the lower half of her left leg sported a sheepskin-lined brace. Multiple sclerosis had forced her into early retirement several years ago. Her fifteen-year-old son spoke when she squeezed his hand, but only to correct his name.

"Ben," he mumbled, a furious blush rising to obscure the acne on his chin. Stuffing his hands into the overlong sleeves of his polo neck, he stared at the muted television as his dad urged Sanne and Nelson to make themselves comfortable.

"Can I get you a cup of tea?" Wilf began to pour from a cosy-covered teapot without waiting for an answer, adding milk and placing a biscuit on each saucer before passing the cups around.

Feeling as if she'd strayed into some surreal photo shoot from *Good Housekeeping*, Sanne took a sip of her tea and tried to settle the cup back on its saucer without clinking it. Tactical Aid had already cleared the house, but the atmosphere in the room was so strained that she half-expected Natalie to burst out from behind the bookshelf. A glance at Nelson told her he was similarly unnerved. With Eleanor's advice still at the forefront of her mind, she swapped her cup for her notebook and signalled the start of the interview by uncapping her pen. She and Nelson had already decided that a direct approach would be best. There was little to be gained by meandering around the subject, with Natalie's photograph smiling out from the newspapers on the coffee table.

"I know this must be difficult for you all, so thank you for agreeing to speak with us," she began. "Can I ask when you last saw Natalie?"

"She came for lunch, a week last Sunday," Barbara said.

"Have you spoken to her since then?"

Barbara shook her head, one hand absently tousling Ben's fringe. "No, but that's not unusual. She's looking for work, and the job centre make her go in every day. She can't always afford a taxi over here, and the buses are few and far between."

"She doesn't drive?" Nelson caught the detail as eagerly as Sanne. The only vehicle registered to Rudd was his van, which meant that the couple were either reliant on public transport now or on the lookout for a new vehicle.

"No. She passed her test a couple of years back but never got a car."

Sanne thumbed through her notebook and scanned the details of Andrew Culver's post mortem. According to the pathologist's timeline, Culver had been murdered the day after that Sunday lunch. If Natalie had prearranged a date with him, it was likely she had been aware of Rudd's intentions during the visit to her family. Wary of Barbara monopolising the interview, Sanne aimed her next questions at Wilf and Ben. "How was she on the Sunday? Did you notice anything strange about her behaviour or about anything she said?"

"She was just Nat," Wilf said. His eyes strayed to the tabloids on the table and remained focused there as if he couldn't quite believe what he was seeing. "She helped make the gravy and washed the pots afterward."

"She played on my Xbox with me," Ben offered, when his dad trailed off.

Sanne was jotting everything down, no matter how trivial. When nothing more was forthcoming, she changed tack and took out a photograph of Steven Rudd. "I'm sure you already know, but we think Natalie might be involved with this man. Has she ever spoken about him, or perhaps brought him here?"

There were head shakes all around. Barbara glared at the image as if her fury alone could tear it asunder.

"He'll have caused all this," she said, her voice a thin hiss of rage. "You mark my words, it'll be nothing to do with our Natalie. Have you even considered that, eh? That he's probably got her locked up or something? You splash her face all over the news without ever thinking that she could be a victim too! It was the same with that Culver lout, dragging her into all sorts. She's been back on track since she split with him."

Wilf tried to put his arm around her, but she batted him away and drank her tea instead. Ben shrank from them both, pulling at his woollen collar as the colour flooded his cheeks again.

Nelson leaned forward, his hands empty and wide apart. "At this point, we're keeping all lines of enquiry open. We're not sure exactly what's going on, and we're as concerned for Natalie's well-being as you are, which is why we really need to find her. To that end, can you think of anyone she may have turned to for help or shelter? A close friend? Perhaps another relative? Or any place in particular that she has ties to?"

After a nod from Barbara, Wilf supplied a couple of names and addresses and ventured Bradford as another city that Natalie was familiar with. To their knowledge, she had no psychiatric problems and had experienced no recent traumatic events. She didn't drink to excess, always smoked outside, and swore that she hadn't touched drugs since a short-lived rebellious phase several years ago.

"Just look at her!" Barbara jabbed an insistent finger at the mantelpiece, prompting Wilf to take down a framed family photograph and hand it to Sanne. It was a studio portrait, everyone in their best outfits and smiling on cue. "Does she look like someone who could stand by and let a man be stabbed to death?"

Sanne didn't try to provide an answer. She'd been on the force long enough to know that criminals rarely stood out in a crowd, that the man or woman next to her in the queue at the chippy, the one exclaiming over the price of cod, could be capable of the vilest act. Using a smudge of dust on the mantelpiece as a guide, she put the photograph back in its place and gave each family member one of her cards.

"You need to contact us immediately if you hear from Natalie or if you think of anything that might help the investigation," she said, as Wilf ushered her and Nelson into the hall.

"Will you let us know if you find her?" he asked.

"Of course." Sanne shook his hand, his calluses rough against her palm. "Thank you for your time, and for the tea."

He escorted them out, barely letting them cross the threshold before shutting the door behind them. Momentarily dazzled, Sanne stood blinking in the glare of the snow. As the spots left her vision, she turned to Nelson, who looked as bemused as she felt.

"Days like this, I'm glad that my family's only half-cracked," she said.

Nelson shook his head, his cheeks puffing out and then deflating as he exhaled. "I doubt we'll hear a thing from Barbara. Natalie could turn up for tea and she wouldn't tell us. Ben may be a better prospect, though."

Sanne held the gate for him. "He was like a cat on a hot tin roof, wasn't he? I'd suggest a separate interview, but he'd need a guardian present, and no prizes for guessing who that'd be."

"Mummy dearest."

"Aye. We'll have to run it by the boss. See how she wants to play it."

Nelson drummed on the roof of the car. "We better get those names back so the TAU can make a few house calls."

"Yup. And then it's an afternoon out at the canal for us." Sanne grinned at his dismay. She far preferred fieldwork to office work. "Don't be so mad. Look, the sun's almost out."

He followed her upward gaze and got a face full of snowflakes for his trouble. "You're very mean to me," he said as she started to laugh. "I might trade you in after all."

CHAPTER TWENTY-ONE

"So, who was it?" Emily dropped her fork onto her plate. She'd arrived home earlier than Meg had expected, to prepare a lunch that now sat untouched in front of her. Sensing what was about to come, Meg had only nibbled a piece of the quiche's crust, and even that was sitting like lead in her stomach. The rich smell of oily cheese and spinach began to make her queasy. She pushed her plate away and looked across at Emily.

"It was my brother, Luke," she said. She had already decided to come clean the moment Emily raised the subject. "He wanted money that I don't have."

Emily folded her cloth napkin along its creases and set it by her knife in a series of deliberate movements. She had schooled her expression so well that Meg had no idea what she was thinking.

"Has he done it before?" she asked eventually.

"Yes, several times. It started when my dad left."

As careful as Emily was, she couldn't conceal her distaste. Meg had seen it flare in her eyes on too many other occasions to mistake it now.

"So he was the one who ransacked your house?"

"Yes." Meg could feel the argument coming, but she couldn't do a thing to stop it. Besides which, she knew she deserved whatever Emily might throw at her.

"Why didn't you tell me? Did you tell Sanne?"

Meg's painkillers were long overdue, and her head pounded as she tried to answer honestly. "Because he's my brother, Em. I didn't want to shout it from the rooftops."

"But you told Sanne."

"Yes, I told her. She's a detective. I asked for her help."

"And your mum's fall…" Emily spoke slowly, as if pulling the dates together. "Was that anything to do with him?"

Meg nodded, the motion sending stars spinning across her vision. "I didn't want you to know. I was hoping he'd crawl back under his rock and that'd be the end of it. I never wanted to drag you into this."

"You didn't trust me."

"No, I do trust you, I just—"

"How can I believe a word you say?" Emily's voice rose without warning, and Meg shrank back, too recently damaged to cope with the threat. If Emily noticed, it changed nothing. "You lie and you lie to me, and all the while you're running to Sanne behind my back."

"It wasn't like that." Meg could summon little more than a whisper, the reasons why she had lied slipping like sand through her fingers, until one truth caught and caught fast. "I don't want this," she said, and even as she spoke, something seemed to loosen inside her, something that had been battened down for months as Emily tried to mould her and adjust her and fix her.

"What exactly *do* you want, Meg?" Emily pushed against the table, jarring the plates and cutlery. "No ties or commitments, and a quick fuck with Sanne whenever you feel the urge?"

"Leave Sanne out of this," Meg snapped. "Think whatever you like about me, but this has nothing to do with her."

"Just give it time," Emily said in a mocking singsong. "You'll realise that's another lie."

Meg lowered her head, all but admitting that Emily was right, because Sanne was there at the back of everything, and Emily had never quite measured up. Guilt and regret hit her hard enough to double her over. "I'm sorry," she said. "For all of this, for everything."

"So am I." Emily's voice had regained its edge. "But I think you should leave."

Using the table for leverage, Meg pushed to her feet and walked unsteadily into the bedroom, where she threw toiletries and a handful of clothes into a bag. She couldn't carry much, and Emily made no attempt to help her as she returned to the living room.

"I phoned a taxi for you." Emily was curled on the sofa, her face pale but her expression indifferent. "I told him you'd wait down in the lobby."

Meg had no response to that. She left her key on the kitchen table and closed the front door quietly behind her.

❖

The TAU officer on the towpath with Sanne was a good foot taller than her. Every now and again he remembered to slow his pace in deference to her inferior stride, but for the majority of the afternoon she had been hurrying in his wake like a toddler lagging behind an impatient parent. It was a problem she had never experienced with Nelson, who almost equalled the man's height but somehow managed not to make her feel small.

"Hey, Graham, it's this one!" she shouted above the chug of a narrowboat braving the ice, as he barrelled past the gap in the hedge that led to their next warehouse.

With traffic grinding to a standstill in the snow, EDSOP were working on foot, each available detective assigned to a TAU officer and two uniforms and given a list of buildings to serve search warrants on. Sanne's first warehouse had belonged to a meat-packing company, and more than an hour later, she could still smell raw mince and innards. Somewhat predictably, she had found neither Rudd nor Acre hiding among the sausages. Warehouse number two was marked as derelict.

"Are you sure this is it?" Graham asked, retracing his steps with obvious reluctance.

Sanne had memorised the directions before setting out. She gave him a look that stopped him in his tracks, and then she squeezed through the hedge.

He might not have been the brightest spark on the TAU, but he knew how to kick a door down, taking point with his baton in one hand while his other rested close to his Taser. He yelled a warning into each of the dingy offices attached to the main warehouse, sending birds squawking for the rafters and rats sprinting for cover.

Sanne shone her torch across the floor, searching for footprints or recent signs of inhabitation: a fire pit, takeaway cartons, human excrement. She saw nothing of the sort, and a mounting sense of futility made her tear her list as she scribbled a line through the building's name. EDSOP didn't have the people or resources for this. It was a massive city-wide manhunt being undertaken by a handful of detectives and whatever additional manpower could be scrounged from departments with none to spare. Rumour had it that neighbouring forces were being asked for assistance, but every force had its own problems, and at this rate it was only a matter of time before the next body showed up.

"What a waste of a fucking day." Graham spat his gum into the snow and immediately began to chew a fresh piece. "Those idiots will be in Tenerife by now, getting a tan while we wade through shit looking for them."

"Yeah, probably." Sanne thought nothing of the sort, but it seemed easier not to argue. "We should start heading back. We're at least an hour from the van. We'll miss our lift if we leave it any later."

"Sounds good to me." He set off at a fair clip and was already out of sight when her mobile rang.

"Hiya, Nelson."

"Hey, partner. How's the knucklehead treating you?"

She laughed, relieved to hear a friendly voice. "I think most of his brains are in his boots. What are you up to?"

"We've called it a day. We're about half a mile from the van. Well, I think we are. The map is a little vague."

"The map or your understanding of it?"

He huffed indignantly, but then his voice turned serious. "I'm actually phoning to warn you."

Sanne hesitated, midway through the hedge. "Warn me about what?"

"Zoe."

"Oh God, what about her?"

"She's on Jay's team—they went out after you—so she'll be on the van with us."

"Great." As Sanne spoke, a thorn snagged her trouser leg, ripping a hole behind her knee. She yanked the cloth loose, muttering half to herself, half to Nelson. "Perfect end to a perfect bloody day."

❖

Thornbury House was a family-run bed and breakfast that prided itself on reasonable prices, locally sourced food, and above all, its setting. Hidden in an acre of land on the outskirts of Sheffield, the converted barn had views over the hills and provided easy access to the Snake Pass. Meg and Sanne had spent a week there one winter when snow had caused havoc over the tops, and it had become Meg's refuge whenever the weather left her stranded. With her brother still evading the police, and with Sanne having more important things to do than ride to her rescue once again, Thornbury had been the first place she contacted.

The elderly Pakistani taxi driver had taken one look at her in the apartment lobby, clucked his tongue, and picked up her bag. To her relief, he wasn't the chatty type, but he parked within a hair's breadth of the hotel's entrance before running round to open her door.

"Beautiful, eh?" Breathing deep, he patted his chest and made a show of filling his lungs. "Maybe you can smile again here."

She did smile for him then, her nerves soothed by the sight of the peaks rising from the valley, white and endless.

"Much better." He grinned, revealing betel-stained gums, and offered her his arm to escort her to the front desk.

Once she'd been booked in and fussed over by the proprietor, Meg embraced the solitude of her hotel room like a long-lost friend. She locked the door and sat on the bed in a patch of sunlight, staring at the hills until she noticed the tears splattering on her jeans. Unsure why she was crying, she wiped her face and went over to the window. Cold, woodsmoke-tinged air drifted in when she opened it, and birds chattered in a nearby hedge. It began to snow again as she stood there, a heavy burst of fat flakes that rapidly filled the footprints someone had left across the lawn. With nothing more pressing to do, she dragged one of the armchairs across and draped a blanket over it. A complimentary selection of homemade biscuits rekindled her appetite, so she brewed tea to go with them and set everything on a tray. Cocooned in the blanket, with biscuits to dunk and the snow bringing an early dusk, Meg could think of only one thing that she was missing, but she left her mobile untouched in her pocket and didn't call her.

Nelson met Sanne at the entrance to the canal basin car park, looking cold and thoroughly miserable.

"We're just waiting on Mike's team," he told her. "They ran into resistance at a friend of Acre's and had to call for backup."

"Everyone okay?"

"One minor dog bite, one arrest, and no sign of our perps."

Sanne kicked at a can buried under the snow. "Same here, only with less excitement and no dog bite." She stepped side-on and displayed her ragged trousers. "A hedge bit me instead."

"Ouch. Bet that's draughty."

"It is, rather."

Nelson glanced back into the car park. "Zoe collared me just now and asked after you." He faltered as if wary of saying anything else, but he'd always been one for doing the right thing, even if it meant giving someone a gentle shove. "Maybe you should go and talk to her, San. She seemed really upset."

"Probably a hangover," Sanne muttered. She jabbed the can again like a sulky teenager and then bared her teeth in a rictus grin. "Okay, okay. Where was she?"

"Picnic bench on the far left."

"Ten minutes." She set off in the direction opposite to his. "If I'm not back by then, please come and rescue me."

Although the farthest reaches of the car park were unlit, Sanne had no difficulty spotting Zoe. Hunched atop a picnic table with her feet propped on the bench, she had her back to the officers chatting in small groups around the van. A cigarette burned in her fingers, and several freshly discarded stubs were scattered beneath the bench. The crunch of Sanne's footsteps made her look up. She quickly extinguished the cigarette in the snow and stayed where she was, allowing Sanne to meet her on the level for once.

"Hi." She twisted her bottom lip between her teeth, smearing them with lipstick. "If you want to shove me into the canal, I'll completely understand."

Sanne turned her head to consider the logistics. "It's icy. You'd probably bounce straight back out."

Her candour alleviated some of the tension. She declined the offer of a cigarette, but plucked the lighter from Zoe's clumsy fingers and sparked it up for her.

"Thanks." Zoe exhaled her smoke high into the sky. When Sanne didn't speak, she assumed the initiative. "I don't actually know what to say, which is a first for me. 'Sorry' seems a bit shit, but for what it's worth, I really am. I swear I didn't know what'd happened to Meg. I never would've—" She cut herself off to pull on her cig. "Well, yeah, anyway, I'm sorry."

Confounded by the inarticulate monologue, Sanne brushed the remaining snow from the table and nudged up beside Zoe. Working as a detective had taught her a lot of things, one of those being that life was too short to hold grudges.

"It's partly my fault," she said. "I shouldn't have given you the wrong impression. My head's been up my arse, with everything that's happened to Meg and with the case, and I'm crap at all this…" She floundered for the right word.

"Dating malarkey?" Zoe suggested.

"Yes, exactly."

Zoe blew out a smoke ring. "I'm usually so good at it."

"I didn't mean to wreck your average." Sanne shrugged. "You should probably write me off as an aberration."

"I don't think you count if you're not really available in the first place," Zoe said quietly. She nipped out her cigarette and got to her feet. "Y'know, when you talk about Meg, your entire face changes."

It was a few seconds before Sanne dared to meet her eyes. "It does?"

"Yep. You'd be terrible at poker."

Taking the offered hand, Sanne slid down from the table. "I always lose at cards, whatever the game. At least now I know why."

"I had a boyfriend like that once. I'd take him to the cleaners every time we played, and he never had a clue." Zoe stopped suddenly. "That other thing I said last night, about you being—"

Sanne broke in, not wanting to make her repeat it. "I remember."

"It wasn't true. No one's ever said that about you." Zoe shook her head. "That ex, he yelled it at me when I dumped him. Fucking hell, I always thought he was such an arsehole for it."

"Did he ever apologise?"

"No, never."

"Well, you've apologised, so let's forget about it, okay?"

A stifled sniffle from Zoe prompted Sanne to fish in her pocket for a clean tissue. She handed it over like a flag of truce.

"Come and sit on the bus," she said, once Zoe had stemmed the flow of mascara. "It's bloody freezing."

Zoe nodded, but she was watching her colleagues at the van, and she didn't move. "Can you tell I've been crying?"

Sanne stood on tiptoe and cleaned a black streak from Zoe's cheek with her glove. "Not anymore."

The gesture brought a proper smile to Zoe's face. "God, you're cute as a button," she said. "I hope Meg realises how lucky she is."

CHAPTER TWENTY-TWO

As the security barrier at HQ rose to admit the van, a weak cheer sounded from those on board who'd managed to stay awake.

Sanne nudged Nelson, whose snores were more audible now that the engine was idling. "Come on, sleeping beauty."

He stretched, smacking his sticky lips together. "Hmm. What time is it?"

"Almost seven." She ducked as someone swung past with a rucksack. "Leave your paperwork with me. I'll probably be camping out here again tonight."

Gratitude brightened his face. "That'd be great, if you don't mind. I just need to nip in and grab my keys from my locker."

They navigated the frozen car park, gave a perfunctory flash of their ID at the front desk, and squeezed into the lift with a bunch of drowsy, shivering officers. No one else got out at their floor. The EDSOP office smelled stale after a day of standing almost empty, and they both jumped like thieves caught in the act when George shouted across to them.

"So close," Nelson muttered. "I was so damn close."

George already had his coat fastened and his cap in hand. "Front desk buzzed about ten minutes ago, asked me to collect a couple of guests for you. There's no one else here, so I stuck around to babysit, and now I'm going home." He beamed, patting his cap into place. "Oh, I made them a brew and put them in Interview Two."

"Wha—?" Sanne stared at his rapidly disappearing form.

"You're welcome!" he called as he stepped into the lift.

He'd left the door to Interview Two ajar, but Sanne guessed who was in there even before she saw the glass of orange juice on the table and the scuffed Nikes beneath it.

"Hi, Ben," she said, draping her coat over the back of an empty chair. "Wilf."

Wilf stood to shake her hand and nod at Nelson. He seemed to have aged in the scant hours since their interview, his grip diminished and his face ashen.

Nelson pulled up another chair, all thoughts of home banished without complaint. "What can we do for you?"

"Barbara doesn't know we're here," Wilf said, his head twitching toward the door as if she might barge in at any moment. "We've had reporters ringing or knocking on all day, so she took a couple of sleepers straight after tea. That's when Ben told me, and I called in sick at work to bring him here." He was a nervous wreck, and an intermittent vocal spasm choked his speech. His foot tapped incessantly, until Ben put a hand on his knee.

"It'll be fine, Dad." Ben waited for the motion to cease before he turned to Sanne. "I just have to tell you what happened, right?"

"Yep, that's right." Sanne had a good idea of what might be coming. "Why don't you start at the beginning? Take your time, and don't mind us if we make some notes, okay?"

He nodded, and the words tumbled out of him in an agitated staccato. "I saw our Nat with that bloke. She came round when Dad was on shift and Mum was at my aunt Sandra's."

He paused, leaving the room so quiet that Sanne could hear the ticking of his watch. Thrilled by an actual witness confirming the link between Rudd and Acre, she had leaned forward without realising.

"When was this?" she asked.

"Teatime, Monday just gone. I didn't know who the bloke was then, I swear I didn't."

"It's all right. You're not in any trouble," she said quickly, seeing him starting to panic. "Monday was the first time we heard anything about Steven Rudd, so you couldn't have known."

"Natalie doesn't have a key to the house," Wilf said, filling a gap in the explanation and allowing Ben time to compose himself. "Barbara took it away after she stole from us to buy drugs. She hasn't had one since."

Sanne noted the detail, but her focus remained on Ben. "What did Natalie want?"

Ben gulped half his juice, keeping hold of the glass as he continued. "Money. She said she was skint and desperate, and she cried a bit because Andy was dead. I brewed up and made sandwiches. Steve seemed okay at first. He's a footy fan, like me."

"So you were chatting?"

"Yeah, just about stuff. Sheffield Wednesday, United. He's a United fan, but I told him they were rubbish."

"They are," Nelson said, making Ben smile. "Did you give Natalie the money she asked for?"

The smile vanished. "I work weekends at the chippy, and I'd saved about fifty quid. She took that and then started asking for more. She knows I go to pick up Mum's incapacity benefit, but it's not due till tomorrow."

It was only the slightest hint, but it stopped Sanne's pen dead on the page. If Ben hadn't been a minor, she would probably have sworn.

"Ben, was Natalie planning to come to the house again, or did she ask you to take that money somewhere once you had it?"

Ben didn't answer. He put his glass down and scrubbed his palms on his trousers. There were tears in his eyes when he looked up. He knuckled them away, his wet fists remaining clenched afterward.

"You're safe here," Sanne said, quietly. "No one's going to hurt you."

His breath gurgled as he swallowed a sob, prompting Wilf to move closer and take his hand.

"Rudd had a knife." Wilf's voice shook with impotent fury. "He held it to my son's throat and made him promise not to say anything."

"He cut me," Ben whispered. Keeping a firm grip on his dad's hand, he used his other to lower the polo neck on his sweater, revealing an inch-long scab. "And our Nat did nothing."

His sense of betrayal was harder for Sanne to witness than Wilf's outrage. She could imagine Ben concealing the wound from his parents, unable to explain how it had happened, and convinced that Rudd would return to make good on his threat.

"They're renting a flat," Ben said, sounding firmer now, as if resolved to get to the end. "Four A Eustace Street, above that row of empty shops. I'm supposed to go there tomorrow in my dinner break."

"Excuse me." Nelson bolted for the door, a note of the address clutched in his hand. His urgency made Sanne shift in her seat, the logistics of organising a raid warring with her desire to see the interview through to a proper conclusion.

"What are you going to do?" Ben asked. He rubbed his neck, worrying at the scab's edge and bringing a drop of blood to the surface.

"We'll go there tonight," she said. "You and your dad are welcome to wait here, or you can go home with officers who will stay with you."

"Will they get Steve if he comes to our house?"

"Yes, they'll arrest him if he comes anywhere near."

Ben appeared to consider that for a moment. "And our Nat too?"

"Yes."

He didn't seem overly concerned by that prospect. He straightened his sweater and wiped the smear of blood from his finger. "We should get back," he said to his dad. "In case Mum wakes up."

"Good thinking, son." Wilf patted Ben's knee. "Was there anything else you needed, Detective?"

Sanne snapped her notebook closed. "Half an hour to get Ben's statement typed up, and a couple of photographs of his injury. If that's okay with you?" She directed this last at Ben, who nodded. She shook both of their hands again: one coarse and tremulous, the other smaller and steady. "I know it can't have been easy coming in here, but you've done the right thing, so thank you. Sit tight, and I'll be as quick as I can."

Once in the corridor and out of earshot, she sprinted to her desk. On the opposite side, Nelson was cradling his mobile against his shoulder as his fingers battered his keyboard.

"Eleanor's on her way—she's sorting the warrant—and I'm on hold with the TAU sarge," he said. "Carlyle, Jay, and Scotty are coming in as well."

"Fab." Sanne started her own computer, feeling slightly dubious now that she'd had a few minutes to reflect. "Hell of a risk to take, wasn't it? Giving that address to a fifteen-year-old kid, even if he is your brother and you've got him at knifepoint?"

"Yeah. There's every chance they've moved somewhere else." Nelson sounded equally cautious. "Or maybe they'll think him even less likely to tell anyone what's happened, now he knows they're capable of murder."

"It's possible."

Nelson held up a finger and adjusted his mobile. "Yes, still here," he said into it. "That's great. I'll pass it on to the boss. Thanks." He dropped the phone into his hand. "At any rate, it's the best lead we've had. Get cracking on your statement, San. The TAU will be here in an hour."

❖

Located half a mile from Malory in an area earmarked for demolition, Eustace Street was an ideal place for anyone wanting to avoid inquisitive neighbours. It comprised three boarded-up shops opposite a row of boarded-up terraced houses, and its sole sign of inhabitation was a slowly revolving advert for *Booze and Fags* that sat above the corner shop. Waiting out of sight on the next street, Sanne held her gloves in her mouth as she fastened her stab vest. Happy with the fit, she let Nelson help her into her coat before shoving her gloves back on.

"I think she might actually explode," he whispered. They were both earwigging on the argument raging a few feet away, while feigning obliviousness.

Thanks to a large-scale brawl in the city centre, the TAU had only been able to spare three men. Eleanor had spent the last twenty minutes alternately railing at the most senior of them and consulting someone on the phone. Now, with the air of a decision finally reached, she slapped the cover over her mobile and gestured everyone closer.

"Right, the top brass are happy with our risk assessment and keen to get this case closed, so we're going ahead as planned. Teams of five and four: Carlyle, Sanne, Nelson, Graham, and Col are through the front, and everyone else takes the back." There was no need for further instruction. Strategy and the layout of the flat had already been discussed at length, and standing around in sub-zero temperatures wasn't doing anyone any favours.

The snow was soft enough to muffle footsteps, allowing Sanne's team to approach the entrance of 4A in near silence. Using a pair of bolt cutters, Graham snipped the padlock fastening the security grille and winced at the squeak as he pulled it open.

"Go, Col," he said, stepping aside to allow his colleague to ready an enforcer ram.

The door shattered in three strikes, the clash of metal still ringing in Sanne's ears as Graham disappeared into the darkness, the bob of his torch tracking his route up a flight of stairs. Col sprinted after him, their shouted warnings a familiar battle cry.

Keeping her torch centred where she needed to place her feet, Sanne took the stairs two at a time, hurtling through the left-hand door as Carlyle and Nelson took the right. She and Graham tossed the double bedroom, overturning a soiled mattress to expose the frame's slatted base and the empty space beneath it and then pulling open the wardrobes. There was no time for Sanne to think, no time to be afraid. The thin light from the bulb swinging overhead showed no other hiding places, and Graham instantly yelled, "Clear!"

An echoing "Clear!" rang out from the living room, raising the hairs on the nape of Sanne's neck as Graham approached the bathroom door. There were only four rooms in the flat, and two of those had already proven empty.

A sudden thud behind her sent her spinning around, before she realised it was just someone kicking open the kitchen door. She turned back to the bathroom in time to see Graham boot his way in, but he stopped so abruptly on the threshold that she almost slammed into him.

"Aw, fuck." He clapped his hand over his nose.

Staring into the darkness, Sanne heard a rattle of an ancient extractor fan and felt the draught from the broken bathroom window. Seconds later, the smell hit her.

"Jesus," she whispered. She kept her teeth clenched, trying not to breathe in the sickly-sweet odour of decaying flesh. "It must be in the bath."

Sweat gleamed on Graham's forehead as he took hold of the dirt-grey shower curtain, his Taser primed and aimed. He yanked on the material, sending hooks flying onto the tiles and the shower curtain sailing over his head. Thick globs of fluid splattered across his face. As he realised what they were, he leaned over the sink and began to retch.

"Shit," he gasped between bouts of coughing. "Clear?"

Walking closer, Sanne lowered her baton and shone her torch into the bath. "Yeah, clear," she said, and then, into her comms, "We've got a body here." Bare legs, positioned wide apart and speckled with patches of green, led up to grossly swollen genitalia. "White male, stab wounds to the abdomen and torso." The man's bloated belly was oozing fluid onto the porcelain, its smell forcing Sanne to recoil as she studied his face. The slip of slackened flesh had rendered his features grotesque, pulling at his mouth and cheeks to give the impression of a melted waxwork. It took her a full minute to mentally fix everything back into position.

"Fucking hell." She pushed her comms, her head reeling. "Boss, you need to come and see this. I'm pretty sure we've found Steven Rudd."

Chapter Twenty-three

"What a bloody mess." Crouching by the bath, Eleanor took a final, long look at the photograph in her hand and then stood without touching anything. She hadn't yet given her opinion on the comparison, and Sanne couldn't tell if she was referring to the body or to its potential implications for the case.

"Is it him, boss?" Carlyle asked from the doorway, evidently unwilling to take Sanne's word for it.

Eleanor shoved the photograph toward Carlyle and gestured for him to move closer. "Either that or he's got a fucking twin. Has he got a fucking twin, Sanne?"

Sanne didn't have a clue. She threw a desperate glance at Nelson, who shook his head. "I don't think so, boss."

"Okay then," Eleanor said. "In which case, I can only assume that Natalie Acre is responsible for Rudd's murder and—who the hell knows? Possibly the murders of three other men." She raised her voice above the ensuing murmurs of speculation from the EDSOP detectives crowded around the door. "I didn't see this coming either, but given the manner in which Rudd has been posed and the fact that we were as good as told where he'd be, I think Acre has sent us a clear message."

Eleanor had never been known to back down from a challenge, and despite her exasperation she was moving with more energy, her expression animated. If Natalie had thrown down a gauntlet, Eleanor would happily pick it up and slap her with it.

"Rudd threatened Ben early on Monday evening, so he was still alive then," Sanne said. She'd just worked out the timeline, and it had given her the creeps. "Acre planned this to perfection. I bet she murdered Rudd as soon as she'd fed Ben this address. She must have done, because she can't have predicted how long Ben would sit on the information."

"She made sure it was us who found him, as well," Eleanor said. "She obviously couldn't turn the heating off—there's no thermostat anywhere—but she used the fan to cover the smell, and the glass beneath that window suggests it's been broken recently. She didn't want anyone jumping the gun and calling the landlord out."

Finished with his analysis, Carlyle began to clean his hands on a sanitary wipe, even though he hadn't put them anywhere near the body. "Meanwhile, she's had two clear days to find herself another hiding place," he said. "We need to pin down more of her local contacts and liaise with West Yorks police, too, if Bradford is a possible safe haven."

Eleanor nodded. "SOCO are ten minutes out. Leave the bathroom to them, but fingertip every other room. If Acre likes to play games, she may have started another breadcrumb trail somewhere." Her shoulders dropped and she looked suddenly exhausted again. "I don't know what the brass will want to do about this. It's possible they'll put the entire case up for review."

Sanne groaned, along with her colleagues. An outsider nosing through and picking fault with every step of the investigation was no one's idea of fun.

"Just be prepared for that, and for the media fallout," Eleanor said, "because the press are going to have a fucking field day."

Two hours trapped in the flat's stifling heat left Sanne feeling as if she'd never rid herself of the smell of dead body. She could taste it at every breath, and it seemed to cling to the inside of her nostrils. As Nelson approached the final cupboard in the kitchen, he looked similarly green around the gills.

"Milk pan, roasting tray with half a spud still in situ, and a cheese grater." He shut the cupboard. "How about you stay with us tonight? We don't have a spare room, but we do have a comfy sofa and a shower that Carlyle hasn't been in."

"I wouldn't want to impose," Sanne said, though she very much did. The thought of another night shivering in Interview Two was less than appealing.

"It's true you'd be a terrible burden, but I think we'd muddle through."

"In which case I appreciate and accept your offer." She took a step back to survey the room. "Are we done? I want to try to catch Meg."

"We're done." He held the door for her, and they went out onto the landing. Scotty and Jay were already there, a solemn shake of their heads summarising their search of the living room. Leaving them to wait for Eleanor, Sanne dodged the two SOCO conferring on the stairs and took shelter beneath the tattered awning of a neighbouring shop.

The first ring of Meg's phone sounded far too loud. It was getting on for midnight, and Sanne had no idea whether Meg would still be awake. She held her breath as the call was picked up, dreading Emily coming on the line.

"Hey, San." Meg didn't sound as if she'd been sleeping, and she made no attempt to lower her voice.

"Hey, you. Just checking in."

"I'm fine. Everything's fine," Meg said, a little too brightly. "Are you camping at the office?"

The false cheer immediately put Sanne on alert. "No, I'm still at work. Did you end up in the spare room again?"

"Sort of." Meg sighed. "Y'know, I always forget that you're a bloody detective."

That was enough to make Sanne really worried. "Meg, where are you?"

There was a lengthy delay before Meg answered. "Thornbury House."

"Thornbury? Why the hell are you—Oh shit, did you have the talk?"

"Aye," Meg said quietly.

"And what? She kicked you out?"

"It was more of a mutual decision." Meg's tone aimed for pragmatism, but fatigue underscored her words. "I don't feel very well," she admitted.

"Does your room there have a kitchenette?" Sanne asked, starting back toward the flat.

"Yes, but, San, you don't—"

"I'll see you in half an hour."

❖

It was several minutes before Meg opened the door of her hotel room. Waiting in the corridor, laden with shopping bags, Sanne heard a geriatric-esque shuffle across the carpet, followed by the rattle of the security chain and snap of the bolt. Helping the door on its way with her foot, she stared in dismay as she set eyes on Meg.

"Oh, sweetheart," she whispered. She dropped her bags and gathered Meg into a careful hug.

"I didn't want to bother you." Meg's lips were scratchy and dry against the snow-dampened skin of Sanne's neck. "I didn't want to drag you out here."

"It's no bother, you daft bugger." Keeping a firm hold of Meg's hand, Sanne led her to the bed, where she settled her onto pillows that bore a well-established indentation. The swelling to her face was less pronounced, but it was her unkempt appearance, shaking hands, and sallow skin that worried Sanne. "You look like crap. When did you last have something to eat?"

Meg blinked as if baffled by the question. "I dunked a couple of biscuits. I can't really chew, and I didn't want to go to the restaurant, not like this."

"Well, fortunately I came prepared." Sanne collected the shopping bags and hauled them to the kitchenette. "Semolina or soup?" she said, holding up a tin of each.

"It's one o'clock in the morning, San."

"Yeah, but I'm starving, you're on the verge of fading away, and we're both in jobs where we get to eat breakfast at midnight. So, semolina or soup?"

Meg chewed her lip. "Have you got jam?"

"Raspberry." Sanne tried not to show her glee. She'd bought the jar in a last-minute flash of inspiration.

"One of my favourite school dinners," Meg said with nostalgic reverence. "Please tell me the jam is seedless."

Sanne rolled her eyes at the unnecessary query and set the semolina to heat in the microwave. "Where are your painkillers?" Following Meg's pointed finger, she found a plastic bag stuffed with underwear, along with a small toiletries wallet. "Is this everything? The sum total of your worldly possessions?"

"That was as much as I could carry. There's a change of clothes in the wardrobe too."

"Fucking hell." Sanne took the toiletries into the bathroom and stayed there, her fingernails digging into her palms, until the urge to rant about Emily ditching Meg in such a state had dissipated. There were two sides to every story, and she'd barely heard one of them yet. She busied herself sorting out pills, waiting for the ping of the microwave before returning to the bedroom to dole the semolina into two bowls.

"Here you go." She set the tray on Meg's lap, and Meg leaned over the bowl to let the steam bathe her face.

"God, that smells good." She stirred a healthy dollop of jam into the pudding, grinning as it turned pink. "You don't know what you're missing," she told Sanne, who was eating hers plain.

Sanne shrugged, taking another spoonful from her own bowl, relishing the taste of something she'd not eaten for years. "So, what happened?"

Meg used a finger to retrieve a stray blob from her tray, but she didn't prevaricate for long. "The talk didn't go very well," she said with wry understatement. "Emily was pissed off that I'd not told her about Luke, and she figured out what had happened to Mum and was pissed off that I'd lied about that as well, and then she managed to blame you into the bargain."

Sanne lowered her spoon. "Oh, no. Oh, shit. Meg, I'm so sorry. Do you want me to phone her or something?"

"What for? To file an appeal?"

"Well, yeah, in a manner of speaking." Sanne frowned. "Would it help?"

Meg set her tray on the bed and pulled up her knees. "What if I was guilty as charged?"

"You?" It had been a long day and Sanne was knackered, but even so she was usually better than this at following Meg's dubious grasp of logic. "I thought I was the villain here."

"Not really. She dragged you into it as someone else to be mad at, but—I don't know, San." Balancing her chin on her knees, Meg caught and held Sanne's gaze. "I think I may have committed relationship suicide."

"Hmm." Sanne scratched her cheek and decided to settle in for the long run. Having plumped up a couple of pillows beside Meg, she shuffled into place and held her arms out. "C'mere and tell me all about it."

That made Meg smile. She leaned her head against Sanne's chest, saying nothing as Sanne stroked her hair. Little by little Sanne felt her relax, until eventually she spoke without prompting.

"I did like Em, I really did, but I suspect I liked the novelty of the romance even more."

Sanne couldn't help it. She laughed. "You? Cynical-to-the-bone Megan Fielding enjoyed being wooed?"

"I know, I know it sounds daft, but for a while there it was nice to come home to someone, and to get chocolates and flowers, and to go out for meals for no reason."

"Like a proper couple," Sanne said, the light beginning to dawn. It was something that she and Meg had never done. They were best friends who occasionally slept together, but they'd never been exclusive or held hands in public or bought each other Valentines.

"Exactly." Meg toyed with a button on Sanne's shirt. "It was all the other crap that came with it that I couldn't handle."

"Such as?"

"Such as, I don't think I was ever good enough for her, or good enough at being in a relationship. It wasn't Em's fault." She hesitated as if reconsidering that and peeked up at Sanne. "Aw, fuck. You'll think I'm stupid."

Sanne already had an inkling of what was coming. "Try me."

That was all the encouragement Meg needed. "I want to get my hair cut short again, San, and eat what I like, and wear what I like, and swear, and spend time alone without needing to explain why, and be a cynical shit, and talk with my mouth full, and not think that the sun shines out of everybody's arse because it doesn't and there's no point pretending that it does." She ran out of breath and had to stop, but she was starting to smile.

Sanne smiled with her. "That's my girl."

"And that was the other problem," Meg said quietly. "I think I'll always be your girl."

When Sanne managed to respond, her voice sounded rough and unfamiliar. "Do you really mean that?"

Meg took her hand, the strength of her grip giving credence to her answer. "Yes, I really mean that."

"Oh, thank goodness." Relief made Sanne speak without thinking, but she didn't want to try to analyse this in any case, to start worrying about how things might work or whether they even would. For now, the glimmer of hope was enough.

"Everything old is new again," Meg murmured. She sounded contented, her body resting heavy and snug against Sanne's.

Sanne hugged her closer and kissed the top of her head. "Oi, we're only thirty-three. Less of the bloody 'old'!"

CHAPTER TWENTY-FOUR

Four-and-a-half hours of solid, dreamless sleep, a kiss goodbye from Meg, and the reopening of the Snake Pass saw Sanne arriving at HQ full of optimism, prepared to take on whatever the day might launch at her. She hadn't even unfastened her coat when Carlyle fired the first volley.

"The boss wants to see you in her office."

Sanne pulled her gloves off slowly. "Did she say when?"

"As soon as you got in." He made a point of looking her over. "You might want to smarten up first, though."

She felt her face go hot. After ripping her trousers at the canal, she'd had to recycle the pair she'd worn to search the wasteland, and there was something splattered on their hem that had proven resistant to hotel soap. Sidestepping Carlyle, she headed for the relative safety of the women's locker room, where she combed her hair and scrubbed futilely at her trousers. The sudden switch from the cold air outside to the warmth of the office had left her cheeks pink, and they stayed pink even when her embarrassment had faded. After a few minutes with no improvement, she gave up and knocked on Eleanor's door.

"Come in."

Sanne entered the office to find three men seated around Eleanor's desk. She recognised one as Eleanor's immediate superior, but the other two she had never seen before. Instinct and her experience as a uniformed officer kicked in, and she clapped her heels together and straightened her torso. She didn't salute, but it was an effort not to.

"You wanted to see me, ma'am?"

Eleanor nodded. "You know DCI Litton. This is DI Southam and DS Rashid."

Although Sanne acknowledged each of the introductions, she didn't move any closer. Her boots felt as if they had lead weights attached to their soles. The smell of bitter coffee and an aftershave that stank on a par with Carlyle's had obliterated the clean apple scent that she always associated with the room.

"We've been discussing your interview with Natalie Acre," Litton said.

Sanne had already guessed as much from the file open in front of him. Even from a distance she could identify her own handwriting. She said nothing, not wanting to exacerbate matters by acting defensive.

"You didn't interview her under caution," Rashid said. His accent, clipped and proper, suggested that he didn't work locally.

"No, I didn't." She stepped forward, irritated both by the question and the ambush. "At that time there was no reason to suspect Acre. As I explained to DI Stanhope on Tuesday night, she came in for interview voluntarily. I only recorded the audio to be thorough." She caught an approving look from Eleanor, but it vanished when Litton snapped the file closed.

"You'll surrender your files on this case to DI Southam and make yourself available for interview with DS Rashid, should he request it."

"Yes, sir." Sanne met his stare as she answered. As far as she was concerned, they could all fill their fucking boots. She'd started this case under an improvement notice, and her investigatory processes and paperwork had been meticulous. If anyone found a T that she'd not crossed, she'd give them a tenner.

Litton stood, prompting the other two men to do likewise, one clasping Sanne's file, the other a disc upon which, she assumed, was Acre's interview.

"I expect hourly updates." Litton fired his parting shot in Eleanor's direction and left with his underlings tagging behind him.

Eleanor waited for a count of ten before leaving her desk and shutting the door. "Try not to worry," she said, sinking into the closest chair.

Sanne took the one next to Eleanor and planted both feet flat on the floor to stop her knees from knocking. She wasn't stupid; she understood what the meeting had been about and the role she'd been cast in. "Should I be worried?" she asked.

"Honestly?" Eleanor rubbed the bridge of her nose. "I'm not sure. Litton asked to see your personnel file, so he knows about the three-month warning, and you're the only detective to have spoken to Acre at any length."

"I'm also the one who pulled together two seemingly disparate murders and named Acre as a suspect."

"True, but that could go against you if they want to play dirty. You hit on Acre because of something you'd missed when you interviewed her, something at the back of your mind that you should've connected sooner."

"Bloody hell." Sanne shook her head in dismay. "How long have we got?"

"Forty-eight hours. If there are no major developments in that time, Litton is planning to release your name to the media. He won't even need to assign blame; if he mentions your disciplinary notice, the papers will undoubtedly do that for him, and then the shit will really start to fly."

"Shit always rolls downhill, boss."

Eleanor smiled sadly. She was almost as close to the bottom of that hill as Sanne. "Don't I fucking know it?"

❖

Fingers of sunshine creeping beneath the hotel curtains made dust motes dance at the foot of Meg's bed, giving her an idea of how late it was. She hadn't meant to go back to sleep, had insisted to Sanne that she would get up and get stuff done, although the specific nature of those tasks had remained vague. Sanne had grinned and tucked the covers back around her. Warm, cosy, and completely at peace for the first time in weeks, Meg had gifted herself a short lie-in that had apparently stretched for several hours.

Rolling onto her back, she tensed with the expectation of pain, but the bulge around her fractured ribs was less distinct, and a bearable ache had replaced the stabs of agony that had been hobbling her for the last two days. Her mobile rang from the bedside table as she was experimenting with wiggling her toes, and she answered when she saw Detective Fraser's number.

"Morning, Meg." Fraser was a cheerful sort who had been checking in with her on a daily basis, if only to offer assurance that his team were still working on her case. "I have good news." He cleared his throat as if wary of sounding too buoyant, but the switch from his usual script already had Meg scrambling to sit up.

"Did you find him?"

"We've arrested him," Fraser confirmed with unmistakeable satisfaction. "He tried to sell your car to a dealer, who recognised him from the photograph we'd sent out. He's been taken to the main custody suite in Sheffield. He'll be interviewed and charged, and—if I have anything to do with it—he won't get bail."

Meg touched her face, her fingers tracing the sutures in her cheek. "Please tell me you'll have something to do with it." She didn't know anyone else on Fraser's team, and she trusted him implicitly.

"I'll be interviewing him. My intention is to get him remanded until trial, and he's looking at a lengthy sentence."

"So I'm safe to go home?" She kept her voice low, almost afraid of jinxing things by saying the words aloud.

"Yes, you're safe to go home." His answer had such conviction that it damped down all Meg's doubts, and she switched straight to the practicalities instead.

"When can I have my car back?"

Fraser chuckled at her pragmatism. "It's been impounded at our lot for processing. We should be able to release it in about a week, but I'll see if I can hurry things along for you."

"That'd be great." She swung her legs out of bed, eager to make headway on a mental to-do list that was growing exponentially.

As her feet touched the carpet, she hesitated. "Thank you. For everything."

"Not a problem. You take care, and I'll be in touch."

She was by the window before he hung up, pulling back the curtains and shielding her eyes against the brilliance of the sun on the snow. She called Sanne first, leaving a message when the answer phone came on, and then she scribbled down her tasks before she forgot them: to resume work for the next day's shift, to sort out a rental car, and to try to collect the rest of her things from Emily's. Realising that she'd omitted something of vital importance, she rapped her forehead with her pen and searched her phone's directory. Marvin—chief proprietor of *Hairway to Heaven*—answered promptly.

"Hiya, Marv," she said, pen poised above her list. "I know I'm on the last minute, but is there any chance you can squeeze me in for a short dry cut?"

❖

"I think it's safe to assume that Natalie Acre is extremely proud of her accomplishments." Eleanor flicked to a new image in what had become something of an endurance test for the detectives and officers squeezed into the briefing room. A pre-dawn post mortem of Steven Rudd had found a plastic-wrapped SD card lodged at the back of his throat. The card's single folder, labelled *All My Own Work*, contained a horror show of photographs depicting the aftermath of each murder—including Rudd's—in graphic detail.

Contemplating the picture that Eleanor had paused on, Sanne struggled to reconcile this grinning version of Acre, her tongue touched to the tip of a blood-coated knife, with the tearful woman who had presented herself for interview. Sanne thought herself a reasonable judge of character, but she had to admit that Acre had utterly beguiled her.

When she looked away, Fred caught her eye and smiled at her, pushing up his chin and indicating she should do likewise. Despite Eleanor's attempts to keep a lid on matters, news of the deadline imposed by the Detective Chief Inspector and the potential consequences of failure had soon spread around the office. EDSOP was a close-knit team, and its members hadn't taken kindly to a threat made against one of its own, no matter how veiled. Even Carlyle seemed to consider it a personal affront, which had surprised the hell out of Sanne.

"The acute downward angle of the wounds and the residual traces of soap lather found on the body suggest that Acre murdered Rudd while he was taking a bath," Eleanor said, returning Sanne's attention to a clinical shot of Rudd's punctured torso. "That would explain how he ended up in there and probably rules out a further accomplice. No heavy lifting was required to position or pose the body, so we're now operating on the belief that Acre is solo and low on money. That means she has almost certainly stayed local, and that, ladies and gents, is where you come in."

As Eleanor turned off the screen, Carlyle hit the lights and began to hand out assignment sheets.

"This list contains the address of every hotel, motel, bedsit, B&B, and fleapit in the city," Eleanor continued. "Meanwhile, the really lucky ones among you are going to Bradford to cover similar ground with West Yorks. We have several more known associates—primarily friends and relatives—to interview, courtesy of Acre's phone records and a little pressure applied to her father. For the EDSOP detectives, there's a separate breakdown of their names and addresses on page two." She folded her arms, waiting out the rustling of paper and whispered discussions. Silence fell in fits and starts and then completely. "I'm not really one for profiling or for putting much faith in psychological claptrap, but even an idiot could predict that Acre will be aiming to go out with a bang. Consider yourselves targets and take all reasonable precautions. If in doubt, call for backup. Thank you."

Allowing the room to empty around her, Sanne skimmed the details of those designated to her and Nelson: two of Acre's old school friends, a cousin, and the landlord of the Dog and Duck. All of them resided on Malory, and there was a three-digit code providing a link to the notes from any previous interviews they'd had.

"Got some reading to do before we go anywhere," Nelson said, watching the officers file out.

"I know. How about we split them two each and lead the interviews accordingly? You take the first pair."

"Sounds sensible. If anything flags from the notes, we can prioritise that address."

"Right." Sanne felt better for having a plan. The more she had to do, the less likely she was to find herself rocking in a corner. The briefing had taken two hours, and sifting through transcripts would eat into even more time. Factoring in the travelling and the interviews themselves, she and Nelson would be lucky to get their visits completed before the end of the day.

"Sanne?" Nelson's quiet question forced her out of her panicked calculations.

"What?"

"It'll be okay."

She nodded, too unsure to actually agree with him. When he lowered his head, she dried the sweat from her palms and began to read.

❖

Meg didn't know what stopped her on the mat. She just stopped, leaning back against her front door, one hand splayed on the wood as if to keep herself from pitching forward. Dappled sunlight made the hallway cheerful, but it also cast a halo on the scuff mark where Luke had bounced her head off the wall. She stayed motionless as she strained to listen for the slightest out-of-place sound. There was nothing, and Luke was definitely still in custody; after parking on the drive, she had called Fraser just to make certain of that.

"Fuck it," she whispered, infuriated by the uncontrollable physiological reaction that had tripled her heart rate and turned her into a mouth-breather. Sealing her lips, she walked straight into the kitchen, pausing only when the first piece of glass crunched beneath her boot. This time around, no one had tidied up for her. Sanne hadn't had a chance to, and Emily obviously hadn't given it a thought. Amid the congealed clumps of blood and vomit, there was pasta and glass stuck fast to the tiles, the overall impression that of a collage created by an imaginative but disturbed child. A cocktail of copper and ammonia burned in her nostrils, redolent of a weekend night-shift, nothing she had ever expected to experience in her own home.

She gave the worst of the mess a wide berth, heading for the sink, where she ran the water until it steamed. She added bleach to a bucket, swishing it around to make it froth, grateful for once that its faux-pine scent was strong enough to override everything else. Brush and dustpan in hand, she started with the loose pieces of debris, sweeping them into piles and then sloshing water on the more persistent stains. She ignored her back when it began to hurt, persevering through the pain until nothing remained but spotless tiles and a half-full bin bag.

It felt weird to stand there in her kitchen, as if she should be finding something else to do, or finalising a schedule for Emily's approval. For the moment, though, her plans involved lunch and a brew, and then she might go to the supermarket or maybe just laze around on the sofa with a book and order a takeout for her tea. Sanne was likely to phone at some point, but she'd probably keep her distance for the first few days, not wanting to imply that Meg needed a babysitter to hold her hand.

The thought made Meg look down at her fingers, at the filthy nails and the skin chafing from the bleach. She smiled and tucked them beneath her armpits to warm them. If she was being honest, she liked having her hand held, and she could only imagine what Sanne's reaction would be if she ever found that out.

CHAPTER TWENTY-FIVE

If the traffic's not too bad, we might make the Dog and Duck before Happy Hour," Nelson said, rummaging in his pockets for the car keys.

Sanne swore beneath her breath as she slipped on the frozen pavement, catching herself on a lamppost and grazing her hand. It summed up their afternoon perfectly: one step forward and several back, with a lot of mucking around in the interim. Their interviews with Acre's cousin and one of her school friends had proven fruitless, and it had taken them a couple of hours to track down the other friend, whose history of mental illness had led to her being hospitalised following an overdose. The pub landlord had agreed to speak with them but warned them that he would be busy from seven thirty onward.

Footsore and hungry, Sanne sank into the car seat and rubbed her temples. She was tired of watching the clock, tired of the ever-present fear, but mainly just tired. The sole saving grace of the entire day had been Meg's message about Luke, though she hadn't yet had a spare moment to return the call. She let her eyes close and waited for Nelson to start the car.

"Here, get this down you." His instruction was accompanied by a savoury smell that set her mouth watering. He passed her a large mug filled with chicken and vegetables, along with a fork. "Brown chicken stew," he said, in answer to her questioning expression. "Abeni always makes too much."

She nodded blissfully, already chewing. "Aren't you having any?"

He started the car and pulled away from the kerb. "I'll eat mine later. I think your need is greater."

She wasn't stupid enough to argue. "Take a left at the end," she said, and shoved in another mouthful.

❖

"Can't say as I'm shocked. There was always something a bit off about that one." The Dog and Duck's landlord, Larry Sutton, wiped ale-froth from his moustache with the back of his hand. According to the case files, he hadn't been spoken to since Rudd had been named as a suspect, but he was clearly fond of chatting and needed only a cursory prompt from Sanne to get him warmed to his theme. "She had shifty eyes, even when she was with Andy. She'd come to the bar all smiling-like, but you'd catch her looking at you sometimes and it'd just stop you cold. She had plenty of the men in here wrapped around her little finger. Made me sick how they'd follow her about with their tongues hanging out. Though, come to think of it, I never saw her with Steve."

"Really?" Sanne asked, genuinely surprised. Like most of the local landlords, Larry's loyalty was to his customers rather than the police, but while he wasn't keen on giving specifics or naming names, he didn't seem to miss much.

"I suppose they must've been in here together at some point. They just weren't an obvious couple or anything." Larry offered her a pork scratching from the bag in front of him.

"No, thanks, I've just eaten." She waited as he crunched his own, wondering for how long Acre had had Rudd in mind as a potential accomplice. Long enough, apparently, to be careful about showing any overt signs of friendship. "You know your regulars well, don't you?"

Larry grunted as the scratching cracked into pieces. "I thought I did. Turns out two of them are psychos, so…" He shrugged.

"Aye, good point." This time, Sanne accepted a scratching. Her dad had put a packet of them in her Christmas stocking every year: pork scratchings at Christmas, and a bag of scampi fries for her birthday. He had done all his gift shopping down the pub. The taste and texture made her stomach crawl, but Larry toasted her with the last of his pint and she knew she was safe to push him further.

"Obviously we're trying to find Natalie before she can hurt anyone else," she said. "Can you think of friends or family members that we might not know about? People she might have mentioned or met up with in here?"

"Well, I'm not sure. Give me a minute."

As Larry procrastinated, Nelson reached across Sanne. "Here, let me get that, Mr. Sutton." He took Larry's empty glass and made a subtle exit toward the bar.

"Don't get many of his type in here," Larry muttered, watching him order his pint. Larry's right forearm bore an "English and Proud" tattoo, and in the last forty-five minutes he had scarcely made eye contact with Nelson. He settled back in his seat, his posture more relaxed, and bit into his final scratching. "Nat knew loads of folk," he said, using half of the pork rind to pick his teeth. "But she weren't close to many. She shagged around, which pissed off a lot of the women."

Sanne nodded and handed Larry the page of contacts. "Is there anyone you can add to that?"

"Hmm. Nope, that's all of them, I reckon." He pointed to one of the names. "Wouldn't bother with her. She OD-ed last night."

"Yeah, we know." Sanne wished they had come here first. Larry could have saved them a lot of hassle. She tapped the paper, thinking. "You said she'd upset some of your regulars. Were there any she bore a particular grudge against?"

"Half the men who come in here, apparently." Larry guffawed, noticed Sanne's unamused expression, and thought a little harder. "There was Portia Cocker, off Balan," he said, his shoulders still wobbling with mirth. "And Darcy and Marcy Wilkes, twins off Benwick and Pellinore. Nat used to be thick as thieves with the three of them, but something went on and they've not spoke in ages. The girls stopped coming in eventually."

"That's brilliant. Thanks." Sanne pushed her pen into her notebook, giving Nelson a cue to return with the fresh pint. She set her card on a neighbouring beer mat. "If you remember anything or anyone else, please give me a call."

"Will do." Larry took a long swig and belched. "Right, I best get back to it."

Nelson waited until they were in the car park before holding out his hand for Sanne's notes. "Darcy, Marcy, and Portia? Seriously? The boss is going to think we're having her on."

"Better than nothing, I suppose." Sanne kicked at the slush, her enthusiasm for the new lead rapidly deflating. "We can nip round to see them in the morning if nothing else comes up." She checked her watch: almost 8:00 p.m. By the time she got home, it would be well past ten.

"You're not sleeping in Interview Two again," Nelson said, tracking her thoughts.

"No, I'm not. I'm going home to my own bed. My neighbour must be sick of feeding my chooks by now."

"I did wonder." Nelson unlocked the car. "I was thinking about them just last night."

She put a hand on her heart, horrified. "While you were eating chicken stew?"

"Well, yes." He grinned. "Don't act so appalled. You've got a tummy full of it!"

"Mm, it was good too. You'll have to give me the recipe for when Git Face turns up his toes."

It was Nelson's turn to look appalled. "You wouldn't eat your own rooster!"

"Probably not." She fastened her seatbelt and stuck her feet on the dash. "The little bastard would choke me to death just to spite me."

❖

Sanne sank onto her pillows with a sigh that was positively indecent. Getting into bed on a winter night was one of her favourite things. She had often joked to Meg that being buried in a pair of pyjamas with a quilt tucked around her would see her happy for eternity. She wriggled lower, nudging the hot water bottle until it was warming her feet, and pulled the bedding up to her chin. Having stood abandoned for four days, the cottage had thick frost on both sides of its window panes, and the bedroom was so cold she could see her breath. The irregular clanks of the radiator promised eventual heat, but she couldn't remember ever having to wear gloves and a woolly hat to bed before. She plucked a glove off with her teeth, dialled Meg's number, and quickly put it back on again.

Meg answered on the first ring, sounding far more buoyant than she had of late. "Hey, you. Did you make it home safe?"

"I did, and I'm just thawing out. What are you up to?"

"Oh, I'm sat in front of the fire, so I'm toasty warm." Meg chuckled and then hiccupped. "Also I've treated myself to an Irish coffee or two, which has made me a bit tiddly."

Sanne's hat slipped over her eyes as she shook her head. "And you call me a lightweight."

"Balls to it, I'm celebrating," Meg said, unrepentant. "I'm a free woman, I have my house back, I'm going to work tomorrow, and Luke's application for bail was rejected."

"Hey, that's fabulous!" Sanne shoved her hat up, instantly regretting her enthusiasm. "I mean about the house and Luke, not about Emily. That's still shit." She cleared her throat. "Uh, isn't it?"

"Not especially," Meg said. "It's nice to be me again."

Sanne smiled. "Did I tell you how much I'd missed you?"

"In not so many words, yes."

They were silent for a minute, the background crackle of Meg's fire soothing and peaceful. There was so much that Sanne wanted to confide: the three-month warning that might yet cost her her job, everything that had happened with Zoe, the possibility of being made a scapegoat for the failings of the case, her confusion over what Meg might want from her and what she wanted from Meg. Instead, she yawned and kneaded the hot water bottle with her toes.

"You should be in bed if you're up early tomorrow," she said.

Meg yawned as well. "I know. I was just waiting for you."

Sanne stared at the ceiling, her lips forming words in a soundless rehearsal. After counting to ten, she bit the bullet. "Do you want to go out for dinner one night?"

"What, like grabbing a chippy or something?"

"No, not like grabbing a chippy. Like a proper restaurant, with cutlery and cloth napkins and a menu that doesn't wipe clean."

"Sanne Jensen, are you asking me out on a date?" The amusement in Meg's voice was unmistakeable.

"No, no, not really a date." Sanne's tongue seemed to be twisted around her teeth as she tried to backtrack. It was too soon, and Meg had only just come out of a relationship, and Sanne should've waited for her to make the first move. She struggled to sit up, tangling her legs in her sheets and accidentally launching the hot water bottle halfway across the floor. Then she froze, and she thought: fuck it, time to grow a pair. "Actually, yes, a date. I am asking you out on a date."

"Well, then, I accept," Meg answered, without a hint of indecision. "Let me know when you've chosen a suitable establishment."

"Oh. Okay. Okay then, I will." Sanne rolled her eyes at herself. "For fuck's sake, Meg, I feel like a geeky teenager."

Meg cackled. "Aw, you're doing beautifully. How red is your face?"

"I don't know, but it's hot, and my back's all sweaty."

"I think that's the most romantic thing anyone's ever said to me."

Sanne kicked her legs free and straightened her quilt. "Sod off. I'm going to sleep now."

"Will you call me tomorrow and whisper sweet nothings into my ear?"

"No, I won't. I'm hanging up. Go to bed."

"Night, love," Meg said, her voice more serious. "Be careful out there."

Sanne switched off her lamp. "I always am, and I'll see you soon. Sleep tight."

Chapter Twenty-six

The selection of pastries sat largely untouched in the middle of the table. Eleanor had also provided fresh milk and brew supplies, but her generosity had failed to lift the mood among her detectives. Even Fred, whose appetite usually knew no bounds, had merely nibbled at the edge of a croissant before dropping it onto his plate and wiping his fingers. Tabloid and broadsheet newspapers were piled beside the pastries, their headlines ranging from crude to cerebral, but their editorials consistent in questioning the police's ability to apprehend Acre.

The six a.m. briefing was for EDSOP only, and Sanne looked around at the haggard faces of her colleagues as they cradled mugs of strong coffee. Most of them would depend on caffeine to fuel them through another eighteen-hour day, and none of them would be home early enough to spend any time with their families.

"If there's a bright side," Eleanor said, "we're overdue another body, which may suggest that Acre has decided to quit while she's ahead."

"Or that we just haven't found it yet," Mike Hallet countered. "Given her choice of vics, she's probably diced up some poor bugger that no one will miss, just to put a roof over her head."

Eleanor stirred another sugar into her coffee. "Damn, Mike, always my little ray of sunshine." She tapped the rim of her mug with her spoon. "Can we have a quick summary of where we're up to, please?"

When no one else took the initiative, George cleared his throat. "We were in Bradford most of yesterday, and we're back there again today. We've had a few unconfirmed sightings of Acre around the East Royd area, so we're interviewing the people who phoned them through and going door to door. It'll probably turn out to be nothing." He shrugged in apology. "Most of the sightings reported to the hotline came hand-in-hand with a request for a reward. These latest calls could be an organised group of chancers trying their luck."

"Follow it up anyway," Eleanor said. "But don't hang around if they are mucking about. Sanne? Nelson?"

"We have three names from our Dog and Duck interview to chase down," Sanne said. "They're ex-friends of Acre, and she does seem like the vindictive type, so it's worth a shot."

"Good." Eleanor moved straight on, continuing around the table until the team had covered what little progress there had been. With the exception of Fred and George, everyone would be staying local, canvassing with uniforms or working on the contacts list from the previous day. There were no new leads beyond the unreliable sightings and a handful of interview possibilities.

Eleanor gathered her paperwork and held it close to her chest. "I'm sure you've all met DI Southam. He and DS Rashid are carrying out a full case review, and we are expected to cooperate without question. If they want your files, hand them over. If they want to speak to you, try to sound coherent. And if they want a brew, point them in the direction of the kitchen."

"Will they be assuming the lead, boss?" Fred asked, his arms folded in defiance.

"Yes, I have no doubt that they will." Eleanor was obviously trying not to focus on anyone in particular, but her gaze kept returning to Sanne. "DCI Litton has called a press conference for seven a.m. tomorrow. I expect he will hand over the case publicly and take the opportunity to detail the myriad ways in which EDSOP have fucked up." She raised a hand at the inevitable outcry. "I know, I *know*, but when is this shit ever fair? Until we are officially told otherwise, we work the case as usual. Any more questions? Okay then, let's get back out there. Sanne, a word please."

Sanne nodded, remaining in her seat as the team filed from the room. When Carlyle had pulled the door closed behind him, she walked across to Eleanor. It seemed to take an age to cover the short distance.

"Have you been in touch with your Federation rep?" Eleanor asked.

"No, ma'am." Speaking to a rep would have meant acknowledging what was about to happen, but Eleanor's simple question opened up a brutal truth: in less than twenty-four hours Sanne would probably be suspended, pending an investigation. She would lose Nelson, along with her position on EDSOP and any chance of building herself a career.

"Make it a priority, Sanne. Contact him before you do anything else."

"I will, ma'am." She tried to match Eleanor's urgency, but the mere thought of involving a Fed rep was anathema. How could she defend herself when she hadn't done anything wrong?

Eleanor paused with her hand on the doorframe. "Litton's clever with this sort of thing." She spoke in an undertone, forcing Sanne to step closer. "Chances are he'll start laying the groundwork today, which might bring you some media attention. If anyone approaches you, give them the number for our press office."

"Yes, ma'am."

"I don't need to tell you to keep your head down and do your job, do I?"

"No, ma'am." Sanne managed a wan smile and held the door open. "Once more unto the breach, eh?"

Sheffield Royal's A&E was almost exactly as Meg had left it. The cubicles on Majors were all occupied by elderly patients with genuine ailments or by thirty-somethings with bellyache; a variety of early morning slips, trips, and back pains were languishing in Minors; and two of the three patients in Resus would probably die there. On the plus side, Donovan was skiing in Klosters, and the breach manager had yet to put in an appearance.

"I'll kill every one of you bastards! I know where you fucking live! Just let me out! I want my mum!"

Sitting at the nurses' station, Meg mouthed along to the tirade, which had been repeated like clockwork every three minutes since the start of her shift. The police officers outside the cubicle had given up trying to placate their fifteen-year-old ward and seemed content to let her tire herself out.

"I bet it feels like you've never been away." Liz set a mug of tea in front of Meg and cupped Meg's chin to bring her face into the light. "You did a real number on yourself, didn't you?"

"Yeah, you could say that." Meg braced herself for an inquisition, but Liz seemed disinclined to pry.

"I hope Emily's been spoiling you rotten."

"Well, uh—" Meg winced as the tea scalded her tongue.

Liz slapped a hand over her mouth, looking stricken. "Oh fuck," she mumbled between her fingers. "Oh, fucking fuck."

Meg laughed and pulled Liz's hand down. "We split up on Wednesday, and I am shocked, nay, appalled that the grapevine hasn't got wind of it. What is this hospital coming to?"

Liz grinned in relief. "Well, we've all been busy picking up the slack for doctors who decide to go on the sick."

"One bloody shift! I was rotaed off for the other two."

"Yeah, yeah, whatever." Liz nudged her. "So, how's your lovely police officer friend?"

"Sanne is very well, thank you."

"I always liked her."

"I'm sure she'll be happy to hear that." Meg leafed through a heap of notes until she found the right set. "Now, if you'll excuse me, I have to help Asif fish a pea from a small child's nose."

She departed with as much dignity as she could muster, the sound of Liz's giggles following her into Minors. Once out of sight, she allowed herself a smile, relishing the buzz of the busy department, something she'd missed after only three days away. Guided by the frantic shrieking, she drew back the curtain on Minors

5 to find a terrified child being held in a headlock by his mum, as Asif—possibly even more terrified—approached the bed with a pair of forceps.

"Dr. Fielding, welcome back." He beamed and shoved the forceps into her hand. "Left nostril," he added in a whisper.

"Wonderful." She smiled at her struggling patient and searched her pocket for the ever-present bag of Haribo. The child stilled as she rustled the sweets, his brand recognition apparent despite his age. "Which do you like best? I think the cola bottles are the nicest."

"Eggs," he mumbled. "And bears."

"Eggs and bears it is." She offered him the bag, letting him select his own. "Now," she said as he stuffed a handful into his mouth, "about this pea…"

Sanne finished the last of her water, wondering whether it would be impolite to drop an ice cube down her neck. Darcy Wilkes's living room was best described as "subtropical," its steamy atmosphere enhanced by the racks of wet washing leaning against the radiators and by the pan on permanent boil in the kitchen. Nelson, usually so disparaging about the cold, had soaked one handkerchief through with sweat and was mopping his brow with a second. Oblivious to their discomfort, Darcy—wearing Capri pants and a top marginally larger than her bra—smacked the leg of her youngest child as he tried to steal the last biscuit, and sent him away screeching in outrage.

"Where was I?" she asked, not waiting for an answer. "I swear down, it's like a psychic link between me and our Marcy. I knew the minute she went into labour with her first—that's Leo—because I had the most terrible belly pain. Our Sid reckoned it was trapped wind, but I said 'no, call our Marcy,' and sure enough her waters had just gone."

"Wow," Nelson said. "That's uncanny."

Sanne murmured in accord. Engrossed by the seconds ticking away on the mantelpiece clock, she had phased out much of Darcy's monologue. "When did you last hear from Marcy?" she asked.

"She texted me this morning. Leo's had a bad chest so he's been off school, and the baby's wheezy too. I'll give her a ring later and see how they are."

"Okay then." Sanne clapped both hands on her knees and stood up. "Thank you for taking the time to speak to us."

"My pleasure." Darcy got hold of Nelson's coat sleeve. "Do you think I'm in danger, Detective?"

"No, it's very unlikely," Nelson said, easing from her grip. "Just keep your doors locked and phone nine nine nine if you have any concerns."

Nodding, she noted his advice in the margin of her television guide. "Say hello to our Marcy, will you? I'd nip round, but I don't want to break my neck on the ice."

"Not a problem."

Sanne stepped out of the front door into clear, cold sunshine. Clouds were skimming across the blue sky, propelled by a brisk easterly wind. It was a perfect January day, and she would have given almost anything to be up on top of Kinder Scout, knee-deep in snow and nowhere near the slush-covered pavements of Malory Park.

Nelson donned his shades. "Shall we ditch the car and walk round to Marcy's? It's not far, and we have plenty of time before your Fed rep's due in."

"Sounds good to me." She pulled out her own sunglasses, turning the world rose-tinted as she put them on. "I suppose one bright side of being suspended would be having more chance to exercise."

"You won't get suspended, San," he said, in a decisive tone belied by his troubled expression. "It won't come to that."

"I hope not."

She didn't tell him about the missed calls piling up on her mobile, calls from unknown numbers that implied Litton's groundwork was indeed falling into place. They walked on without speaking, Sanne effortlessly navigating an estate that seemed as familiar to her now as Halshaw. The weather hadn't tempted many residents from their houses; the only people they passed were a postman and a pair of uniformed officers. Sanne slipped her radio earpiece into place, listening to the chatter on the channel, but the exchanges were dominated by routine address confirmations and background checks, and she pulled the earpiece free again as they turned onto Pellinore Walk.

"Déjà vu," Nelson said.

"Aye."

Even if Sanne hadn't remembered which of the flats was 26B, one of Andrew Culver's neighbours had given the game away by decorating his wheelie bin with leftover crime scene tape. Marcy's address was at the bottom of the walk, where tiny terraced houses replaced the flats and where someone was playing R&B at an ear-shattering volume.

"Number three, white door." Sanne glanced at her phone as it began to ring again, but slipped it back into her pocket unanswered when she saw the "anonymous" tag.

"Everything all right?" Nelson asked.

"Yep." She knocked hard on the door. "God, I hope our Marcy's the quieter of the two."

"Stands to reason, growing up with Darcy." Nelson checked his watch. "We should try to keep this short and then set off back to HQ."

Sanne pressed the bell, holding it down longer than was necessary. "Assuming she opens the door." When a figure appeared in the hallway, Sanne eased off on the bell and then watched with mounting impatience as a key was fumbled and dropped. "For fuck's sake, it's not like this is a surprise visit."

Nelson touched her arm. "How about I lead this one?"

She nodded, already ashamed by her outburst. If she had tried to speak, she would probably have sobbed. Nelson, displaying composure enough for the two of them, greeted Marcy with a warm smile and held out his ID.

"Do you want to come in?" Marcy asked, although she didn't move to allow them through. Shielding her eyes from the sunshine, she blinked myopically as if she had forgotten what daylight looked like. Her outfit was far more conservative than that of her identical twin, but her mismatched socks and the shrivelled specks of food on her sweater suggested that her two sick children were proving hard work.

"We can't really do this on the doorstep," Nelson said. "We won't take up much of your time."

"Okay. Sorry." She stepped back, running a hand through her tangled hair. "Everything's a bit of a mess. Leo's off school with his asthma, and the baby's caught something as well."

Nelson wiped his feet on the mat, even though the carpet was grey with dust. "We know, Darcy mentioned that. Like I said on the phone, Miss Wilkes, it's just some routine questions."

"Marcy." She managed a tight smile. "Can I get you a drink?"

"No, thank you."

Sanne also shook her head, taking the chair closest to the door to allow Nelson to sit opposite Marcy. He thumbed to an empty page of his notebook.

"Okay, I'll try to keep this brief," he said. "Can you tell me when you last heard from, or saw, Natalie Acre?"

Marcy's gaze flitted to the ceiling as she struggled to remember. She had the bleary detached bewilderment that Sanne recognised from years of nightshifts.

"It was a good while ago, I think. We used to meet up in the pub, but then we stopped doing that."

"Why did you stop?"

"It was all Portia's fault," Marcy said quickly. She paused to drink from a mug of black coffee. "She accused Nat of sleeping with her fella, which Nat hadn't, but then our Darcy sided with Portia and dragged me along."

Sanne leaned forward, intrigued. She was about to challenge the account when Nelson did it for her.

"That's not how your sister or Portia saw things," he said. He flicked back a couple of pages as if to refresh his memory. "They both insisted that Natalie was in the wrong and that she continued a relationship with Portia's husband after the marriage ended."

"No." Marcy shook her head, adamant. "That's not how it happened. It's not. Nat's all right. She didn't do nothing wrong."

Sanne frowned. "So have you remained friends with her? Perhaps without the other two knowing?"

"I really wanted to, but I couldn't." Marcy worried at the patchy gloss on her bottom lip. "Darcy would've battered me."

"And how did you feel when you saw these murders reported in the news, with Natalie named as a suspect?" Nelson asked.

Sanne watched Marcy's knuckles whiten around her mug. Her answer came in fits and starts at first, with a stammer punctuating her denial of the allegations. It might have been a natural, nervous response to police presence, but her frequent eye contact didn't tally with that. After taking a sudden deep breath, she managed to provide a cogent answer.

"I don't go to the Dog and Duck anymore, and I haven't seen Nat in months." She nodded toward the baby monitor on the shelf beside her. "Will this take much longer? Katy's due her feed any minute."

"Just a few more questions." Nelson gave her his best placating smile. "Haven't heard a peep out of them, have we?"

"They're fast asleep. They're both good kids." She pointed at the photograph above the fireplace, a studio montage of a proud brother cradling his new sister.

Sanne barely noted the image. Her attention was fixed on the baby monitor as she strained to detect the slightest transmitted sound. Despite the green light on its base, the familiar snuffles and grunts of a sleeping baby were strangely absent, and a cold fear slithered along her spine when she realised why. Silently taking out her notepad, she scribbled a question and held it up for Marcy and Nelson to see: *Is she listening*?

All the colour drained from Marcy's face, and she swayed, grabbing hold of the sofa. Sanne made a frantic gesture to Nelson to keep talking, and wrote another message: *Is she with the children?*

Tears started to run down Marcy's cheeks as she nodded, but she managed to answer Nelson's questions about which school Leo attended and who his favourite football team was.

"My girls are mad on Sheffield Wednesday," he said, his voice remarkably calm. He shook his head vehemently when Sanne stood up, but he couldn't say anything that might alert Acre.

For her part, Sanne fell back on a tried and tested tactic. "Do you mind if I nip to your loo?" she asked. "I've got a bladder the size of a thimble."

Marcy wiped her face. "No, that's fine. It's upstairs."

"Smashing. Thanks." Sanne caught a glimpse of Nelson's expression and immediately looked away. To hear him speak, though, she would never have guessed that anything was wrong.

"Marcy, can I ask you about other friends of Natalie?" he said. "Is there anyone she might turn to for help? Anyone in particular that she was close to?" He passed Marcy his contact list as a prompt, and she understood at once, reading out names at random and embellishing with addresses and any other details she could think of. She seemed far steadier now that someone had realised what was going on.

Nelson coughed when Sanne reached the doorway, but she ignored him. They couldn't safely have any kind of discussion or argument, and she couldn't see any alternative course of action. They could try to take Marcy from the house and return with backup, but Acre was likely to kill the children in the interim, and Marcy would undoubtedly refuse to go anyway. If they opted to leave the house and keep it under surveillance, they gifted Acre three hostages again rather than two.

"What about Bradford?" Nelson asked. In an implicit signal of consent, Sanne heard him move to sit beside Marcy, aiming his voice directly at the monitor. "Did she have contacts there?"

Shutting the living room door behind her, Sanne hesitated in the hallway for a second, gulping for air. She unfastened the press studs on her baton and CS gas, leaving them loose but still in their pouch. No one would go to the bathroom armed to the teeth. Then, as ready as she was going to get, she took the stairs two at a time, making no attempt to disguise her approach.

Three doors came into view when she neared the landing. Following the tinny echo of Nelson's voice, she approached the farthest. She had no plan, just a vague hope that Acre might hear her coming and choose to hide somewhere apart from the children. The door of the third room, already ajar, swung open under her hand, and the gauzy green light from the closed curtains showed a bedroom decorated with aliens and spaceships and exploding stars.

"Don't fucking move!"

The hissed order destroyed Sanne's hopes in an instant. She stopped dead on the threshold.

"I mean it! I will cut his fucking throat!"

Sanne's eyes struggled to adjust as a lamp was switched on. When they finally focused, she wished that they hadn't. Sitting on a toy chest against the opposite wall, Acre was holding Leo on her knee, one hand covering his mouth and wrenching his head back, the other keeping a knife poised at the corner of his jaw. She had bound his hands with tape, and he was shuddering uncontrollably, his gaze set on an invisible point beyond Sanne as a spreading patch of urine darkened his pyjamas. Every time he swallowed, blood trickled down the knife's blade. His baby sister was asleep in a crib by the wardrobe, apparently unharmed.

"Does your partner know?" Acre asked. "Did that stupid bitch give me up?"

"No! No, he doesn't know anything." Sanne kept her voice to a whisper. If Nelson stopped the interview, she dreaded to think how Acre would react. "I came up to use the loo, and I thought I heard one of the children. That's all, I swear." She indicated the monitor. "I must have heard that instead."

The reminder worked. Acre spent a long moment listening to Nelson and Marcy, and then smiled broadly as if satisfied that Sanne was telling the truth. "Well, what the fuck do we do now?"

"Natalie, please." Sanne instinctively raised her hands. "He's only a child. Please let him go."

Acre tilted her head, her expression amused as she appeared to consider the request. "Uh, no. I've never liked him. He was always such a cocky little shit."

"Okay, so you've taught him a lesson." Her hands still out in front of her, Sanne took a step forward. "Swap him for me. No, no, think about it," she said, persevering over Acre's laughter. "You kill a kid, and everyone will hate you. You kill a police officer, and some of the folk out there will love you for it. You'll be a hero to them."

"Maybe I'll kill all three of you." Acre twisted the knife, forcing a thin sob from Leo. "It's not like I give a fuck."

"You will, though." Sanne began to unzip her stab vest. "You know you're going to prison, and you will give a fuck in there." She felt the weight of the armour divide as the zip opened. The thin shirt beneath was wet through and stuck to her torso. "If I take this vest off, can I come over to you?"

Acre jerked Leo to his feet, but the knife was no longer in contact with his skin, and she nodded slowly. "It'll hurt," she whispered, nicking her tongue with the blade. "I'll make sure it hurts."

Sanne ignored the performance and the threat, concentrating on Leo instead, now held by his hair at arm's length.

"Come kneel by the wall and I'll let him go," Acre said, her teeth and lips blood-coated and her eyes bright with exhilaration. She shook Leo to emphasise her instruction, his skinny legs continuing to quiver even after she'd yanked him upright again. He didn't make a sound. Too traumatised to cry or beg for help, he fixated on Sanne as if she were the only person left alive in his world.

"It'll be okay, love," Sanne told him. "You're going to run straight downstairs to your mum, all right?"

He grunted, the only sign that he had heard her, and then jumped as her vest hit the floor.

"Wall. Now." Eagerness made Acre's voice rise. "I won't fucking tell you again."

Sanne had already gauged the distance: three steps to Leo, seven to the wall. She took the first step as a cold draught rippled goose pimples over her arms, bringing with it a familiar smell that nearly made her sneeze.

"Jesus," she whispered, so close to Leo now that she could almost touch him.

The next command came from behind her, an urgent "Go!" that propelled her forward in a mess of outstretched arms and skidding feet. She collided with the child, driving him to the ground as Carlyle sprinted past.

"Move! Run!" Sanne hauled Leo to his feet and launched him out the door. She lunged toward the crib, but a burst of CS gas half-blinded her, and something thick and hot splashed across her face. A strangled cry from Carlyle made her spin. She saw his body fall to the floor just before Acre's fist slammed into her cheek. She weaved, stunned, Acre's hold on her shirt the only thing keeping her upright as black stars sparked across and then faded from her vision.

"Bitch!" Acre screamed, her eyes streaming. She slashed wildly with the knife, opening cuts on Sanne's arms and chest. Heedless of the wounds, Sanne punched Acre in the jaw. She dodged a reckless return and grabbed Acre's throat with both hands, digging her fingers into the soft spots and squeezing hard. Acre struggled, kicking out viciously as her mouth flapped and her eyes bulged. Somewhere far away, Sanne could hear Nelson shouting and doors banging, but no one seemed to be coming to help, so she bashed Acre's head into the wall and then retched when Acre retaliated by thumping a knee into her abdomen.

Winded and gagging, Sanne let herself drop, slipping from Acre's grasp and beyond the arc of the blade. Her options limited, she aimed for Acre's legs, diving forward in a clumsy tackle that forced Acre to the floor. They landed badly in a twist of limbs, and Sanne yelped as she felt hands grab her shoulders and drag her clear.

"Stay the fuck down! Stay down!"

Sanne didn't know whom the command was aimed at. She ducked, but the hands quickly released her, and the boots hammered past.

"Stay—"

A sudden pop and the crackle of electricity made her look up, and she watched Acre staggering backward, the twin probes of a Taser deeply embedded in her chest, before two uniformed officers wrestled her to the carpet.

"Sanne!"

Nelson's shout came from behind her. Still on her knees, she scrambled over to where he was crouched beside Carlyle.

"Oh shit," she whispered.

Carlyle was semiconscious and covered with blood that was still pouring from a wide gash in his throat. Nelson shook his head, his hands slipping as he tried to apply pressure.

"Fuck." Sanne scrabbled about for clean clothes, towels, anything, and settled on a pile of disposable nappies, folding two into place and letting Nelson reposition his hands.

"I can't…it's not working," he said.

"Fucking hell. Where the fuck are the paramedics?" she yelled to no one in particular, clamping her hands atop Nelson's.

"Three minutes!" an officer shouted back, as he dragged Acre toward the doorway.

Sanne swore again. "You'll be fine, Sarge," she said. "You'll be fine. Just hang on, you'll be fine."

The room was quietening as most of the officers left with Acre and the remaining ones fell silent. Every gurgled breath Carlyle took sounded like a tiny victory, and the howl of approaching sirens sent a murmur of expectation through those gathered around him.

"They're here now. They'll get you patched up." Sanne was starting to shiver, her blood streaming down to mingle with Carlyle's. She kept her hands in place until gloved ones prised them away, and then she slumped back against the wardrobe and let the medics work. She hadn't noticed it before, but Carlyle had removed his boots to tiptoe upstairs, and one of his navy blue socks had been wrenched off, leaving his foot bare. She couldn't see the missing sock anywhere.

"San?" Nelson said quietly, lowering himself to her level and touching her shoulder.

She pulled down her shirt sleeve and rubbed her eyes with it. "Are the children okay?" Her voice was so hoarse she hardly recognised it, but she couldn't remember screaming.

"Safe and sound. The baby slept through most of it." Nelson took her hand as they watched medics strap Carlyle to a wheeled chair and rush him from the room. "Come on. Someone needs to have a look at you too."

She shook her head. Nothing was hurting, not really. "I'm all right."

"You're bleeding."

"It's mostly the sarge's." Her breath hitched, but she managed to stop herself from crying. "I should never have come up here,

Nelson. You said no, and I should never—I smelled his nasty fucking aftershave. That's how I knew he was there. I was only ready to move because the smell of him makes me feel ill." Guttural sobs finally overwhelmed her. When Nelson pulled her into his arms, she buried her face in his chest and wept.

"If we're playing the blame game, it was me that sent the text asking for backup," he murmured into her hair. "And then I couldn't get upstairs fast enough to help you." His torso heaved as he tried to settle his breathing. "Acre didn't care who she hurt, San. She'd have killed those children without blinking."

"I know. God, she nearly did." Sanne sniffled and tugged Nelson's sleeve. "And you did help. You helped a lot."

He didn't seem convinced. "Leo caught me on the landing. By the time I got in here, it was all over."

"No, the sarge would've died without you. And anyway, Abeni might be happy to hear that you arrived late to the party." Sanne shifted to examine the damage to her arms. Her shirt was in tatters, her face was throbbing, and she felt sick. "On the other hand," she whispered, "Meg's going to fucking kill me."

CHAPTER TWENTY-SEVEN

"Ta-dah!" Feeling justifiably smug, Meg placed the specimen pot in front of Liz, who eyed the snot-covered pea with disdain.

"That's disgusting."

"That cost me half a bag of Haribo," Meg countered. She rattled the pea against the container. "I think it was worth it, though."

"If you say so. Sign this for the renal colic in Four, will you?"

Meg autographed the prescription chart obediently. Everyone knew that nurses were the ones in charge of the department. "What's going on with the boys in blue?" she asked.

The police officers were still on duty by Majors 7. Having spent much of the morning chatting or playing on their phones, they were now conferring in hushed tones, their earpieces pressed in place.

Liz jangled the keys for the drug safe. "No idea. I've been inserting a catheter for the last twenty minutes."

Curiosity got the better of Meg, and she beckoned one of the officers over, a lad who didn't look old enough to shave. "Is everything okay?"

He was obviously upset, his voice tremulous as he answered. "They've arrested the Slasher, out on Malory, but two of the Special Ops detectives have been hurt. I think she's stabbed them."

Meg sat down so abruptly that the officer caught hold of her arm.

"Easy, Doc. What's the matter? Do you know someone on EDSOP?"

"Yes. Detective Jensen." She searched through her pockets for her mobile, throwing her steth, a tongue depressor, and the bag of Haribo onto the desk, scattering sweets across her paperwork. "The injured detectives, are they male or female?"

"Don't know, sorry. It's mayhem on scene, and we're only catching odd bits on the channel. You'll probably find out before we do."

He returned to his colleague as Meg finally pulled out her phone. No missed calls, no messages. She sent Sanne a text: *Call me*, and was about to try her number when the Bat Phone rang. Unsurprisingly, the red standby was for the first of the injured detectives.

"Male, approximately forty years old," Meg repeated in a monotone. Her pen went on recording the details while her brain failed to process any of them. "Do we have anyone else en route?"

"Six-year-old with minor injuries, and a baby girl coming in for a check-up," the dispatcher said. "And another detective, but I think she's still on scene."

Meg closed her eyes. "Any word on her condition?"

"Walking and talking. That's all I know, sorry."

That was more than enough for Meg. She hung up and methodically returned her kit to her pockets. She'd stopped hyperventilating by the time she reached Resus, and the pins and needles were fading from her fingertips. The bays had filled up during her escapades with the pea, and she checked the board, glad to have a task to keep her occupied.

"Eight-minute ETA on a hypovolaemic detective with a lac to his throat," she said to the F2 on duty. "Hey, don't look so worried. We'll be able to squeeze him in somewhere."

The paramedic adjusted the blanket around Sanne's shoulders. "Sure you don't want those painkillers?"

"I'm sure." She tried to get up as Nelson came back into Marcy's living room, but he motioned for her to stay put. "Any news?" she asked him.

"Not yet."

"I need to contact Meg. If she's got wind of all this, she'll be panicking." She displayed the remnants of her mobile phone, smashed beyond repair. "I can't remember her number, though. I usually can, I know it, but it's just gone."

Nelson sat beside her on the sofa. "Don't worry, we'll have you at the Royal in no t—"

Eleanor strode into the room, cutting him off. "I might've bloody known it was you two," she said without preamble. "I didn't have any grey hairs, not a one, until seven months ago." She didn't have many now, but neither Sanne nor Nelson contradicted her. "What's the damage?" she asked the paramedic.

"She needs a few stitches, but most of the lacs are superficial. She was lucky."

"Good. Can she travel with me?"

"Uh." He glanced at Sanne and shrugged when she nodded. "Yeah, that's no problem." He made himself scarce without being told, leaving space for Eleanor to sit.

"The paramedics managed to stabilise Sergeant Carlyle," she told Sanne in a milder tone. "He should be at the Royal by now."

"Thank you, ma'am." Sanne didn't know what else to say. In the last ten minutes, all of her faculties seemed to have deserted her, and fast-fading adrenaline and the warm solidity of Nelson's body were the only things keeping her upright.

Eleanor shot a pointed glance at the blood leaking through the bandages on Sanne's forearms. "Yes, well, there'll be plenty of opportunity to discuss your risk-assessment process and strategic decisions at a time when you're not bleeding onto a witness's upholstery. Given our current run of luck, we'll probably get sued for the dry-cleaning bill." She sighed, letting her hard-nosed cynicism slip for a moment. "Actually, from what I've heard, Marcy Wilkes is singing the praises of all three of you, and there are plenty of people outside who are willing to listen."

"There are?" Sanne turned to the window, but someone had closed the curtains. "Blue flashing lights do tend to draw a crowd."

"Most of them are press, Sanne."

"Really? They got here quick. How the hell did they—Oh." Sanne felt Nelson tense as he worked it out too. "Someone had already tipped them off for Litton." She stated it as a fact, too tired to be pissed off.

"In all likelihood." Eleanor didn't sound upset either. If anything, she seemed rather pleased. "The DCI may have inadvertently done us a favour, though. The media are keen to write a hero into this sordid little saga, and they've been directed to Malory at a very opportune moment."

Sanne shook her head. "Boss, I can't. Not right now."

Eleanor stood and smoothed the creases from her coat. "I'm not asking you to say a word. Just walk out, keep your head up, and let them take their pictures. Litton will say his piece, I'll get to say mine later, and the rest will fall into place." She smiled, not presenting the scenario as optional. "Ready?"

Sanne let Nelson help her to her feet, grateful for the arm he kept around her. They walked out into the hallway, dodging forensic markers and bags of kit dumped by SOCO.

"Try not to scowl at anyone," Eleanor said, and opened the front door.

For the umpteenth time, Meg checked the clock on the wall. Plugging the hole in Duncan Carlyle's neck had been a useful distraction, but now that that crisis was over she'd resigned herself to watching the seconds pass by. Thanks to Nelson, ambulance dispatch had phoned Sanne's ETA through: a sedate twenty minutes, relayed eighteen-and-a-half minutes ago. Meg pulled off her apron, washed her hands, and—unable even to pretend that she had anything better to do—went to wait in the corridor.

The rattling approach of a wheelchair with a dodgy footplate forced her attention away from the ambulance bay.

"Minors Two is free for her." Liz bashed the chair into the wall in an attempt to park it. "Do you think she'll need this?"

Meg smiled. "I think she'll be safer without, but thanks anyway."

"Speak of the devil." Liz hit the button for the doors, and Meg turned so abruptly she almost gave herself whiplash.

Sandwiched between Nelson and Eleanor, Sanne was walking mostly under her own steam, but her face was ashen where it wasn't bruised, and she was placing her feet with exaggerated care. Unconcerned by her audience, she stumbled into Meg's embrace, and Meg held her close, kissing her cheek, her hair, anything she could reach without hurting her. She smelled like a war zone: blood and sweat and a chemical trace that Meg couldn't identify. Whispering a jumbled litany of apologies, she clung to Meg's scrubs for a few seconds before managing to stand independently.

"Can I see the sarge?" she asked.

Meg silently collected on a private bet and then led her by the hand into Resus. "Two minutes," she said. "He's full of morphine, and he's going to theatre soon."

Sanne checked Carlyle's monitors with the skill of someone who'd spent far too much time in hospitals, before walking over to speak to him. Meg couldn't hear the words, just an indecipherable murmur as Sanne touched his arm, but she saw his lips move in response and the ease of Sanne's smile.

"Right, you, time to go," Meg said. "You're losing more blood than he is."

Sanne left the cubicle without protest, her stiff upper lip enduring right up to the moment where her legs buckled and Meg had to dart forward with Nelson to catch her.

"Can someone grab a trolley, please?" Meg shouted. She cradled Sanne's head as Nelson lowered her to the floor, where gravity revived her within seconds. "There you are." Meg stroked Sanne's forehead, making her blink. "Y'know, you're heavier than you bloody look."

❖

Sanne stared at the needle above her arm, an evil little thing that seemed designed to inflict maximum discomfort.

"So, let me get this right," Meg said, apparently unaware of the torment she was inflicting. "You went upstairs on your own?"

"Yes."

"Knowing there was a serial killer up there?"

"Yes." Sanne ground her teeth as Meg jabbed the needle in and injected something that stung like fury.

"Sorry. Should've warned you about that." Meg didn't sound very sorry. She selected a hooked needle trailing a line of thread but lowered it again when Sanne flinched. "Look, I'm not mad at you, love. Not really."

Sanne tried to bite her lip but caught the thickened part where Natalie had punched her. "She had a six-year-old boy, Meg, with a knife stuck into his neck, and I didn't even think. I begged her to swap him for me, and I didn't think about what might happen after that."

"No prizes for guessing what did happen." Meg's fingers were gentle where they touched Sanne's cheek. "You could've been killed."

"I know." The painless glide of the suture thread through her skin mesmerised Sanne. What had happened that afternoon, and all of its potential and actual consequences, hadn't really sunk in yet. They tugged at her like the needle Meg was wielding, but she couldn't feel their sting.

"What would I do without you?" Meg asked quietly. She made several attempts to tie off a knot before setting the needle aside and using a paper towel to dry her eyes. She blew her nose and then clasped Sanne's hand. "Will you please consider that, the next time you pick a fight with a psychopath? You're only little, and I don't have a cat, so I wouldn't even turn into a crazy cat lady. I'd just be on my own and broken-hearted, and I'd have no one to dunk my HobNobs with."

Sanne somehow managed to nod, laugh, and sob simultaneously, producing a sticky concoction of tears and snot. "I promise I'll consider you and your HobNobs," she said.

Meg dabbed beneath Sanne's nose and then swapped the tissue for the needle. "Me and my HobNobs appreciate that. Now hold still."

❖

There was something about a mug of tea that provided untold comfort, even if the taste of it wasn't particularly pleasant. Ordered to sit out four hours of observational bed rest, Sanne let the brew warm her hands and savoured every calming sip. Meg, having finished her shift, sat dozing with her feet on the bed. She stirred on occasion to ensure that Sanne was behaving herself, and she'd even managed to find a packet of biscuits for Sanne before falling asleep.

"Hello? Sanne? Are you in this one?"

The voice outside the curtain was so unexpected that Sanne missed her mouth and dribbled tea down her chin. She was still wiping up the last drops with her bandages when Zoe stuck her head into the cubicle.

"Hey, you!" Zoe whispered, creeping past Meg to plant a careful kiss on Sanne's cheek. "If it isn't Scrapper Jensen, as I live and breathe."

Meg stirred and chuckled. "Scrapper Jensen?"

"That's what my shift's taken to calling her." Zoe grinned. "You must be Meg. It's an absolute pleasure to meet you." She shook Meg's hand and then pulled out a bunch of tulips from behind her back and offered them to Sanne. "I'm glad you're okay."

"Me too." Sanne took the flowers, trying not to laugh at Meg's perplexed look.

"I can't stay. We're on our way across to Pellinore to guard the scene." Zoe sighed. "Trust us to miss all the excitement."

She departed as suddenly as she'd arrived, with a blown kiss to Sanne and a wave to Meg. Once the curtain had stopped undulating in her wake, Meg leaned back and exhaled.

"She was…" She cast about for the right word.

"Tall?" Sanne suggested.

"Well, she's certainly that. I take it she's a friend of yours?"

"Sort of, yes." Sanne waved the tulips in surrender. "It's a long story."

She was saved from further explanation by Eleanor stepping into the cubicle.

"It's like Piccadilly bloody Station in here," Meg muttered. She sacrificed her seat for Eleanor, who graciously pretended not to have heard her.

"You look brighter," Eleanor told Sanne. "And by that I mean less unconscious."

Sanne winced. "I didn't think you'd seen that, boss."

"It was just a little faint," Meg said. "Nothing to be ashamed of, Sanne. It happens to the best of us."

The look Sanne gave Meg prompted Eleanor to interject smoothly. "I've spoken to DCI Litton, who asked me to pass on his thanks for your courageous and selfless actions this afternoon. He would have visited in person, but the media are demanding much of his attention." She paused to allow that to sink in.

Sanne gaped at her before realising that some sort of acknowledgement was called for. A tentative "Oh" was all she managed.

Eleanor nodded. "The police surgeon has examined Natalie Acre and deemed her unfit for interview until tomorrow afternoon at the earliest. I'll be conducting the interview with DS Rashid, but if you'd like to observe, be at HQ for one thirty."

"She wouldn't be in the same room, would she?" Meg asked, before Sanne could respond.

"No." Eleanor looked straight at Meg, obviously understanding her concern. "Not this time." As Meg relaxed back against the wall, Eleanor reverted to her usual, less formal tone. "You'll need to give a statement, Sanne, and there'll be an investigative process to determine any lessons to be learned from what's happened, but I don't think you have anything to worry about."

The pressure that had been sitting on Sanne's chest for the past thirty-six hours seemed to dissipate, leaving her so light she felt she might float to the ceiling. "Thank you," she said, still bordering on inarticulate.

Eleanor stood to leave. "I suspect Sergeant Carlyle will be undertaking a self-defence course, but I very much doubt that you'll be required to attend one." She examined the buddy splinting on Sanne's ring and little finger. "Boxer's fracture?"

Sanne nodded. “I broke it on Acre’s jaw.”

Eleanor’s laugh was uncharacteristically raucous. “Good for you.” She set Sanne’s hand down again. “I’ll see you tomorrow.”

“See you tomorrow, boss.”

As the tap of Eleanor’s heels faded, Meg began to collect Sanne’s belongings. “Come on. I’m taking you home, where we might actually get some peace.”

Sanne eased herself upright. “Can we stop for chippy? I’m starving.”

Meg held Sanne’s coat open for her and then set to work on its zip. “I’m sure we can manage that.” She pulled Sanne’s hood up. “Wait here in case the press are lurking. I’ll bring my car to the ambulance bay.”

“I thought your car was impounded.”

“It is, so I rented something sleek and shiny.”

“Oh God, really?”

Meg laughed. “No, it’s a Ford Focus, you pillock.” She kissed the top of Sanne’s hood. “Be ready to make a hobble for it when I beep the horn.”

CHAPTER TWENTY-EIGHT

Meg pulled into the disabled parking spot closest to the entrance of HQ and left the engine running.

"What?" she said to Sanne's disapproving frown. "I'll only be here for thirty seconds, and you've been stumbling about like an octogenarian all morning." Her fingers drummed an unrecognisable tune on the gearstick, her feet providing an intermittent accompaniment.

Sanne, already a bag of nerves, took her hand and stilled its movement. "You don't have to come and pick me up. My car's here. I can drive myself home."

"Uh-uh. Not with a broken finger. Not for forty-eight hours."

Sanne puffed out her cheeks and released the air in a manner she hoped was suitably disdainful. "Did you just magic that figure out of your arse?"

"It's possible that I might have, yes." Meg unclipped Sanne's seatbelt for her. "Great, that's settled, then. Text me when you're done." She took Sanne's lapels, pulled her close, and kissed her, a shy kiss on the lips that became bolder when Sanne reciprocated with enthusiasm.

"Mm, that was for luck," Meg said, when they eventually parted.

"Right." Sanne rearranged her coat, trying to compose herself, when all she wanted to do was drag Meg behind the nearest wall and kiss her some more. "I'll see you later."

Walking across to the main building, she listened to the crunch of Meg's tyres on the ice and then the steady acceleration away as they found traction. She'd put on her woolly hat and wrapped a scarf up over her chin, but a variety of double-take reactions told her that most of the people entering and exiting HQ recognised her. It wasn't surprising, considering that her image had featured in all of the morning's newspapers, the tone of the accompanying reports a far cry from what they would have been had she not thrown a spanner into Litton's works.

The officer at the front desk greeted her with applause, but she saved her brightest smile for Nelson, who met her in the lobby. She hugged him tightly, finding the confidence to dispense with the woollies and walk with her head held higher.

"The sarge sends his best," he said as the lift doors closed, granting them privacy. "I dropped by for a visit on my way in. Apparently the food is inedible and he didn't sleep a wink, but he seemed happy to be here still, regardless."

"Does he remember much?"

"Enough." Nelson smiled. "He mentioned the nappies."

"Oh, hell. But then again, desperate times…" She re-pressed the button for their floor as the lift stopped. "You never said, yesterday, how did he even get into the house?" It was something that had nagged at her; she hated loose ends.

"Marcy had left the back door unlocked." Nelson shuffled closer to make space for a group of officers. "She'd been planning to grab the children and make a break for it if Natalie ever let her guard down. Carlyle was only a couple of streets away, so he got there first and let himself in."

Sanne shook her head, impressed at Nelson's ability to keep his cool and multitask. "You must've sent one hell of a text."

"Let's just say it was comprehensive."

It was Saturday, but every desk in the EDSOP office was occupied, with a cacophony of ringing phones and Fred's off-key singing creating a lively atmosphere. Sanne hadn't even taken her coat off before George swooped, embracing her with such vigour that both her feet left the floor.

Fred hurried over. "Put her down, you daft sod. She's all beaten up and bruised." He patted her shoulder gently and unruffled her coat. "There's cake and loads of biscuits in the kitchen—mine and Martha's treat—and Eleanor said to tell you that they're starting at two."

Too keyed up for cake, Sanne bypassed the kitchen and headed for the room adjacent to Interview One, where she took a seat in front of its one-way mirror and chewed the skin off her thumb until Nelson joined her.

Eleanor abhorred bad timekeeping. At precisely 1:55 p.m., she and DS Rashid arranged their paperwork on the table of Interview One. Four minutes later, a knock on the door brought them to their feet. A uniformed officer escorted Natalie Acre and her lawyer into the room, and Eleanor made the introductions necessary for the recording.

"It's all so civilised," Nelson said, echoing Sanne's thoughts. "Look at her. She's a multiple murderer capable of disembowelling a man and leaving him for dead, and she's sitting there like butter wouldn't melt in her mouth."

Dressed in custody-issued grey sweatshirt and jogging bottoms, Acre folded her hands in her lap and watched the preparations with an air of indifference. She seemed smaller than Sanne remembered, less alive somehow without the knife and the attitude. Purple bruising covered one side of her jaw, and there were clearly delineated fingerprints around her neck. She looked as battered as Meg had the night of Luke's assault, but there was no trace of shock or horror in her gaze. There was no emotion at all.

"Is this where you attempt to get inside my head and figure out why I did it?" she asked, before Eleanor had even uncapped her pen.

Her lawyer almost choked himself in his haste to interrupt. "Ms. Acre, we discussed our approach to this."

"What, no comment?" Acre laughed at his dismay and studied her newly trimmed fingernails. "I think they caught me red-handed, *Gavin*." The emphasis she put on his name would have made any man's balls shrink.

"Okay." Eleanor opened her hands in invitation. "Why *did* you do it? Why did you murder Andrew Culver, Marcus Jones,

Daniel Horst, and Steven Rudd, and attempt to murder two of my detectives?"

Acre responded eagerly, her answer so fluid it almost seemed rehearsed. Leaning over the table, she spoke in a lover's whisper, seductive and intimate. "Haven't you ever wondered what it feels like? Before Andy, I spent ages wondering whether I could do it, whether I had it in me, and with him it was more to check things out, y'know? Something to get my feet wet." She rocked back suddenly and laughed. "And it was so fucking easy and *so* good. It's like being drunk and high and having the best fuck all at once. After that, I think I must have got a taste for it. My mum always did say that I had an addictive personality."

Watching Acre chuckle at her own insight, Nelson ran a hand over his brow as if trying to ease away the ingrained frown lines. "I can't tell whether she's insane or flat-out evil," he said in an undertone. "I spend my days thinking about what might be for tea, and she's planning to kill someone because she's curious to find out whether she can."

"It's easier if there's a reason," Sanne said, Acre's performance compelling and repulsing her in equal measure. "For us, I mean. Revenge or rage, something specific and sort of understandable. This—this I'll never understand. I'm not sure that I even want to. And if you and I can't, can you imagine someone like Adele Horst trying to come to terms with it?"

He shook his head. "I know what you mean. And despite everything Acre is saying now, she's deranged enough to enter a not-guilty plea just for the drama of a trial."

"I've no doubt that she will. She'll probably claim diminished responsibility. It's one trial I'd be happy to stand in the witness box for, though."

Nelson had just opened his mouth to respond when Acre's enthusiastic wolf whistle interrupted him.

"Now, that's a good one." Acre flipped a photograph around to show her lawyer. Whatever its subject, it made him recoil and run a finger around his collar. "I caught the light just right."

"How did you choose your victims, Natalie?" DS Rashid had spread a selection of images across the table, but if he had hoped to evoke some sign of remorse, his tactic had failed spectacularly. Acre was picking them up and admiring them one by one.

"Andy and I were old friends, but you already know that," she said. "Jonesy came over to cadge booze and got more than he bargained for. Hadn't really planned for him, but I reckon it worked out all right."

"And Daniel Horst?" Eleanor asked.

Acre traced the edge of Daniel's photograph. "Everybody wants their five minutes, don't they? No one gave a fuck about Andy or Jonesy, so I told Steve that I needed to aim higher. I'd seen that God-bothering twat out on the estate, and honestly"—she looked upward, her hands clasped in front of her—"it was like someone had answered my prayers. Boom! National news."

Eleanor took her time writing a note, refusing to give Acre the satisfaction of a reaction. "So, did Rudd just outlive his usefulness?" she asked at length. "Or were you annoyed that he was getting all the credit?"

Acre clicked her fingers in agreement with the second point. "It was funny at first, everyone thinking he did it, but then it started to piss me off. He drove and he fucked, and that's all he did. Are you writing that down?" She slammed a hand onto the table, startling Rashid. "Write that down!"

"It's noted." Eleanor's voice was as smooth as glass.

"My brother gave you that address, didn't he? The snivelling little shit. Have you met him and my dad?"

"No, I haven't."

Rashid pounced on the theme. "Is that where your hatred of men stems from? Your father and your brother?"

Acre arched an eyebrow. "Who says I hate men?"

"Well, all your victims are men," he said, immediately wrong-footed.

"So, what? You're thinking my daddy touched me or beat me?"

"It's a possible motivating factor, yes."

"He didn't," she said. "He was nothing. He was like beige fucking wallpaper: there, but just in the background for my mum to scream at."

"So your family life was troubled?"

Acre made a point of turning to Eleanor. "He's boring the shit out of me."

Eleanor nodded. "Were you planning to kill Marcy Wilkes and her children?"

Acre gave a nonchalant shrug, but the question seemed to have reignited her interest. "I'd been trying to work that out, the legistics."

"Logistics," her lawyer corrected, and then gulped almost comically when she glared at him.

"I reckoned I might be able to chop them and freeze them, especially the kids, once I was ready to move on."

For a protracted, horrible minute, Sanne thought that she might be sick. She closed her eyes, swallowing down the slick rush of saliva and waiting for the pounding in her head to lessen. "How long had she been there?" she whispered to Nelson.

"Since Tuesday," Nelson said. "She forced her way in and kept one of the children with her twenty-four seven. She couldn't let Leo go to school, so Marcy had to make up the asthma story."

"Almost four days. Jesus, they were on borrowed time, weren't they?"

"Very much so. They were incredibly lucky that our visit didn't spark the fuse."

"Maybe us ringing ahead gave Acre the time to fix a plan," Sanne said, trying not to imagine the terrible burden of three deaths on her conscience. By contrast, Acre was chatting about the rubbish sacks she had found in Marcy's kitchen, apparently untroubled by any of the anguish she had caused.

Sanne pushed her chair away from the mirror. She'd heard enough. "I know I'm neurotic and spooked by my own shadow at times, and that I need a regular kick up the arse, but bloody hell, Nelson, I'd rather be all that than anything like her."

He muted the sound from Interview One. "I don't know about you, but I think I'd prefer to skip the rest of this one. What would you say to a cuppa and a piece of Fred's cake?"

She turned from the mirror without sparing Acre another glance. "Are you brewing?"

"Go on, then, seeing as you've got a wounded paw."

"Then I would say that's a perfect idea."

❖

Crouching out of sight beside her Land Rover, Sanne checked her hair in the wing mirror for what she swore would be the final time. The muted street light cast a convenient shadow across the week-old spread of yellowed bruising on her cheek and hid the bit of hair that kept standing up no matter how hard she tried to stick it down. Everything was arranged, and nothing would go wrong, or so she had been telling herself throughout the drive over. The restaurant, recommended by Eleanor of all people, had been booked since Monday. With the official review of the Acre case still ongoing, Sanne's shift pattern had reverted to weekdays only, guaranteeing her this Saturday off. She had almost forgotten what working regular eight-hour shifts felt like.

After giving her head a last, optimistic pat, she collected her bag from the passenger seat. Her stomach fluttered as she straightened, a little dance of apprehension that couldn't be blamed on a light lunch and a long afternoon jog. She was bloody ravenous, though, now that she thought about it.

The gravel on the driveway, newly liberated from the ice, crunched beneath her boots, but it began to snow again as she reached Meg's front door, the first delicate flakes carrying a promise of a far heavier fall. She knocked and took a step back, her hands out of sight behind her. Meg must have been waiting, because the hall light came on immediately and the door opened a second later.

"Bugger, I'm sorry," Sanne said. "I'm looking for Meg Fielding. A scruff about my height with messy hair. I think I've got the wrong house."

Meg stuck two fingers up at her and performed a dainty twirl. "Do I scrub up well or what?"

"You look gorgeous. Did you treat yourself to a new outfit?"

"What? This old thing?" Meg held out the sides of a tailored jacket to reveal its satin lining. She looked like the cat who'd got the cream and accessorised it with a rather tasteful shirt. "It cost me an arm and a leg," she admitted.

"Worth every penny." With a flourish, Sanne presented the bouquet she'd been hiding. "These are for you." She set the flowers in Meg's arms and gave her a chaste kiss on the cheek. "Oh, and this." She pulled a small chunk wrapped in gold foil from her coat pocket.

Meg set a hand on her heart. "Really? Your very last Rolo? Sanne, it's too much. You shouldn't have."

"I'm attempting to woo you." Sanne squinted up at her. "How am I doing?"

"Marvellously," Meg said through a mouthful of chocolate and clotted caramel. "You ate the rest of the packet, didn't you?"

"Yeah. Nelson and I got peckish on a stakeout yesterday." Sanne rubbed her cold hands together. "Your chariot awaits, Dr. Fielding."

Meg dashed inside to grab her coat, came back out still holding the flowers, and disappeared again to put them in water. She reappeared with her coat half-fastened. "Okay, I'm definitely ready now." She took Sanne's hand and squeezed it. "Where are we going?"

"It's a surprise."

"Is it Abdul's?"

"No, Meg, I'm not taking you for a slap-up kebab."

"What about Frydays?"

"It's not a chippy either."

"That's me all out of ideas, then."

Sanne opened the Land Rover's door for her and went round to brush the snow from the windscreen. "You need to think bigger," she shouted through the glass. When she got in and turned the ignition key, the Land Rover spluttered and failed to start.

"Alternatively, we could eat whatever mouldy sandwich is stashed in your glove box," Meg said.

Sanne was too busy cursing to dignify that with a reply. She turned the key again, stomping on the accelerator when the engine showed signs of willing, and the car rattled into life with a cough and a puff of exhaust smoke.

Meg cheered and fastened her seatbelt. "Onward and upward!" She grabbed the dash as the wheels skidded in the fresh snow. "Onward and sideward!"

Sanne snorted and then started to laugh. "You're not helping."

"Don't mind me. I'm just happy to be here." Meg reached across and stroked a curl of Sanne's hair. "Here with you, in your knackered car, in the middle of a blizzard, heading out into the unknown."

Sanne caught Meg's hand and kissed it. "We have the best adventures, don't we?"

Meg smiled at her, entwining their fingers. "Always."

The End

About the Author

Cari Hunter lives in the northwest of England with her wife, two cats, and a pond full of frogs. She works full-time as a paramedic and dreams up stories in her spare time.

Cari enjoys long, windswept, muddy walks in her beloved Peak District and forces herself to go jogging regularly. In the summer she can usually be found sitting in the garden with her feet up, scribbling in her writing pad. Although she doesn't like to boast, she will admit that she makes a very fine Bakewell Tart.

Her first novel, *Snowbound*, received an Alice B. Lavender Certificate for outstanding debut. Her second novel, *Desolation Point*, was shortlisted for a Goldie award and a runner-up in the 2013 Rainbow Awards, and its sequel, *Tumbledown*, was a runner-up in the 2014 Rainbow Awards.

Cari can be contacted at: carihunter@rocketmail.com

Books Available from Bold Strokes Books

Cold to the Touch by Cari Hunter. A drug addict's murder is the start of a dangerous investigation for Detective Sanne Jensen and Dr. Meg Fielding, as they try to stop a killer with no conscience. (978-1-62639-526-8)

Forsaken by Laydin Michaels. The hunt for a killer teaches one woman that she must overcome her fear in order to love, and another that success is meaningless without happiness. (978-1-62639-481-0)

Infiltration by Jackie D. When a CIA breach is imminent, a Marine instructor must stop the attack while protecting her heart from being disarmed by a recruit. (978-1-62639-521-3)

Midnight at the Orpheus by Alyssa Linn Palmer. Two women desperate to make their way in the world, a man hell-bent on revenge, and a cop risking his career: all in a day's work in Capone's Chicago. (978-1-62639-607-4)

Spirit of the Dance by Mardi Alexander. Major Sorla Reardon's return to her family farm to heal threatens Riley Johnson's safe life when small-town secrets are revealed, and love may not conquer all. (978-1-62639-583-1)

Sweet Hearts by Melissa Brayden, Rachel Spangler, and Karis Walsh. Do you ever wonder *Whatever happened to…*? Find out when you reconnect with your favorite characters from Melissa Brayden's *Heart Block*, Rachel Spangler's *LoveLife*, and Karis Walsh's *Worth the Risk*. (978-1-62639-475-9)

Totally Worth It by Maggie Cummings. Who knew there's an all lesbian condo community in the NYC suburbs? Join twentysomething BFFs Meg and Lexi at Bay West as they navigate friendships, love, and everything in between. (978-1-62639-512-1)

Illicit Artifacts by Stevie Mikayne. Her foster mother's death cracked open a secret world Jil never wanted to see…and now she has to pick up the stolen pieces. (978-1-62639-472-8)

Pathfinder by Gun Brooke. Heading for their new homeworld, Exodus's chief engineer Adina Vantressa and nurse Briar Lindemay carry gamechanging secrets that may well cause them to lose everything when disaster strikes. (978-1-62639-444-5)

Prescription for Love by Radclyffe. Dr. Flannery Rivers finds herself attracted to the new ER chief, city girl Abigail Remy, and the incendiary mix of city and country, fire and ice, tradition and change is combustible. (978-1-62639-570-1)

Ready or Not by Melissa Brayden. Uptight Mallory Spencer finds relinquishing control to bartender Hope Sanders too tall an order in fast-paced New York City. (978-1-62639-443-8)

Summer Passion by MJ Williamz. Women loving women is forbidden in 1946 Hollywood, yet Jean and Maggie strive to keep their love alive and away from prying eyes. (978-1-62639-540-4)

The Princess and the Prix by Nell Stark. "Ugly duckling" Princess Alix of Monaco was resigned to loneliness until she met racecar driver Thalia d'Angelis. (978-1-62639-474-2)

Winter's Harbor by Aurora Rey. Lia Brooks isn't looking for love in Provincetown, but when she discovers chocolate croissants and pastry chef Alex McKinnon, her winter retreat quickly starts heating up. (978-1-62639-498-8)

The Time Before Now by Missouri Vaun. Vivian flees a disastrous affair, embarking on an epic, transformative journey to escape her past, until destiny introduces her to Ida, who helps her rediscover trust, love, and hope. (978-1-62639-446-9)

Twisted Whispers by Sheri Lewis Wohl. Betrayal, lies, and secrets—whispers of a friend lost to darkness. Can a reluctant psychic set things right or will an evil soul destroy those she loves? (978-1-62639-439-1)

The Courage to Try by C.A. Popovich. Finding love is worth getting past the fear of trying. (978-1-62639-528-2)

Break Point by Yolanda Wallace. In a world readying for war, can love find a way? (978-1-62639-568-8)

victory
EDITIONS

Drama

MATINEE BOOKS

MYSTERY

erotica
EROTICA

BSB
SOLILOQUY
YOUNG
ADULT

BOLD
STROKES
BOOKS

LIBERTY
EDITION